the
Enigma
Rising

Breakfield and Burkey

BOOK 2: Award Winning Techno-Thriller Series

Published by

ICABOD Press

ISBN: 978-1-946858-28-3 (Paperback)
ISBN: 978-1-946858-05-4 (eBook)
ISBN: 978-1-946858-06-1 (Audible)
The Enigma Rising was previously published under a different ISBN

Library of Congress Control Number: 2013920609
Cover, interior and eBook design: Rebecca Finkel, FPGD.com

Second Edition
Printed in the United States

TECHNO-THRILLER I SUSPENSE

Novels by Breakfield and Burkey in The Enigma Series
www.EnigmaBookSeries.com

The Enigma Factor	*The Enigma Beyond*
The Enigma Rising	*The Enigma Threat*
The Enigma Ignite	
The Enigma Wraith	**SHORT STORIES**
The Enigma Stolen	*Out of Poland*
The Enigma Always	*Destiny Dreamer*
The Enigma Gamers	*Hidden Target*
A CATS Tale	*Hot Chocolate*
The Enigma Broker	*Love's Enigma*
The Enigma Dragon	*Nowhere But Up*
A CATS Tale	*Remember the Future*
The Enigma Source	*Riddle Codes*
	The Jewel

Kirkus Reviews

The Enigma Factor In this debut techno-thriller, the first in a planned series, a hacker finds his life turned upside down as a mysterious company tries to recruit him...

The Enigma Rising In Breakfield and Burkey's latest techno-thriller, a group combats evil in the digital world, with multiple assignments merging in Acapulco and the Cayman Islands.

The Enigma Ignite The authors continue their run of stellar villains with the returning Chairman Lo Chang, but they also add wonderfully unpredictable characters with unclear motivations. A solid espionage thriller that adds more tension and lightheartedness to the series.

The Enigma Wraith The fourth entry in Breakfield and Burkey's techno-thriller series pits the R-Group against a seemingly untraceable computer virus and what could be a full-scale digital assault.

The Enigma Stolen Breakfield and Burkey once again deliver the goods, as returning readers will expect—intelligent technology-laden dialogue; a kidnapping or two; and a bit of action, as Jacob and Petra dodge an assassin (not the cyber kind) in Argentina.

The Enigma Always As always, loaded with smart technological prose and an open ending that suggests more to come.

The Enigma Gamers (A CATS Tale) A cyberattack tale that's superb as both a continuation of a series and a promising start in an entirely new direction.

The Enigma Broker …the authors handle their players as skillfully as casino dealers handle cards, and the various subplots are consistently engaging. The main storyline is energized by its formidable villains…

The Enigma Dragon (A CATS Tale) This second CATS-centric installment (after 2016's *The Enigma Gamers*) will leave readers yearning for more. Astute prose and an unwavering pace energized by first-rate characters and subplots.

The Enigma Source Another top-tier installment that showcases exemplary recurring characters and tech subplots.

The Enigma Beyond the latest installment of this long-running technothriller series finds a next generation cyber security team facing off against unprincipled artificial intelligences. Dense but enthralling entry, with a bevy of new, potential narrative directions.

The Enigma Threat Another clever, energetic addition to an appealing series.

Acknowledgments

We are grateful for the support we have received from our family and friends. We look forward to seeing the reviews from our fans. Thank you in advance for your time.

Specialized Terms are available beginning on page 375 as a reference for the reader, if needed.

Advice, Like Medicine, Needs to Be the Right Dose

Thiago stared at his most recent picture of his beautiful daughter, Lara, as if that alone would bring her back. In the photo her long auburn hair, slightly wavy like his, big chocolate eyes with lashes that needed little cosmetic enhancement, and generous mouth with perfect teeth smiled out at him like she had a secret. Lara was around 1.7 meters and trim, with a well-proportioned figure he feared too many young men would notice when she went away to university. Her grace when she walked and her lilting laughter, to say nothing of his wealth, made her a very sought-after heiress, whom he'd overprotected her entire life. He missed that laughter in their home. The four months that his daughter had been gone had felt closer to a year.

Lara was brilliant in her subjects, fluent in English, Portuguese, and Spanish, with a stubborn streak that matched his own. Hard-headed when it came to her dreams of modeling and being an actress. As if he'd allow his daughter to ever pursue a career like that. Maybe if her mother had lived, these pursuits would have been nipped in the bud and channeled into her legacy. Thiago knew she was more than capable of stepping into his shoes one day and taking over his interests in his iron, steel, and petroleum business. She knew a great deal about the business, the social requirements, and many of his associates. She simply didn't want it like she had when she was younger. Most likely because he wanted her to do it, the same way he had pushed her into college.

He hoped his lunch meeting with Otto today would provide a new option for locating Lara. As wealthy and powerful as Thiago Bernardes was in Brazil, and throughout Latin America for that matter, he hadn't been able to find his daughter. He'd been able to keep the fact that she was missing from the press and friends with the contrived story of her vacationing at a spa. How much longer that would work was an open question. Oscar, the head of his security team, had done some digging and tracking, discreetly of course, but had no real leads.

Otto was visiting for an update on the financial investments that his firm provided to Bernardes Ltd. They'd been friends for many years, and Otto had advised him well for investments. Thiago knew, however, that Otto had many inroads to information sources. As Thiago entered the restaurant, he was delighted to see that Otto was already seated. Otto stood to shake hands as he approached.

"Thiago, my friend, so happy you could meet with me today. The cuisine smells amazing, and I hope you have a recommendation," Otto said as he shook hands with his old friend.

Thiago responded with a slight smile, "It is very nice to see you again. We get together in person too rarely, my friend. Yes, of course I have my favorites which I will recommend."

They sat down and glanced at the menus briefly while giving the waiter their drink orders. The waiter provided a list of the specials and indicated he would be back with their drinks and to take their orders.

"Business, by all reports, appears to be good here in Brazil and throughout South America. Your investments, I am happy to report, are doing quite well, and I have a few items for your consideration. But, before all of that boring discussion takes place, tell me about yourself and your lovely daughter, Lara. I thought perhaps she might be joining us today." Otto smiled, pleased to be there with his old friend.

A shadow crossed Thiago's face, deepening the lines of stress. "Business is very good, Otto. Lara, however, is a different matter. I was thinking of confiding in you and seeking your counsel. I require your utmost discretion, however, if we continue with that discussion. But let's order lunch first, shall we, and discuss lighter topics."

"Of course. I have never broken a confidence of yours. Problem with Lara? From all you have told me over the years, I find that difficult to believe."

The waiter interrupted when he returned with their drinks. They both chose from the specials offered, with the waiter indicating they would be most pleased with their choices. When the waiter left, they toasted their meeting and discussed the weather and such as they waited for their meals. Though Thiago looked less robust than usual, Otto strived to keep the conversation casual. Their luncheon was served, and they were left in peace to their corner of the restaurant.

"Thiago, this salmon is excellent. How is your swordfish?"

"Very nice. To be honest I have yet to have a poor meal here. Consistently delicious though a bit pricey on some dishes. I find these days my appetite is not what it once was, so this always tempts me to eat more."

"Ah, so how is your progress on overcoming your health challenges? You look a bit tired, but I would attribute that to worry from what you indicated before lunch."

"The doctors were not encouraged at my visit last week. Some recommendations have been made, but I fear that the end is closer than they are willing to admit. That is another of the reasons I would like to discuss Lara with you and see if you have any options I might explore."

"Your health is critical so of course you must either seek other medical opinions or adhere to their recommendations."

"I have consulted with two other doctors, and they are all aligned in the treatment methods. They all indicate I can overcome this issue, but I need to reduce my stress, exercise, take their silly pills, and rest more. I am doing my best to adhere to their guidance and am scheduled for some additional procedures in a few weeks.

"Otto, Lara is missing. She has been for months. So far, all my efforts haven't resulted in any leads on her whereabouts. Due to my health problems and lack of finding Lara, I have also redone my will naming you as the executor. I have no other choice until Lara returns."

"There are courses of action for your health. That is good. Executor of your estate? That seems extreme, but I will honor your wishes for the time being. Now what about Lara? What is the problem? I would like to help you if I can."

Forcibly calming himself and taking a breath, Thiago succinctly stated, "Lara ran away four months ago. I have kept it out of the press, but have no leads on where she is. I am so worried, I am starting to neglect the business and imagining all the worst for my princess."

He paused again, then continued, "I have Oscar on it, but he has found nothing of any substance. He tracked her on a flight to Argentina before he lost her."

"Oh my! I am so sorry. Do you know what she took with her? Was there an event that caused her to leave? You two didn't butt heads, did you?"

Shaking his head and looking very sad, he responded, "She took two suitcases filled with clothes, her passport, her credit cards, which she has not used since the purchase of the airline ticket, and a few thousand U.S. dollars cash.

"To be quite honest, we did have an argument. She wanted to try her hand at modeling and acting, but I could never allow my daughter to do that. I put my foot down and reminded her of her responsibilities to the company and our people. We stood toe to toe, with me giving orders and her saying she was grown and could make her own choices. I told her my expectations. My last words were to forbid her to pursue modeling and acting. She glared at me and told me I was impossible and then she ran from the library to her room. When I got up in the morning, I didn't see her and figured she was cooling off. When I returned from work that evening, she was gone with no word to any of the staff. I then discovered the missing luggage and the other items."

Otto empathized, "You've had no word, no calls from her? Are you sure that she wasn't taken? How could she escape the scrutiny of her bodyguard? She adores you. I am surprised she wouldn't have at least called you to say she was alright."

With tears coming into his eyes, Thiago said, "She's been outsmarting her bodyguards for years, though not in public. Even during her time at the university, she adhered to the security requirements. Oscar and I both believe she left voluntarily. The words were terribly ugly between us. I told her she would fail and then come begging for help from me. At one point during our argument, she said she didn't need me and could get by on her own."

"I understand. Sometimes when we are mad we say things that we would never otherwise say. I am sure it was the case on both sides of the argument. So Oscar has had no success. You believe she left on her own. Overall, she has been discreet and thus is not immediately recognized, so no paparazzi interest, I would guess. How do you think I can help you?"

"Otto, I am confident that you have resources outside of the financial investments with which we have always dealt. Perhaps you can make some discreet inquiries. Keep an eye out for her. I do not want it in the press. It is far too private and that would further alienate her, I fear. We have been fortunate to not be a targeted family, as some of my associates are."

Otto sat back and thought for a few minutes. Could he use his resources to help here? It was different than other activities his team was involved with, but then again perhaps not so much. His team was the best at getting information, but to be discreet would take time. Perhaps JAC and Quip would have some ideas, he thought.

"Thiago, this is not an area in which I or my associates would normally get involved. However, I have known you for a long time and Lara since she was very little. I have a couple of folks that I might be able to have work on it. It will take time though, especially if you do not want the press involved.

"Doesn't she speak several languages? This is important to potentially discover where she might have traveled to. Do you have some current photographs of her? Exactly how much cash do you believe she left with? She aspires to be a model and an actress, right? Did she do any acting in school?"

Thiago nodded and said, "She is fluent in several languages that would allow her to easily fit in anywhere in North or South America. She did not act in any school plays, but said her whole life was like playing a role. Sadly, though she inherited the looks of her mother, she also got her tenacity from my side of the gene pool."

They both grinned, knowing that trait was well engrained in the both of them. It contributed to their success in business. Their discussion continued down the business path as the main objective for their lunch when it was originally scheduled. Otto wanted to gather his thoughts as well as give Thiago a chance to recover his composure after telling of the disagreement with his daughter. As they finished up their conversation, paid for their lunch, and readied to leave, Otto ventured forth with an offer.

"Thiago, I will have my team make some discreet inquiries."

"I understand, Otto, and I appreciate that it will take time. She could be any place and doing anything to reach her dream. Money is no object so please let me know your fees for this."

"Do not insult me with fees for doing a friend a favor. If the team incurs costs then you can reimburse us for those, but no fees. You do have to make a promise to me for doing this." Otto knew that the longer she was gone, the greater the risk at her recovery, and he wanted to push Thiago.

"Of course, anything! What do I need to promise?"

"That no matter how long it takes, and it could take some time to maintain your requested discretion, you will do what your doctors say so that you can see her when she is found."

"That is not fair. I can hardly control that."

"You will adhere to their requests, and I will have a doctor I know review the treatment recommendations as well. When she is found you can readdress your will. Agreed?"

As they stepped outside, Thiago seemed reinvigorated, "Alright. I agree. Thank you, Otto. I will send some information to you. Please provide progress updates. Oscar is at your disposal if needed."

CHAPTER 1

We don't need no stinkin' badges

Juan and Carlos were fidgeting and distracted while waiting on the plane. Their home away from home did not provide much in the way of amenities, since they wanted as little attention as possible out here in the Chihuahuan Desert of Mexico. Besides, they didn't want to have an electricity bill for this unmarked landing strip they had spent so much time getting ready. The idea was to have it look deserted from the air as well as on the ground. Any time there was work to do, they showed up with their own water truck and portable generators. This allowed them to be self-sufficient for as many days as needed.

Carlos had become rather proficient at borrowing satellite communications time, so their voice and data connectivity never suffered because there was no phone line available. Actually, Carlos had been a telecommunications specialist in the military. He was quite clever at setting up complex signaling schemes that were encrypted and got bounced several times around his ground links to cloak the true location. When they sent a plane off or when they had a plane on approach, he insisted on radio silence. Being naturally cautious, he felt this minimized the possibility of the wrong people triangulating their location based on radio communications traffic. That left them with a lot of time on their hands to worry about what might go wrong with the shipments.

Carlos was practical, thoughtful, and the consummate worrier of the two brothers. Juan, on the other hand, never showed up properly prepared for any situation. Thus, he improvised a lot to compensate for his cavalier approach to most everything. The result, however, gave him great adaptability to any given set of circumstances. His sense of humor, coupled with his knack of getting out of touchy situations, made him an excellent resource for this kind of work. Juan's natural abilities to adapt and excel at almost any sport, whether physical or social, made him the person everyone wanted on their team. Juan's charming wit and personality was always a hit with the ladies. This unfailing charm of his could usually be counted upon to get him out of difficulties, which he seemed to court more times than not. Born in Mexico but educated both there and the United States allowed the brothers to work easily in either country. They preferred Mexico.

The rest of the ground crew in their private location in the Chihuahuan Desert was comprised of Vaughn, Don, and Ron. They were referred to as the On-Brothers, though they weren't even closely related. They didn't quite seem able to make it with the ladies or possess the commonly accepted social behaviors needed for romance. Indeed, from time to time Carlos and Juan were asked if the On-Brothers were gay. They weren't, but the absence of social skills only left them each other to live with. Their favorite game was mental cruelty. They'd take turns belittling one another, usually as a game of two against one. Their eccentricities could be entertaining or tiresome, depending upon the circumstances. Carlos had gotten into the habit of letting them know when they could devolve into their ritualistic verbal combat and when they could not. Whenever a landing was expected, the dialog became informational only among them, so that Carlos wouldn't lose his temper.

At one point Carlos and Don had been equal partners in the business. Don would zone out from time to time, taking as much as six months off, leaving Carlos to run operations. Vaughn showed up one day after his marriage had failed and fell right in to the new line of work. His temperament was the opposite of Don's. Don was introspective, fairly well-read, and when his pockets were full of money, he would simply leave if nothing was going on workwise. Don had come to Mexico seeking mystical enlightenment from the Yaqui Indians but stayed because of the peyote. One time he had even lived as a hermit in a cave along the Rio Grande and lived off the land wearing just a loin cloth. However, after six months, he was driven to return to civilization primarily because he couldn't get his major food supplement, Fudgesicles. Vaughn couldn't read very well so the material had to have lots of pictures of women, and the more naked those were the better. Ron was like a puppy dog no one wanted, but for some reason he fit right in to round out the On-Brothers trio. The trio was mostly unfit and scruffy looking. Not candidates for inclusion in GQ Magazine.

Carlos had an unusual birth defect. For all his planning and efforts to contain and control himself in a situation, when he lost his temper it triggered an adrenaline leak into his system, doubling his strength and giving him the moniker Raging Bull. Juan loved to tease his older brother, but he had to be careful that he didn't push the wrong buttons on Carlos. The one time was quite enough and ever since then they'd worked together like well-oiled machinery. Carlos, at a lean 1.83 meters, muscular, with black hair and a mustache, and Juan, at 1.52 meters, stocky but muscular, black hair and clean shaven, could easily be candidates for GQ Magazine when they cleaned up. Neither of them had problems attracting females and they thoroughly enjoyed them.

"Where the hell are they?" asked Carlos. "I don't know why I let myself get talked into using gringos for this operation. You know they can't be trusted! If they screw this up…"

Juan interjected, "Then we won't have to worry about them ever again. Look, you don't fly into the U.S. looking like us without attracting attention. They are wanted fugitives with nowhere else to go. They can't go back to where they came from, and we are the only ones who will work with them after the Mexican police started cleaning house. After the enemies they made at the Night Owl shoot out, their ONLY option is to work with us."

Juan looked up at the clouds moving in and added, "I sure don't like the looks of the weather. These clouds have the look of nympho cumulus all over them."

Carlos stared at Juan for a moment and said blankly, "… nympho cumulus?"

Juan, not changing his studying of the cloud formations, said, "You know, fucking thunderstorms," to which Carlos rolled his eyes at being pulled into Juan's gag.

"But anyway, just so you know, I am glad we have that remote detonation device hidden in the plane as our failsafe. Good thinking, bro."

Carlos settled down a bit after Juan's statements. Juan was right, where would they go if not back here? JC and Robert were larger-than-life men who had played it fast and loose. The U.S. Feds were after both of them. If it hadn't been for Juan's plane and some low-level flying, JC and Robert would be parked in the same cell block with Charles Manson and his friends.

JC was a small-time crook who was looking to hit the big time. At 1.84 meters tall and 113 kilograms, he was an imposing individual. His size coupled with his outgoing and hyper personality made it seem like he sucked all the air out of any room he entered. His jokes were desperately off color but his laughter was so contagious that everything seemed alright with everyone. He liked to pay for everything when he was out with the gang and it earned him the nickname On-Me JC. In fact, he was so extravagant in his spending that he always needed more money, which led him into dealing drugs. His first wife didn't quite get the hang of his changed lifestyle and didn't want to join him down that path.

The big score he needed to put himself into the elevated role he envisioned came with a cash price he couldn't deliver. So JC, being the resourceful individual he was, killed two birds with a single stone. According to federal testimony, JC murdered his wife for the insurance money and used it to finance his first big drug deal. His second wife, who was almost the same age as JC's oldest daughter, didn't seem to mind JC's undocumented business activities. She thoroughly enjoyed spending the money it brought in. JC was always talking about his new acquisitions.

At dinner one night with 15-20 close friends, JC told everyone about the new Cadillac he had just ordered with every upgrade possible.

JC told everyone, "You should see this new Caddy I have coming in. Man-o-man, it's got EVERY possible option you can think of! The only one I couldn't bring myself to get was the automatic douche. I don't want an automatic douche."

His wife and daughter laughed the hardest at this, as they did with all his antics.

JC's drug dealing connection was Juan out of Mexico City. They shared the same passion for flying, which is why Juan picked up JC one day at Dallas Love Field Airport, just one step ahead of the feds and flew him to Mexico. It was quite a haul that day since Juan also brought along another social climber, Robert.

Robert was somewhat quiet and withdrawn, moody. A moderately built ex-military gunnery sergeant and sharp shooter, there wasn't anything he didn't know about weapons and how to effectively use them. All Robert ever talked about was being in financial investments. Word was that after Robert left the service financial investments was exactly what he did. He robbed banks, 20 to be specific. His assembled team would blow into a bank masked and heavily armed, hold a few hostages, and grab everything of value in under eight minutes. Then they'd take someone's car out of the lot and drive to where their car was located. The story goes that one of his team members got drunk one night and described in too much detail one of the robberies to a lady who happened to be an undercover cop.

The police broke in on Robert and held him at gunpoint while they searched his apartment. The SWAT team recovered several weapons and some C-4 explosives. One SWAT team member brought a locked briefcase over to Robert and asked him to open it. Robert was being held down on his stomach with his hands cuffed behind him with two H-K semi-automatic weapons pressed to his head.

Sensing the irony of the situation, Robert told the guy, "You can open it if you'd like. I'd do it but I'm busy right now."

The guy said, "Ok I will, but first let me bring it over here and put it next to your head" which he did.

Robert, not one to let the moment slip through his fingers, quickly added, "Hey man, before you open it can you put your fingers in my ears? I hate loud noises."

Robert was out on bail and trying to buy a drink using only coins at the local bar when he bumped into On-Me JC and Juan.

Robert was due for sentencing the next day and was trying to have one last drink with the few quarters he had left before he went in. When Juan and JC couldn't stand to watch the pathetic activity of Robert trying to pay for a drink with loose coins, they both covered the tab.

Juan was never able to miss an opportunity to have a dig at someone and, knowing a little about Robert, said, "Boy, some bank robber you are!"

The absurdity of the situation made everyone laugh and of course that was their evening toast at every round of drinks ordered. JC and Robert really seemed to hit it off as drinking buddies.

Juan sized up the bar crowd and knew something was wrong. He was pretty sure that his two new friends were being watched, which meant so was he. But ever the party animal and with someone else to rock out with, he ignored the feeling. The night got louder and louder. Juan even bought drinks for the DEA, the Feds, and the undercover police, pretending he was just being sociable to the crowd watching their antics. Around midnight a couple of small caliber weapons went off in the bar, which quickly emptied the place.

Juan orchestrated the exit and took his two new friends straight to the fully fueled King Air twin engine parked at Love Field and promptly took off. He filed his flight plan while taxiing down the runway. He dropped from radar shortly after crossing the DFW city limits, and no one picked him up again until he was on the ground at the landing strip in the Chihuahuan Desert of Mexico. Juan was right. Robert and JC had no place else to go.

The On-Brothers came rushing in to say that a plane was on approach and everyone rushed out to see if it was theirs or someone unwanted.

"Right, saddle up!" Carlos shouted as he strapped on his favorite Colt 1911 semi-automatic pistol and grabbed his other weapon of choice, an H-K semi-automatic assault rifle. Everyone else saddled up as well in case they needed to greet intruders.

CHAPTER 2

The less you have the more there is to get!

Carlos was a little on edge with receipt of this shipment. He'd been trying to push this band of misfits into becoming a powerful cartel that could broker anything for a price. They struggled to move up the food chain and only got marginal jobs that lacked prestige, in his mind. Carlos and Juan simply didn't have the political connections that the older families had.

They also didn't have the resources of the drug lord growers. They were deficient in the financial backing needed to take on the bigger deals, which required larger aircraft. Carlos's business approach focused on small deals with thin margins, but more of them done faster than anyone else could. Thus, the group was really only a small mom-n-pop retailer in a business dominated by large cartels who bought wholesale closer to the source and drove up the margins. Carlos and Juan knew that they wanted to do more wholesale buying and selling. Success with that would allow them to move away from the frontline dealing, which was too close to the focus of the federales.

Ron interrupted to say that the plane was on approach, a cigarette awkwardly dangling from his mouth as he spoke. Ron was the most stable of the On-Brothers. To further his role and assert his leadership, he'd been trying to learn how to smoke. You can always tell when someone is not comfortable with something because they act like they are learning. Everything about their actions is unnatural. Unfortunately, Ron had been learning to smoke for 24 years. He still didn't get it.

Ron informed, "The plane is approaching for landing, Carlos. We don't have any unusual activity in the area."

Carlos nodded, then directed, "Let's get ready. I want to see my shipment. We need to turn this around according to the timetables we talked about. Our U.S. buyer, Joel, is expecting this shipment. I want this plane moved to the underground hanger for refueling and light maintenance. I don't want the aircraft to almost get to the destination or not be able to return with our profits."

The On-Brothers had done a pretty good job of building a nice underground facility for their operations out here in the Chihuahuan Desert. Carlos hadn't wanted the staging facility visible from a passing airplane or satellite. He'd required the underground construction to accommodate a couple of planes, their all-terrain vehicles, and modest accommodations. This permitted them to remain out of sight, except for aircraft takeoff and landing. The On-Brothers weren't very innovative, but if you told them exactly what to do and where, they could be relied upon to deliver good results.

The plane rolled up and before things could be fully secured, Carlos was looking inside the plane for the drugs. But the plane was empty. Carlos walked carefully and deliberately back to the underground hut and sat down at their conference table. Robert and JC came in, along with Juan and the On-brothers.

Carlos asked, with a polite air of innocence, "Where is my cargo?"

JC flopped down in an extremely well-worn chair and said, "Buddy, we were on approach when Robert saw that the area was surrounded by government troops. I swung in low, and the contact, to his credit, waved us off, which confirmed our visuals."

Carlos restated flatly, "You didn't get my drugs."

JC, getting agitated, said, "We didn't put down in the middle of the troops to get your goddamn drugs because we wouldn't have gotten back out again."

Carlos emphasized again, "You didn't get my drugs."

JC, now really aggravated, barked, "If we had put down not only would they have the plane, but precious me too."

As he looked JC straight in the eyes, Carlos commented, "Don't try to cheer me up. You didn't get my drugs, you gringo moron."

Before JC could leave his chair, Juan and Carlos moved as fast as two mongooses dueling with a cobra in the dance of death. Juan quickly moved in behind JC and held a very sharp knife to JC's throat and prompted him to open his mouth. Carlos slid the business end of his 1911 Colt .45 Combat Commander into JC's mouth. The On-Brothers, somewhat startled by the lightning fast moves of Juan and Carlos, had the good sense to freeze, as did Robert. JC was already properly motivated to remain motionless.

Juan and Carlos had grown up together and had always been very close. The lethal onslaught didn't surprise the On-Brothers, as they had seen these brothers move as one before on several occasions. The Rodriguez brothers were the core of the organization, and they were the last men you wanted to screw with.

After what seemed like an eternity, Carlos managed a slight smile.

"I'll do the talking, JC. Nod your head gently if you understand," Carlos said in a very calm and collected tone. "This is the interactive part of the conversation."

With Juan's knife at his throat, JC gently nodded. The gun and knife were not going anywhere soon.

Carlos educated, "In order to do business with these people I prepaid for the drugs we sent you two after. Not only are we out the drugs but also a big chunk of working capital that I cannot get back since that whole effort is now compromised. You do understand, I can't just call a 1-800 DRUG CONTACT and get a refund because I failed to receive the shipment, right? That means this whole operation failed and with it everyone's profits from it. It also means that our next deal is off because we didn't get the money from this deal. The only thing you did right was to bring my plane back in one piece, so we at least have something.

"I know everyone understands that we don't have a payday until the next deal goes down correctly. Right now I don't have another deal in the works. I doubt the gringo here has any ideas on financing another detail at this point."

Everyone noticed that JC was drooling because he couldn't close his mouth with the gun in place. Juan was the only one with the courage to note the humor in the situation.

Juan looked down at JC with the gun in his mouth and with a wry smile said, "Carlos, I recommend that you clean the gringo slobber off your pistole after this discussion, so the weapon doesn't rust, bro."

As always, Juan provided the right amount of humor to break the tension and get Carlos to settle down. Carlos withdrew the weapon and hastily wiped it down before he returned it to his shoulder holster.

JC, wanting to recoup some dignity from being pinned so quickly and to add to the levity of the improved situation, said, "I'm just glad you used my mouth for the demonstration rather than giving me a rectal explanation."

The quip made even Carlos smile.

Finally, after the laughter settled down, Carlos said, "We need to look at a different line of work. The drug business is already saturated with plenty of people who are entrenched, and the weapons-running action requires larger aircraft. What we need is a high value transport business where we can make our margins and dominate a market that others haven't pursued."

Robert perked up and suggested, "What about moving currency, precious metals, precious stones? These are high value/low cargo weight endeavors that not many are doing.

"Even the drug dealers are forever looking for ways to launder their money to get it legitimate. Why couldn't we be the go-to-group for moving money? I mean, you can't legitimately cross the border between countries with more than ten thousand U.S. dollars, and most drug cartels make that each day before they have their cornflakes. Once an illegal operation generates good cash flow, the next real problem is how to sanitize the money. Without this, they can't become mainstream.

"The first step in that activity is moving illegally earned currency to areas where it can be laundered. The good part of this is if their business is good, we'd be kept busy moving money for them."

Carlos looked the group over and considered the proposal.

"Not bad, gringo. Hadn't considered you as a man with a brain. It does have possibilities. I might even know where to start with this new business model. Let's get the plane out of sight and let me think about this and discuss it with Juan." Carlos grinned and looked to Juan.

CHAPTER 3

The second mouse gets the cheese

Juan pulled Carlos aside and asked, "How bad did we get hit on the lost drug run? Are we completely cleaned out, or can we still mount this new business venture that Robert suggested?"

Carlos looked around to make sure that no one else could overhear and revealed, "We got hurt, that's true. No, I didn't bet the farm. And no, we didn't prepay everything because I don't ever gamble everything on a single roll of the dice. We have operating capital, but like I said, we need a new line of cargo to transport. The longer I think on currency transport to help launder money, the more I like it.

"I mean, think about it. We are dealing directly with the owner of the funds, moving it for them, and delivering it to a consumer who is going to launder it. We have just eliminated three levels of distribution that we had to put up with in the drug business."

Juan agreed, "Unless we are handling counterfeit currency, in which case the drug model would be the same. You have the producer, the wholesaler, the distributor, and the retailer selling to the end user on the street."

"I hadn't even considered counterfeit currency. Sometimes you amaze me, little bro. Let's keep our options open on that line of business as well. Right now though, I want to go talk to the drug cartel that just got hit for the drugs we couldn't get and were likely confiscated."

"WHAT? They owe us money or the drugs. Why would you want to talk with them?"

Carlos smiled and patiently explained, "The federales are on to them, and time is running out. Who better to solicit business from than someone who is being stalked by the federales? They need to take their liquid assets and move because if they don't the federales will close in, take everything, and put them in jail for a couple of centuries. We can help them move their currency, and possibly them, to a new operations area where they can restart their business.

"In fact, we should start soliciting all the drug cartels with this approach since it is easier to stalk and arrest if the prey is too static. Our business motto is Mobility for peace of mind. The faster you move, the more times you move, the harder it is to find and catch you. We are enablers of this new business model. Besides, they owe us a chance to recoup our losses. What better way than hiring us again."

Juan studied Carlos for a minute, then wondered, "Ok, it sounds good. But, if we are just money movers then someone else will come along, and we will have the same problem we have now, competitors. How do we move ahead of the continual newcomers that are bound to want a piece of our action?"

Carlos suggested, "We need to be more than just money movers. We need to have a laundry machine, relocation planning, and emergency transport options as part of our service offering. We are going to have to add some new connections, so I need you to run down some information."

"Like what kind of information?"

"We need some contacts in some of the usual offshore banking organizations that are sympathetic to taking large cash deposits for a small percentage. We don't need a huge inventory of places around the world, just a couple of reliable contacts, preferably in our own backyard in the Caribbean.

"I want you to take Robert and JC with you to completely understand air traffic patterns into and out of these areas, local orientation to currency movements, and bankers we can trust. If the banks are too large then there are too many prying eyes, but if the banks are too small then they can't explain the large influx of cash nor will they be able to exchange it effectively. I want you to act like this is our money. In fact, that is a good idea. If we have our money in this laundry machine, we can sell this business proposition far easier, as well as protect our investments. I mean, we might want to be legit someday too.

"Also, we need to learn about moving money securely electronically. At some point we will need to upscale the money-hauling business, and I don't know enough about that yet so keep an eye out for us to be able to learn more about that. I will do some research as well."

Juan declared, "I better get started right away. There is a lot of territory to cover and people to meet."

Carlos finished, "And I have to go sell this to the drug lords before they get grabbed up by the federales. Oh, and by the way, I only gave the drug cartel half of the money up front and told them the other half would be in the plane to be surrendered upon inspection of the goods."

Juan looked incredulously at Carlos and asked, "So you put the money in the plane for delivery once we got the drugs? Where did you put it? I didn't see anything like that before they took off or after they landed."

Carlos smiled at the private joke, then enlightened, "It wasn't there because I didn't send it. I figured on our first time we would put up only earnest money we could afford to lose, if everything went wrong."

"So, what if the deal had gone as planned? They weren't about to give us credit, and you would have put JC and Robert in an awkward position. What would you have done then?"

"JC and Robert would have been put on the spot. But they are only gringos. They would have had to call me to ask for the location of the rest of the money. I would have said that the money was in transit or some such nonsense. They could then offer that the drug cartel should only give us half of the drugs if they weren't comfortable with things. I was reasonably sure that we could have gotten half the shipment loaded at a minimum. If we could have moved it, we could come back for the rest. If the drug cartel didn't like the offer, the worst they would do is kill JC and Robert and keep our aircraft. The best would have been that they loaded half the goods, and we made our profit. We couldn't pay for the whole load before we moved half of it anyway so it was a calculated risk. And yes, I was gambling with JC and Robert. Sometimes that's how things roll. Any other questions?"

CHAPTER 4

Mobility for peace of mind

JC asked, "Juan, what are we doing here? We flew all this way to meet someone in a Holiday Inn bar?"

Juan was slowly nursing his drink so as to keep his head about him. This was not a party trip. The last thing they needed was an argument in this place.

Without looking at JC, Juan asked, "Did you get the information we needed on flight traffic in and out of this place? That should include names, places, time schedules, and payments expected. Can we fly in unexpected and undetected, move a lot of illegal cargo to our target destination, and leave without a lot of questions? Did you get all that?"

JC sighed and confirmed, "Yes, Juan, I have all of that information. Robert is doing his piece to confirm maintenance potential and ground movement personnel who can be trusted. So, who are we trying to meet with? I thought we had everything."

"We need someone to accept what we are transporting, and I have to be sure that we can trust them. We need to meet face to face, and I want to talk to him before we do our first test run. If I don't like what I see and hear, we move on to Panama and write off the Cayman Islands for money laundering. We might do that anyway if this clown doesn't show up pretty soon," Juan informed JC.

JC stood next to Juan and ordered a drink. Neither of them spoke to each other, since both were lost in their own thoughts. Patience was not a strong suit for either of these men, and Juan was about finished waiting.

A deep timber voice behind him said, "Mr. Juan, I presume?"

JC and Juan turned around to greet the individual but lowered their gaze in order to actually see the man's face.

"My name is Phillip Johnston. I'm sorry I'm late. My boss, Denali, dropped his cell phone overboard while fishing, and I had to deal with getting the replacement and reprogramming it for him. So, what are we drinking, gentlemen?" Johnston enquired.

Johnston seemed to suffer from short-man syndrome and was doing everything possible to try and enhance his deficiency.

Juan instinctively grabbed JC's massive arm to get his attention and without a spoken word sent JC off to a table. Then Juan indicated for Mr. Johnston to join him at an empty table in the corner. Juan took the seat in the corner with Johnston facing him.

Juan gathered his usual charm and offered, "No worries about the timing. I was just relaxing here. What would you like, sir?"

Johnston clapped his hands together and with a grin that would only have endeared him to a cockroach said, "How about my favorite local adult beverage, Jamaican rum?"

Juan could already tell that this was going to be a long, trying evening with this person. He started off the conversation asking about Johnston's past history once the drink was served.

"You seem like a bright lad, but you have no accent that I can place. I can tell you are not from around here."

Johnston was obviously pleased with the impression that Juan had received. He launched into a monologue using Spanish, English, French, and Portuguese to cover his diverse background. Johnston ended up trying to explain his reason for moving to the Caymans by using a joke requiring a play on words and a certain amount of classical art education on the part of the audience.

Johnston said, "So after my classical art business went under, I was baroque and out of Monet."

The humor fell so flat as to be pathetic. Johnston laughed at his own joke so hard that he spilled his drink. Juan looked at Johnston, and then JC, who had heard the attempted humor as well, and then back to Johnston. After Johnston regained his composure and another drink, Juan decided enough history had been learned. Moving on to his objective for the meeting, Juan figured if they didn't get to the business at hand and discover if this clown could help them, they might as well go on to Panama tonight.

Juan verified, "Of course. So now you work in a banking institution here on the island, correct? I am told you have certain knowledge and skills in handling large inheritances. Is that true?"

At the question, Johnston went from rodeo clown to serious business man capable of in-depth financial discussions in sub-millisecond time. He could smell the sweet odor of success close at hand.

Johnston reassured, "Of course I can help you with managing your inheritance. What type of transactions do you need assistance with? Are they electronic transfers or physical deposits in cash, or gold, or diamonds? What level of funding, frequency, and availability will you require? Also, what kind of investment risk do you favor for your portfolio? I am well-versed in handling large inheritances and being most discreet for my clientele."

Juan was quietly stunned at the complete change in Johnston. He was also impressed at the range of questions being asked. This was the type of information Carlos wanted to know about.

Juan nodded and stated, "Now we have something to talk about. So tell me just how much record keeping and intrusive reporting do we need to endure here at your bank if we, in fact, wanted you to manage our inheritance? I must tell you we are a close family who takes our privacy very seriously. So seriously that we are in the process of moving our inheritance from our native country to a more understanding and sympathetic financial institution. So far, I like some of what I am hearing. So please tell me more about your services, customary banking fees, and, most importantly, your discreetness, sir."

The next two hours passed very quickly. Juan had the information requested by Carlos and additional details that were in the category of nice-to-have information. Finally, Johnston made his farewells, but not before inflicting another joke on Juan with again the same effect. Juan tried to smile as if it totally made sense. After Johnston left, JC rejoined Juan.

JC interjected and chuckled, "It occurs to me that Johnston needs to keep smiling all the time so no one tries to pull a condom down over his head by mistake."

Juan granted, "No arguments from me, buddy. If he can do what he said, then I think we can overlook his personality disorders. But frankly, I'd rather have my head shaved with a cheese grater while chewing on aluminum foil than listen to another one of his jokes."

JC toasted Juan silently with his glass in complete agreement.

CHAPTER 5

Sometimes winning the game is about beating the clock

Carlos could tell this was not going to be an easy discussion. Jesus Ruiz was thoroughly distracted and almost incapable of focusing on their conversation. The knife Jesus held to Carlos's throat was tolerable when standing still, but unnerving while milling around. It was standard practice when meeting with Jesus and mostly for show.

Carlos said, "Jesus, thanks for letting me in to speak to you. I know you have a lot on your mind and that you don't have a lot of time to spare."

The comments had the desired effect of getting Jesus to stop pacing and focus.

Jesus said, "I let you come in here because you said you had something I would find valuable. So, let's get to it. I do have a lot on my mind right now so if you don't start explaining you won't get a chance to talk."

Carlos coolly looked down to the knife held at his throat and calmly suggested, "If you're that busy, I can come back another time. Of course, I already know who is hunting for you. The federales busted your drug operation, rounded up all the farmers, and have started squeezing all their known associates and family members. They are currently getting warrants and reinforcements readied to finish off your organization."

Jesus lowered the knife, and Carlos could see a little flicker of fear across his eyes.

Jesus smirked, "Do you really think I'm frightened by them? They who have been on my payroll for the last ten years? I'll be back on top again. This is just a temporary setback. Every business has them."

Carlos responded with conviction, "Not this time. The federales are not taking any chances. Due to political pressure and NAFTA agreements, they have invited in the U.S. Drug Enforcement Agency to help make an example of you and your export business endeavors. Most of the politicians and police that were on your payroll have all been jailed if they didn't get shot while running. Those not jailed are now enthusiastically working in what has become a seriously large military operation to come in here and finish you off. It's not clear if their intention is to take you alive."

Jesus displayed another fatalistic smile. "Here I thought you were visiting to get your money back that you lost in the raid."

"I didn't think it would do any good to ask, but since you bring it up."

Jesus put the knife back to Carlos's throat, then added with malice in his voice, "Better tell me what's on your mind, Carlos, before I lose my temper. Just so you know, it better be good!"

Carlos ventured, "I can fly out your hard currency to an off-shore bank that I have. I want ten percent of everything I move. I would point out that everything I move to your offshore account is everything that the federales can't take away from you."

Jesus slowly removed the knife from Carlos's throat. He walked around pondering the offer.

Carlos continued, "Your group here is no match to what I've seen the federales assembling. It looks to be a full-scale operation with artillery and air power. If we can get all your money out of reach of the federales, you can comfortably buy your way to freedom. That is unless, of course, you want to stay here in Mexico and put your trust in the judicial system. Nothing said that you and your money can't go together."

"Keep going, you have my interest, Carlos."

"There is nowhere here in Mexico or the U.S. that you can take your money that they won't try and confiscate it. I can take it out in one big haul or do it in several trips to minimize the risk of being intercepted. It's your call. The machinery to hide and launder the money is your best option over staying here and being killed while fighting against the federales. In fact, I'm not sure that you won't be killed even if you surrender. I'm pretty sure that your money will never be found after the raid is over. Just as likely, they will divvy it up and report that it wasn't here when they closed your operations."

Jesus looked at Carlos and reflected, "You know, you remind me of your dad sometimes when you are putting your case forward so convincingly and passionately. You never knew him as a grown up, what a shame.

"I hated hearing that he had been killed by the police in the campus demonstrations of 1968 in Mexico City. He argued for rights and justice, but all it got him was a stray police bullet. He bled out before anyone found him or could do anything about it. He wanted things to be better, and he detested the government even though they gave him the money to go to school. I guess he was angry because it felt like the government was trying to buy him off for his father's death.

"Your abuelo was the epitome of the true government believer who always tried to do the right thing. You know, he was pretty sure that his last assignment to guard Leon Trotsky was a setup. Those Russian bastards knew where Trotsky was and that there would only be one duty bound guard left to overcome to assassinate him and that's what they found; one dead Trotsky, one dead guard, and your abuelo. I guess that murderous psychotic Stalin slept much easier knowing that there was no one left to contest his stranglehold on the country. I've never had any use for Russians since then.

"This money laundering scheme of yours doesn't involve any Russians, does it?"

Carlos shook his head then said, "No, Jesus, it doesn't involve using or trusting any Russians. So do we have a deal?"

"Yeah ok, for the sake of your dad, we have a deal. Seven percent of everything you help me get out is your cut."

"I said ten percent not seven percent."

Jesus left Carlos on the patio. He told Carlos to help himself to the wet bar and to have a seat. Carlos smiled as he reviewed the conversation and thought of the approach he might use with the visit to the next drug leader. Jesus walked out with a small yet heavy briefcase, which he handed Carlos along with an envelope.

"Here you go, we have a deal. Ten percent just like you asked."

Carlos looked at the briefcase and questioned, "What's this? I was expecting more than this."

Before Carlos could add anything else, Jesus smiled, "It's the money you paid down for the failed drug deal. You are the only one to actually come back here and offer me something I really need. Well, we need to be on good terms if we are going to pull this off. Agreed?"

Carlos smiled, nodded, and then said, "Agreed, Tío. Where is the money you want moved? How soon can we go?"

"I want to start tonight by moving half of the money since I also know that there isn't much time. Can your team be ready that quick?"

"Yes, sir. They are already standing by waiting for the phone call to go. If you want, we can leave sooner than that."

"No, I want the plane here at dusk, we load it up, and fly out after dark. Your people will be ready to take delivery once we land? Because as soon as that is done, I want to fly back and take the rest out, so this is going to be a tough forty-eight hours. Do you understand?"

Carlos agreed, "Yes, Tío, I understand."

"And don't call me uncle again, nephew. This is strictly business and you better not mess up."

CHAPTER 6

Finding something is as much a science as an art

On his August return flight from São Paulo to Zürich, Otto not only thought about how to approach finding Lara for Thiago, but reflected on the evolution of his organization. Thiago's knowledge of the capabilities of the family business, known as the R-Group, was limited to the branch that handled his investments, Ronnie, Ltd.

The family business, now in its third generation, had begun with the financial arms that had taken advantage of the encryption capabilities of the Enigma Machine. The machine had been captured by the three men who founded the R-Group. The families of the three men had fled Poland during World War II and that entire experience had shaped how they conducted business. Over the years they had certainly done many things that preserved the financial wealth of their customers, but also participated in activities that helped thwart those considered evil, such as the Nazis. The R-Group code of conduct was based on maintaining the balance of power for economic and human conservancy.

The business had evolved over time to include not only the financial arms based in Switzerland, but also real estate all over the world, communications, and information brokering as paid services. As technology evolved and shrunk the world in many ways, their team of family and selected contractors had kept pace and stayed one step ahead of all others, even those within the intelligence divisions of various countries. The projects they took on were by mutual consent of the inner circle, or family members in power. The organization's resources could perhaps help Thiago, but Otto needed to insure that by doing so nothing else would be compromised.

When he'd spoken to both Wolfgang and Ferdek before his flight home, they had agreed to support the effort, provided that other assignments were not impacted. The world, they had reminded him, continued in economic turmoil with new players vying for dominance. Some of these new players held a myopic view for their own benefit rather than the benefit of man overall. They'd suggested a joint collaboration meeting that included Quip, JAC, Erich, Petra, and Jacob via a secure conference call.

Otto slept for the last hour of the flight, but outlined in his dreams how the problem might be approached. He woke when the plane landed, quickly cleared customs, met Haddy with the car at the terminal curb, and they headed straight to the operations center. As his right hand in all things, he briefed her on the results of the meeting he'd completed.

Otto, in his prominent European manner, briefed his immediate team on his luncheon with Thiago in São Paulo as he delivered their new assignments. He provided photos and the history of Lara's disappearance to everyone. He suggested that the team should keep an eye open and an ear to the ground for information on Lara.

He assigned the primary responsibility of locating Lara to Quip and JAC. Quip, information scientist and the R-Group's bleeding edge creator, was a lean 1.8 meters with chiseled features and long blond hair tied back with a leather strap. Quip was into mastering technology to do his bidding. He'd cultivated his nickname over the years with his outrageous commentary. R-Group's cyber assassin Julie, also known as JAC, was a master identity inventor. She was a lithe 1.7 meters, with short, wavy, light brown hair and a heart-shaped face with an engaging smile that turned heads. Between identity changes she also worked in intelligence gathering, interactions with customers on confidential deliverables, and was adaptable to any situation with her girl-next-door look. These two, who over the years had worked projects together, were only too eager to accept such an assignment. Each had some ideas of what was needed and what could be leveraged. They conducted a brief discussion with Oscar and obtained the details about how he had tracked Lara to Argentina before losing her. After that call, Otto outlined their assignments as well as solicited their ideas.

Otto started, "So Quip, for the near term I want you and JAC to focus on this Lara disappearance. I wanted all of the team to be aware of the activity at a high level, but since Petra and Jacob are on vacation in Acapulco, I saved the extra details for you."

Quip asked, "This girl disappeared? What is going on down there in the Caribbean, anyway? I recently heard several Mexican police channel exchanges about movement with the drug lords in that region, with money missing and increased drug trafficking in Columbia and the Dominican. New players are trying to be identified as a part of our normal information trolling. Now this well-connected Lara Bernardes has gone missing. So are we to assume that the Bermuda Triangle has widened its reach to cover all the territory to the Sea of Cortez? Is this a new consequence to global warming or a sign that we will get additional requests?"

Otto, somewhat vexed at the comment, took a deep breath and continued, "Thiago Bernardes is not only a long-time customer of Ronnie, Ltd, but is also a close, personal friend. I have known him and Lara for a long time. This is a personal issue for me and a point of honor. I would like to know if you can work to help find her."

JAC, sensing Otto's irritation, placated, "Yes, of course we can, Otto. While I won't speak for Quip, I would very much like to help, and the more difficult the challenge the more gratifying when we succeed. Don't you think, Quip?"

Quip was somewhat embarrassed by his glib comment and offered, "Otto, I apologize for the impertinent remarks about your longtime friend. Yes of course, I would like very much to help in this matter. But where to start? I mean, from what you are telling me she fell off the grid, and even the head of Thiago's security team has no leads after months. My first guess is that he wasn't hunting for her in the right way. She left no trace of her old personage, as evidenced by the fact that they cannot track her with credit cards and state ID, so the answer is she is now living under a new identity."

JAC said, "Agreed. She must have known that if she used anything from her old life that it would lead Oscar straight to her. Otto, how much urban survival training did she receive from the security team and Oscar before going AWOL?"

Otto asked, "Urban survival training?"

It was now JAC's turn to be more informed, so she clarified, "She is an heiress to a large corporate conglomerate. Thus, she is automatically a target for kidnapping, extortion, and assassination. I would suggest she had security around her 24/7, as is the standard procedure. The security team would have typically educated her in how to handle herself if she were grabbed. So how much training has she had? If it is a little, then she may be a kidnapping victim after the money she had ran out. If she had a lot of urban training, then she may still be moving below the radar and continually covering her tracks."

"But Oscar and the security team have no evidence of kidnapping and certainly no ransom demands," Otto reaffirmed.

"Understood. They may not have any ransom demands yet, but in that part of the world kidnapping and extortion are a way of life for the rich and famous. We must assume that she cannot stay under the radar indefinitely because she wanted to be a model and most probably a movie star. At some point, even with her limited exposure to public media hounds, someone could identify her and take advantage. My concern is that we may not be able to find her in time."

Quip volunteered, "I have an idea how we can change the game in looking for her, but it is going to be slow, even with the help of the Immersive Collaborative Associative Binary Override Deterministic system, my old buddy, ICABOD. I want to use some leading edge but imperfect facial recognition algorithms to hunt through the human flotsam and jetsam that goes through that female meat market world of modeling to see if we can get any leads."

"What do you mean, imperfect facial recognition algorithms?" Otto asked, interested with the possibilities.

Quip continued, "Well, facial recognition can yield roughly an 89% success factor when in use with this kind of search. One can't hide the cheek, eye, nose, ear, mouth, and chin design structure which makes a human unique, unless plastic surgery is involved. We have to presume she would not have enough funds or likely a true desire for that sort of makeover. However, she certainly could significantly change her recognizable appearance with hair style, color, contacts, makeup, or other props such as hats or glasses to distort the analysis process.

"There has to be a good picture of the subject to work from and a good picture to compare to. The likelihood that we will be lucky enough to find an automated match quickly is rather small. We have the two photos provided, both of which are straight on face shots, with the most current being three years old. I have software that can gently age it, but modeling poses tend to be more profiles, or a head tilted in some way to accentuate what is being sold.

"Certain views have been found to be the best for selling. Sort of like watch ads, which usually show the time on the device as ten minutes after ten and thirty seconds. Fashion has some similar standards that are used, as do other venues in which female models are used. Even though it is slow, it is certainly better than waiting for her to use an old credit card."

"I agree, Quip. That is one good angle to cover. Most pictures for magazines, sales brochures and so forth are digitally transmitted and catalogued these days. It will take time to tap the various systems and film over the last few months in which she might appear.

"I, however, am better at people hunting on foot, so I am inclined to operate in the possible areas to which she would gravitate. The fashion spring and summer shoots would be my best vectors, I think, to start asking questions with her picture in hand."

JAC feverishly took notes on how to track the venues for the major fashion magazines and best city routes. Quip could use that same list for his data-hunting process.

Otto, now encouraged by their stream of ideas, summarized,

"So it looks like Quip can search common area pictures and modeling specific shoots where she might either be a hired model or an on-looker. JAC can probe the modeling scene at ground level. Both of you need to exchange leads and additional ideas frequently so as to enhance the search results. With these ideas, I feel certain additional options will present themselves.

"We need to track the areas eliminated and provide that as a progress update with the reasons why. Now remember, this is just to find her, not to approach her, at least not yet. It would be unfortunate to find her only for her to get spooked and disappear again. Agreed?"

Quip and JAC both nodded, letting the thoughts sink into their approach.

"JAC, how are you going to flash Lara's picture around and ask a whole lot of questions on where she might be, yet not raise suspicions that might get back to her?"

"My alter-ego here will be that I am a fashion designer look-ing for the right spokesperson for my new clothing line. She has caught my attention, and I want to see if she is up for the role. But I have been unable to find her attached to an agency." JAC flashed her megawatt smile with confidence.

Both Otto and Quip were aware of how convincing JAC could be when she was in a role. She was also an artistic dabbler of sorts, so a few quick designs for a pseudo-fashion look would be easy. If she needed a wardrobe for any reason then she would call upon those resources.

Otto then allowed, "Ok, I'll leave you to it. Please keep me informed of events and any progress on locating her. Thank you in advance for working on this."

CHAPTER 7

One step leads to another, but it is the direction that matters

Simone stared into space while seated at the hotel bar. For several months her problem had been persistent, not enough income and unrealized career dreams. She was trying to slow down on her third drink, but she needed to get to a certain mental state before Spencer came and got her. As an undiscovered model, she knew that the margaritas packed more calories into her system than she'd exercise off, but she needed the numbness alcohol provided for the pending photo shoot.

She'd left home after graduating from university with her business degree to follow her dream of modeling and possibly finding her way to an acting career. She laughed bitterly thinking back on her dream, and wondered how she had ever thought the career move was viable. What's that old Chinese proverb? she thought, Be careful what you wish for, you just might get it.

She continued going to go-sees for gigs, but there was always someone else chosen for the prime role. She was considered attractive with her mixed heritage of South American and Mexican and a toned body just short of athletic. Her generous mouth and bedroom eyes, as one photographer had commented on her, had landed her some paying shots for lingerie. Her smile was charming, framing perfect teeth, but her cleavage had been perfect without artificial enhancement. She wasn't built like the rail thin models that most fashion photographers preferred.

She followed the shoots for all the spring and summer fashion lines from the South American to the North American coasts. Though her funds had dwindled significantly, she was able to travel with the other models for the selection process done at each of the shoots for filler models and the ongoing search that was done for new faces. The second and third-tiered jobs did pay a little, but after the photo shoots there was always some photographer that asked if anyone wanted to make some extra money tonight. She lowered her gaze to the drink and sighed. At one point here in Acapulco she'd needed the extra money, and that was how this slippery slope she was on had started.

The extra money was usually for semi-nude photo shoots which were reasonably tame, but she knew if she wasn't mindful it could lead to other shoots that weren't as innocent. She had met Spencer at one of these shoots, and he'd promised that his connections could land her into a prime acting role. He'd struck up a conversation and empathized with her at one of her lowest points, and she'd agreed to move on toward her goals. Now she was having second and third thoughts, especially after the impromptu breakfast with one of Spencer's starlets this morning.

The starlet, Rita, had stated flatly that Spencer was an accomplished predator. Spencer was a beefy 99 kilograms at a mere 1.52 meters and always poorly dressed. His long, oily black hair was thinning, and he was constantly trying to fluff it with his greasy hands. The patchy mustache and beard thankfully covered up his unbrushed teeth and poor complexion. Despite his looks, he could entice people into adult entertainment venues by preying on their dreams. Males and females who dreamed about making the big time were always easy targets for Spencer and his adult entertainment machine.

Rita told Simone that Spencer was the writer, producer, and director of smut films, and he had no shortage of voyeur clientele for his porno output. He had a gift of calming the natural fears of an unsure participant in the sexual scenes he dreamed up but wanted others to act out. The promise of money made the effort rewarding for the participants, but his ability to exploit the ambitions of these vulnerable people was his genius. Of course, all the promised money never materialized, so the poor participants kept coming back to earn a little more or maybe get discovered so they could get on with their lives and put this shabby episode behind them. Some did escape, but he'd set his trap to get Simone and keep her under his control.

Simone let one tear slide down her cheek for her self-loathing in taking a wonderful human experience and letting a deeply disturbed individual distort it with base, foul, and coarse intent to serve it up to a paying clientele. She had watched his productions. He had tempted her with minor cameo roles as he tried to seduce her into begging for a larger, more graphic role.

His adult entertainment productions had become more profitable ever since he stopped trying to write himself into the script. The story, Rita related to Simone that morning, was that when he wanted a certain type of performance from a male on the set, he would pull down his own britches to give a demonstration. It should be noted that, in this of all professions, size REALLY does matter. But for all the attendees on the set it was all perfectly obvious that Spencer was desperately underpowered as a male, and the demo went limp, so to speak. Before they'd parted, Rita suggested that Simone really consider herself and what she wanted and asked if this was the right avenue to choose.

Simone could see it was time for Spencer to show and discuss her role for the scheduled filming. She just couldn't find the discipline in herself to face Spencer and his entourage of human junk. His two brothers-in-law had learned the lighting and sometimes ran the cameras when Spencer was helping stage the scene. Their sister, Spencer's wife, had died in bed when her cigarette set it on fire. If she hadn't been so drugged up and drunk, she might have escaped alive.

The adult entertainment distributors, Bob and Estella, would be there too to see that their particular taste was captured in the production. They were always mesmerized when Spencer used the buggy whip in scenes, their preference being for heavy S&M. She glanced down the front of her gown to see the almost-healed bruise the buggy whip had left on her breast. A mistake, Spencer had reassured her. She needed the money, but all she was willing to do was another cameo role and not have to get close to the buggy whip.

The drink was almost gone, and Spencer hadn't shown. Perhaps he'd been distracted, she hoped. Since he was late she thought she might return to her room and worry about finances tomorrow.

"It looks like your glass is empty. Would you permit a stranger to buy you a fresh drink, madam?" Carlos smiled at the pretty lady. "My name is Carlos. If you will excuse me for being forward, you are stunning."

Simone studied his face, looking to see if she knew the stranger. Their eyes met, and she could hardly believe that this powerful, good looking and tastefully dressed man was addressing her as a lady. She realized she'd forgotten she really was one. Before Simone could answer, a heavy hand grabbed hold of her arm. She tried to pull away and failed.

"Let's go, Simone. I have a perfect gig for you this afternoon," Spencer said with no greeting. "In fact the crew is waiting on you now."

Carlos, completely unimpressed with Spencer's interruption, continued, "And if the drink refresh finds favor with you, perhaps you would consent to have a little dinner as well?"

Spencer was in a hurry and fairly annoyed at Simone, but this new guy was really chafing him.

Spencer asked, "Was I talking to you, buster? Simone works for me and right now we have work, so bugger off!"

Spencer turned to leave and tried to pull Simone from the stool.

"Simone. I like the sound of that name. Simone, will you have dinner and drinks with me? I think we should get to know one another better." Carlos smiled at her again, ignoring Spencer.

Carlos reached for her hand, and with all the chivalry that can possibly be packed into one moment, took it and gently kissed it. Spencer was absolutely astonished. Simone, who could no longer see, hear, or feel Spencer, was enchanted.

"Yes, sir knight," Simone said to him with a charming smile.

Carlos, enthralled by her voice and smile, smiled back at her. For all the impact that Spencer had on these two, he might as well have been a bar stool. Spencer was a man who was usually cold and calculating, rarely impulsive. However, the sequence of events had swept him up into a rash action that he soon regretted. Spencer tried to push Carlos away and at the same time pull Simone along to exit the bar. Carlos didn't have the time to intercept his temper before his adrenaline leak launched his muscular body into overdrive.

Carlos caught Spencer's hand just above the wrist and crushed the two forearm bones together, causing excruciating pain. Spencer released Simone and quickly tried to retrieve his mangled arm that no longer responded to neural impulses. With his other arm he hurled a poorly aimed punch that merely grazed Carlos's head. Carlos couldn't stop himself and before Spencer could do anything else, Carlos caught Spencer by the throat and lifted his body off the floor. Spencer, struggling for air and with only one good hand left to try to free his windpipe from Carlos's death grip, suddenly found himself pinned against the wall. Spencer was flailing and gasping. Carlos, with Spencer braced against the wall, stared into his eyes and smiled.

Carlos quietly assured, "I'm quite sure you won't be joining us, but I will take you up on your offer to buy dinner for us to make up for our poor introduction. Nod your head if you understand, as this is the interactive part of our discussion."

It was all Spencer could do to make the requested movement.

Carlos grinned. "Good. Now use your good hand to reach into your pocket for your dinner contribution so we can leave. It would be unfortunate if you don't have any money on you."

Spencer, still gasping for air and being held almost one meter off the ground, found the strength to find the money to give to Carlos. Carlos smiled a terrifying smile and hurled Spencer towards the end of the bar, where the heavy oak stopped his forward progress.

After the incident had been concluded with Spencer's road trip into the bar, Simone's eyes clearly indicated that she had been impressed while watching the exercise. Carlos came over to her, smiled and simply snapped his fingers to bring her out of her daze.

Carlos offered, "I hope you're hungry, Miss Simone. I know I'm starved. So where can a gentleman take a beautiful lady of good breeding for dinner? We have much to talk about."

CHAPTER 8

Sins of the father
can follow the sons forever

"Dr. Pettingrübber, the briefing is ready to begin in the Omega Room, sir."

"Thank you, Stacy. I'm on my way."

Dr. Eric Pettingrübber was abruptly stopped by a remembered conversation he once had with his father on proper meeting etiquette. Hans von Pettingrübber maintained that a meeting would begin when he arrived so there was no need to have a staff member come and fetch him. Of course, Hans von Pettingrübber was a Standartenführer, an SS Colonel in the Intelligence Section of the Waffen SS for the Eastern Front in Russia during World War II. Von Pettingrübber, as he preferred to be called, had been spared the public trials of high-ranking SS officials because of his usefulness in the intelligence business. He'd been assigned to gather military grade intelligence on most of Eastern Europe during the Cold War.

Hans von Pettingrübber's career at one point seemed doomed when he tried to alert the German High Command of an eminent Russian counterattack planned for October to November of 1942. He simply couldn't get anyone to believe that the whole Russian Army was going to fall on the left flank of the German 6th Army at Stalingrad. After the fall of Stalingrad, von Pettingrübber's reports carried much more weight and were taken quite seriously. He was very well-schooled in the intelligence gathering business along the German Eastern Front. So much so that the Americans wanted him working for them after the war ended.

Due to the risky nature of Hans von Pettingrübber's work for the Americans, young Pettingrübber was sent to the States for schooling and distanced from his father's work. Young Pettingrübber had earned a Doctorate in Behavioral Sciences from Johns Hopkins University. Like his father, he had a talent for the intelligence business.

It was a short walk to the Omega Room. Once in the room he took a seat off to the side so as to remain low key. The presenter abruptly stopped the chit-chat to greet the good doctor.

Dr. Pettingrübber said, "Please, just Eric will be fine. Can we get started?"

The presenter, Travis Marshall, pleased at being able to address the doctor as Eric, quickly proceeded to the chart deck and presentation.

"Ladies and gentlemen, we have started seeing some unusual activity in the Mexican and Caribbean areas. Both our electronic surveillance and ground operatives have noticed some anomalies with regards to the drug cartel leaders throughout the region.

"To be more specific, the drug lords are vanishing. At first, we thought that this was the normal drug cartel turf war activity where one is disposed of by another and the balance of power simply shifted. But for the last few months, one drug lord after another just drops off the grid, and usually just ahead of when the Mexican drug enforcement officials are ready to do

a comprehensive raid to shut the target down." Travis left up
the chart that depicted the range of local drug lords that had
vanished.

One of the attendees asked, "How do we know that it isn't
just inside trader information and that the Mexican drug enforcement officials aren't in on the scam?"

Travis nodded, "Then we would be seeing pay off dollars
going to the officials in at least some of the instances. This usually
becomes obvious at some point, which it has not in any of the
current cases. Plus, the Mexican drug enforcement officials
trashed almost the entire personnel infrastructure and replaced
them a year ago with what is believed to be reputable law
enforcement individuals.

"Additionally, our own DEA personnel are in there, at the
request of the Mexican government, and they confirm the claims.
Everything is as it should be, but there just aren't any drug
lords to arrest and, more importantly, all their liquid assets are
missing as well."

That sparked another attendee to disapprovingly question,
"So how long have the drug lords been practicing this Houdini
routine? A couple of months is what you indicated? Then why
are we just now hearing of it and why are we only seeing part of
the picture? With all of our operatives and intelligence gathering
activity that we brag about; a bunch of drug lords just check out
and we don't know what happened? Do we need to get a note
from someone's mommy that answers will be found?"

Travis, a bit flustered at the comments, continued, "We
have not focused on this as it is not really our jurisdiction, and
frankly there is no corresponding activity to match against. No
dead bodies, no gang hits, no money left behind, and no money
surfacing again, which suggests a well-designed exit strategy.
Problem is, it is not just one of them but all the top players.
We've never see anything like this before."

Dr. Pettingrübber enquired, "Do the Mexicans have the resources to work this issue, or are we being asked to help? I mean, I would like to know what is going on, but is it really our issue? With all the mandatory budget cuts that we have coming, we need to pick and choose our battles carefully. We simply don't have the resources to run down every anomaly on the planet."

The discussion continued and opinions were gathered. Travis promised to provide everyone with the summary and presentation materials before the end of the day. It had been a lively topic.

After the meeting, Dr. Pettingrübber returned to his office and signaled Stacy that he was not to be disturbed as he closed the door. He removed a cell phone from his highly secure safe and launched a special encryption program that blinked when it was ready. He placed a call to a speed dial number from the contact list of one.

"Hello, Mr. Monty. I am always pleased to hear from you. To what do I owe the pleasure of your contact, kind sir?"

Dr. Pettingrübber responded, "You know it would be easier for our conversations if I had a name I could use for you. I find talking to you a little awkward since you know my avatar name, but I don't have one for you."

"I know it's you when you call since your encrypted voice call must complete the electronic handshake before it can speak with my device. But perhaps you're right, Mr. Monty, and please forgive my thoughtlessness on this matter. I would not want our relationship to suffer from my rudeness. Please call me Otto for ease of conversation."

"Otto. I like that. It seems to fit well. So, Otto, I have been alerted to some curious events in an area that we have interest in, but need to keep our distance for a variety of reasons. It occurs to me that you and your organization might be able to do some discreet prowling in the Mexican and Caribbean drug arenas to see what is going on. I don't have a great deal to go on, but that always gets your team interested, doesn't it?

"Over the last few months, six top-tier drug lords have vanished out of the Mexican drug business. There is no trace of them or their assets, and payoffs to local officials haven't been found. We would like very much to know where these people and their assets landed. Please add this activity to our existing contract statement of work and label it the Houdini Project. We will use the standard drop-box transfer method once the report is done. Please let me know when you have something, Otto."

Otto confirmed, "That is, of course, acceptable. It may take a bit of time, but we will put the best folks on it. Can you send me the details of the six vanished souls and possibilities on which ones might be next to our secure drop box?"

"I will send it now, yes. It aligns with the Mexican government raids, so potential names will also be included."

"Thank you, Mr. Monty. Good evening, sir."

CHAPTER 9

Mistakes are doorways to discovery

The first-class flight from Zürich to Acapulco was perfect for a late summer, well-deserved vacation. During their flight, Petra and Jacob discussed the myriad of events that surrounded them and their budding relationship. Both had grown up sheltered for reasons of the family business. They were both brilliant information technology specialists, with skills that highly complimented each other. Each was passionate about knowledge overall, but had limited experience in the ways of love.

This trip was to help them understand how relationships evolved and even blossomed into forever love. But they lacked the experience of knowing what they gained or lost from opening themselves up to one another. In their own way, each was enamored with the other. Physically they were definitely well matched. Jacob was tall and athletic, with dark wavy hair and deep blue eyes, while Petra was rather petite, well-toned, with long blonde hair and brown eyes flecked with gold. They complemented each other in all ways.

Petra discussed her fear that Jacob wouldn't trust her, as she'd kept his background identity hidden when she'd first discovered she was attracted to him. Jacob reassured her that was in the past and they were moving forward. Jacob indicated his reluctance to commit to a relationship until he felt settled in his work. He was also concerned that she'd lived a far more affluent lifestyle than he felt comfortable with. Finding out he was actually a descendent of one of the founding members of the R-Group, as Petra was, disconcerted him to a degree. But he'd found family that he'd thought did not exist.

He believed in the overall charter of the R-Group, but wondered if he would be as valuable as Petra and Quip. Quip had demonstrated his capabilities with his insightful methods of adopting technology to snoop in networks all over the world and garner selected information. Petra was an encryption expert at the absolute top of the field. Jacob himself was a technology tester, programmer, and information flow specialist. He also knew that if Otto, Ferdek, or Wolfgang passed away, the burdens of the R-Group would pass to Petra, Quip, or himself in turn. The agreement among the team to shelve the SECcoin had demonstrated how much power the R-Group held. This troubled him from a vast responsibility perspective.

Their discussion had cleared the air to a degree as they'd eaten, sipped wine, laughed, and kissed now and again during the flight. Both Petra and Jacob wanted to see if they would grow closer on this trip. As busy as the business was, taking this time away together placed some work at possible risk. Each had focused their lives on their work to this point. They were committed to trying to explore the possibilities of a personal life together.

Jacob and Petra settled into their suite in Acapulco, complete with a private Jacuzzi. Acapulco was a beautiful setting, often referred to as the Mexican Riviera, and Divers Resort was truly elegant. The beaches were pristine, the sun shone brightly, and the people looked happy. Haddy, Otto's wife, had really outdone herself with these accommodations. The bar had a perfect view of the cliff divers, as stated in the hotel brochure. It was a place neither of them had ever been, and they hoped to explore it and their feelings together without work interruptions.

Jacob suggested, "Let's spend the day on the beach near the pool bar. I'd like to swim a little and maybe try to learn some of the water sports using their equipment. How do you feel about that, Petra?"

"I'm not a big fan of stingrays, jellyfish, or squid so I'll stay closer to the pool, but only if you'll put this SPF 200 on me so I don't get skin cancer. Ok?"

Jacob studied her a minute and answered, "Yes, my darling. I wouldn't want anything like a nasty sunburn to mar your creamy skin or prevent me from touching it."

Jacob helped Petra get settled near the pool in a comfy lounger under a large umbrella and then went to try out the water toys. Petra mused to herself, Boys with toys. She smiled at her man's efforts to learn how to use a sail bolted to a surfboard.

The problem with poolside service in resorts anywhere in the Caribbean or on the Mexican coast like this one, was that prompt service was an oxymoron. Petra finally got up to get a drink ordered at the bar so she could enjoy it that day.

While she waited for her beverage, a gentle, friendly voice said, "I was wondering how long you were going to last out here without a drink. Hi, I'm Simone. I can tell you're not from this part of the world because you were expecting poolside service."

She offered an engaging smile that normally made people warm to her. Simone truly liked people. This lady she had spoken to looked nice and her companion had been very kind before he'd left for the water sports.

Petra responded, "Hello, Simone. I'm Petra and you are correct. I'm not from around here. We are here to recharge our batteries, so to speak."

Simone said with an impish grin, "Yes, I noticed your man. He seems quite nice, though not brown enough to suit my tastes, in case you were worried."

Petra grinned, "I wasn't worried. So, is your significant other also out playing in the ocean? I can't believe he would not be in close proximity to such stunner like you."

Simone laughed, "Like your man, mine is also a treasure! My prince called and asked me to meet him here because he wanted to celebrate our two-month anniversary and his most successful business deal to date. I've never been so happy. I know you must think me silly for telling you all this, but I'm so proud of him and his successes! He pulled me out of the worst possible circumstances, and he loves me for who I am. You have no idea what that means to someone like me."

Simone's eyes glistened with moisture, but she did not shed any tears. Petra observed that Simone was quite pretty, with hair black as coal tight against her head in a long braid. Her make-up was a little heavy for Petra's taste but accentuated her pretty face with hollowed cheeks that defined her thinness. Petra could see that Simone had no pretense and was quite genuine. However, as in all social encounters, particularly with females (ok males too), she couldn't help but compare herself to Simone.

Her quick inventory took note of Simone's hair, facial features, mannerisms, and wardrobe. They were both pretty striking women, tastefully attired for the beach setting. Petra grinned as she thought of 'Salt and Pepper' as nicknames for them.

Simone seemed ready to share her innermost feelings and gave her trust up front. Petra was more guarded and did not easily share, holding her trust more as collateral. She returned with her drink and settled back under the umbrella as Simone stretched out on the chaise next to her.

"So what does this prince of yours do, Simone? Is he a foreign diplomat? Is he a real estate broker? A handsome airline pilot? Or is he from a wealthy family that is part owner of this wonderful retreat? Inquiring minds want to know."

Simone, excited to brag on Carlos, said, "Oh no, he is his own man! He's worked his way up in the finance world and is now at the top of his game. You should see how hard he works! Many times we have had to cancel or postpone our time together, but he always calls me to say how much he loves me and he always makes it up to me.

"We have wonderful weekends together and he usually brings a gift. Not very much and hardly ever expensive, but that's what is so thrilling for me. The fact that he stopped whatever he was doing long enough to get a small gift to bring back to me. Well, this time he called me and said meet him here.

"When I got here, everyone called me Miss Simone this or Miss Simone that. It is terribly exciting for me to be catered to by people at the directions left by my man. I adore him."

The two ladies smiled at each other and with the clear lines of battle now behind them, they could be friends.

"Simone, I think we should become friends. I like your enthusiasm. It sounds like you have a wonderful life. Happy anniversary, by the way. My mother always said to remember the important times and mark them."

"Petra, I would like a friend. Thank you. Tell me about yourself."

Petra and Simone sipped their drinks and exchanged information. They had fun laughing at stories and getting to know the parts each of them was willing to reveal. Petra found it quite nice to have a female friend to chat with and grew more comfortable as the afternoon wore on. Simone was delighted at finding a friend as well and shared many things with Petra, though nothing about Spencer. Petra told her some about her home in Europe and a little about her work. Simone talked about her desires and of course, Carlos. Several hours had elapsed when Jacob waved that he was returning his surfboard to the vendor.

"Well, it looks as if Jacob is finished with the toys for a while. It has been great visiting. Perhaps we can get together tomorrow morning as well?" Petra suggested as she was putting her stuff back into her beach bag.

"Carlos should be here tonight so how about the four of us get together for dinner, Petra? Say around seven here at the hotel? The food is pretty good, and they make great margaritas. If it doesn't work, call the desk and leave a message for Carlos and Simone in room 114."

"I think that is a great idea. I am sure Jacob would enjoy meeting you and your Carlos. I will call if we cannot make it. We are in room 640. Thanks for the afternoon."

CHAPTER 10

Life is one big experiment

Simone reassured Carlos that this was just a fun social encounter with new folks and no high finance pressure deadlines. Carlos struggled getting into character for the casual dinner but had settled into the role by the time the hostess seated them. Petra had similar concerns from Jacob, but his issue was one of wanting her alone and naked. Once introductions were completed with the obligatory handshakes, they settled in, ordered drinks and moved past the first meeting anxieties.

Simone was the talkative, social animal of the bunch and quickly had the conversation rolling along. In fact, Simone was so loquacious that the others had trouble finding an opening in her monologue to get a word in edgewise. Petra smiled at the ease with which her newfound friend made everyone comfortable. She related the story of their meeting by the pool and the crazy people they'd observed. They all chuckled at the animated delivery.

Jacob finally found an opening and asked, "So, Carlos, I understand that you have been quite busy these last few months in the financial sector. I don't wish to pry into your customer/consultant relationships, but can you tell us about your area of expertise?"

Petra sensed that Jacob simply could not turn off work. She knew that he was interested, and he had spent a great deal of time using his technology insights in the finance sector. He was always the one looking for business expansion possibilities, more so now that he was a part of the family operation. She smiled, confident that he would graciously handle this portion of the discussion.

Carlos warmed to the polite way that Jacob asked and responded, "I've worked a long time at modest financial consulting jobs, and in the last six months I have gravitated towards financial management of large inheritances. People that I've grown up with are coming into large inheritances as they lose parents or take over family trusts. I've been advising and consulting with these clients and friends. Luckily, each one in turn gives me a referral that brings me new opportunities. As in a lot of professions, if you work hard and pay your dues the rewards seem to find you. Business, as they say, has been good. And you, Jacob, can you tell us something of your profession?"

Jacob was delighted with their dinner companions and the shared discussion. He was still a guarded individual but saw no reason not to respond.

"I'm something of a high tech specialist in digital security, though I do enter other avenues in technology, as it makes sense."

While Jacob spoke, Carlos only seemed focused on Simone's arm as he slowly and gently stroked her smooth skin with the back of his hand repeatedly with tender, erotic intent. Jacob and Petra noticed, and the distraction made it difficult for Jacob to speak, as his mind was wandering elsewhere. He and Petra had limited public displays of affection, but somehow he found this gesture something that could be reassuring.

Jacob continued, "I get called in to a variety of companies, a lot of banks actually, to do what is called pen-testing or penetration-testing of digital security systems. I find it challenging and a fun profession. Just me against the security defenses, and after I'm done I write my report and deliver the findings to the customer so they can strengthen their defenses against the bad guys. I also review programs and write them as needed to help customers as required."

Carlos was still fixated on stroking Simone's arm with the back of his hand, but he obviously concentrated and listened to Jacob. He sensed that this Jacob was not one to talk about his success unless it struck the right chord. Carlos found that interesting in this new gringo acquaintance.

Without moving his gaze from Simone, he suggested, "So this penetration-testing, I would think, entails slowly and deliberately getting close to a target to, say, observe all the appropriate details that can be viewed from a cursory look. Perhaps gently touching the target here and there to see if there is a reciprocal response or maybe an invitation. It would seem appropriate to also inspect as much surface area as possible, at least visually, so a detailed memory map can be created and, if the target is receptive, perhaps to offer to enter deep enough to continue the exploration but not provoke alarm in this penetration exercise."

Carlos's description of the activity caused Jacob's mind to shift to what Petra had pulled him away from to attend this dinner. He could sense that Petra was blushing and saw her pulse quicken in her beautiful, creamy neck. Technology gone erotic – who would have thought?

Still stroking Simone's arm, Carlos continued, "I can see where such a penetration exercise would require the utmost discretion by the one doing the penetration of a well-defined target so that the compromise could be conducted over and over without being refused the exclusive access to the tenderest areas of one's business.

I would expect that the intruder would want to withdraw as gently as he had penetrated so as to keep the target receptive to future penetration exercises. Wouldn't you agree?"

Jacob swallowed to gain composure over his runaway thoughts. Petra was silent but totally focused on this description, and her blush was deepening. Simone was too enthralled by his fingers across her arm to even notice the effect that Carlos was having on their dinner companions.

Jacob responded with a grin, "Yes, I would totally agree on that approach. Your description is most interesting. Honestly, I'd not taken that view of it myself."

Carlos stopped the gentle stroking of Simone rather abruptly and addressed Petra, "So Madam Petra, can you tell us about yourself? I sense you are drawn to this accomplished gentleman, but I can't believe that you are a penetration taster as well?"

Simone quickly leaned over to Carlos and whispered a little too loudly, "Tester, mi amor! Not taster!"

Before the conversation could go further Petra said in her very charming voice and with an impish grin, "I am adaptable and definitely drawn to him, though not a taster like he is."

The brief second of silence was washed away by a torrent of laughter.

Carlos grinned and asked, "I am curious, Jacob. Do you do independent contract work? I actually have need of such a skillset in my new capacity."

Jacob blinked and had to refocus his thoughts on the directional conversation change. This Carlos had a quick mind and worked at multi-levels, which Jacob appreciated. With it now directed back to him, he responded.

"Well, I have done independent contract work in the past. I usually get an ok from my company before I do so, in order to avoid any conflict of interest issues."

Carlos offered, "Forgive me, but in my evolving role as a financial consultant I have been put on the board of directors at a banking institution. I am compelled to provide the best and most comprehensive security for my clients' money. People don't think about things like that once their money is in the bank. They simply presume it secure. In my new role I am forced to consider the bank's security as well as the client's money. With the experience you have outlined, it does appear clear that this is an important aspect to consider. I see value in engaging your services to evaluate my bank's security. So how can we make this happen?"

Simone was a little let down at Carlos's change in direction away from a fun casual dinner with new friends. She was very proud of Carlos, but did want him to relax. And she wanted to make certain that Petra wouldn't be offended by the business detour.

Simone sweetly suggested with a gentle smile and big eyes, "Honey, can we talk business some other time? I mean we've just met these nice folks that are here on holiday. I'm sure the last thing on their minds is going back to work. Please?"

Carlos smiled softly at Simone and her gentle request.

Looking at the new acquaintances, he expressed regret, "My apologies, Petra and Jacob, but Simone is right. I didn't mean to be boorish or rude in my conversational topics."

Glad Carlos wasn't offended, Simone added with a grin, "You are just like your brother sometimes, delightfully risqué and naughty. By the way, wasn't he coming here tonight as well? Where is he?"

Petra asked, "Are we given to understand that there may be another person with the same je ne sais quoi as your Carlos?"

Simone laughed, "Juan is such the ladies' man, which is likely why he isn't here. You can't help but love Juan, but my heart belongs to this man. Carlos is my prince and the only one for me."

Carlos smiled at the thought of his brother and presented, "The difference between us is I was looking for Miss Right, and Juan is always looking for Miss Right Now."

Again the table erupted into laughter. As often happened, Carlos eased into the shift of conversation using his missing brother as the target.

Carlos sighed and with a look of concern replied, "It is a shame that he and I have a long standing vendetta that must be resolved soon. Juan showed up one day with a five-meter-long recreational vehicle fully outfitted for a hunting trip. Now I'm not too bad with a weapon and a static target, based on my military training, but he wanted to hunt the fastest animal in North America, the pronghorn antelope. I should have known better, but I agreed that we should bring along my old partner, Don, to provide local color.

"Our destination was a large cattle ranch that permits antelope hunting in northern Mexico. Predictably, Juan started slugging down cerveza even before we get out of the driveway, to the point I wouldn't trust him to drive. We finally get on the ranch property. I'm driving down this gravel and dirt road looking for antelope. The nice thing about a recreational vehicle is that while I was driving he could excuse himself to the bathroom and avoid my stopping every ten kilometers. Well, he goes back to relieve himself of the back of the vehicle.

"Don and I are driving along at about seventy-two kilometers per hour looking for antelope, but I'm not really watching the road.

"Don hollered out, 'Carlos, slow down for the cattle guard coming up.' I hit the brakes a little too aggressively but got the vehicle's speed down to cross the cattle guard comfortably. Juan stormed out to confront me while I'm still driving. It is at that point he vowed vendetta and that he will extract revenge. He was wet from his chin all the way down to his belt loops and obviously furious. Don and I looked at each other then back at Juan.

"Juan shouted, 'You knew I was standing back there taking a leak and you deliberately slammed on the brakes. I went flying backwards into the little tub right behind me. So there I am on my head, in the tub, but I'm still peeing and can't stop because it takes a while to empty five cervezas from a bladder.'"

Everyone laughed at the picture this tale painted. Jacob and Petra hadn't met the man, yet the story was so funny. Petra and Simone had tears running down their cheeks and struggled to get their giggles under control.

Carlos added with an almost straight face, "I shouldn't have said anything at that point but I couldn't resist. I commented on his apparent low pressure for urination. That a man in his prime, in that position, should really be able to soak his hair and not just hit under his chin."

Again, the table erupted in laughter. It took a while for everyone to regain composure with Simone and Petra giggling out portions of the story, which started them laughing all over again. They continued light conversation over dinner, desserts and after-dinner drinks before Petra and Jacob left for their room.

Later that evening Juan and Carlos were having drinks at the bar in a quiet corner so no one could overhear their conversation.

Juan angrily asked, "So what ARE you thinking? We've got this swell gig setup making money from these drug dealers by moving their goods. We get a nice percentage for the effort. We've even gotten seats on the board of directors of the bank based on all the inheritance monies we have been directing there. Hell, we might even get to be respectable bankers! So what is going on with this Jacob character and you hiring him for consulting? You don't know him at all. Hell, you just met, and he is a gringo to boot."

Carlos looked at Juan and patiently explained, "So when the commissions run out because there is no one left to help move their inheritances, when we have made all the introductions so all our customers are now dealing directly with the bank, what do you think will happen? How long will the bank keep us on the board if we are not bringing in new customers? You need to understand, we are working ourselves out of a job! We need to be thinking about our next steps, our future."

Juan sat back and digested the comments, then retorted, "I hadn't thought of it in those terms. But what is the Jacob angle? A pen-tester? Whatever the hell that is! And his babe, Petra, what did you say she told you she did? She does encryption algorithms to protect electronic data and secure transmissions? How is he or she going to help us with our looming problem?"

"Juan, I want to leverage our bank privileges while we have them. I want this guy to help show us the bank security vulnerabilities. Then we will use those vulnerabilities to take all that money from our drug dealer clients and electronically transfer it somewhere encrypted so we don't get traced. The bank would only prosecute if the customers want to work with the police. What do you think the chances are that those drug dealer clienteles are going to want to do that?"

"Ok, but you can damn well bet they will bring their own associates to hunt us down and kill us to get the money back. Or just kill us. You know how easily amused they are," speculated Juan.

"With all their funds in our hands, don't you think we could easily hideout with our own private army? We can go anywhere in the world. They won't have the resources to locate us."

Juan raised his glass to Carlos and saluted the brilliance of the plan.

"Bro, why didn't you say this in the first place? But one thing, I want to make sure that Phillip Johnston gets the blame for the money being stolen so that the first thing the drug lords do is execute him. Would that be ok?"

"Juan, you drive a hard bargain, but because it's you, ok. Here I thought it was only me that was annoyed by that little man."

The two toasted the planned success and called it a night.

CHAPTER 11

Opportunities always look bigger going than coming

Otto walked into the command center following his discussion with Mr. Monty. He was trying to recall what Quip had said about some activity in the Mexican and Caribbean region. He hated to take resources from searching for Lara, but Quip was known for effective multitasking. Sadly, Otto feared that he was getting too old and perhaps missing details. From what had been discussed previously, many of the tasks would be automated for Quip's portion of the Lara effort.

"Quip, I need you to look into some unusual activity in Mexico," Otto stated after joining Quip in the operations center.

"What am I looking for, Otto? We are talking about a region that is fairly unusual by most standards."

"Your dear friend, Mr. Monty, has contacted me and asked that we look into drug lords and their money vanishing from Mexico. I suspect it will extend across the Caribbean, but he did not bring that up. Apparently for the last several months, one drug lord after another just drops off the grid, along with their accumulated wealth."

"Could it be the normal drug cartel activity where they take each out until the winner just takes over? There has been some buzz for many weeks now regarding drug lords and money movement. No specifics though. Why are we being asked to help in the area rather than the officials running those countries? Is the U.S. DEA involved? Monty is not DEA, but he should be tied into their intelligence gathering. For the record, he is not my dear friend. I do like picking on him though." Quip added a grin and suppressed a chuckle thinking about his last encounter with Mr. Monty.

"My dear Quip, this is accounting forensics that we are being asked to look into. Money just doesn't disappear from the balance sheet without a corresponding entry somewhere else. We are interested in the somewhere else of this missing drug money and the top tier drug lords themselves. If it was just one drug dealer making a run for it with his ill-gotten gains, then, yes, you are correct, the U.S. DEA and Mexican police can run their operation without any help from us. However, since it is a steady stream of drug dealers with their money vanishing that means that some kind of well-run organization is at play. A new organization we aren't aware of makes me very nervous, especially with the potentially huge sums of money. We want to know everything about them. Wouldn't you agree, Quip?"

"I totally agree. New bad guys, hmmm, my favorite. Should I alert Jacob and Petra? When are they due back from their vacation anyway?"

"That's right, they are down in Acapulco, but they've only been there a short time. Perhaps it would be a good idea to get word to them in case your reconnaissance efforts need some field work to help get answers. You go ahead and start. They really aren't due back for two more weeks, but I'll contact them and ask them to stay a few more days in case we need eyes and hands in the area. Besides, who wouldn't want to spend a little more time in the Caribbean on R&R?" Otto grinned at finding a way to keep Petra and Jacob in a romantic setting.

"I can start. I presume this is not a higher priority that finding Lara. JAC is sending updates on locations that have not gained us any ground, so we are eliminating some cities and countries."

"Correct. Please don't stop that effort. Let's just fit this one in as well."

Otto returned to his office and launched an encrypted call to Petra.

"Hi, Otto. Checking up on me, or is there something else going on? Jacob and I are still keeping an eye out for your friend's daughter, nothing yet. No pretty models either, though some are expected soon for the upcoming photo shoot season. I related that to JAC."

Otto recounted the new assignment received from Mr. Monty and Quip's primary role for tracking large fund transfers and so forth.

"I was calling to see if you and Jacob might be willing to stay a little longer there in Acapulco in case Quip comes up with a few leads that you could run down for him. You might have to go to Mexico City or somewhere else in Mexico, which should be a quick hop from where you are staying."

"Oh darn! Otto, you mean we have to stay here a little longer?" she asked sweetly as she struggled to contain her exuberance.

Otto, sensing her pleasure at the request, smiled. "My dearest Petra, I can just picture you doing your happy dance. I trust you can break the news gently to Jacob so he won't be as disappointed that you are both to stay a while longer?"

Petra giggled, "Actually, Otto, we met some interesting people here, and after they learned that Jacob is a pen-tester they wanted to know if he would do a security analysis on their bank. Frankly, the whole set of circumstances seem a little odd, but it wasn't too stray of a request. They are willing to pay for the service. You know Jacob. A few days away from his computer and his hands itch."

Otto focused, "Indeed. A Mexican bank?"

"No, a bank in the Cayman Islands. Jacob is not sure about the request being legitimate so we wanted to discuss it with you. We had planned to phone you later. They will provide private transport. They seem to have their own planes so it is not a small business. We are trying to gather some additional details."

Otto responded, "Interesting. Let me send a contract, under Resource Security Service, to you with proper T&C's for use in your discussions with these people. I would very much like to have some internal reconnaissance on this bank so we should try and have you both work this piece of business. Yes, this has possibilities, young lady, and we need to see where it will take us."

CHAPTER 12

Successful gamblers
know when to fold 'em

JC and Robert approached Carlos to ask if they could talk. The evening was early and things had been going quite well for a change. Carlos was apprehensive upon their approach but agreed.

JC openly began, "Carlos I want you to know that I – we – both appreciate all that you and Juan have done for us. In these last seven months you guys got us out of some serious trouble in the U.S. and have given us fair pay for work that isn't too hard to do."

Carlos interjected with a smile, "So you're here to give me a rebate?"

JC and Robert grinned a little. JC was obviously the spokesman of the pair.

"Actually we want to leave the group. We came to you as we want your understanding and approval. It has nothing to do with you, Juan, or the team. It's just that, well, I'm homesick and want to go home. Robert feels the same way. We mean no disrespect to you, Carlos, or Juan. We just want to go home."

Carlos saw Juan prowling a ways off. Juan displayed a keen interest in the serious discussion and was ready to provide backup if needed. Carlos indicated with a shake of his head that Juan should stay put for the time being. Carlos moved his gaze from JC to Robert and then to his glass of wine while thinking of the right sort of response. These poor gringos had proven quite useful.

"I am not surprised at your request, but I had hoped that you might come to call Mexico home. Especially after all we have been through. I understand your desire to return home. I too have had similar feelings for my home village, which I can no longer return to.

"I should point out that law enforcement will be waiting for you since you are fresh on their minds. Your escape made them look foolish. You do get that you can't just go home and step back into your old lives, don't you? Anyone who knew you and any one they can use to bait you into returning to your old lives is being watched. Anyway, how much have you saved to try and take back home? I suspect that the amount is not nearly enough to keep you and your loved ones safe." Carlos sounded like a concerned parent.

JC presented, "We've each got about a quarter million stashed with that bank we've being flying to with the inheritance valuables. We are following your example of keeping ahold of our money so it can't be grabbed."

Robert added, "We also thought about getting new identities so we could go back as new people. So long as we don't draw any attention under our new identities, we should be able to remain under the radar. Neither of us have wives or girlfriends anymore, nor do our families want contact to any great degree at this point."

"I don't understand. This desire to return home is not for families or love? What are you going to do once you get back to the States with your new identities? You can't just go get a day job because that seems too out of character. Pilots in the United States have to have background checks, which new identities rarely pass. You can't go back to your old locations and friends because the federales are hoping you'll do just that.

"Even with what you have saved, which is commendable, you don't have enough money to retire. So logic suggests that you will end up in your old line of work: robbing banks and running drugs. You can do that from here, and it doesn't require an identity change. With moving out the drug lords, the drug market could become lucrative again. We could hook back up the drug business, use our U.S. contact, Joel, and you could run it from here with our infrastructure. Of course, I'll want a cut of the profits." Carlos grinned and yet still looked sympathetic.

JC and Robert looked at each other at the thought of the proposal. They had not considered some of the points that Carlos brought up. Neither of them shook their heads in denial of Carlos's statements. He waited a while to let them mull the proposed transfer of the business.

Carlos emphasized, "However, if you still want to go, then I understand and approve. But here is the deal. Don't come back here under any circumstances. You two cannot come back, ever."

JC was taken aback a little and asked, "Why couldn't we come back? I mean, I wasn't planning on coming back. Like I told you, I'm homesick and don't want to come back here. No offense, Carlos."

"The rule stands. If you leave, don't come back. I will shoot you on sight with no questions and no discussion. Do you understand?" The look in Carlos's eyes meant business.

JC and Robert gave a puzzled look first to Carlos and then to each other.

Carlos clarified to make certain there were no doubts. "If you didn't save enough to retire then you will be back at your old jobs, where you will get sideways with the federales again. Once you are caught, one of two things will happen. The first is, they will throw you in jail for the rest of your lives. The second is, they will offer you a deal to help bring down our organization for the chance to be with your friends and family in a normal life again. If you show up down here again, I will be forced to assume you cut a deal to sell us out to the federales. So as soon as I see you back, you're dead. Now do you understand?"

JC and Robert realized that Carlos had painted a fairly bleak future for them and nodded their heads. They needed to be certain that they wanted to make that one-way trip.

Carlos soothed with a partial smile, "I have enjoyed working with you boys and even have some trust in you for protecting our organization here. The only time we ever had a problem was when JC drooled on my pistole. I won't insist that anyone stay who isn't one hundred percent committed to working for this group. So if you must go, I understand, but my council is that you take the offer I made earlier rather than go back. At least you have a chance here to be your own person. The ladies here can be quite heartwarming. It is your decision. I suggest that you talk it over and tell me in the morning. Comprende?"

They both nodded and left, already talking between themselves.

CHAPTER 13

Study situations from the outside – inside you can't see the trap

Juan sat down with Carlos after the other two had left. He ordered a cerveza which was promptly brought by the cute waitress.

Juan asked, "What the hell was all that about? As serious as all of you were, I'd have guessed they were either asking for your daughter's hand in marriage or they wanted you to participate as a third member in their gay tidings' duo. I know the first isn't possible. I am quite certain that I don't want to know your comment on the second possibility since I would NEVER be able to un-hear it."

Carlos looked straight into Juan's face and in all seriousness responded, "Actually, they wanted to know if they could have your hand in marriage because they both wanted you in their gay tidings ménage à trois."

Juan snorted up his nose and, inserting his index finger down his throat, made a gagging gesture with a noise to indicate that the contents of his stomach were about to be ejected. There was a momentary pause before they both erupted into spasms of laughter.

Once Carlos could breathe again, he enlightened Juan. "They are looking to move on and go back to the States. I made them a counter proposal of reestablishing the drug smuggling business, and we get a percentage. Then they said something that caught my attention. They talked about how they had thought they might get new identities. They have already placed money in our bank to draw from and have saved a nice, modest sum. However, they gave me an idea.

"Juan, I've been thinking about this bank heist operation we are looking to do. Stealing the money and running like we discussed before. I don't want to take all this money and end up living in a private prison of my own making. I want the money, sure. I think you do as well. I also want to have it enrich my life and be free to travel and do things without an entourage of bodyguards. At some point I do want someone to come forward to ask for my daughter's hand in marriage. That's not going to happen if they can't get past the guard dogs placed there to keep me safe from assassination."

They were both silent for a bit. Carlos had struggled with this for a while. Juan studied his cerveza and slowly nodded his understanding of the crossroads at which they had arrived.

"Well, there is nothing to say we can't stay at this a while longer," Juan offered as an option. "I have been meaning to tell you that we are now getting inquiries from the South American drug dealers about our Inheritance Export Service. So we have a new group of customers that could easily extend this a year, maybe two. New customers, more money, and we plan our next move very carefully."

Carlos educated Juan, "Well, that's the other problem. The amount of money we are bringing into the bank is now starting to be a problem. As the quantity goes up so does our visibility, and that usually brings the sovereign investigators. The bank has to do something with the money, and I fear they are starting to struggle with the amounts they have to discreetly invest. I think we need to reevaluate our success and try to figure out how to change our business model to be a more global player.

"So it looks like we have two options to consider. The first is to simply grab the money that we have helped move to Cayman Bank and run like hell. In doing some research, I stumbled onto what I have learned is an identity laundering service that might make this option a game changer. As an added piece of insurance, we clean our identities like JC and Robert before we exit. That way, wherever we land it is with fresh identities, including history and documentation. We could maybe even do an identity cleaning on a periodic basis and move on so as not to get too comfortable.

"The second option is that we stay in the game, continue to run Inheritance Export Service and look for new bank partners to reduce our exposure from the one bank. Maybe even incorporate this identity laundering as a new offering for our clientele. This means we branch out and explore new opportunities outside the Mexican and Caribbean universe we currently know and lessen the dependency on this narrow customer market."

"Ok. So what do you want me to do?" Juan asked.

Carlos suggested, "We need to know more about the identity laundering service I found. Maybe check into the one that JC and Robert are considering. Let's see what it is that we are buying and maybe even establish a couple of IDs for each of us, so if we have to run at a moment's notice, we have that all taken care of. I would expect good quality IDs take time, so we need those done before we make up our minds as to which option we choose. I need you to run down some sources to determine how much and how reliable these services are."

Juan agreed with a nod, then asked, "What else are you working on?"

"I need to get that bank pen-testing assignment going. Knowing the security of the bank is an important aspect as all our wealth is in one place. Then, I need to find some new bank to spread the risk across and set us up for being a global player. Let's try and get back together in a week and discuss where we are. Deal?"

"Deal."

CHAPTER 14

The difficult business decision – to build or to buy a solution

The Chinese Chairman, Lo Chang, was rather pleased with himself. He liked to watch Nikkei move around, and the two of them had learned to trust each other ever since she had been rescued from the Russian, Grigory. Of course, the Chairman never really ever trusted anyone, least of all a 158 kilo white tiger. His two associates, Won and Ton, had sedated her and brought her to the chairman after Grigory's untimely demise at the claws and teeth of Nikkei. Nikkei was always slightly sedated so the relationship with the Chairman could evolve without another incident.

Tranquilizing an animal as big as Nikkei was something of an art. Unfortunately, Nikkei came around faster than Won had anticipated when she was removed from Grigory's clutches. The animal might not have reacted so violently if Won hadn't stepped on her tail, which was hanging out through the bars of the cage. Nikkei absolutely hated having her tail messed with and re-enforced that sentiment by lunging at Won and batting him hard enough to have him standing on his head rather than his feet. Before Ton could stop him, Won went back at the animal to try and secure her from reaching through the bars again.

Won didn't have his temper in check, leading him too close to the cage. Nikkei's paw shot out and then down so fast Won never even saw the movement. Even though both Won and Ton were trained martial arts experts, their job with the Chairman demanded it, they were simply no match for the white tiger's reflexes. Won stood there for a moment in disbelief and turned to face Ton. Won had been raked down the left side of his face and over his shoulder to mid-torso with just enough depth in places to have blood squirting out. Ton screamed in horror as his twin brother slumped to the ground. Ton collected himself and pulled Won away from the cage and started wrapping the worst wounds with his own clothing. If the white tiger hadn't been for the Chairman, the animal would not have made it back to China.

The Chairman believed that young interns were the best investment you could make in bringing on new associates. You could train them, mold them, work them hard, pay them modestly, and in many cases trust them if you could start them young enough. Won and Ton were born to a family who couldn't really afford to send them to advanced schools. This had allowed the Chairman to convince the parents their boys would be looked after and given the education they deserved. They would never see their sons again. The boys were old enough to understand the transaction and young enough to be trained properly.

Won and Ton were twin brothers, and the Chairman saw that it might be advantageous to having two associates that looked identical. All that changed when Won was raked by an enraged Nikkei. Ton had offered to have a similar wound done to himself so he could match his twin brother. The Chairman turned down the generous offer from Ton but was flattered none the less. Ton and Won were identical in everything else.

When the organized coup d'état of Grigory had eliminated him from the Russian Mafia organization he had built, the Chairman began installing his own people, and instructions were issued through Won and Ton. In so doing the Chairman had the organization operate the way he wanted, but he was kept insulated from the operational issues. To anyone doing business with the identity laundering service, Won and Ton were the customer-facing operations managers with a European flair.

The Chairman had anticipated correctly that his country needed such a group to provide false and laundered identities to his fellow countrymen as much as other nationalities throughout the world. It was imperative that such an organization needed to have a non-Chinese flavor to it, so if it was exposed no blame could be pinned on China. Of course the profits could not then be funneled directly back into China. The Chairman smiled that the result of this rationalization ironically benefitted his personal fortune.

The service began as a part of Grigory's old Dteam organization. The other business elements had remained with the Russian operators or had been simply disposed. The main business locations had started off in the big cities like New York City, Moscow, Paris, London and others in the United States and in Europe, the Middle East, and Africa. But the managers started seeing business opportunities in other large cities in Latin America such as São Paulo and Mexico City. In fact, any city with a population over five million was targeted as high potential for interest in these services.

Won and Ton were pressured by the Chairman to expand revenues by taking on new markets. They began building branch offices in these new target markets. The process of identity theft, alteration, and laundering was well understood, but staffing these locations with trusted employees was the problem. Hiring someone you hardly knew and entrusting them with your intellectual property for identity laundering was even more difficult in practice than it sounded.

The other related issue to identity laundering was the subject's money. There were the fees, of course, but then there was the need to also launder their money. Once a customer completed the identity laundering process, they wanted to enjoy their life with their resources readily available, just cleaner. The Chairman could see the demand rising for this next logical piece in the service, but Grigory had not left behind any legacy infrastructure toward that elemental need of a customer. Today, customers were managing that aspect themselves. Some were even successful. The Chairman had sent for Won and Ton to discuss this aspect and the options that might be pursued.

"Gentlemen, we need to add financial infrastructure to our identity laundering service, but we will have special requirements. I want to be able to articulate our banking services to our customers up front in our discussions with them. We need a banking partner that has a good, reliable reputation, but that is not quite legitimate. Funds will require access from anywhere in the world and have impeccable accounting standards, but only for us and our customers. Certainly not for any sovereign tax entity. We need security for us and security against all outsiders. Do you both understand what we must find in our new banking partner?"

They both nodded in agreement with the Chairman.

Lo Chang continued, "I want to place a call to a long-time associate of mine and ask for his counsel in this matter. He may have a brilliant suggestion that is already available. Please listen but do not speak until after we hang up."

The Chairman placed the call using a secure device and loaded the appropriate encryption program.

"Good morning, Chairman Lo Chang. How good of you to call, kind sir. It pleases me that you remembered my birthday and are calling with well wishes. I find it astonishing that with everything you have going on, that you would set aside time to call an old friend to wish him a happy birthday," the male voice said with sincerity.

The Chairman was at a loss for words, but responded with a note of sincere regret, "Otto…I didn't realize that today was your birthday. Allow me to congratulate you on having made it this far."

Otto followed up with a chuckle, "Chairman, I was only teasing you. It is not my birthday, but you call so infrequently I thought I might jest with you a little bit so as to re-establish our relationship. So how can I help someone of your wit and honored status today?"

The Chairman breathed easier as he sensed the mirth in their exchange. "Ah. Western European humor again. It is a difficult concept. I'm sure it wouldn't be so difficult to comprehend if it was funny. But no matter, sir, you tried.

"Actually I called for some of your wise counsel on a topic that I do know you excel at: banking. More specifically, discreet banking that is fully accountable to its customers' needs and most importantly, secure from sovereign tax authorities' inquiries. I would be most grateful for your thoughts on these matters."

Otto said, somewhat deflated in his tone, "Oh, Chairman Lo Chang! Is this all I can do to help you? Why, this is no more an assignment than what I used to teach school children on how to use a telephone directory. I should be happy to show you how to use the new generation telephone directory lookup that leverages an Internet search engine for such a query. I am sure your two associates, Won and Ton, who are standing there in the room with you, could easily perform a highly selective search that would return more useless information than you could bargain for."

Won and Ton both displayed inaudible fear and anxiety on their faces as the Chairman rolled his head with annoyance at having been caught so easily at the deception. He nodded to the boys to reassure them they had done nothing wrong.

"Otto, I can see I have caught you on a difficult day, but I wasn't going to ask for a favor without some compensation for this knowledge of yours. This banking endeavor of ours would not be a onetime activity, but on-going. I am looking for introductions to trustworthy people and their financial institutions. We both know that is not casual information that can easily be retrieved from an Internet search engine."

Otto enjoyed the cat and mouse game, but this was potential business and he was interested.

"Chairman, why didn't you say so in the first place? Of course I have contacts that I can introduce to you. I trust that it would not be you but instead Won and Ton, which is why you have them in the room listening. Very well, let's discuss the fee for this type of information as well as the associated meeting rules."

"Well, since this is only information and none of your regular services, I should think that a reduced fee would be in order. What are your thoughts, Otto?"

Otto replied, "It has always been difficult to challenge your logic, but consider the fact that all information has a freshness factor associated with it. So the fresher the information, the more current and thus more value it is. My dear Chairman, it does take work to deliver fresh information and current contacts. That, by definition, means services. Wouldn't you agree?"

The Chairman quietly clucked his tongue and slightly ground his teeth before he responded. Won and Ton were watching his every nuance.

"Well, Otto, again your logic is difficult to refute. The standard fee shall apply then. The fee transfer will be completed in two business days. When can we expect our highly valued banking information?"

Otto enjoyed the conversation that played so well into the mainstay of the business.

"You should expect it to arrive through our normal courier service by the end of the week. Agreed?"

"Agreed. May your days be long and vital, Otto."

"And to you as well, Chairman."

Then, as a last delight of the conversation, Otto added, "Oh, and Chairman. It was your speaker phone that gave Won and Ton away. The audio pickup was too good, and I could hear them breathing. My ears are quite keen. Good day, sir."

After the Chairman disconnected from the call, he lowered his gaze on Won and Ton. "You may both be martial arts masters but as Ninja stealth warriors you are like two hippos in a wind chime factory! Gentlemen, can you try and develop those skills?"

Both Won and Ton were embarrassed but solemnly nodded. They bowed deeply as they left.

CHAPTER 15

Sellers and buyers, both sides of the same coin

Carlos eyed the twins suspiciously, "So, gentlemen, we meet at last. I was beginning to wonder if this was an honest enterprise or not. I found our last two cancelled meetings highly annoying and an unwelcomed waste of my time, but I assume that in your line of work trust is your most important asset. I have to believe that you were really at both meeting locations, but wouldn't reveal yourselves until you were sure I was a legitimate customer and not some undercover federale. Your call on the burner phone was quite surprising since I had only un-wrapped it thirty seconds earlier. So that tells me that you evaluate your customers before accepting them as clients in the identity laundering service you have established. My compliments to your thoroughness in your craft. I have need of such measures."

Won and Ton were silent and inscrutable during this opening comment. Ton was the designated speaker in most of these types of discussions.

Ton finally spoke. "Mr. Carlos, we take our trade very seriously because our clients need us to be thorough. We run a business that does not advertise in the telephone directory or the Internet, nor do we have a regular place of business with our company's logo out front. When people come to us, they want peace of mind and to escape from who and what they were. We are gatekeepers to that doorway into a new life. So not only do you have to trust us, we have to trust you. So tell us, now that we have trust, how can we be of assistance?"

Carlos presented, "I have need for some new identities for myself and my associates that will allow us to, how should one say, go out and reinvent ourselves and to put distance between ourselves and some modest character blemishes unfairly awarded in our youth. I need to know how long will it take to receive a new useful identity? How much down payment as an act of good faith? Lastly, of course, how much in total?

"I would assume that yours is a cash and carry business. However, I am curious to know if currency is the only medium you deal in or would precious metals or stones be accepted as payment?"

Ton responded, "We have no experience with grading gems or weighing gold or silver, but let us confer with others in our organization before we give you an answer to that question. One of the questions you also need to answer for us is what kind of new identity do you require?"

Carlos, thinking what that might mean, asked, "What do you mean, what kind of identity?"

"Mr. Carlos, we build different types of identities for different circumstances and, of course, there are price differences. For instance, you may simply want a new passport so when traveling you can leave one country and enter another as a different person. Simple passports are a modest twenty-five thousand U.S. dollars.

"However, you may have need to completely leave behind your identity because of modest character blemishes, which means that driver's licenses, credit cards, bank accounts, as well as work and residence history, in addition to the passport, would require changes. We farm new identities like this so people can easily get through the identity doorway to their new life.

"Farming new identities may include a past existence of someone who died early in life, but we gather those terminated identities and continue their existence over time to create the illusion that they are growing up, going to school, taking out loans, medical visits, and so forth, even though these personal milestones are only electronic in nature. We create this history, so a full new identity comes with a believable past, making the transition more complete for the identity traveler.

"These efforts start at two hundred fifty thousand U.S. dollars. We tend to recommend that people use our service rather than invent something on their own since they are usually in a hurry to escape their past. In our experience, people who are in a hurry typically make mistakes in laundering the identity themselves. The identity farming process also takes into account that you wouldn't want to run into an acquaintance of the deceased while using the new identity, so we also cross-check your target destination and your new proposed lifestyle to minimize a chance encounter.

"We understand that past circumstances are such that details cannot be discussed, but the more we know of your past, the easier it is to camouflage you in your next identity. It's the details that a novice in the area of identity laundering typically misses, causing them exposure to past elements rather than an escape in total. Mr. Carlos, we cannot guarantee that our high-end service will be one hundred percent flawless due to the imperfect history growing of a deceased person. We will, however, provide you with more of a believable past that will last longer than if you try to do it yourself."

Carlos smiled at the merchant pitch and the thoroughness delivered. "I did not realize identities were available à la carte. So I would expect then that the full identity laundering exercise would take longer to accomplish than a simple valid passport. Yes?"

Won nodded in acknowledgement, but it was Ton that affirmed, "That is correct. So how can we help you?"

Carlos said, "Well, I have several needs and you have voiced several things worth considering. My most immediate need is for a long-term friend who has, shall we say, run out of options and needs to start fresh again, but has limited funds. For him, I believe the new passport and its price would be a good fit, plus, I would get to see the process as we move forward."

"We understand your caution and welcome the opportunity to demonstrate our skills in delivering a new passport, Mr. Carlos. When can your friend be brought in?"

"Perhaps I should explain. Past indiscretions have made public appearances a bit too awkward, so I was hoping to bring you pictures and personal statistics that you could work from rather than risk his detection by traveling here. Additionally, time is of the essence since he is staying with me, so I could be compromised by association. While we have had a long association I am anxious to have him on his way. I hope you understand."

Won and Ton both nodded.

Ton acknowledged, "We understand your position. Very well, we require sixty percent down to begin work with the country of origin desired. The balance is then due one week following receipt of passport-grade photos of your friend, during the delivery of the product. Do we have a deal?"

"I was hoping for a faster turnaround than seven days," voiced Carlos.

Ton justified, "You should understand that we don't have the necessary equipment here to deliver a suitable passport in that time frame. At a high level, we call in the particulars on an encrypted voice channel accessing one of our range of automated, encrypted voice response programs that generates a package for an information mule to deliver to us. The information from the mule and the photographic image are fed into high-end laser printers, and government-grade documents come out the other side.

"All our proprietary technology is in our highly secure data center, and the printers to turn out the work are in several business locations for final printing, security verification, and delivery. We transport everything via encrypted files, but the final finished package is delivered via an analog information mule that cannot be traced over the wire. We find while this approach is more secure, but it does take a little more time. I trust you approve of our methodology?"

Carlos nodded his approval, then commented, "Yes, quite. Here is the package that I need built for my friend Phillip Johnston and here is your fifteen thousand U.S. dollars in down payment."

"Thank you, Mr. Carlos, for your business. We will meet you here in seven days with your product and collect the balance of payment."

Carlos grinned at the fulfillment of his private joke, then confirmed, "Agreed."

As Carlos stood to depart, Ton presented, "By the way, we have a new service that has just come online for people needing to export their personal financial resources in such a way as to not alert government regulators. Would you or your friend also need these services?"

Carlos sat back down. The comment had excited his interest. He then qualified, "So you are an interesting group of merchants.

Is this a complementary service to the identity laundering or is there a fee as well?"

Won and Ton both suppressed their smiles, as Ton explained, "Importing and exporting personal financial resources is a service we offer, but it is done on a percentage basis starting at eight percent for anything up to one million U.S. dollars. We offer reduced rates as low as a five percent fee for over ten million U.S. dollars. Additionally, we provide very competitive rates of return for standard market risk but do offer more aggressive rates of return, depending on your appetite for investment risk. All of our offerings are cloaked under very strict bank secrecy laws by a sovereign nation who understands the needs for privacy."

Carlos nodded thoughtfully and said, "You have given me much to consider, gentlemen. So, may I ask, how is the move of personal financial resources conducted? Is it the physical movement of hard currency, diamonds, artwork, and precious metals or is it only electronic transfer of funds? And how many electronic transfer points do you use to disguise the point of origin?"

Won and Ton looked at each other before Ton said, "Your questions indicate you may have some very special needs. Allow us to confer with our operations director to see how we can best serve them. For the most part, we are only set up to electronically move wealth."

Carlos smiled, then submitted, "Gentlemen, it is true that I have special needs, but I also offer some…unique services to my customers. In this cottage industry of mine, I move financial assets that are not in a liquid state to be electronically transferred. The services my organization offers might be a nice augmentation to your portfolio and, more importantly, we could be in a position to have your company augment my service offerings. I see potential synergies between our organizations from which we could both profit.

"So yes, socialize my proposal with your operations manager and perhaps we can talk further at our next meeting. Good day, gentlemen."

Carlos rose and started to turn to leave. Won and Ton rose as one and both bowed.

Ton said "Good day, sir."

CHAPTER 16

What you give is what you get

Carlos had always been a little standoffish when growing up. As an adult, he portrayed himself as a little too serious for most peoples' tastes. Juan was the daredevil who always pushed the envelope, but no one could resist his charm. Between the two of them, they balanced each other out and made a formidable team, whether it was business or social.

This was Jacob's first meeting with them together. It was an introductory event prior to completing the actual contract and assessing fees for the possible work effort by Jacob.

Jacob's years of experience made him exceptionally versed in penetrating-testing as a data and network security exercise in any financial environment. He wanted to let Carlos complete the summary of his expectations and describe the planned work effort. Juan was quiet but seemed unusually alert in this formal setting. Jacob had met him once before in the hotel bar but found him reserved. Jacob was focused on Carlos's words.

Carlos opened the discussion, "This is our first lead effort at the bank to evaluate their security. Juan and I have moved a lot of close friends, relatives, and friends of relatives' wealth to this institution. We want to do our appropriate due diligence to make sure there is low to no risk and where there is risk we want to understand our options. I have checked your references and we have what I would consider a good social relationship. More importantly, our ladies have a good social relationship and frankly, that is just as important.

"Now, Juan here thinks you're just a nerd with a computer but is willing to give you the benefit of the doubt so long as you don't use too many big words or senseless anachronisms."

Juan and Jacob both chuckled at that remark. Carlos was quite adept at putting people at ease, Jacob noticed.

Jacob queried, "May I presume that this will be a non-covert operation? I mean, there are two schools of thought here. One is covert, or undercover, and the other is non-covert, or simply above board. The penetration techniques are slightly different depending upon if everyone knows that the activity is going on or if you want to keep all activity secret.

"Some places don't want to alert their own people to what is going on, so as to really stress test not only the technology but the people as well. They want to see if their people can be easily socially engineered into giving up user IDs and passwords, defeat alarm and video feeds, and basically simulate a real attack.

"My question is based on time and effort to do the penetration-testing. It is faster if you, Carlos and Juan, simply bring me in as a consultant, and only people with a need to know are advised of my work activity. I get passwords and access quicker that way so I can begin work sooner. The covert operation takes more time and is closer to a mock robbery than a security evaluation. Personally, most of my customers prefer an above board security analysis because everyone is on board with the process, and we get results faster which also means the effort costs less in billable hours."

Carlos and Juan studied each other just long enough for Jacob to understand that they had not thought about the differences of a covert effort versus a non-covert one. Silently the men appeared to reach a decision, but Carlos remained the spokesperson.

"Jacob, we need to look at all the security attributes, but I think we want an above board approach. Your report will be for our eyes only. Juan and I will deliver the results to the board of directors at the end of the engagement. Now even though we will be escorting you in, we still need observant eyes looking for physical security flaws, if they can be identified. Is that an inappropriate request or outside your skillset?"

"Well typically, gentlemen, my assignments are from the inside so that no time is wasted trying to simply gain access to the facility. I also try to be aware of my surroundings so I can include any observations that may be pertinent to security discussions. My efforts won't have the look and feel of a James Bond film, but we will be able to move deliberately and without fear of discovery. Getting caught in a covert operation would not be pleasant. With a signed contract, if I'm caught, the agreement will get me out of trouble, but it will point them at you two for authorizing the operation. Some are very fussy about security breaches and tend to take out their hostility on those involved. I recommend that we go with the non-covert operation."

Carlos studied Jacob, taking his measure, then agreed. "Good counsel, Jacob. We will go with your recommendation for a non-covert operation. I will alert the bank's IT department of our arrangement. When can you travel, sir? Our preference is to begin as soon as possible. Let us know so that travel and accommodations can be arranged. Let's talk tomorrow. Agreed?"

"Agreed. I will outline the contract guidelines and estimate time to be spent. Petra has also agreed to be a part of the review and remote support if you agree. Travel costs are your responsibility and will not be a part of the fees unless we need to define that separately. Do we?" Jacob looked to both Juan and Carlos for confirmation.

"We will cover all the travel, no problem. Juan will likely fly us all there. Petra seems like a great asset. So glad to have her eyes on this as well, even if remotely. Until tomorrow then."

CHAPTER 17

Trouble shared can be trouble halved

As had been their habit for several days, Petra and Simone had met by the pool for a late brunch, swimming before the sun became too intense for Petra, and then engaging in girl talk. Petra was impressed with Simone's charm and sweet nature, as well as her ability to find something fun to discuss. Simone seemed to like having a girlfriend almost as much as Petra. During this initial conversation this morning, they had discussed their men working together and fashion.

The contract for the review of the bank in the Cayman Islands had been finalized. Petra would be doing a review of the report was prepared to remote in as necessary. Jacob had left it open with Carlos that if needed, she could travel there as well to observe.

Having just finished a few laps, Petra was lathering back on the sunscreen. Simone didn't seem to need any at all. They were different, mused Petra, yet comfortable. The tenure of their discussions had changed as they became more comfortable with each other, almost to the point of sharing confidences.

Simone asked, "How long have you two been married, sweetie?"

Petra gave her a quizzical look and asked, "Married? Do Jacob and I look married?"

Simone smiled and nodded, "Well, our men just left this morning, and it appears you are already longing for him like the wife of a great lover. So my intuition tells me that you miss him and can't wait to call him. Maybe even talk naughty to him over the phone. You both look very much in love. You are here in Acapulco at a reasonably expensive resort. It occurs to me that this is probably a well-deserved honeymoon. Am I close?"

Petra was not used to being analyzed by anyone. She was certainly delighted to be alone here with Jacob and to be learning about them as a couple. It almost scared her that it showed in some way, especially to a stranger. Few people could hit the target on her feelings. Jacob was one in many instances and now this new friend. Obviously she should think about that more and school her features better.

"We are not married, yet." For some reason she felt a blush rising. "I mean, we haven't really talked about it. After our last assignments, we both agreed we needed to get away and re-charge our batteries, so to speak." Petra paused and then decided to share a bit and see how that went. "But yes, I do already miss him, and… yes, I do love him."

Simone giggled a little at Petra blushing. "Sweetie, I so understand and am happy for you. When Carlos and I first got together I could hardly bear to have him away. His banking trips took him away too often and for far too long to suit me. He has done so well and I'm so proud of him. Carlos and I aren't married either, and it isn't a subject that we have talked about at all. He is so kind and attentive to me, like Jacob is with you.

"I guess I was hoping you were married, so there might be a chance for me. I worry that I am not the kind of girl that a man as good as Carlos would want to marry. Before Carlos, I was struggling trying to break into a profession that doesn't require much brains. I have a good education, but Carlos doesn't discuss with me the details of his work. Jacob and you seem to talk the same business language. I guess I am just not good enough for Carlos to have that level of confidence with me."

Petra bristled a bit and felt oddly protective of her new friend. "I think you are wrong. Carlos wants you. I've seen it in his eyes and the way he stares at you when he holds your hand. I noticed it the first time we all had dinner together. You seem like a very nice girl, so I don't understand your statement regarding 'not the kind of girl that a man as good as Carlos would want to marry'. You two seem comfortable with each other and from that, all else will come.

"Anyway, why would you say that Carlos doesn't want a girl like you? You are caring, engaging when you talk, interested in what people have to say, certainly attractive to the male species, judging from the visual inventory taken when you walk by. From outward appearances you are quite beautiful, and I am a bit envious, truth be told. Do you have some defect that you clearly hide quite well?"

"My past is something of a problem that I don't like talking about. Carlos has no interest in my past before we met, and that works for us right now. It isn't, however, necessarily a good foundation for a forever thing." Simone averted her eyes and fiddled with her bracelet.

Petra thought about what it meant to have a friend. This was new ground for her, and her background experience didn't help too much. But, she knew from being with Jacob that if a person revealed something about themselves, it helped to create a bridge on which to build trust. When she had withheld knowledge about Jacob's family origins, he had taken it well as to the why, but it had bothered him that she didn't trust him enough to talk openly to him. She liked Simone and didn't know if it would be a long-term friendship, but she wouldn't have the chance if she didn't try. She also knew the limits of how much she could reveal from a business perspective.

"Simone, I grew up in a very sheltered manner. Though my parents loved me, they protected me and had designs on my life. Fortunately, their goals and my goals aligned, but I too have struggled with sharing in my relationship with Jacob. Jacob is the first man I have wanted a relationship with, even to the point of thinking of us as a long-term couple. That is part of the reason we took this trip, at least for me. He too grew up sheltered, so for us revealing thoughts and feelings is new. I have traveled, seen many beautiful places, but feel most comfortable with a computer in hand. You are my first girlfriend and in this I also struggle with how to behave to create a lasting friendship."

"You are so together though, Petra, you always seem comfortable. Pretty and elegant and refined. Me, I like to talk, as you know, but it is to keep things focused on something other than me."

Simone seemed to be gathering up some courage to speak, so Petra kept silent.

"See, I have been trying to make it as a model, following the fashion shoots around for months prior to meeting Carlos. It just isn't working out the way I thought. The modeling business is brutal, and I found myself always competing and losing out to younger women that looked more like coat hangers than real women."

She laughed, then said, "I have a shape that I guess doesn't lend itself to standard modeling. If one hits it big then everything lines up in front of you, but if one doesn't then you are starving because there is little money for those not chosen to model. I was lucky to get some paying lingerie shoots, but that is not like a frontline premiere model, most of whom are under eighteen. If they are a prime face or body for a designer, then they are well-protected. If one is an extra, like I am at this point, then there are offers after the scheduled shoot by some lower ranking photographer for afterhours shoots. Translated, as I discovered, to mean semi-nude or nude shots.

"I am not terribly shy, and I like how I look, so that in itself is not bad. The money from that helps, but it's skimpy too. I learned those connections can lead to other jobs as an exotic dancer, filming or other adult entertainment, which is really out of my comfort zone. There was a crazy, low-life man taking advantage of a girl when she was down, who made it seem like a path to lots of modeling and acting work. I was almost ready to make that mental shift. It was a low point for me and I could see no other way to achieve my dream.

"Then Carlos rescued me. When Carlos introduced himself to me that night, he changed everything for the better. I assume he has deduced that my past was in the adult entertainment world, but he has never asked and I have never volunteered."

Petra was dumbfounded by this revelation. It never occurred to her that Simone had struggled with something that scary. Petra felt herself a late bloomer with her relationship with Jacob. She couldn't imagine how difficult it would be to make those types of decisions.

"Simone, I might be prying, but do you have any family to support your dreams?"

Simone shrugged and again fiddled with her bracelet. "My family stated that I couldn't possibly want to pursue such a stupid dream and basically forced me to leave. Now they wouldn't take me back anyway. That is not important. What is important to me is Carlos."

"I can see that," Petra laughed. "And I am right there with you. I do think though you cannot escape your past or your family. Is Carlos your first love?"

"He is. And I am pouring all my romance readings and dreams of having and holding a man into this relationship. I know that Carlos is a very experienced and pleasing man. We have a lot of fun together making love and being experimental," Simone informed her friend with a knowing grin.

Petra raised her brows and looked serious as she stated, "Really! I myself have no knowledge of romance readings, nor have I really had dreams of being with a man. Jacob and I simply connected. Hard to explain, but he was not in my plans. Perhaps you can enlighten me to some of these finer points of the sexual parts of a relationship. I can work almost anything out with a computer and do magic with programming, but men are very different. Actually, men are a lot like computers since you have to turn them on to talk to them."

"Well, we might work on that discussion with our dinner and drinks tonight," laughed Simone. "Since we are on our own, girl talk seems to be in our future. I will share what I know, but with a drink or two that gets a bit easier to discuss, wouldn't you agree?"

"I don't know, but I am willing to explore this. I would be a bit shy about the photos you have alluded to doing. Can you tell me more about your experience, perhaps over dinner? Again, I am not trying to be nosey. I do need to get out of the sun and take care of some things before we meet."

"Of course. I feel I can tell you most anything. Now get out of the sun before you get burned. You have the creamiest white skin, not made for tanning. We will talk more this evening. And Petra, wear something slinky and elegant, because I already picked out a beautiful dress from ones that Carlos bought for me. We will take care of each other."

"Alright, I will! See you later. Call me."

Simone motioned her away. Petra had some updates that Jacob wanted done, and she decided that some of what Simone had said might be useful to the Lara project. Her comments might give Quip some additional places to search. There were some similarities, but Simone was obviously a native Mexican and very different than the pictures of Lara Otto had provided. She smiled to herself at having a new friend.

CHAPTER 18

Logic is a contrast to most thought processes

Otto began, "Andrew, I have asked you here as a consultant on this project. As always, I respect your complete discretion on this exercise. I would very much appreciate your extensive telecom and satellite expertise in our investigative efforts on this project. Quip found some peculiar events in the Caribbean area, and it doesn't follow an expected pattern.

"Quip, I need you to introduce Andrew to ICABOD and have the three of you capture and interpret the activities you have been observing. My expectation here is to determine if these events are leveraging some cloaking activity. Our thinking, Andrew, is if we can penetrate these events perhaps we can understand more clearly the underlying intentions. Gentlemen, are we clear what is to be done?"

The sour look on Quip's face betrayed his annoyance at having to work with Andrew. He knew he needed the experience to help better understand communications transmissions. He just knew that Andrew grated on his nerves most times, yet was funny as could be at other times. He nodded his agreement to Otto's summary of their activity. Andrew, on the other hand, was delighted to be working with Quip and couldn't wait to see ICABOD in action. Quip was a lot of fun to needle.

Andy beamed like a kid in a candy store as he said, "I have often thought y'all had some swell technology here so I am ready to go to work, sir!"

"Andy, we are fairly informal around here, so please just call me Quip."

Andrew slightly raised his chin, almost as if snapping to attention, and stated, "Sir, back in Georgia we enlisted men would all agree that you are the tall hog at the trough around here. My momma would box my ears if I had forgotten my upbringing and that means I say sir!"

Quip, on one hand, liked the compliment and yet on the other knew instinctively that Andrew was yanking his chain. "Quip. Quip is just fine, Andy. I am calling you Andy like you asked me to."

Andrew was obviously amused at the effect he had on Quip. "Young feller, you're repeating yourself. That seems to be a habit with you from what I've seen. Have you thought to have that checked out?"

Quip, visibly agitated and totally off topic, stammered, "I am not repeating myself. I am not repeating myself!"

Otto, unable to resist interjecting into the hazing that Andrew was giving Quip, said, "Quip, you are repeating yourself."

Andrew's face broke into a wide grin as he added, "Oh come on, young feller! We're just having a little sport with you. Aren't we, Otto, sir?"

Otto gave them a fatherly type of smile, then chided, "Now boys, it's time to come in from playing outside and go to work."

"Quip, you know having you repeating yourself like that reminds me of my cousin Jimmy D., who also had some speech problems. I'll never forget the story he tells about landing his first job selling bibles door to door to the surrounding towns where we lived.

"Ol' Jimmy D. has a stuttering problem, and the sales manager didn't want to give him the job. Jimmy D. begged and agitated until the sales manager finally said ok, offering him a commission-only position. That cagey sales manager figured that since Jimmy D. stuttered so bad no one would buy anything from him, but Jimmy D. agreed to the proposition.

"Well, that first week Jimmy D. is selling as many bibles as the number two sales guy, after two weeks he is selling as many bibles as his best sales guy, and after three weeks he is selling as many bibles as the whole sales team. Well sir, that old cagey sales manager hauls Jimmy D. into his office and puts the obvious question to him asking how someone with a severe speech problem was able to out sell all the seasoned bible sales guys. Jimmy D.'s response was priceless, so I want to make certain I get it right."

Andrew parroted Jimmy D., "Well mister sales manager… I…I…I…g-go up to the house li…li…like you taught me and I knock real hard. When they answer the door I go into my sales routine and say I'm sel…sel…selling bi…bi…bles ma'am. Wou… wou…would you li…li…li…like to b…b…buy one or…or…or… would you li…li…like me to read it to you? And you know, mister sales manager, almost all of them want to buy that bible from me right then and there but couldn't read it until later."

Otto broke into a grin, but Quip was desperate to try and suppress his laughter. In the end they all lost it. Andy did have a way of telling stories that was irresistible. They all took a breath, ready to refocus on the real task at hand.

"Come on, Andy, let me introduce you to ICABOD. Otto, if you want to come back after we've had time to take a look and evaluate, that works. I know you are busy."

Otto left feeling confident that the boys could work together alone. Quip showed some of what ICABOD could do, and Andy commented on the capabilities. A while later they were both pouring over the satellite information trying to make sense of it. There was a specific sequence of data that Andrew was highlighting to Quip with all pretense of the country boy removed for the moment.

"Look at this, Quip! Someone is stealing transmission cycles as though they are a legitimate signaling end point. The content is fine but the ID markers are bogus." Andrew pointed to the specific areas of interest on the screen. "This means someone has figured out how to get some of the communications satellites to carry their voice traffic. And look here! They have gotten into the proprietary signaling programming to turn off satellite tracking. Basically, the satellite is being told, don't look here, don't track this, and is obeying those commands! Wow, this guy is really good! This makes it seem like the satellite works for the hacker."

Quip watched with interest as ICABOD mapped out the scene from a low-earth orbit, or LEO. This was new data for ICABOD to maintain for future efforts, and Quip wanted it trapped as a correct reference in the library.

"Does that mean that we can't track this hacker's movements? So now what?"

Andrew reverted to his good 'ol boy routine and said, "Now young feller, I didn't say we couldn't follow the hacker. I said he told the satellite not to look in certain areas. But what your hacker here doesn't know is that if you take all the non-mapped areas together, one after the other, you get a trail or corridor that starts at one end and ends up in another. Basically, we have a map of the hacker's path based on areas he didn't want to be tracked in, but as we capture and store them rather than relying on the satellite's historical data, that is exactly what he gave us."

Quip realized that Andy's observation was very astute. He also noticed the change in Andrew's communication vernacular and recognized how he'd allowed his chain to be yanked. Later he would admit to Otto that having Andy on this assignment was a good idea. He was now also in a position to figure out how to yank Andy back, but for the time being he let Andy continue.

The consummate professional now, Andrew continued, "So it looks like the no-track zone begins here in the Chihuahuan Desert, yet ends here in the Cayman Islands. Since it is a straight line with rapid and consistently timed movements from one area to the next, I'd hazard a guess that it is an airplane. Most likely a twin engine since you wouldn't want to go swimming if you had engine trouble. It looks capable of a cruise speed of about 325-350 knots. Probably something like a King Air or maybe a light jet."

Quip was annoyed with this much conclusion from Andrew ahead of his own evaluation, but ICABOD seemed to concur.

He was interested so he asked, "So how do you know just how fast this supposed plane has to be flying?"

Andrew, still staring into the 3-D ICABOD screen, said without looking at Quip, "Well, young feller, if you watch the time each of these zones is blocked out and take a distance reading for each and leaving some margin for error in each no-track zone, I come up with each zone being similar in diameter and each is in a no-track zone for the same period of time."

Then Andy added with a degree of good ol' boy sarcasm, "Now if I use my ciphering skills that momma taught me, I take that twenty kilometer, times minutes, times the number of zones that ICABOD has spotted. I should be able to use my times table for a total distance and speed of the aircraft so long as I remember to carry the naught like she taught me."

Quip felt Andrew yank his chain about his ciphering, but just then ICABOD confirmed the calculation with a dialog balloon above the tracked area. Quip was ready to go to the other room to pout when Otto walked in.

Otto asked, sensing some tension from Quip, "So, how are you doing, gentlemen?"

Before Quip could admit to being humbled, Andrew blurted out, "Otto, sir, you should see what Quip has uncovered with this highfalutin contraption of his! We got ourselves here a real smart hacker that has learned to cover his tracks with a U.S. based satellite. Old Quip here wasn't fooled a bit. Ain't gonna be no work left for someone like me if Quip and his ICCYBOB machine can always figure everything out. I might as well call it a day, boys."

Otto looked at Quip, who could hardly restrain his emotions of annoyance, irritation, admiration, and humbleness at the generosity of Andy's description of the afternoon activities and telling Otto that it was all Quip. Otto knowingly grinned at the two and asked Quip to escort Andy out of the ICABOD center.

As Andy was leaving, he turned back to Otto and said, "Otto, this is one talented hacker that your boy Quip found. I wouldn't mind spending some time with him or her. This person might make a nice addition to my staff actually. Not certain yet how the hacker is doing it. I'm going to have to noodle on it for a while. Thanks, young feller, for introducing me to ICCYBOB. Very cool machine."

CHAPTER 19

Things just get bigger when ignored

Thiago Bernardes watched the video glass of the large black obelisk that was his desk. There were several video feeds from his many operations around Brazil, as well as current events, email, and instant messages from key people. The doctors monitored his condition and he abided by their rules. To reduce his stress he had delegated some of the responsibilities, which sadly resulted in some additional internal politicking. He finally decided that he needed to speak to Otto regarding the organizational politics he faced as an excuse to also get a status update on the search for Lara. He placed the call, with the audio piped to an immersive audio system to provide higher quality conversation.

Thiago waited for Otto to answer, which he did on the second ring. "Otto, good afternoon, thank you for taking my call, young man."

"Young man, that is very kind of you, my friend. Thiago, how are you feeling? The doctor I recommended indicated you had engaged his services and are progressing. Of course he would provide no details to me."

"I do feel better, Otto. My appetite has improved, and I like his no-nonsense methods. So thank you for the recommendation. The new team of doctors are all consulting regularly. I am, however, at work, which is a good thing.

"That actually brings me to one of the reasons I called. I have a board of directors meeting coming up in a few weeks. I have delegated responsibilities to others to a degree as doctors have recommended, but I am afraid that the board members are growing more impatient with me. They insisted on adding a succession plan for the company to the upcoming agenda. It is apparently the top priority for discussion either because there are increased rumors regarding my health or someone suspects that Lara is not willing. Though it is my company, it is incorporated, and the board of directors has a significant level of oversight and responsibility to the shareholders. I held them off during the last quarterly meeting, but it needs to be addressed at this meeting.

"Which brings me to the other reason for my call. From our prior discussions you know that Lara is my choice for succession. I have tried to be patient as your team works it, and I know from Oscar that discussions between him and your team have occurred. Have you any news that would help me?" Thiago implored.

Otto knew the pain his friend was feeling, so he kindly related, "Thiago, just because we find her that does not mean all will be better. She stormed off in a rage to prove something to you. If I know anything about strong-willed young women, there is no guarantee that everything will be fine when she is located.

"In answer to your question, no, friend, we have not turned up anything, but we are still engaged on the effort. At this point it is more of a process of elimination of where she is not. I know you understand that when we do find her, she may have found a comfortable life that she is unwilling to abandon. That said, have you given any thoughts to what our next steps would be once we locate her?"

Thiago sighed, "You use the term when and not if, which makes me believe that your team finding her is a very real possibility. So, based on that, when you find her, I want her immediately brought home to me. I will make amends with her. Other than obligatory work items, I have thought of little else."

Otto took a deep breath and concentrated on how not to offend as he inquired, "My friend, do you hear yourself? What would you have me do? Use a tranquilizer gun to sedate her like some wild animal? Don't forget that I too am a father of a proud, strong-willed daughter, and I don't think you have thought this through. I can tell you that forcing her, or kidnapping her, against her will can only exacerbate the situation. Once reunited under duress, you will have an argument that will make the last one pale by comparison."

Thiago sighed, then acquiesced, "You're right, Otto. It would only make things worse than they are now. It seems I need your counsel again, old friend. Tell me what I should do to make things right again. I desperately want her back, but not as a caged animal. I love her too much to see that."

"Let us find her and reason with her on your behalf. I imagine that getting her to listen may be a colossal task that probably would be best done by another female. Assuming that her pride is at stake, I suggest that if she will listen to this associate of mine, Lara might be agreeable to a phone call to just talk with you. If we can get her to have this phone call with you then you must be available at any time and already have your thoughts mapped out beforehand.

"What I mean is that you have to rekindle the fond memories you two have had together and not let the immediacy of the phone call lead you to offer to buy her love back. I would recommend honest feelings of loss, remembrance of those fun times together while she was growing up, and how much you care for her. You must allow her to speak honestly as well. She is an adult and this is a two-way street. This conversation structure provides you a chance to do some serious emotional fence-mending. I suspect if that is not the result of that call, it will probably be her last."

Thiago exclaimed, "You really believe it is that critical?"

"I do. You must also resist the temptation of insisting or even asking her to come back, because it will devolve into yet another corporate-negotiated deal. You need, for the sake of both of you, to put all the emotional baggage on the table. If she does not volunteer it, then ask what she thinks the next steps should be for you both. She may need some more time to think, as I would expect the phone conversation will be disorienting to her emotional state. Small steps here will go a long way to repairing the damage done to your relationship. You must provide open dialog and allow her to do the same. I imagine that the hardest thing for you will be to listen to her hurt feelings and maybe that is all you will achieve on the first call."

Thiago was unable to speak as the tears ran down his face. He was saddened anew to think that his daughter might be found and yet lost to him forever.

Otto sensed the emotional impact and responded, "You are an accomplished speaker and you know how to articulate to investors and corporate bankers, but this time you are up against your toughest audience, your daughter. She will sense manipulation, insincerity, and salesmanship if you do not deal with her honestly."

After a few minutes of silence to allow Thiago time to regroup his emotions, Otto decided to shift gears in the conversation.

"So you voiced some concern regarding the upcoming board of directors meeting. It occurs to me that for the line of succession topic, you could apply a very good stop-gap measure that should hold the board at bay until you can speak to your daughter. Let me conference in a trusted associate of mine who might help with a delay tactic for you."

Not waiting for agreement, Otto made certain Thiago could hear the request.

"Wolfgang, can you join us in a conference call, sir?"

Wolfgang joined the call and Otto said, "Thiago, I would like to introduce my associate, Wolfgang Mickelowski, who is also a part of Ronnie, Ltd."

"A pleasure to meet you, Wolfgang," Thiago responded.

"Wolfgang, you have been briefed on Thiago's daughter and are aware of his company as you have supported both investments and reviews of his account."

"Yes, of course, Otto. How may I help you both?"

"Thiago has a board of directors that is insisting upon discussion on a succession plan in their upcoming meeting. Thiago, of course, wants his daughter in that plan, which is not viable at present. What ideas or thoughts would you have on other options that might be taken?"

Wolfgang responded, "Thiago, first of all, I want to convey my support to a good end result with Lara. Our team is really hard at work on this issue and has taken it very personally.

"With regards to your upcoming meeting, are all the seats filled on your board at present?"

"Actually, Wolfgang, they are not. Otto, I apologize. I should have indicated that at first. I do have a seat open and am required to nominate someone for the seat this week. I have never had a nomination of mine refused," stated Thiago.

Wolfgang and Otto were already aware of the seat on the board and had discussed options the previous day. It was not uncommon for a board to get antsy when their CEO had an extended illness. It also meant it was ripe for corporate takeover if the board was not supportive of the current CEO. As with many of their customers they helped plan well in advance of requests. It made the R-Group and their working subsidiaries even more valued.

"No apology needed. Honestly, this may then work toward your favor, Thiago," suggested Otto. "Would it make sense to perhaps nominate Wolfgang to that board position with the purpose of then leveraging him in your succession planning discussion or as a diversionary tactic on your part? We would, of course, understand and agree that Wolfgang would only remain in this position until Lara is located and next steps are determined. You will, however, need a good story as to why you aren't nominating Lara to the position at this time. But I will leave that discussion point in your capable hands. I think this is in line with the responsibility you gave me when we last met as well. Do you agree, Thiago?"

Thiago, somewhat hesitantly, asked, "Ok, so while I appreciate the idea and it seems viable in the short term, how do we unwind it once this is all in place? I may be too optimistic here, but I am hopeful of Lara returning. If her seat is filled by Wolfgang, what would we do then? I do not want to have the board second guessing my strategies of course."

Wolfgang answered, "That is the easy part. As soon as everything in that area has settled, and she is ready to take on that responsibility, then my health issues will preclude me from remaining on your board of directors. I will simply step down, making way for her. Thiago, let's be clear I have plenty to do in my current capacity. This additional duty would be for your benefit, but only on a short-term basis."

"I believe that answers my question quite clearly. Thank you, Otto, and thank you, Wolfgang, for a viable option. Wolfgang, can you provide me your background information tomorrow morning, so that I can get this idea for feedback from some of my trusted members? There may well be push back since you are unknown in this region of the world."

"I am honored to do so."

"Perhaps it would also be useful for your team to review the board members for any indiscretions. I know you had done that as each board member was appointed, but it might be more useful to get current information or insight to alliance shifts."

"Thiago, I believe that seems prudent," agreed Otto.

"Thank you. Otto, please let me know of any updates on Lara. I do value our relationship in business and as a confidant. Good day, gentlemen."

CHAPTER 20

Illusions can be shattered with technical reality

As Carlos had arranged, Jacob was greeted at Cayman Bank by Phillip Johnston and escorted inside to the data center. Security here had a very different look to it when compared to U.S. banks. Jacob was not surprised that there were several checkpoints requiring IDs, badges, and signatures before proceeding past heavily armed guards. He was using the name Jacob Funston on this trip, and the identifications passed without a hitch. Jacob silently thanked JAC yet again for her efforts. There were only two classes of people in this part of the world; the very rich and the desperately poor. In several Latin American countries, the middle class had devolved to the lower class, with very few exceptions. He suspected it was better to display heavy armaments that discouraged ill-advised assaults. Jacob mused to himself that in this part of the world point and click had an entirely different kind of meaning for security.

Johnston was animated, which Juan had suggested would be the case. After they had met and moved through the process, Jacob wasn't impressed with his escort and his obvious need for conversation.

"Well Mr. Funston, what do you think so far? Pretty impressive security measures, wouldn't you say?"

Jacob responded, "I don't typically see armed guards at every checkpoint, nor have I seen the bank and the data center in the same location. Usually the data center is in a business park separate from the bank's customer-facing area."

Johnston nodded but explained, "Our thinking is to use one set of guards to protect both customer and operations. It simplifies our logistics by putting everything in the same building. In this part of the world there are only two property types, commercial grade for business use and everything else. You don't save anything by putting the bank storefront in a commercial area and the data center in a business park because there is no cost differentiation between the two. Another challenge we face is getting utilities that work all the time. Providing utilities to a business is hard enough, but to two buildings could cause one to tear their hair out."

Johnston halted to show off his highly polished dome of a head as proof to his statement, but grinned. At this point, Jacob averted his gaze from Johnston's bald head in order to control his laughter. He remembered Juan's comment that dealing with Johnston was like having your head shaved with a cheese grater while chewing on aluminum foil.

Trying to change the subject, Jacob asked, "Where can I set up shop and begin my analysis? I am anxious to get started. The sooner I start, the sooner I can get back to my lady and our vacation."

Johnston gave a series of highly exaggerated eye winks to Jacob, intended to indicate the depth of his own romantic prowess.

"Yes of course. Right this way, Mr. Funston. We have a technical briefing set up for you by the head of our data center to explain the layout. After that we can get you plugged into the core of our data network. Now, a key point for you is that we like to shut down promptly at four o'clock each afternoon so contractors and guests need to leave at that time. Only in-house security gets to remain and this place gets locked down. So, unless you want to sit here in the dark until the next day, I suggest that you wrap everything up before then. Have I made myself clear, sir?"

Jacob said, "Quite clear, kind sir. By the way, please call me Jacob."

Johnston clapped and rubbed his hands together as if that totally made the difference in their relationship.

Through his gnomish, toothy grin, Johnston said, "Ok, let's go to the briefing. Let the games begin!"

Jacob was completely focused on the penetration-testing at Cayman Bank, going through it by the book. After a few hours he started to notice some strange activity. Actually, what caught his eye was the lack of any strange activity. In fact, there were no anomalies captured in the logging servers, and the network traffic was so formal as to be almost sterile, as if it was only a recording being played for someone's amusement. There were no error messages logged, no failed connections, no re-tries highlighted, and no lost services.

Jacob looked closer at the log files and saw some anomalies. He noticed that all the logs files were in fact the exact same file with only date changes. Someone or something had tampered with the logging and that usually meant that someone was doing something they didn't want discovered. Jacob launched a protocol analyzer to view and capture packets transported across the wire in real-time mode. The packet capture data was quite revealing.

Jacob located secondary traffic on the data center backbone and identified that it was using a different subnet mask that allowed it to run transparently under the production servers. This was a clever cloaking ruse used to hide in plain sight, but certainly not brilliant by any stretch of the imagination as the traffic was un-encrypted, thus easily interpreted. During the remaining few hours of the day he pieced together several transactions trying to determine exactly what was happening. However, his progress was interrupted by Johnston, who arrived to escort Jacob out for the day.

Johnston cautiously asked, "So are we having fun yet? What do you think so far?"

Jacob responded a bit guarded, "Well, so far everything seems to be in order."

Johnston clapped his hands and rubbed them together as if he was adding more oil to them.

With a grin that looked remarkably like a Halloween pumpkin carved using a dull deer antler, he excitedly added, "I knew it, squeaky clean, right? It has taken me years to work into this position and all that hard work has paid off. I'm sure to get a bonus when this report hits."

Jacob revealed, "However, I'm not yet finished and would like to return tomorrow. Will that be possible?"

Johnston was a little deflated but asked, "But you just said everything was ok. How much more time do you need?"

Jacob smiled, "Oh, it shouldn't take more than half a day. Once those traces and captures are completed I can go back to my room and start writing up the report. Same time tomorrow morning, sir?"

Johnston was a little sullen but managed to respond, "Yes of course, at nine in the morning."

Back at the hotel Jacob established a secured conference call with Otto, Quip, and Petra.

Jacob related, "In doing this pen-testing assignment here at Cayman Bank, I am seeing a lot of abnormalities in the data traffic, as well as tampered log files. Quip, can you turn ICABOD loose on this place and see if he can understand the patterns that I am seeing?"

Petra asked, "What do you mean, patterns? What did you find?"

Quip asked, "Yeah, what did you find at this unknown to me Cayman Bank? I've been focused on two other projects and have not kept up with your current events. I thought you were on vacation and wouldn't pester me."

Jacob responded with a chortle, "Now, Quip, you know how it is, work is never too far away. Otto suggested that I take this pen-testing assignment for this Cayman Islands bank for a financial adviser named Carlos Rodríguez. Petra and I met him and his lady friend Simone at our Acapulco resort. I was flown to the Caymans by Carlos and his brother, Juan. I was at the bank today escorted by the local contact, Phillip Johnston. During the testing, I found there are two sets of information flows, one perfect for the visitors and one that is all over the map. My field of expertise is single to multiple-intrusion events, but this is more like accounting sleight of hand if I'm reading this right."

"Hold on now," Quip responded," Cayman Bank in the Cayman Islands? Precisely where in the Caymans? Oh, never mind, I have a lock on your cell phone location and…huh, that's interesting. That is quite close to the satellite blackout tunnel end that Andrew and I tracked an aircraft to. Let me tell you what we have so far, and let's see where the overlaps are.

"Andrew and I tracked a satellite blackout tunnel that started in the Chihuahuan Desert of Mexico then ended in the Cayman Islands. We were looking into why several drug dealers were vanishing with all their loot as part of an assignment from our favorite Mr. Monty.

"You're on vacation in Mexico, but actually doing some data center pen-testing in the Cayman Islands. During your pen-testing, Jacob, you discover some weirdness at Cayman Bank, which is close to where the satellite blackout tunnel ends.

"You know what they say about coincidences. They are always well-engineered."

Petra added, "Jacob, didn't Juan and Carlos take you to the Caymans in their plane?"

Quip interrupted, "What kind of plane? Was it a fairly big twin engine or small corporate jet?"

Jacob responded, "Yes, it was a large 12 passenger twin-engine plane that certainly had been well used as a freight dog plane, but it was comfortable. We didn't have much trouble with the customs inspectors when we got there, come to think of it. We were actually waved on through without so much as a second glance."

Otto suggested, "It appears to me that we have some common ground on these two situations. Quip, can you assist Jacob with his testing exercise using ICABOD to ferret out the truth? Petra, can you see what you can do to help interpret the findings with Jacob for his report? Jacob, you need to give some thought as to who is or who are the perpetrators in this before delivering your report."

Jacob asked, "What do you mean, Otto?"

Otto said, "You were hired to examine the bank for security holes by someone who is new to the bank. It could be that Juan and Carlos are setting the stage to exploit your information for personal gain. It could also be that they were brought in precisely to have a fresh set of eyes dig into the goings-on at the bank, and these issues have been going on for some time. It could also be that they have no knowledge and are simply being cautious, or a combination of any of these.

"Petra, you've been somewhat quiet on this conference call. May we have your thoughts and observations?"

Petra said, "Honestly, Otto, I was just thinking about how much we like Carlos and his girlfriend, Simone. Considering their country of origin, they have been open and communicative. Carlos, according to Simone, has been having some financial success and she is quite proud of his achievements. Juan, I have met, and he was fine at first meeting. Jacob has had more interaction with Juan. They have been more of a social connection at our resort, with this request for consulting based on dinner conversation regarding Jacob's abilities and work expertise. Simone has made a real effort to befriend me. We are going to dinner later together since Jacob and Carlos are away.

"It does now occur to me how little we know of them. Quip, can you have ICABOD do a little digging on these folks? But I have to say that I hope you don't find what I am afraid that you might find."

Otto offered, "I understand how you feel, Petra, but not knowing the truth would hurt more. Don't be so glum. Enjoy the time and the people while you can, because it's gone all too quickly."

Quip responded, "Yes, I can certainly meet both of your requests. I will do the background checking first. Petra, since you are planning dinner with Simone soon, I will send anything that would raise a flag right away.

"Jacob, to map the environment requested, can you send me the IP addresses you are attached to with your traces as well as the location of your programs that you obviously loaded earlier today. Use our secured point that we established when you were last here, please. I should have something for you relatively quickly."

"Quip, I will send the information shortly. Petra, have a nice dinner and relax some. I know you are enjoying Simone's company, and you are in a fairly public location to say nothing of the security that is at the resort," offered Jacob.

CHAPTER 21

Learning often opens the door to failure

JAC and Quip continued their efforts to find Lara. Quip was having limited success with the facial recognition software, due to the volumes of data being scanned and compared. They had conducted daily morning calls to track their progress and direction since the project began. Each day they found at least one location that was eliminated from where she might be found. The process was slower than either of them cared to admit.

JAC asked, "Anything yet from ICABOD with the adaptation of the facial recognition programs?"

Quip replied, "Nothing substantial yet. I'm not just searching general public photos but also publishing companies, photographer databases, printers, proof-agents, clothing designers, marketing groups, and even the databases of some models who have their own libraries. When you mix in multiple photo-shoot circuits over six months there's a lot of territory to cover. As you suggested, I am sticking to the photographers that use North American and South American beach locations for this time of year and the upcoming season being captured.

"I know that you eliminated Hawaii and California, which are prime targets for many fashion shoots. Right now, Santiago, Cancun, Puerto Vallarta, Cabo San Lucas, and Acapulco seem to be the most active territories for modeling work. I am uncertain if that is due to the time of year, fashion season, or simply location preferences.

"Oscar indicated that Santiago was the last known destination of Lara. My guess is that it is too close to her home. I suspect that she moved on with another identity. While I'm not giving up on finding something in Santiago, I am concentrating on North American photo shoots for the time frame we have been given. How are the on the ground, face-to-face activities and interviews going, JAC?"

"I did eliminate the U.S. locations, plus access in and out of the country is tougher there than other places. Santiago did have some interesting shoots, but I came up empty. I arrived in San Miguel de Allende last night and will work through the other Mexico locations based on timing and travel access. I would estimate no more than two days per city unless I find several shoots, which would require speaking to more people.

"Did you get a chance to have those designer samples run for me? I want some tangible evidence that I have a solid product line. I have been showing the photo and my sketches. I think that having a few pieces of the fashion line will help me fill the role better. Folks in Mexico are inherently distrustful. Fortunately, Lara is also very pretty in the pictures I have which makes some of the photographers look twice."

Quip said, "Where did you get this beachwear, loungewear, and lingerie line of yours? I mean, some of this looks quite good, but I do not want to have to fight copyright stuff with a well-known designer. And yes, they were run and should be in your hands by tomorrow at the hotel you alerted me to last night. By the way, I used Haddy to help with the fabrics and color choices as well as confirm the sizing to fit Lara, as that was so out of my knowledge base, JAC. Haddy thought the sizing would be useful if you needed to convince her she was the only model you could use."

JAC chuckled, "The fashion design and fabric manufacturing classes I had in college weren't wasted, huh? These are all mine, Quip, so copyright them for our team. Good insight on the sizing. Please thank Haddy."

"Well don't give up the day job just yet, young lady. They look very innovative to a mere male such as me. Ok, I need to let you go so I can deliver my search results on another project. Let me know when you receive the merchandise. I will keep you apprised of any hits by the program and send along any pictures that are possible Lara matches."

"Thanks, Quip. Talk later."

CHAPTER 22

Honest feelings are not always from the honest

Quip launched a secure conference call and looped in Jacob, Otto, and Petra to discuss the findings on the peculiar activity at Cayman Bank, and the players Phillip Johnston, Simone, and Juan and Carlos Rodriquez. The findings of these searches were within an hour of the requests, which pleased him.

Quip opened the discussion, "Your suspicions were right, Jacob. The computer activity you spotted under the radar at the bank WAS accounting sleight of hand. The program being used was a decimal rounding program from our old friends at the Dteam used to divert third, fourth, and fifth decimal point earnings from a bank account to another destination. Petra just confirmed the program's usage since it had part of her code in it, along with yours.

"Upon closer inspection it looks like your contact Phillip Johnston is the instigator. With this little handiwork, he is building a nice little nest egg for himself. Here's the funny part – it's in his name with no outbound wire transfers to get it out of Dodge. I mean, what a maroon this guy is. Even a first year junior internal auditor should be able to trace this.

"So I looked into this Johnston guy. He has been at the bank for three years now, but it looks like he has been trying to engineer himself into this position ever since he got there, probably with this idea in mind. You'd think that with three years to plan he would be a little more creative and stealthier than this. I know of people who make crossword puzzles that are more innovative than the guy who did this clumsy piece of work.

"Oh, and the other thing is he seems to be taking principle from six accounts that have come online over the last six months, along with the rounding decimal movement. These accounts indicate that Carlos and Juan Rodriquez are the financial sponsors of record for these accounts. All of them are classified as inheritance type accounts with huge balances."

Otto asked, "What did you discover about Juan and Carlos?"

"That's another odd series of issues. Juan is mostly a flyboy pilot with lots of certifications, including one to fly Boeing 727 aircraft. Apparently he got that from a major carrier just before that airline collapsed. He has been practically non-existent since then but does surface every once in a while when he flies into U.S. airspace to party in Dallas, Texas.

"Carlos, however, came out of the Mexican military. Haven't found his last rank yet, but he was a part of the communications group where he received special training with U.S. counterparts. His record contains notations that he showed a very high aptitude for satellite and wireless communications in hostile climate conditions, and promotion was considered to an officer's rank. He was subsequently thrown out of the military, apparently for fighting and landing issues with a squad of eight soldiers in a bar one night. He had minor cuts and abrasions and was treated and released. The squad was hospitalized with one man still in rehabilitation."

Jacob questioned, "Fighting and landing?"

Quip laughed, "Yeah, fighting and landing. Carlos did the fighting and the other eight soldiers did the landings. It might not have been so bad for him if the commandant's son hadn't been one of the landees. Apparently he is quite the scrapper, Jacob. He did all of this with no weapon in hand. His file noted that his allegiance was to himself rather than the Mexican Army.

"Simone is listed in the resort with Carlos as Rodriguez as well, like they are married, but I cannot locate anything to substantiate that yet. Plus, Petra had said that they weren't married in her summary note to me regarding conversations between her and Simone.

"Anyway, Carlos has only surfaced in the last six months or so in this financial advisor role. Now he and Juan have accounts at Cayman Bank, but all I see going into the account are the commissions they are collecting up front when the accounts are opened. Looks like the account disbursements are legitimate and indicate a comfortable lifestyle. So I don't really see anything to suggest that Juan and Carlos are working a scheme together. Frankly, I am rather relieved that they are not scheming with Johnston since both of them appear to be much smarter.

"Over the last six months, several drug dealers and their liquid assets have been leaving Mexico through some unidentified conduit. In that same time frame, large cash deposits are being shepherded into this same Cayman Bank. There is also no evidence to suggest that Juan or Carlos have legitimately earned the designation of financial consultants, or we would have seen some evidence of this type of education or experience in their backgrounds. They only popped up on the grid six months ago and are moving millions into a country known for its bank secrecy laws.

"So, I would put it to you all, I suspect these are the money-moving magicians for those drug lords based on what we have so far. There is nothing solid to back up this statement. We all know already that I do not believe in coincidences."

Neither Petra nor Jacob liked the evidence nor the conclusion offered by Quip. Otto sensed the dismay of everyone with the resigned sighs heard over the call.

Before Otto could voice what everyone was feeling, Quip added, "Let me go on record as having said dammit! Dammit! Dammit! I happen to like Juan and Carlos from everything I've seen so far, as well as from what Petra and Jacob have relayed in conversation. Add in the fact that I am convinced that Carlos pulled off an amazing satellite cloaking event to shield the plane his brother is flying that significantly impressed Andrew. And, well, I have a sneaking admiration for these two rogue scoundrels."

Otto chuckled, "How uncharacteristically chivalrous of you, Quip. But thank you for voicing our collective feelings. So now, my wards of the R-Group future, what do you propose we do about this? The overlap of portions of our current assignments is interesting and worth leveraging.

"Mr. Monty is pressing for some progress on the whereabouts of several drug lords and their missing assets. We have some entity laundering money that seemingly coincides with drug lord disappearances. We have an annoying, not too bright, bank official in an untidy affair concerning the criminal use of decimal rounding software. And we have two rogue scoundrels that we would like to extract from their circumstances because… well, just because. Does that capture all the elements that are on the table?"

Each of them listened from their various locations and were making their plans based on the overall results found. In their own ways, they struggled to wrap their heads around the coincidences of these events in these places.

Jacob interjected, "Quip, thank you for my answers in this matter. I need to get to the bank on time in the morning and pull a few more traces to complete my testing analysis. I want to deliver my results to Carlos and Juan as soon as possible. Otto, let me deliver the report before you talk to Mr. Monty. I agree that Carlos and Juan are worth extracting. I have a pretty good idea of what needs to happen next, so wish me luck."

Petra added, "I am off to dinner with Simone. I will update you on any new discoveries."

CHAPTER 23

Unescorted ladies can often handle things perfectly

Simone had called Petra and suggested that they meet at the bar for a drink before going to dinner. She also suggested they might want dinner at a restaurant adjacent to the resort. The ladies arrived at the bar at the same time and greeted each other like old friends as they exchanged hugs and kisses. They were beautiful in their resort dresses, long hair and makeup. They located a quiet table in the corner of the bar and ordered white wines. Simone sensed that Petra was distracted and in typical Simone manner tried to lighten the mood.

"Petra, please tell me what's on your mind. I'm here for you and I'm a good listener."

"I guess I just miss Jacob, and I'm ready for a bit of your insight into men. However, you had indicated that we might have dinner outside of the resort. Let's get that squared away and perhaps we can chat about my relationship questions then," Petra replied honestly.

"I was thinking that it might be really fun to watch the cliff divers. I was told that the best viewing is from a restaurant located next to but off the resort property. If you are agreeable, then let's see if we can confirm the location with the concierge. They are supposed to have a mixed crowd of resort customers and locals. I heard there may be some models and photographers that just arrived for a shoot later in the week for four of the major fashion retailers for their summer lines."

"Ah, so you still want to pursue your ambition. A little exposure to the modeling opportunities that might be available, as it were?" Petra laughed. "Sure we can do that if the concierge agrees that it is close enough. I don't think I could walk far in these heels."

They finished their wines and went to the concierge. Miguel, the on-duty clerk, was full of information about the restaurant and its attached dance club, the schedule of the cliff diving, as well as an offer to take them over and pick them up when they called that they were finished.

"Señoritas, The Dive is a very nice restaurant that caters to our resort crowd but also to those staying in Acapulco. The dancing is lively, the diving is wonderful, and the food delicious. Between us, the view of the divers is far better from there than here, but please don't tell my manager. As you ladies are not escorted tonight, per messages I see in your files, I am happy to escort you over in our golf carts and return you when you are finished. Simply tell the hostess and she will contact me," Miguel conveyed in a most charming manner.

"Thank you, Miguel," Petra said. "I think that is ideal."

Miguel took them to The Dive and made certain the hostess would contact him. The hostess escorted them to a prime seat over-looking the cliffs and indicated the divers would be performing at the top of the hour. The waiter took their orders for food and beverages quickly and promptly returned with their drinks.

"This is so beautiful, Petra. I am glad we can see at least two of the performances of the divers. They are amazing even from our resort."

"I agree. I think it is well worth the look and the thrill when they dive toward the rocks. I am not afraid of much, but I don't think I would willingly make that dive," agreed Petra.

"What about you and Jacob, what are you afraid of there? We spoke earlier that your relationship is rather new. Is that part of your concern or just your lack of experience that you alluded to earlier?" Simone sweetly inquired.

"Simone, we really have no troubles, but it is a new relationship. Frankly, I have little experience in relationships with men, period. Our lives are complicated, but I do want him in ways I never imagined. He is an ardent lover and seeks to please me. How do I know if I am really pleasing him? I don't want our relationship to fail because of something I did or something I didn't do. Do you know what I mean?"

"I think I understand and honestly, I can relate. Carlos too is very attentive to my needs and desires, even those I couldn't possibly identify or speak to. I think some men give as much as some women do when their feelings are involved. I try to mix in new activities and might suggest you do the same to expand your bedroom repertoire. I think though that each couple has a range of experimentation that is agreed to consciously or unconsciously. One of the things that Carlos said during our first night together was that I could ask him for anything at all when we were making love. Essentially, he said there were no limits between us," Simone grinned.

"Well, Jacob never said anything like that, but he has certainly never said no to anything I have tried, nor have I to him. Perhaps we can share some specifics."

The ladies were interrupted with their dinner and refills on their wine and the first show by the famed cliff divers. For the next hour while they enjoyed the meal, they had a fairly frank discussion on sexual techniques and innovations. Some parts of the conversation erupted in laughter at the very idea of this or that, especially when Simone suggested modest introductions of special outfits or toys rather than using the big bang theory, which was everything all at once.

Petra judged her own bedroom techniques as very basic and almost naïve when compared to Simone's tutorial on accelerated skills. Petra surmised that Simone had the benefit of several partners, lots of reading, or some exaggeration. Petra wasn't certain if friends exaggerated with each other as a rule of thumb. Petra did not have that skill. Simone also discussed additional details regarding some of the semi-nude photos she'd had taken, which were very basic compared to what a friend of hers had experienced, who became something of a porn star.

Both ladies felt increasingly comfortable with one another as they exchanged several discreet confidences. Simone expanded on her desire to model and become an actress if possible, but not a porn star, which she had apparently been offered prior to hooking up with Carlos. Once they finished and the sun was setting, they decided to go to the dance area and listen to music and have another drink or two. Petra demonstrated her early dance training that had helped her walk without tripping. Simone had mentioned she too had early dance lessons, but did not expand on that discussion with any details.

They arrived at the crowded dance floor. As they looked around for a place to seat themselves, a couple of nice looking, well-dressed men asked to join them at their table. Both girls were not here looking for men and declined with grace. They spotted an open table and proceeded to claim it as their own.

"Simone, this is a nice place. Great for people watching."

"Yes, and the music is loud enough to dance to but not too loud to hear ourselves talk. Those two guys were really scoping us out. I am so glad you didn't want to have them join us."

"We are doing just fine getting to know one another without worrying about two men we have no interest in. There are lots of pretty girls in here that really look as if they'd like the company. Look at that pretty blonde dancing over there. Wow, I am amazed she can stay in the front of that dress. How does she do that?" Petra questioned.

"Oh, I'm sure she uses that body spray glue. It basically keeps her tits in place by holding them to the sides of the dress. It is a trick some models use," Simone clarified without thinking and before she had located the girl Petra referenced. When she located the object of the discussion, her eyes widened as she said, almost with panic in her voice, "Oh my god. That's Rita. What's she doing here?"

Petra, immediately alerted, asked, "You know her? She sure is pretty, but that outfit is really revealing, and those five inch heels, how is she dancing so easily? How do you know her? If she is a friend, you can invite her over if you want."

"Rita is a really nice girl and I do like her. She is also a renowned porn star, the one I mentioned earlier. I met her when, as I mentioned before, the possibilities for extra money looked to be toward nude shots and movies without clothes. She actually warned me off, I think, because she has a good heart."

With tears welling up and her embarrassment rising, she continued, "She recognized that I am really not cut out for that venue of acting. I like her a lot, but with her here, I suspect others that I have no desire to ever see again are here as well. I think we should go. This can't be a good sign."

Petra recognized the panic rising within Simone and patted her arm. She knew of some of the history and Simone's shame at even considering that avenue as a way to become an actress. But running away was likely not the answer. Here they were in a public place and no one would bother them unless they allowed it.

"I think we should enjoy the music and at least finish our drinks. Relax a bit, I don't think we will be bothered with all these people around," reassured Petra.

The song ended and Rita thanked her partner and started to walk toward them to one of the tables close by. She was about to sit with two other girls when she saw Simone and her eyes widened. Rita looked around and then decided to come to their table.

"Oh, Simone, how nice to see you. You look lovely, as always." Turning toward Petra, Rita said with an honest smile, "Hi there, my name is Rita. Are you friends with Simone?"

Petra smiled and said, "Yes, Simone and I met here in Acapulco. Nice to meet you, Rita. How do you dance in those shoes? Please sit down and join us a minute."

Rita laughed, "Dancing is fine, just keep on the toes. The walking is the real killer, especially if the surface isn't smooth.

"How are you, Simone? I didn't expect to see you around here. I figured the argument with Spencer would keep you well out of his purview. You aren't meeting him, are you?"

"Heavens no. I had no idea that this would be a hot spot. Is he here? Please tell me he's not here. I really don't want to see him," Simone said with her voice on edge.

"I haven't seen him, but he could show up. Though this place is a lot nicer than where he usually travels. He does have a new film he has concocted and he wants me to consider being the lead. He is hunting for new talent in case I turn him down. Petra, as pretty as you are, please tell me you too are not looking to become a movie star. He'd try to pick you up in a minute and lie every step of the way. I told him no new films until he paid me what he owes me. The bastard! "

"Thank you for the compliment, but no, not my style. But you, Rita, you are a movie star? What is the new film that you are considering? Do you not have a contract where he would have to pay you?"

"Ok, now we have two very naïve girls. Yeah, we have a contract of sorts, but it means nothing. Right now I am popular, which forces him to pay me something. In the business of adult entertainment films, though, there is more drama outside the film that one could imagine. The acting talent used is a bit different than what Simone, for example, wanted. And because Spencer is my agent/manager I am stuck, to a degree. My goal is that someone will see past the skin part to the acting part.

"This new theme he has is so not original. I don't think it is worth the time it will take. For me the money would need to be very good and up front."

"Really?" asked Petra. "I have, like, no experience in this area at all. Can you tell me some of the details?"

"Petra, I don't think you really want to know this stuff. Rita, how else are you doing? Any new photo shoots that you might be involved with or suggest to me? I heard that several of the fashion folks were doing summer shoots here very soon."

"That is really why I am here, Simone, to work on gaining a top campaign. They pay so much better and you don't have to pretend to be a pretzel to get the shot," Rita giggled.

"Ok ladies, now I really want some details. Pretzel seems rather descriptive. I have had just enough to drink where I suspect this will be funny," Petra implored the ladies.

Laughter ensued with Simone and Rita shaking their heads. A look passed between them that suggested Petra was so not aware of the darker side of adult entertainment. Rita decided to go for the shock value description, which also should remind Simone that this was really not her career avenue. Rita thought they both seemed like really nice ladies. Nice ladies hadn't crossed her path much nor tried to interact as friends might. Especially not with Spencer's crowd of misfits.

"Ok, I will outline the planned story line as it was related to me. But, girls, you need to tell me when it is simply too much. Of course, the beet red color of your faces should be the tell-tale sign."

They all giggled and ordered another drink for this descriptive discussion. Petra thought if nothing else it would be fun telling the story to Jacob later. Plus she was sort of having fun just being with the girls.

Rita began matter-of-factly, almost clinically, "You both know that guys really like fantasies. So if they can think it, they want to see it. I personally think that the girl on girl thing is perhaps one of the top things that guys just love imagining, seeing or experiencing. Spencer's idea is along those lines. Like usual, he expects all the cast to understand what he wants with his outlines, or he is happy to demonstrate his ideas. It's what really makes him so creepy, 'cause he is so not buff or built like the other guys used as props in these types of films.

"Ok, in scene one, these two girls somehow decide they want to get into a strip club. They are some classy girls that want to check out the wild side a bit. Two guys looking for some hot little pick-ups negotiate with the girls to act as escorts. You know, girls have a challenge getting into a strip club without a male escort. They sort that out with a wink and promise for events later. That settled, they all go in and find a table close to the stage where the club girls perform. In a gentlemen's club it is all about imagination since touching is not openly allowed. The better the dancer is at projecting eroticism with sensual moves and looks, the better the tips and customer drink consumption.

"One of the performers takes a fancy to one of the guys and goes over to offer a special on a lap dance."

"Excuse me, Rita. Lap dance?" Petra asked.

"Umm, yeah well. That is where an exotic dancer provides a very close dance for a specific man…well, or lady. I don't do exotic dancing in clubs but girls I know that have say it pays really well," clarified Rita. "I do know that handling a male that has been watching a lap dance or a stripper after the fact can be a very intense sexual experience."

"Ok, thanks. Please continue. This is quite interesting," reflected Petra.

Rita elaborated, "Well, Spencer's plot lines haven't evolved very much. So the new story goes, that the guy asks the dancer to do a lap dance for one of the girls he helped escort into the club. He wants to get her all excited so that he can have a chance with her. The dancer begins her routine, really getting into the game. The more erotic her dancing the closer the two girls get as if protecting each other and they hug and hold each other. They are supposed to get so wrapped up in the dance that pretty soon their lust takes over, and they are exploring each other."

"Really, this is permitted in a gentlemen's club?" Petra asked with a bloom in her cheeks and fanning herself with her hand.

Simone said, "I haven't been in one, but I would doubt that a no touch place would allow that."

They both nervously laughed, then turned to Rita for clarification.

"Ladies, it is a porn movie where anything goes. It doesn't matter if it is what one can do in a real club. Though with enough money anything is possible from what I have seen and heard.

"So the girls are supposed to ignore the exotic dancer, or one of the guys just takes her right there. The two girls are to then erotically explore each other as they move clothes aside or remove them, then the guys will join in after the girls have moaned and groaned with repeated orgasms. That is why Spencer is looking to source additional ladies as dancers in the background and as my main partner. He wants me to be one of the ladies who then takes on one or both the guys in the wrap-up scenes," Rita finished with a laugh at the looks on Simone and Petra's faces.

"And you're saying that guys like this?" Petra asked. "I had no idea. Simone, is this true?"

"I have no first-hand experience on this but from my readings and certainly comments from Spencer, I'd have to say yes." Simone then said, "This was the main reason that I decided that this was not the kind of filmmaking I could do. I like having fun and all, but that is outside of my comfort zone. Rita, how do you do it?"

Rita shrugged, "At first I was nervous and actually hated it, but I grew up with some abuse and sex way too early. Now I simply have my mind someplace else. I treat it like a job, but I don't like it. I just do it well. My real choice is to find something better so I can move out of this business."

They were so absorbed in the discussion that they all jumped as a hand rested over Rita's right shoulder. Petra looked up and saw an extremely unkempt man with dirt under the nails of his beefy hands. His shortness and his roundness made his wrinkled clothes look awful. Petra shuddered and immediately lost her entire wine buzz. She glanced at Simone and saw fear in her eyes even as her facial expression became distant but composed.

"Rita, my dear, here you are," the man loudly stated, "and with a pair of pretty ladies too. Did you find your own co-stars, honey?"

"No, Spencer, just speaking with some folks that asked me a question," she said as she rose. "I need to get back to my group. Nice talking with you both," Rita added as she walked away.

He immediately took the seat Rita vacated and said, "Ladies, my name is Spencer, and I can make you both a lot of money. You can be stars in my new film because you are simply…" He stopped and stared as he recognized Simone. His lip curled, then relaxed as he finished, "Beautiful. Simone, I hardly recognized you all dolled up. How are you?" he reached over and tried to stroke her arm before she pulled away.

"Spencer, you can leave. We didn't invite you to join us. Our escorts will be back shortly, and they wouldn't like seeing you sitting here," Simone spoke bravely.

Spencer said, "Why, Simone, I am shocked and dismayed by your attitude. After all we have been through and the number of times I have come to rescue you from your emotional meltdowns. All the times I have tried to get just the right star vehicle to launch your career and you show me no gratitude. Why, you haven't even introduced me to this charming lady who is sitting here with us." Spencer took Petra's hand and kissed it with all the charm of an eel before she pulled it back.

Spencer gave the ladies an oily smile before he taunted, "Oh, I get it. You are doing your own recruiting for that movie I told you about. My dear Simone, I can see you have done some homework on the terrific cinematic role we last discussed and that I just know you were made for."

Spencer turned his attention toward Petra and continued, "The story line is quite original and I have cast this most ambitious lady in a journalistic role as a star reporter for the Evening Post. The Chief Editor is the romantic love interest and Simone is *The Star Reporter* who desperately wants on the Editors' Evening Post. His Evening Post." Spencer laughed at his play on words. "But his tragic addiction to cocaine has taken the wood out of his Evening Post. Simone is tried and true to her one great love even though his cocaine habit has taken her from being a star reporter on that Post to simply being a meter maid watching the futility of someone trying to shove an oyster into a parking meter. She cannot bear to see him fall from so powerful a position, and so she takes on a female lover to be satisfied."

Petra was appalled. She opened her mouth to speak, but nothing came out.

Spencer seductively stated, "I know you will be just wonderful as Simone's lover in this epic masterpiece. I am so confident in your ability to adapt to this role that I am even willing to do a few test shots at my own expense just because I can see terrific chemistry here. Ladies, please bring your drinks and let me introduce the lighting and production team that will be totally captivated by your ravishing charm. I would pay, but I didn't bring any cash with me from the studio. No matter though. Your careers will be such that soon people will be begging to pay for your dinner and buy you drinks."

Simone smiled as she'd discovered the perfect opening. It was so clear to her now.

"Ahh, like the time that guy let you pay for my meal? By the way, how is the arm, Spence?"

Spencer by nature was a weasel and accustomed to being rebuffed. However, he recalled the night that Carlos had crushed his arm and had him pinned to the wall. The memory was like a light switch that instantly turned pain onto his face and mannerisms. Spencer visibly struggled to keep his emotions in check regarding that event.

Before he recovered his composure, Simone added, "Yes, Spencer, perhaps you're right about people throwing me money to have dinner with them."

Simone turned to Petra and related, "Spencer was so thoughtful to pay for Carlos and me to have dinner that evening. And, such a gentleman he was! Why, Petra, Spencer saw the look in our eyes and knew that a romantic prince had arrived for me and insisted on paying for our evening and then promptly withdrew without even waiting for our thank you."

Spencer had taken all the ridicule he could stand at this point and reached into his coat and pulled out a nickel-plated, pearl-handled automatic pistol. Standard armament for a pimp in a cheap whorehouse. He kept it out of sight of the casual patrons and waitstaff, but easily visible to Simone. Simone froze, which immediately placed Petra on high alert.

Spencer informed them in a very agitated but low-grated volume, "I am armed now after that little event with your stallion. You can tell him if I see him again, the outcome of our meeting will be quite different, you perra!"

Petra smiled like a duchess as Spencer's gaze rested on her and then casually knocked over a drink into Spencer's lap. This distracted him just enough for her to jab him quite effectively with a nerve punch, causing him to slump forward just enough for her to then drive her foot straight into his solar-plexus under the table. Spencer landed face down on the table. Petra motioned the manager over to alert him to the man with the weapon who had drunk too much. Petra and Simone quickly slipped out of the dance area in all the commotion and asked the hostess to alert Miguel that they were ready to return to the resort.

As they waited outside for Miguel, they were both quiet. Simone hadn't recovered from the events of the evening or from seeing Spencer. Petra wondered how she would explain this to Jacob or the others. She usually stayed out of physical trouble, even if she was capable of handling those types of situations.

As Miguel dropped them off and they parted each to their own room, Petra smiled at Simone, "Same time tomorrow, my friend? We'll start at the pool. You do seem to know all the right people and I am having such a good time getting to know them."

CHAPTER 24

Always earn favors in advance of needing them

JAC retrieved the package sent by Quip from the hotel concierge and returned to her room to inspect the contents. She examined the items and was so excited seeing her design creations in finished form. The fabrics used were wonderful and helped bring out the best in the designs.

She smiled, then praised to the air in her room, "Not bad, say I."

In her mind she replayed and laughed at that vulgar phrase of Quip's, Keep this up kid and you'll be wearing diamonds as big as horse turds. As she finished that thought she was reminded that she needed to check in with him. JAC dialed Quip on their special cellular encrypted channel.

Quip answered, "Hi kid, how we doing? Did you get the package and were the results to your liking?"

JAC heartily replied, "Yes, Quip, everything is here and it is perfect. Thank you so much. This portion of this assignment is so much fun. I missed the early morning shoot, but there is another one slotted a couple of hours before sundown so I will end up there. If I have no positive hits there I think that I will move to the other locations you suggested. I was thinking Acapulco, and I'll say hello to Petra and Jacob, maybe bunk with them.

"Still no positive IDs from the facial recognition program, I take it?"

Quip said, "Nothing positive or a total match yet, but I found some high-ranking possibilities with one photographer. I sent the address to our secure place and a couple of extra pictures that you might want to print out if you can.

"I know you are working the plan. Leverage your new fashion line. The more folks you ask, the better chance you have of getting a real lead. The program is working within ICABOD to hunt out lots of picture files from fashion lines and retail fashion mailers. I really lucked out in finding that treasure trove of photographers and files containing new-look models in three different sources. That resulted in that possibility that I sent you.

"Someone has seen her and taken some photos in the last six months or so. The only other possibility is that she slipped into another new identity or maybe even gave up on this dream completely. If we can't get a positive ID, then maybe that is what has happened."

JAC said, "I don't think she's the kind of person who would completely abandon her dreams. Usually when that happens the person goes home to people who want them back and that chapter is closed forever. I have to believe that the drive is there and that she is still trying to make it work."

Quip suggested, "Ok kiddo, let's run with it and see what we can find. Good luck hunting today.

"You know, if you do make it to Acapulco you might want your own room. Give the lovebirds the alone time they need, no matter how much they both like you."

"I hear you."

JAC packed up some of her merchandise in a smart-looking backpack and set out to the local shoot sites. She spoke with forty or so models, several photographers, and actually received one, I think I saw her, comment and a reference to the same photographer Quip had uncovered. As she showed some of her samples to the models, she'd received positive responses. She also took several photos of girls with some characteristics similar to Lara, and took some names and numbers for future reference. In the back of her mind fashion might be another avenue that could be pursued. She planned to forward the details and photos to Quip to add to his information databases.

Armed with that information she traveled to Acapulco and arranged a hotel near the address of the photographer. The shoots planned were not near the resort where Petra and Jacob were staying. After she arrived and checked in, she uploaded the information to Quip and crashed, dreaming of being a leading fashion designer, even as she planned to begin early the next morning with the photographer's studio.

She arrived at the studio first thing after breakfast. The place looked deserted, which was further supported with the printed notice of eviction in Spanish on the front door along with a large padlock.

JAC commented under her breath, "Well, this is certainly inconvenient! Looks like models aren't the only ones having trouble making ends meet."

She rapped on the door several times anyway to see if she could gain anyone's attention. She called out for anyone and started to circle the building when she spied a scruffy-looking guy with all his cameras and worldly belongings coming out the back of the shop and headed toward the alley way. She moved quickly that way and noticed how young but beaten he looked. The man was in his mid-thirties and looked fit, though hungry.

He noticed JAC, realized she wasn't an official, and offered, "I'm no longer in business. Can't you read the sign? I'm certainly not hiring any assistants, models, or nannies so thanks for stopping by, but no thanks." He smiled weakly and shifted the equipment he carried.

JAC smiled sympathetically, "Oh, so you don't hire yourself out for photo shoots anymore? That's a shame, I'd heard you had a good eye. I have money too. Oh well, I'm sure I can find someone else to do good quality photographic work for my new fashion line. Good day to you, Mr. Dejected and Beaten."

The comments from JAC had the desired effect on the photographer, who turned back and nearly roared, "Well, why didn't you just say you had work and money? I can still get in through the back door today, so come on in and let's parlay. My name is Manuel Sanchez."

JAC was somewhat amused by the scruffy photographer with his vigorous turnaround and accepted his invitation. They settled down to talk at a wobbly table. JAC told her story to Manuel and showed her fashion line as well as described the type of individual she wanted as the lead model. He suggested some settings that appealed to her.

Manuel listened intently, studied the items and made a few rough sketches that quickly showed he was a seasoned professional who knew his trade, as well as how to plan shots. He suggested some shoot locations as he looked at her like an artist that itched to pick up his camera. The more JAC worked with him and listened, the more she was saddened by his leaving the business. He demonstrated a talent for picture composition and clearly articulated his ideas.

Casually, she pulled out the photo of Lara to see if Manuel recognized anything about this model. JAC explained that she had seen only a few shots of this particular model but wanted to speak with her to see if she would be suitable as a spokeswoman for the product line. Manuel said nothing but got up and retrieved his hardcopy portfolio file. He rifled through it rapidly, then smiled as he located a very promising picture that he presented to JAC.

JAC immediately recognized the resemblance and was excited by the prospect that she might be on to Lara's trail at last. The hair was very different in his photograph and her face was shadowed with a look that was hardly a schoolgirl. But some of the facial structure looked very similar.

JAC smiled broadly at Manuel, then said, "It looks like you, Manuel, may have found her at last! What's her name and when can we talk to her about this role?"

Manuel presented, "She said her name was Celeste, I think, or something like that. A lovely lady suited for specific fashion with her generous bosom. She would be good, from what I recall, for your line, no doubt. I liked photographing her as she was good with responding to requests correctly the first time asked.

"If that's who you are searching for as a model, I am disappointed to say that I have no idea where to find her. I don't even know her last name. She probably moved on to another shoot and another opportunity. These models are always looking for huge discovery. This shot came from a very minor portion of a big shoot several months ago.

"If she was the only person you wanted for this role then I guess you'll be moving on as well. I sense that we won't be able to do any business until you find her. So thank you for showing me your product line, and I hope you will fare well, madam."

He rose and collected his files, then his equipment and moved toward the door, encouraging her to leave first.

JAC interjected, "I'm a pay-as-you-go kind of girl. So how much do I owe you for your time, kind sir? You have been most helpful."

The photographer was obviously torn between the need for some income and his pride as he said, "Madam, no real value was provided since I cannot tell you where she is located. I cannot expect to be paid, but thank you anyway, señorita. Perhaps another time?"

JAC smiled her dazzling smile and then suggested, "You know, I am a stranger in this country of yours and, well, I could use an informed escort with knowledge of where good models can be found, provided he conducts himself as a gentleman."

JAC peeled off two thousand U.S. dollars in travelers checks and placed them in his top pocket. He was too dumbfounded to refuse the generous gift.

The photographer was overcome with emotion but refused to shed any tears in front of her.

"Well, since you put it like that, allow me to freshen up a bit and I will discharge my obligation accordingly. I shall be right back."

He excused himself as he wiped away some tears at finding a new lease on his career within his grasp. When he returned he found that JAC and his picture had vanished.

The photographer smiled as he said to the empty room, "Sweetheart, I would have given you the picture for just one kiss."

CHAPTER 25

It's the little things that get you, possibly protect you

Jacob called Carlos and when he answered said, "Carlos, I have finished my report and would like to deliver my findings. But I think it would be prudent to discuss the report with you before we let anyone else see it, if you have no objections."

Carlos was guarded in his response. "Jacob, I will trust your judgment in this matter. So how about this evening to provide us some privacy to our discussion? No one need know of our meeting since it will not be during regular business hours. Will that be satisfactory?"

Jacob said, "Yes, of course. May I suggest somewhere quiet where we can have dinner along with our discussion? I presume that Juan will be there with you."

Carlos laughed, "A capital suggestion! Now since this assignment includes expenses I would have you pick up the tab and charge it back on your delivery order. That way I don't have to pay to feed us. Juan may or may not join as there is other business he is working at present."

"I'll meet you at our new favorite restaurant here on the island at seven," Jacob chuckled.

Jacob and Carlos arrived at the same time and were promptly seated in a discreet booth away from other patrons. The men were a little on edge. Each was somewhat tense and apprehensive at what the other might think of the discussion.

Jacob asked, "Do you want to talk business first or should the meal take precedence? The reason I ask is that in the U.S. Americans are always in a hurry to talk shop but everywhere else it is typically the custom to enjoy food, wine, and the company before diving into business discussions. Frankly, I prefer the meal and wine first, but you are the customer."

"For a New York gringo, you have learned the protocol of other countries rather well. I agree the meal and wine should take precedence. Juan was not able to meet with us."

Dinner and drinks helped take the edge off their moods. The food was good and the seconds on wine helped them both relax. After the plates were cleared, they sat back, each assuming their positions for the discussion.

"Jacob, I sense there is some concern on your mind about the report content. Otherwise you would not have asked to give a private briefing to me rather than simply sending me the file to review. What should I know, that I don't know?"

"Actually Carlos, there are two pieces of the discussion. For the first piece, I will cover what you do not know.

"There is a somewhat elaborate ruse going on at Cayman Bank, Carlos. I was told to look at certain areas of the network by Mr. Johnston. Then I was restricted to certain servers and only given access to the areas of the network per strict instructions of Mr. Johnston. Everything I was told to look at was in perfect working order with no blemishes. That's the good news."

"So are you inferring that there is bad news?"

"Yes. The bad news is there is other activity going on under the radar, if you will. The short version is that a lot of unauthorized traffic is going on that is being masked by the sanitized stuff I was told to look at. The sanitized traffic and altered log files are all apparently designed to fool an auditor, causing most to not look anywhere else. Additionally, this hidden traffic seems to be focused on diverting interest income, in most cases by the use of a decimal rounding program that I happen to know is from a Russian program delivered from a group known as the Dteam. The Dteam typically sells their applications to the highest bidders or uses them for their own reasons. In this case it appears not to be used directly by them, so it is presumed to be a sold version.

"I also found that actual principal is being skimmed in small amounts that would not be noticed over time. The interesting part of this story is that it is only tapping into the accounts you and your brother have brought to the bank over the last six months. All evidence points to the money being re-routed to an account owned by Phillip Johnston. I checked and found no evidence of inappropriate fund diversions to your or your brother's account. Frankly, this is a rather low grade of financial theft and not very imaginative. I believe though you had indicated to me that Mr. Johnston was your liaison to Cayman Bank."

Carlos sat back and reflected on the information. He mulled different scenarios around in his mind. Instinctively Juan hadn't liked Johnston from the first meeting. He formulated his response to this revelation from Jacob.

"Well, that's unexpected and at least somewhat disappointing," Carlos responded. "I was under the impression that Johnston had proper banking ethics, but it seems that is not the case. You know Juan has never completely trusted Johnston, and the other day I found good reason not to trust him either.

"We had finished up a board member meeting and went to retrieve our jackets from the coatrack. Johnston and I had similar dark suits on and he grabbed my coat instead of his, put it on and walked out ahead of the rest of us. I found his coat instead of mine hanging there and hurried after him to make the exchange. I knew it was his coat because it was so small I couldn't even put it on.

"Juan had watched him put on my coat that dwarfed him so much that he had to push the sleeves up over his wrists to grab his briefcase. It never occurred to Johnston that the coat he put on was not his even though the coattail came down to his knees and his hands were swallowed by the cuffs! Juan laughed as we hurried after Johnston.

"Well, when I grabbed his coat to run after him, in my irritation at him taking my coat, I must have jostled it enough to have his passport fall out of the inside coat pocket. It had to be a phony passport because it had his picture but was from Canada under another name. I didn't understand the significance of the event at the time but now I do. He must be diverting other account holders' monies to his account and had a phony passport made up in order to run.

"I, for one, am glad you have acquired the hard evidence the bank needs to prosecute Johnston. All I had was conjecture of his holding a phony passport, which I did return when we swapped coats. Of course, I showed Juan first so he could back me up as well. He kept a copy of the passport number.

"When I think of how close he came to raiding my clients' accounts after they trusted me to move their inheritances to this bank, I get very angry. Can we reverse what he has skimmed off thus far? I must acknowledge my debt of gratitude for what you have provided me with your efforts."

Carlos smiled at Jacob with open appreciation and ordered another glass of wine for each of them. Once served, Jacob continued with his report.

"It is possible to reverse the effects of the rounding programs and I have put a correction program in to do that if you wish. However, Carlos, I found that is not all of the story. The pirating of those accounts seemed a little odd, specifically since Johnston has been at this bank for several years. The question came to mind – why only those accounts? So I pieced together what seems to be a plausible sequence of events that I wanted to talk with you about.

"Actually, there has been a rather peculiar series of events over the same time frame that involves a group of Mexican drug lords vanishing overnight with all their hard currency and treasures. The six accounts that have been established under your shepherding coincides with those drug dealer disappearances, though none of the account names match directly to the known drug lords.

"My working theory here, Carlos, is that you and Juan flew the drug dealers and their assets to this bank. You enlisted the sympathetic help of Johnston for handling the funds and getting onto the bank board of directors. Johnston is now raiding the accounts with an ambition to steal it all since the drug dealers can't call the police. If that is the correct scenario playing out, you would get blamed for recommending the bank in the first place. So, my question to you is, can you help me fill in the gaps, and more importantly, what should we do about this?"

Trapped by Jacob's surmising the whole sequence of incriminating events, Carlos started to protest, but was glad that the detective work had intercepted his sponsored accounts from being raided. He also recognized he was a changed man since he met Simone and not as antagonistic. It also brought immediately to mind the extent of Jacob's information sources. It seemed a bit more involved than simply testing technology security. It opened the door for some concerns by Carlos as well as what Jacob might or might not propose.

"Thank you, Jacob, for helping to identify the activities of Mr. Johnston. The people I sponsored here would be most unforgiving of having lost their inheritance money to one as unscrupulous as he appears to be.

"As for the other matter, what would you have me do? I am merely helping friends that have come into great wealth maintain their investments outside of the taxing authorities of Mexico, which are quite onerous. I am open to suggestions at this stage of our discussion, but I should probably say that I may not take your advice in this matter."

Jacob smiled, "Well, I've given it some thought and a few creative ideas have occurred to me which you might consider."

For the rest of the evening Jacob outlined the possible scenarios that Carlos might consider in a very straightforward manner. The discussion was lively but never loud or unruly. The risks and benefits of the outlined steps which might be taken was not lost on Carlos. At the end of their discussion they had reached agreement like gentlemen with each receiving at least some of what they felt was required.

CHAPTER 26

Forgiveness is far easier than permission

"Otto, thank you for calling me back. Have you and your team made any progress on the Mexican drug dealer disappearances or what happened to the missing funds?" said Mr. Monty.

"Mr. Monty, sorry to have missed your original call, but we have been busy working on your effort. We actually have an interesting tale to tell on this matter, along with some, well, shall we say, navigational hazards to circumvent in this story. As usual we have comedy, drama, and pathos to convey to you, our customer," explained Otto.

Mr. Monty dryly replied, "Otto, can you just net it out for me and I'll read the unabridged version later?"

"Of course, Mr. Monty. We did our always thorough job for you, and the report is on the way. Talk to you later, sir."

Mr. Monty acquiesced, "Wait, wait, wait! Can I have some details, please?"

"Ah, so you do want the epic story? Well then, let me say we have come across some unusual activities which are tightly entangled. I believe conveying these activities are critical to understanding the results. Are you now interested?"

Mr. Monty, somewhat vexed at basically being told to sit in his chair, replied, "I just said so, though I fear that your Quip is rubbing off on you.

"Please sir, regale me with stories of comedy, drama, and pathos that pertain to our drug dealers and their finances. And no, you need not wait for me to get popcorn for the telling."

Otto smiled, then began, "Well sir, we found the target destination of the drug dealers' wealth. In following the money we have the whereabouts for the drug lords for the most part as well. During our search, we discovered the receiving bank, a bank parasite skimming said funds, and his poorly planned exit strategy. That is the good news."

Mr. Monty responded with a pleased tone, "That is good news, Otto. May I have more details, please? Of course your comment leads me to inquire, what is the bad news?"

"When you provided the details and background for this assignment, you indicated six drug dealers and their funds. We have been able to specifically confirm information on five drug dealers and their funds. So far nothing on a sixth, so more information is required for us to continue on that person and their supposed wealth.

"The skimmer is one Phillip Johnston, who was about to abscond with the drug dealers' deposits dutifully placed in a Cayman Islands bank account. We have a copy of his bogus passport and bank records with log traces that clearly indicate that he had the intention of moving everything and relocating himself to where he could catch the pirated funds. All in all a good day, wouldn't you say?" inquired Otto.

Mr. Monty was impressed with the details to this point, knowing the report would contain specific information that his team could leverage to take further actions as needed. The abilities of this team were undeniably creative and goal oriented.

It was a little disconcerting to know that their abilities extended past the resources of his teams and those of his global peers.

"So how did the funds get there without the Mexican government or the U.S. knowing about it? As the tabloids say, inquiring minds would like to know."

"Ah, a very astute question of you, Mr. Monty. It seems that Mr. Phillip Johnston lured unsuspecting drug dealers to an off-shore bank with the advertised purpose of laundering their inheritances. The result, however, was the five drug dealers were to be scammed out of their savings. After all, they would certainly not call in the police for support. A most unfortunate line of work that this Phillip Johnston has chosen to pursue with powerful people that tend to get even. Our team has neutralized him and his activity so you can deal with him as you deem appropriate. The details are all in the report that we are in the process of finalizing."

Mr. Monty inquired, "So you are saying one got away, and you don't know the location of that drug dealer nor his funds?"

"Sadly that is a true statement, Mr. Monty. We will, of course, continue to look, but any additional details you can provide might increase our ability to locate your sixth drug dealer."

"And you want me to believe that this Phillip Johnston is the sole perpetrator in moving the five drug dealers and their drug money to a bank that he happened to be working at, so he could pirate those said funds? No one else had a hand in it? Is that what you wish me to believe? Otto, really!"

"When we began this discussion, sir, you did say you wanted me to net this out for you, rather than the epic version. This would then be the net-net version of the story."

Mr. Monty was annoyed. He knew there was something missing in this verbal report. He doubted the report itself would have any other significant details. Trust was a big issue between

U.S. intelligence agents and their contractors. The R-Group had significant reach, but in this instance the story had some holes he just couldn't ignore without further discussion.

"Ok, Otto. Let me fill in some blanks to the story that occur to me to make it believable. Phillip Johnston didn't move those drug dealers and their wealth to his bank without external help. There must be at least one more person and perhaps two who are smart enough to transport, I'm thinking airlift, persons of interest and their ill-gotten gains from Mexico to the Cayman Islands undetected by our satellite surveillance cameras or our local operatives. I do buy that he could be responsible for trying to fleece them after they arrived. Is that pretty much it?"

"I would maintain, Monty, you are shortening the story unfairly, leaving too much open to speculation and conjecture."

"Well then I would say, almost well done, except I need the missing drug dealer with his funds and the missing element of the transport that moved the poor unsuspecting drug dealers into the clutches of the nefarious Phillip Johnston. These drug dealers are wealthy because they have a relatively closed community, and we both know they will not share any names with us. I cannot see how your Phillip Johnston could be associated with these dealers in order to complete their transport. I do want him as an accessory to this money laundering and drug lord export business so he doesn't escape jail time. Do we understand one another?"

Otto mused, then continued, "Mr. Monty, you would understand that in my circle of influence there are people of interest with unique skillsets that should be cultivated and not squandered. I must admit that in this sordid tale of people and money laundering, we found just such a person with a unique skillset that we need to bring in-house, so to speak.

"I will further admit that during negotiations for incorporating that skillset there was one drug dealer, a personal relation, and his wealth that needed to be granted an exit provided he never returned to his previous lifestyle. We did, in fact, receive such guarantees, and so I must maintain that those assets are now out of bounds for further pursuit. I trust you will see the wisdom of this course of events."

Mr. Monty was now thoroughly annoyed. "Otto, you can't just dictate to me what the terms of conditions are in a vacuum. I have an ethical and moral obligation to pursue all offenders to the full extent of the law. I can't let you take someone into your sphere of influence just because you need his skillset or what he knows. Where would the world be if governments permitted the gathering of criminals or semi-criminals into their operations just because it suits their current business needs? No, I need the rest of the puzzle!"

Otto sighed, "First of all, in this scenario prosecuting to the full extent of the law is for Mexico first and the U.S. second." Otto paused, letting that reality sink in before continuing, "I would also have you consider; if you were in charge at the end of World War II and you desperately needed accurate intelligence gathering behind the Soviet Iron Curtain, would you have said no to Waffen SS Standartenführer being hired to do your work? Would you have declined the negotiated request to hide their offspring in the U.S.?"

Otto looked up and smiled at Quip, who had been ordered to remain quiet during the conference call. Quip grinned back.

Mr. Monty couldn't speak for a moment, but finally rejoined, "Otto, I see the wisdom you and your team offer. So, I will admit that in the grander scheme of things, what is one or two missing individuals when the bulk of the offenders have been rounded up for prosecution. I concur, Phillip Johnston was the main perpetrator and he will be prosecuted in this matter. I trust that you and your organization will provide the details to substantiate that in the final report to me?"

"Mr. Monty, as always a pleasure doing business with you based on your grasp of irrefutable logic. Have a good evening, sir."

CHAPTER 27

The closer to the event horizon the stronger the gravity pull

The staging area was pandemonium, and JAC was having trouble getting past security. Ordinarily she would just scan her expertly engineered identification and the system would allow her through with no fuss. Sometimes the near field communications (NFC) chip in the ID card took two swipes before she could gain an entrance to some locations. None of this worked, however, if the system was down due to someone else's computer virus, as was the case here. Everything here had dropped back to a handwritten list, being manually checked by five people who had to already know you or the company you represented before they permitted entry. Even her megawatt smile fell flat when dealing with the gate goons.

She muttered under her breath, "A high-tech digital assassin sideswiped by a lousy analog process. Time to break out plan B. I just wish I had a plan B at this point."

JAC felt a slight tap on her shoulder followed by a friendly voice she recognized. "Plan B speaking. How can a local photographer help you, Miss Travelers Checks? Manuel Sanchez, photographer par excellence, at your service, madam."

JAC smiled knowingly, then lamented, "Can you believe these people? Here I am trying to get on site to further my product line, Jacque's Alive, by finding the right model, and the gate goons won't let me in because their systems are down. Argh!"

Manuel gave a quizzical look, then suggested, "Hmm… perhaps a change in tactics is in order. Follow me, stay close, and look bored. As a matter of fact, when we get to the gate goons offer up a bit of a protest that suggests that this is a mistake to come to such a low-rent show and that we would have better luck across town at the other show. Nothing like wounding their pride a little to help get better treatment, Señorita Jacque."

At the gate, before Manuel could put down his credentials, JAC launched into a spoiled designer routine and spoke loud enough for the show promoters to overhear.

"I thought we were going to the high-end session in Cabo San Lucas! What are we doing wasting our time in this backwater show? They aren't even automated here. By the time we finally get in, the girls will be sunburned and totally unsuitable for print work!"

A couple of the show promoters rushed over to help contain the bad press at the gate and immediately give them VIP passes. The ruse worked, mostly because they recognized Manuel and also because JAC came across as a believable designer with that attitude.

Once inside Manuel smiled and winked at JAC, then led her toward some well-dressed folks. He provided some introductions so she could navigate a little more independently among the models and other designers. He watched to see if she needed assistance but mostly renewed his own relationships. As he watched, she deftly worked the crowd with her story but was unable to get any other leads on her quest for her model.

Manuel tried to mingle, which provided her some distance to operate, but he really couldn't focus on much else but Jacque, as he thought of her now. Manuel even caught himself smiling at her movements and the determination she showed for her fashion line. The pieces she'd shown him had some great lines, color, and fabrics, but he wanted to see them on a model. Any model in his mind would do, but she was focused on a specific model. He scouted to see if he could recall any of the other models' faces when he'd taken the pictures that Señorita Jacque seemed to favor.

After a couple of hours, JAC was fairly confident that this show was another dead end, though she had collected information and had asked Manuel to grab some candid shots of a few girls that might fit the need, along with contact information. She'd exhausted her options and was about to head back to the hotel when she was approached by an individual that instantly placed her on her guard. Manuel noticed from his distant location that her manner had shifted to one of full alert. She visibly bristled as the man got close enough to introduce himself. He couldn't identify the man, though he looked somewhat familiar.

"Pretty lady, allow me to introduce myself. I am Spencer and you seem to have caused something of a stir. Apparently you are much like me in that you are looking for someone special for your product line. You may not be having much success with your quest, but I on the other hand have just seen the star of my next picture; you, my fair, porcelain-skinned beauty."

It took all of JAC's martial arts skills of concentration and mastery of emotions to contain her immediate dislike and revulsion for this man.

Her concentration focused, she smiled at Spencer and haughtily offered, "I'm not selling today, Mr. Spencer, but I am buying. I'm looking for a certain model to be my summer fashion line spokesperson. Perhaps you might be useful, however, to look at photos of the model I am seeking, to see if you know her?"

Manuel finally recognized the man. He was very familiar with the greasy Spencer and his product line, so he drifted over to lend a hand if this enigmatic lady needed assistance. While he started in that direction, he suppressed laughter at himself for his chivalrous desire for a woman whose full name he didn't even know.

JAC forcibly slowed her breathing to help choke back her anger and repulsion at this slime ball of a man, then extended the picture of Lara she had taken from Manuel. Spencer studied it for a few minutes and broke into a sickening smile before he laughed out loud. Even though JAC was an arm's length away, she saw his green teeth extended from his scraggily beard as he laughed like a mule. His horrible buffalo breath only added to his creepiness. She was totally torn between leaving him or decking him when he regained his composure.

Spencer asked with a lascivious grin, "This is who you are looking for? I know her. She has done some cameo work for me."

By this time Manuel had moved up close enough and provided JAC a calming effect for the encounter.

With the arrival of Manuel, Spencer repeated, "Yes, I know her. In fact, she is under contract to me. I can see why you would want her as your spokesperson, but I don't know if she is interested in your fashion line. I can try to arrange a meeting and perhaps an understanding can be reached."

JAC, grateful that Manuel provided her an emotional cushion in this situation with this hideous man, related, "Manuel, Mr. Spencer seems to be well acquainted with er…what did you say her name was?"

Spencer, fully into his sleazy, oily character, responded, "Her name is unimportant until she wants to consider your offer. She is under contract to me and my studio. But I fear that if I make introductions, it might lead to me losing my star protégé and my plans for her."

JAC was now in control of her contempt of this disgusting man and suggested, "So we are at an impasse, unless I happen to locate her?"

Spencer's smile was meant to be disarming but only highlighted his sinister intent. He continued, "Well, I can be a reasonable man if properly persuaded. Of course my star protégé would be flattered and maybe even interested in hearing your proposition. And while you are there at my studios, should I get a meeting arranged, you might even reconsider my proposition."

Manuel looked over the top of his sunglasses with a classic nonverbal You're not really gonna buy this shit, are you? expression that made JAC give him a mischievous smile, alerting him that everything would be ok.

Without taking her eyes off of Manuel, JAC agreed, "Yes, I would like the chance to discuss our futures together at our earliest possible time. As to your other agenda item, stranger things have happened, so we can discuss it. However, our meeting needs to be at a common ground location, and I doubt your studio is appropriate. Where and when can we meet you and your star protégé?"

Spencer was a little taken aback and asked, "We? I was suggesting only the three of us will join the discussion."

JAC, fully in charge of her emotions, smiled, "I want Manuel along because it was he who first got me interested in this model. He already has the requirements that I want fulfilled in the shoot of my line. He is also the one who can confirm she is the one I'm after. So yes, of course, we will both be in the meeting."

Spencer gave a sour look, then said, "Ok, we will all meet, but only after I gain her commitment to the meeting. Ordinarily

I would call Manuel here and leave instructions, but since he never pays his phone bill maybe you can give me a number that I can call you on."

JAC provided him her business card and five hundred U.S. dollars as a show of good faith, which Spencer greedily accepted. JAC turned to collect Manuel's arm so as to avoid any physical contact with Spencer and wished him a good day as they departed. Greed was her ally when dealing with this jerk.

After her encounter with Spencer, she had a brilliant idea for a new product line; body condoms. Body condoms that a person should put on before having an encounter with one such as Spencer, so as to avoid any possible skin contact.

CHAPTER 28

Support has many forms yet is always welcome

Carlos answered the phone, "Hi, babe. It is good to hear from you. Do you miss me, sweetheart?"

Simone responded with a tone of urgency, "Hi, honey. Do you have time to talk?"

Carlos questioned, "Uh oh, what's wrong? Are you ok?"

Simone gently laughed, "Nothing wrong but I need to talk with you. It is not a casual conversation either so I wanted to make sure we had time for a discussion."

Carlos said, "I sense apprehension in your voice and at least some gravity in what you are about to tell me. Does this mean that you found someone else and don't want me anymore? Hence the 'dear Carlos' call and my pending dismissal?"

Simone bristled with indignation, then curtly answered, "How can you say such a thing? And how little you must regard my feelings for you that would suggest that all you would get is a long distance call for such a discussion. You are an important part of my life, and you don't get to leave, understand? Now are we clear that this type of conversation is not nor will be on the topics of discussion?"

Carlos mentally backed up a bit and contritely responded, "Rewind, rewind. Let me try this greeting again!

"Hello, sweetheart. How is the love of my life? What can I do to make our travels together more meaningful in this best of all possible worlds?"

Simone was somewhat taken aback, but quite pleased by the greeting. It amazed her the ways that Carlos could change so quickly from one character perspective to another.

"Hi, honey, I miss you terribly. Are you still coming home tomorrow? Or hopefully today?"

"Tomorrow, my love. Do you have something pressing that we need to talk about now? I have nothing but time for you, sweetheart. Please let me know what you need."

"Carlos, you have been so good to me and never even questioned me about my past or about my ambitions, but now I am compelled to tell you some of that past."

"Sweetheart, you have no need to tell me of anything before we met as that won't change how I feel about you. I am happy to listen to whatever you wish to share."

"Thank you, honey. I think this is important. I left home after a terrible fight with my family over my ambitions, and I wanted to prove, if only to myself, that I could achieve my dreams. I've always wanted to be a model and had visions of advancing a modeling career into movie roles and maybe even stardom. When you and I met, I was at a low point in realizing that dream. You immediately captivated my heart, so when you said 'let's go', I couldn't resist. I have no regrets about our life together and, no, I do not want to lose you, but I have been approached by an old acquaintance who insists that a loungewear designer wants to build an entire product launch with me as their spokesperson. This is the dream of a lifetime for me. I do so want to meet with these people to see if this is my destiny.

"Now that I have told you this, honey, I want to know how you feel about my dream. I mean, I know this is not quite fair, springing this on you over the phone when I would much rather look into your eyes and hold your hand. They want to meet later today to discuss a contract. I don't want this to ruin our relationship and that's why I wanted to tell you of my feelings on this, in case it is for real, before I meet with them."

Carlos was somewhat puzzled. "I didn't know this about you, babe. I have seen that dreamy look in your eyes when you see shows on modeling and behind-the-scenes movie making on television, before I do a channel flip. I did not know of your passion for this line of work. You are undoubtedly a beautiful woman. They would be very lucky to have you represent their fashions. So, let's make this simple – Simone, honey, I want you to pursue this opportunity with all the gusto of a hound dog and see where it leads. I will support you in every way that you need, and we will see if it is, in fact, your destiny. You must promise me that you will allow me to stay in your life no matter how famous you get."

Simone beamed with Carlos's support. Those few words from him helped her confidence tenfold.

"Yes, honey, I promise! I do so promise!"

Carlos reflected for a moment, then asked, "Uh babe, when you say modeling, just exactly how much modeling do you have to do and how little do you model in? No, wait! Rewind, rewind the statement! What I meant to say was, honey, I trust you to use good judgment in your profession and that you will insist on a tasteful display of your gorgeous body and not simply a voyeuristic spread. Am I being unreasonable in this request?"

Simone wiped tears from her eyes as she responded, "Thank you, Carlos, for supporting me and asking for some parameters on the modeling I want to do. Yes, I will maintain high modeling standards as a condition of the contract.

"Carlos, one last thing I need for this meeting today. I would like an escort to go with me. Even though I would prefer you I don't want you there to see my disappointment if this is another dead end. So could you ask Juan to be my escort? I know you trust him and, well, I trust him too."

"I will make it so. After we hang up I will speak with him and I'm sure there will be no problem in this request. Love you, babe. I know your meeting will go well. I will see you soon."

Carlos practically yelled into the phone, "No? What do you mean, no? Juan, I ask a simple favor to escort Simone to a meeting and you won't? What's up with that?"

Juan responded, "Look, I just flew back from the Caymans and I'm tired. It is still morning here. As a matter of fact, you woke me up. So, goodbye, Carlos. We can talk again in eight hours, bro."

"Alright, give me JC or Robert's number. I'll ask them to escort Simone to the modeling photo shoot."

Juan, now fully awake, asked, "Modeling photo shoot? As in modeling, babes wearing-almost-nothing-but-a-smile modeling photo shoot? Is that where Simone needs to be escorted?"

Carlos suppressed a grin as he responded, "Yes. Simone has what could be a modeling contract offer, and she would prefer to meet with these people with a male escort. I naturally thought of you. But since you're too tired to escort her to the contract meeting at the modeling photo shoot then I'm sure I can get JC or Robert to accompany her. Get some rest. You must be tired after all that flight time."

Juan sounded indignant about losing out to JC or Robert as Simone's escort. He could sleep anytime. He figured that his only way back in was to raise concern with Carlos.

"JC escort Simone to a modeling event? Are you hearing yourself? I can see the headlines now! That's like inviting Godzilla to downtown Tokyo under the pretext of a light brunch!

"And Robert as an escort for your Simone? The man has the personality that closely approximates a roll of toilet paper!

"It's obviously best if I escort Simone to her meeting just so she isn't embarrassed by having either of them in tow. So what time is the meeting? I mean, I can be ready for Simone in fifteen minutes if need be. I'll even brush all my teeth to make a good impression."

Carlos suppressed laughter as he presented, "Hey, you're not going to take advantage of being in this target rich environment, are you? Simone is looking for a polished gentleman as an escort at this contract meeting, not some horn dog. Can you conduct yourself properly, little brother?"

"Me? Please, bro. Why, I'm as suave and debonair as any high-end airline pilot or international playboy. I'm thinking that I might even bring extra charm to help close Simone's deal. By the way I can be ready in nine minutes."

"I'll have her call you with the meeting time and place. Thanks, little brother."

CHAPTER 29

Searching for good with evil results

JAC said to Quip, "I am sending you a photo I would like you to upload and verify. I think it is Lara. I found the photographer, Manuel. He was the one you said might give us a good lead based on what you found prowling with ICABOD. He did, in fact, have a full hardcopy that was better quality than the partial you sent me. Can you let ICABOD-Face, as I have now coined your facial recognition software enhancement, take a whack at comparison back to our baseline shot of Lara? How soon can ICABOD-Face let me know?"

Quip laughed, "Cute, JAC. I am uploading it now, and it shouldn't take too long to give us a probability rating. Anything else going on, or any new leads?"

"Well, if ICABOD-Face can give us a high nineties rating then there is more work to do to verify the identity, but I think I am close. Call it gut instinct.

"While at one photo shoot here in Acapulco, I met this sleaze-ball that not only claimed to know the girl in the picture but also indicated that she was under contract to him. Mr. Sleazeball calls himself Spencer Perez on his business card, but he wouldn't validate her name until he'd spoken with her. He offered to broker a deal, but I don't want to have to meet with him again if this only a definite-maybe match. This guy grossed me out. Like, his teeth were green, yuck."

"Well kid, ICABOD – I'm used to the shortened version – says it's a ninety-six percent probability that the picture is Lara, so it looks like you'll be making that meeting after all. Talk about good news, bad news. Anything I can do to help make this go a little smoother?"

"Yes, please. I wanted you to run down this sleaze from his cell phone and name. Give me all you can on this creep. I need leverage in my backpack before I go into that meeting because I don't think it will be a pleasant one. His name may be an alias, but Manuel said he has known him by that name for some time. He didn't like the guy either. I also sent the photo that Manuel took of him so let me know what you can find on Mr. Sleazeball."

A short time later Quip responded, "Uh, kid, I'm sending you what I found on Spencer in the fast review. I highly doubt your opinion of him is going to improve after you see it. You got someone to watch your back when you go to the meeting? Because I'm gonna tell you, don't go by yourself. Don't get all riled up at that statement because I know how good you are at defensive moves."

"Why? What did you find on him? Ok, it's coming in now… Oh my god! This isn't a human being! He is a monster out of Greek tragedy! Even if this isn't Lara, we need to get this girl away from this guy. We must figure out what to do about him, so he doesn't get his hands on any more adolescents," JAC committed.

"I am so with you on this one. There is additional data but it all seems to match what I have sent you, just more victims. Hopefully we can come up with something for this animal. Let's take care of business first and locate our missing Lara. Alright? I need to go and work with Otto, but I want you to exercise caution with this sleaze. Call if you need help. I know you are good at your craft but no unnecessary risks. Got it?"

JAC smiled at Quip's concern and respectfully responded, "Yes sir, Mr. Project Manager."

CHAPTER 30

Dear God, I have a problem. It's me.

Petra had spent most of the day outside under the umbrella on the patio of the resort suite. Petra had enjoyed breakfast with Simone that morning, and they'd chatted and lingered over coffee. It was obvious that Simone was distracted. It hadn't surprised Petra when a pool meeting later in the day was declined. Simone had said she had some things to take care of and perhaps some good news to share over dinner. She said something about not wanting to jinx anything by sharing in advance. Simone had smiled and laughed when she'd left saying they should chat around six to firm up dinner plans.

The patio was lovely with its private Jacuzzi, and Petra wished Jacob was there to enjoy it with her. This vacation of theirs had been different from what she'd expected; however, it seemed to be the way of her life.

After Jacob landed the assignment with Carlos and his subsequent trip to investigate in the Caymans, things had been disjointed. He'd be back tomorrow, and their brief conversations indicated his thoughts were aligned with her thoughts on how they would spend the remainder of their vacation. She smiled as she recalled the discussion with Rita and Simone the other night at The Dive, before things had gotten so crazy. Petra wanted to relate the conversation to Jacob and get his reaction.

Without any poolside time with Simone, Petra had completed remote updates to her encryption programs for several of her regular customers. She had also prowled around on their systems that she could easily access, to see if they were plagued by any irregular programs. Most of her customers were also maintained by her and her team, so she realized she would likely find nothing.

She had also worked on the ongoing development of a new routine that combined encryption algorithms along with some code-capture routines designed to be invoked only under special programmed situations. She wanted this completed before Jacob returned so she could get his opinion. She'd worked through the program even after the late luncheon room service had been delivered. It was close to finished when she realized she needed to update Quip on a few items and decided a call would be most efficient. Using her secure connection program from her cell, she was delighted that he answered almost immediately.

"Hi, Quip, how is it going? Are you free for a few updates and status reports for our customers?"

"Petra, of course, for you. You're bored with Jacob gone, aren't you?"

She laughed, "Well, there is that. I can't fool you anymore can I, my friend?"

"Nope, you really never could, Petra. So what have you been up to outside of updating the customer programs we had discussed? I presume you finished them, right?"

"I did complete them. I even checked to see if there was any new activity that our scanning might have missed. I am working on that consolidated program I had outlined to you before we left. I wanted Jacob to take a look at them when he returns.

"He should be back tomorrow. In a conversation we had a short time ago, he indicated that the discussion went well with Carlos and the deal was conveyed to Juan as well. I presume your meeting with Mr. Monty had the proper outcome, or Father would have called me to complain. Otto tends to not call unless he wants a different perspective or for a new assignment. I think he really wants me to have this vacation."

Quip grinned, knowing exactly how much Otto and Haddy wanted Petra to commit to Jacob. It was so obvious from his perspective that Petra and Jacob were well matched. Added to that was Quip's respect for Jacob with his considerable technical abilities that had expanded substantially while they'd worked together in Zürich.

"Oh, he wants your vacation with Jacob to be perfect. I think, Petra, he hated giving you an additional assignment while you were there, but location, location, location always wins.

"Speaking of which, JAC sent a photo of a girl she found in Acapulco, oddly enough, that is an almost perfect match to our missing Lara. Last I heard she was setting up to actually meet with the girl face-to-face sometime today and get her name. JAC was hoping it would help her formulate the next steps to a father-daughter reconciliation. I expect contact from her some-time later today.

"JAC is having so much fun in this role of fashion designer. She really seems to have some talent, from this guy's point of view."

Petra laughed, "Really, our little cyber assassin Julie has other facets to her outstanding skill levels?"

"She really does," Quip suggested with all sincerity. "Haddy and I worked together to bring some of her clever designs into real garments to help her promote her role at the various shoots she has been scouting out to locate Lara. The designs are simple but original, so I am trying to determine how we copyright them.

"Heck, even Haddy is adding her flair of fabrics and colors to really help the designs come alive. I had no idea that Haddy had any talent in that area at all, but she does."

"Haddy and design talent are almost always said in the same sentence, Quip. You've seen all her work in our home, the R-Group offices, and how she always looks so put together. Heck, the only reason my travel wardrobe always looks so nice is due to Haddy. I am surprised you hadn't realized that before.

"I am glad that JAC is enjoying herself. After the long run as a coffee barista, I felt she'd like a change, but fashion design wasn't something I would have considered."

They both laughed as they continued the discussion on what would happen if Julie decided that fashion was more fun than the cyber assassin work at which she excelled. They lamented on how things always seemed to deviate from the plan. They agreed, however, that their overall ability to respond to such changes made their services that much more valuable.

Petra wanted to explain the events of the evening she and Simone had spent at The Dive, but she really wanted to share with Jacob first, so she held back that information. Quip and she had a long history, being so closely related, but sometimes everything wasn't shared.

"So, Quip, how has the adaptation of ICABOD and the facial recognition program worked? Are you pleased with the results?"

"Petra, to be honest it has done better than I hoped. JAC coined a modified name of ICABOD-face, which I rejected as undignified. I do believe these program changes and trolling attributes have some applications to some of the identity theft stuff as well, if needed. I have done some tweaking with it, and it keeps showing wonderful possibilities. I have been assembling different test cases that I hope to use for some of the requests we seem to be getting from the intelligence communities. I will show you when you come back to the lab and get your thoughts. I think Jacob could also help refine the trolling routines, and I need some expanded encryption added by you as well."

"You're right, Quip. We all need to get caught up on some of the new inroads you've made and the enhancement modifications. I think we'll back in a week or so. I also believe that, based on what Jacob and you have said, we need to further explore the satellite communication expertise and how we can leverage it. Have you discussed any of this further with your buddy, Andy?" Petra teased.

"I am not notifying Andrew yet, no." Quip whined, "Otto has asked me the same thing. As Carlos is still in the Caymans, I think we are just fine to put that off for a while. Although I think…"

"Quip, are you still there? I can't hear you. Quip," tested Petra.

"I'm here. Just a second, Petra. I'm getting texts from Jacob. Hold on," Quip said with a tone that immediately meant business.

Petra waited quietly and ran through scenarios in her mind *as to why Jacob had contacted Quip and not her. Was everything* ok? Had something happened to him? She heard the clicking of the keys over the phone connection as Quip obviously responded to Jacob or searched for information. She paced the length of the suite while she waited for him to return to the call. The seconds stretched into very long minutes as she waited. Patience was her strong suit in most things, but not when Jacob was involved, she ruefully thought.

"Petra, I'm back. Sorry to keep you waiting so long. Jacob was texting me some details and needed to see if we had any local medical resources in Acapulco," Quip explained.

"Why? What is the matter? He isn't here, as least I don't think so," Petra interrupted.

"Hold on, lightning brain. Let me explain the details that I know. Jacob is still in the Cayman Islands, though they will be flying back as soon as they can get to their aircraft. It is still several hours until they will arrive.

"It seems there has been some sort of fight. I don't have all the details, but Carlos's brother Juan has been shot, possibly seriously. Juan is with Simone in her suite at present with someone named JC on the way to help treat him. He refuses to go to the hospital so Jacob was asking me if we had any medical staff in our pocket down there, which we do not.

"Carlos sent his guy JC over to help Simone. That is a challenge in many things, but certainly with his brother being shot," related Quip in a concerned tone.

"Oh my, poor Simone. I should go to help. We can talk later," announced Petra with concern evident in her voice.

"Slow down, more information, my dear lightning brain," Quip insisted. "Juan was shot by a guy named Spencer, who may be the same guy that JAC had me research. This guy is a piece of work who is so far into pornography that it made ME sick.

"Simone took Juan back to her suite and has been giving her best medical treatment but complained about the amount of blood she feared Juan was losing. That is why Carlos sent JC to help, as he is less than a couple of kilometers from the resort. Carlos didn't want you specifically to see JC, so he insisted that you not go to help Simone for around thirty minutes. I don't know why. Carlos and Juan have their secrets like we all do."

"Alright, I don't understand, but alright. A guy named Spencer interrupted Simone and me at dinner the other night, but I handled it. Wonder if it is the same one? Hmmm.

"I can call Simone from the phone in the suite and touch base about the rough dinner plans we had. Let her dictate the timing. Am I supposed to know that Juan was shot or what?"

"I think you're going to have to play that by ear. I am going to try to reach JAC when we hang up, as she was meeting with Spencer and the girl, she was convinced was Lara. I'll let you know if she provides any additional details. Perhaps you can tell your dinner story a bit later. Ok, lightning brain, you can go now. Keep in touch though in case things get hairy and you need something."

"Thank you, Quip, I will. I will also leave Jacob alone even though you didn't tell me that. I am sure he has enough on his plate supporting Carlos."

CHAPTER 31

Refuse to enter a battle of wits with an unarmed man

"Juan, thank you for escorting me to this meeting." Simone frowned as she reluctantly added, "This meeting is with someone from my past. Though I would prefer to forget that past, he has declared this is a legitimate business meeting with a modeling contract at stake. Last time I saw him he was carrying a gun, but he promised not to bring it to this meeting. I might be considered for this fashion line's spokesperson from what he said. I don't trust this scum, but I just couldn't pass up the opportunity without seeing for myself."

Juan agreeably offered, "I can play whatever role you want. I can be your escort, or driver, or a cousin, you decide. Carlos asked me to support you in this exercise and that implies, I will defend if necessary.

"Also, uh…he said we were going to a modeling show. If everything goes as it should then I get to cruise for babes, ok? I will, of course, get a taxi for your transport so no worries on that score."

Simone giggled, "Ok, but don't portray me as your ex-girlfriend or ex-lover again to get sympathy from a lady who fills your eyes. That is so deceitful when you do that, Juan."

Juan lowered his eyes, trying to show some semblance of shame, as he admitted, "Oh! So you know about my routine number nine for picking up hot babes. I didn't realize that I was that transparent."

Simone steeled herself as they approached the designated building. It appeared deserted and there were no vehicles or people in sight. There were windows facing the street, but they couldn't clearly see inside from where they stood. Spencer had said it was a space that he used for filming now and again. Juan parked the rental car, and they got out.

"Ok, let's do this, Juan," Simone volunteered with more confidence than she felt as she took his arm.

The door was locked, so they knocked. Moments later Spencer greeted them with some disdain at Juan being in tow. He focused on Simone first.

Using his regular insincere smile, he said, "Simone, how lovely you look. And your escort, may I know your name, sir?"

Juan almost smiled and then offered, "I am Juan Sanchez, the most marvelous man in the universe. Would you like my business card by way of introduction?"

Simone immediately felt the hostility rising between the two men. She was concerned that perhaps bringing Juan was a poor idea. She was determined to put them both at ease.

"Juan, the next thing you know Spencer will be offering you a contract for consideration," she suggested to lighten the intensity.

"Do we have to have this Juan in these discussions? Simone, you and I need to discuss my fee in brokering this deal before the people show up to talk. I want to have my fee in hand before the contract negotiations begin."

Simone, still hanging on to Juan's arm, felt Juan tense. He knew this part of the discussion might come up and what she had said before agreeing to the meeting.

"Spencer, I told you I'm not providing a fee until I hear the sales pitch, the offer, and have all the particulars on the table. Juan is my escort and confidant in this matter. So yes, he stays close for the discussion as my reliable witness for negotiations."

Spencer clucked his tongue in annoyance. "Very well then, let's go inside and await the designer."

They didn't wait long as the taxi pulled up. Spencer hurriedly moved Simone and Juan inside to a table with chairs behind a half wall, where they sat down. Spencer headed back to the door to try advanced negotiations with the new arrivals only to find the fashion designer really had brought the photographer, Manuel. Spencer had trouble covering up his disdain for yet another uninvited male also acting as an escort.

Spencer groused, "Well, I see you brought your photographer. Come on in. I sure hope there's room inside for me, since I leased this space for our private meeting and I am the one to bring everyone together."

JAC smiled and inquired, "So what should I find once we are inside? What is this lady expecting and what are your expectations?"

Spencer smiled, warming to the idea that he would get something out of the deal yet.

"Ah! How nice to have a lady with good manners for business." Spencer cautioned, "But I must warn you, she has brought a business manager of sorts which suggests an aggressive negotiating posture. I had hoped to broker a simple and quick deal, but that may not be the case.

"I suggest that you just pay me a finder's fee, and I will let your two teams hash out the terms and conditions. You are, of course, welcome to hold your discussions in my humble facilities, kind lady. Are we in agreement?"

JAC had been hustled by smoother people than this before and smiled at the hopelessly amateurish pitch. Plus, with the information she'd received from Quip, this worm was getting nothing positive from this deal if she got her way. In dealing with this worm, greed was her friend.

Flashing her smile, she soothed, "Spencer, you have so little faith in the outcome of this meeting! What if the terms yield a brokerage commission far in excess of the measly fifty U.S. dollars I was going to give to you, in addition to what you received last time we met? I wouldn't want to see you forfeit a large commission, so let us go in and discuss. I am quite sure you are going to be surprised at the outcome."

Manuel's amused smile was completely offset by the sour look on Spencer's face as they entered the building. That sum was far less than what Spencer felt this deal was worth, especially since he'd seen this lady's bankroll. Spencer's greed made him try to salvage what he thought it would be worth. They approached the table, expecting to make personal introductions.

Before JAC or Manuel could begin their personal introductions, Spencer blurted out, "Simone is my client and as her manager and contract holder I am here to help set expectations."

Juan, incensed at the rudeness of Spencer, simply ignored him, "We are pleased to have this meeting. Simone, will you please begin introductions while the rest of us listen?"

Simone rose to greet them with a warm smile and began, "Hi, my name is Simone and this is my escort, Juan. May we know your names, please?"

Spencer was furious, but held his tongue as JAC interjected, "How very kind of you to begin with the pleasantries, Simone. My name is Julie, and this is my escort and right-hand man Manuel, who you may have met during a photo shoot. I trust neither of us needs to introduce Spencer as we all already know what, I mean who, he is."

The only one not smiling at the inside joke was Spencer.

They adjusted their seats and again Spencer tried to lead the discussion, but Juan waved him off with a look.

Simone smiled, "Julie, I understand that you have been on something of a quest in search of a model and perhaps even a company spokesperson for your fashion line. Can you tell us why you are here looking for a particular lead model, and how my photo, that Manuel did quite some time ago, was helpful for your quest?"

"What if I show you what I'm thinking about with some of my designs, and let's see if we have some common ground?" suggested Julie.

With that, Julie removed some of the finished sample garments she'd designed, while Manuel retrieved some of the drawings he had made of the planned shots for the garments Julie didn't have completed. At the same time, Julie discreetly took a couple of pictures of Simone and quickly sent them off to Quip for analysis. Simone was so engaged in viewing the sample products, she completely missed the candid phone shots being taken. Juan relaxed as the garments appeared, sensing that Simone was pleased. Even Spencer was impressed by the layout and could almost feel the money in his pocket. Julie was pleased that Simone was so absorbed in the product line and seemingly excited.

Julie asked, "Would it be impertinent to ask that you try some of the items on and let Manuel take some test shots? I presume that Spencer has an area which will afford you some privacy. I have seen only a little of your modeling efforts, and I would like to see if what I have in my minds-eye matches reality with you."

Simone beamed and agreed, "I accept the challenge. Please excuse me while I change. I'll be right back." She snatched up three of the items then inquired, "Spencer, where might I change, please?"

"It's right through that door behind you." Spencer pointed toward the side of the great room.

Spencer was growing more agitated by the delays and wanted to move to the money part of the discussion.

After Simone left, Spencer ventured, "See, I told you she is perfect for the role! We need to talk about my finder's fees and move to the next stage of the discussion so we can all be on our way."

Juan stated dryly, "Why don't we let the primary people talk and arrive at an agreement and you remain quiet until we need to know where the toilet is."

Spencer intently eyed Juan, then snarled, "You aren't much different than the escort Simone was with the last time I worked with her. In fact, your kind is probably the only kind she ever hooks up with. You even look like the last loser that I bounced around in that bar the night she ditched me and the work she'd committed to. I haven't forgotten the money that evening cost me, and this time I want my payment up front."

Juan smirked, then rose, "Coming right up."

Juan was an accomplished taekwondo brown belt, though not actively training any longer, and was extremely good at delivering flying spin kicks at three meters high. The lack of practice, the years, and too much extra weight had brought his kick to half that height, but it was still enough to send Spencer reeling across the room. Spencer grabbed his chest in order to try and breathe again.

"Yes, you picked up on the resemblance, since he is my brother. I always liked hearing how, after your frank discussion with Carlos, you insisted on paying for their dinner. Which arm did he crush when you met? I want to make sure that I take care of the other one this time," challenged Juan.

Julie was interrupted from the scene unfolding by a vibration from her phone. It was an inbound text from Quip, which she quickly glanced at, then smiled.

Julie quickly stood and moved toward where Simone had gone and away from Spencer. Manuel moved to the opposite side from Juan.

Spencer, finally able to restore his breathing, roared, "You're not going to get the chance to work my other arm because ever since that night I carry a revolver. I had always intended to get even with him, but now that I have his smartass brother, I can get revenge twice."

His .38 was out and aimed toward Juan and the direction of the table. Juan started moving toward Spencer and away from the others. Spencer was not much of a marksman, especially in his crazed state of mind. Juan was faster than he appeared. Spencer got off three shots with two going wild but the last one hitting home on Juan, just as Juan landed a kick that sent Spencer to the floor where he passed out. Juan looked at the blood oozing through his clothes and slumped to the floor.

Manuel couldn't believe the speed of the spectacle and looked for Julie to make a hasty retreat. She lay on the floor too, grazed on the head from one of the stray bullets, which had apparently knocked her out. Simone rushed out into this scene dumbfounded wearing what she had hoped would be the beginning of a magnificent new career. Manuel took a few hasty, impromptu shots of Simone before he gathered up Julie and ran from the building.

It took Simone a few minutes to assimilate the scene, but the sight of Juan bleeding drove home the seriousness of the situation and she bent down to tend to him. She looked horrified as she looked up and glared at Spencer

By now Spencer had begun to recover his footing. His shock, and the realization of the results of shooting, had begun to sink in. All the players were down or scattered, and he had no money to show for it.

Spencer declared, "It's all his fault! He baited me and then when I couldn't take it anymore he kicked me across the floor. I had to defend myself! You can see that, can't you, perra? It's not my fault!"

Spencer was shaking so badly from the events that he ran from the building crying, "It's not my fault! It's not my fault!"

Simone comforted Juan and tried to put pressure on the wound. She had a basic understanding of emergency medical treatment, but the blood was pouring out of the wound.

"Juan, what did you do? My poor, sweet dear Juan! We have to get you to a hospital like, right now. Let me throw on my clothes, and I'll get the rental car.

Juan, in extreme pain, managed, "I'm sorry about the deal to represent the modeling line, but I'll make it up to you. I promise you I will, but in the meantime can you take me over to where the babes are modeling? I'm pretty sure that this bullet wound is going to get me sympathy from at least one of the girls."

Simone cried softly over Juan as she tried to lighten the fear growing inside her. She recalled one of Juan's famous pick-up lines.

"You know what your mother always told you about looking for sympathy?"

Juan couldn't help but smile, then replied, "Yes, I know. If you are looking for sympathy you can always find it in the English dictionary between shit and syphilis."

They both chuckled, then Juan coughed, "No, not the hospital, but I do want you to call Carlos on that special emergency number that will get to him anywhere. He may be airborne, but it will still get to him. Tell him what has happened and that you are alright.

"Tell him that JC is closer than he is and ask to have JC come get me and take me to the staging area. He'll know what that means.

"We need to leave here and get you out in case the slime bag comes back and wants me for more target practice. Simone, call him quickly and get dressed. Take that pretty outfit with you, it looks good."

Simone had not considered that they were still there in Spencer's place and that they were at risk. She hastily changed, then managed to help Juan to the car after bandaging his wounds and drove them back to the resort. She asked Miguel at the front desk to help her get Juan to her room. He promised his silence after a generous tip. Then she contacted Carlos. After she related the basic details and cried in his ear, he reassured her that JC would be there soon and that she should do as he asked. Carlos was so much stronger than she was, but she knew his concern for his brother would move mountains. She only hoped he wouldn't blame her and had told him how sorry she was. He reassured her that she was not at fault.

CHAPTER 32

The right place
at the wrong time

JC loaded up the rental car with some heavy-duty bandages and antiseptics, along with a few other items to help treat what Simone had described as a lot of blood. When Carlos had phoned and asked him to transport Juan back to his hotel in Acapulco and evaluate him for transport to their Chihuahuan Desert location, he had no idea of what had happened to Juan. But he was close and needed to respond. Simone was so panicked when he'd spoken to her, he retrieved supplies based on the worse possible scenario. Carlos had said no hospital, unless there was no other choice. Simone was to remain in her suite at the resort until her friend came. Hopefully JC would be gone by then.

Since Carlos and JC had spoken in the Cayman Islands about the possibility of JC and Robert taking on the operations of not only the drug trade, which they were pretty much running, but also a new endeavor for the hard assets, JC had thought of little else. He recognized that the hard assets part was based on the assets already housed safe and sound in their facility.

Carlos said he hadn't spoken to the On-Brothers, but they should have the secured areas finished and divided for storage of the hard assets from each of the drug lords who escaped Mexico and new slots that could be sold to others. The On-Brothers were to take pictures of the individual items in order to demonstrate the safety of the items and complete documentation of the process to have them shipped wherever needed. This would be the cornerstone for selling this service. The movement of money to a different source bank was something Carlos was looking into, but it would be a pass-through transaction, most likely.

Carlos and Juan had been caught and identified for their participation in the relocation of the drug lords, but JC and Robert had not. Carlos offered to leverage that small detail for their benefit. In mulling it over, JC decided it was a pretty sweet deal and Robert had agreed. JC and Juan had returned early that morning from the Caribbean and were to work out details of connecting with some Chinese guys named Won and Ton for coupling in an identity-change offering for other customers expected to get on board in the South American region over time. This permitted several options for services to include protecting hard assets, drug running, money laundering, and identity change. JC and Juan, however, had never hooked up with the men.

JC arrived at the resort and took all the supplies to Simone's suite. Thankfully, it was on the ground floor, so he parked reasonably close. When he knocked, a teary-eyed Simone opened the door.

"Oh, JC, I am so glad you are here. He's still bleeding a lot. I am running out of towels. I tried to keep pressure on it, like Carlos said, but it is so difficult. I am afraid I am hurting him," cried Simone.

"I am sure you did fine, Simone. Take me to him. We'll figure it out."

Simone took JC to Juan, and he did a quick assessment. Juan was weak but he did open his eyes and groaned when JC moved him to get a view of his other side. The bullet was a through-and-through so at least he didn't have to dig out the slug. He applied some antiseptic and then had Simone help pack it with gauze and tightly bound him.

"Hey, JC, guess we'll have to catch up on that cerveza another time, right?" Juan croaked. "I was looking forward to it, but something got in the way."

"Heck, Juan, I know you just wanted to get out of paying like you promised. So, how the hell does a smart guy like you let some bozo get the drop on him with a gun? I thought you were this big, bad hard-ass like your brother," growled JC.

"It was a completely lucky shot for that sleazeball. Tell him, Simone. You were there."

"Juan's right, JC. Spencer is a piece of work, and he totally surprised us all. He even ran crying from the building. Juan is a hero," offered Simone with fresh tears forming in her eyes.

JC acquiesced, "Ok, man, I'll buy it for now. Carlos may have doubts though. So you didn't even kill the bastard, huh? Don't answer, just shut up and listen. You need to conserve all your strength.

"Simone, we're done talking here. I need to get Juan out of here as instructed. I want you at the door to watch for other guests and give me the clear sign after I get close to the door. Then I want you to go to the blue Ford Taurus to the right out of your door and open the door to the back seat.

"Juan, I'm going to pick you up and carry you. When I do, it is going to hurt like hell. You need to try to keep quiet. I'm going to put you in the car, then come back for this stuff," outlined JC.

The transport of Juan to the car went smoothly even as he groaned repeatedly with each step. JC knew Juan's wound would get aggravated as he was jostled. There was no way Juan could walk on his own. He wondered how Simone and Juan had managed as he picked up Juan. JC got Juan settled into the car and returned to the suite. Simone threw herself into his arms and cried. He patted her back.

"Simone, stop now. You stay here until your friend arrives. I will take care of Juan, so don't worry. Carlos is on his way back and will come see you before he meets up with me," reassured JC. "You need to dry those eyes and get changed so he sees your pretty face, not one all splotchy with tear streaks."

Simone laughed a bit. "Ok, JC. Sorry to drip all over you. I will be fine. Go take care of him."

Simone locked the door after he left. She broke down and cried, then went to take a fast shower. She dressed and then panicked as she recalled Spencer was free and knew where she was located. She cried out as the phone rang.

CHAPTER 33

Some things are better left unsaid, some not

Petra took a deep breath before she picked up the suite phone and called Simone. It rang several times. She reminded herself to react to what Simone said, not what she knew so far of the situation. She empathized with Simone and her tender heart. Her concern was rising and then the phone was finally answered.

Petra cheerfully asked, "Hi, Simone. It's Petra. Are you ready to talk about a plan for dinner? I'm getting hungry."

"Oh! Thank goodness it's you, Petra," exclaimed Simone, breathing hard. "I hadn't realized it was so late. There has been so much happening," she sobbed.

"Simone, what's wrong? Why are you crying? Is someone there?"

"No one is here. I need to see you though. Can you come to my room, please?" Simone implored.

"Of course, I will be right there. You sound very afraid. Make certain you look through the door before you open it. I will be there soon."

Petra dashed out of her suite. She took the stairs rather than the elevator to the ground floor. Simone was obviously distraught, and with good reason. She arrived in minutes to the suite and knocked as well as called out that she'd arrived. Simone opened the door after disengaging the chain deadbolt and pulled Petra into the room.

"Oh, Petra, thank goodness you are here. We can't stay here though. I need you to let me stay in your room until Carlos returns. We can order room service if you want to. I will pay for it."

"Of course, we can go back to my suite. What is wrong though? Why can't we stay here?"

"It is a long story and I need to tell you. But do you recall that man we met at The Dive, Spencer?"

"Of course I remember. I hurt him. Why?"

"He knows my suite number at this resort. It was awful. He tried to kill Carlos's brother Juan. He still has his gun and he escaped. Please, please, let's just go to your suite?"

"Alright, grab a few things in a bag and we'll go. You can fill me in on the details."

Simone grabbed up a few items while her hands shook. Petra was concerned about her friend's stability. They quickly returned to Petra's suite. After some quick chatting on food and wine, they ordered room service. They settled into the plush couches near the windows that overlooked the outside personal pool area. Simone looked out, and tears started rolling down her face as she broke down.

Petra sympathized, "Simone, I know you are upset, but nothing you've said makes any sense so far. Why did Spencer shoot Juan? What were you doing near him? I thought he was off limits. How could he have found you? I am your friend and I will do my best to help you, but I need to understand the details."

Simone cried, "Oh Petra, I have made such a mess of things. I don't even know where to begin."

"From the beginning. I don't think I will understand unless you start at the beginning," offered Petra.

"I have made so many bad choices. I thought I was done with that. I thought I had a chance, but I was so very wrong," cried Simone as she started to weep again.

"Enough, Simone! Lamenting poor choices explains nothing and only upsets you further. Everything can be fixed from here forward, but you need to be honest here and work through the details."

"I agree. But I also know that once I am honest, you'll probably ask me to leave. But you are right, I owe it to you. I don't want to lose you as a friend," she sobbed.

Simone took a deep breath, gathered her thoughts, and resolved to tell her friend everything. She was tired of the lies and the fears.

"First of all, my real name is Lara Bernardes. My father is a powerful businessman in Brazil. My mother Simone is dead and has been for many years. I was well educated and groomed, as it were, to take over my father's corporation at some point in my life. But it wasn't my dream. I wanted to be a model and an actress." Lara paused and held up her hand to prevent Petra from speaking.

"No, please don't comment. I have to get this out in one shot while I feel brave. Please let me continue."

Petra went silent and schooled her features to not display her shock at the revelation.

"I ran away from home many months ago to pursue my career choice. I traveled to several locations known for supporting fashion shoots. I was turned down at nearly every one of these because I was not a stick figure. My face was ok for photos but only clothes of certain styles looked good enough on me for fashion magazines or ads. Runway modeling was certainly not going to happen either. Even with the protests around the world of models dying from their bulimia and drugs to keep their weight down, the modeling world is not ready for ladies with natural curves.

"I did a couple of lingerie shots, and even paid for a portfolio to be built that I could carry to go-sees for photographer's consideration. Most of the girls modeling today began when they were children. They've grown into their roles and contacts.

"Then at one shoot, Spencer found me. He empathized with my desires and offered me a chance to at least make some money to eat by doing some cameo shots for his nude magazine publications. I did some partial nude shots, which were good, but I didn't have the temperament for full nude shots.

"Spencer wanted me to do adult films. He had me come to a few of the sets and watch to help, I think, desensitize me to the activity. He filled me up with liquor even to do the still partial nude shots. It didn't help me overcome anything. Honestly, it was disgusting. It was where I met Rita though. Rita knew that I did not have it in me to do adult films, regardless of the money. My upbringing would simply not allow it.

"Rita really wanted me to get out before I couldn't, but I was too proud to go running home, defeated in my desire to be a famous model. I was at an all-time low when I met Carlos. He and I were magic from the moment he spoke to me."

Simone was interrupted as room service arrived. She took the opportunity to wash her face and take a deep breath. She returned to find that Petra had poured them both some wine. Petra raised her glass in a toast gesture.

"Simone, you are being very brave by telling me. Here's to your finishing the story and our working toward a solution." Petra smiled, "Cheers!"

Simone whispered, "Thank you."

Reinvigorated, she continued, "The night I met Carlos I was scheduled to meet with Spencer and do a small adult film clip. I was to be paid a nice fee, though he always reneged on payment for the still shots. When Spencer grabbed my arm, Carlos came to my rescue and beat up Spencer.

"Spencer, always the revenge seeker, left to plot and plan. Carlos and I became a couple. I've accompanied him on several trips as he worked on his financial business, or he left me at an apartment we share. This trip was a celebration of sorts for his business as well as our time together. When I met you it seemed like my life would normalize again, and I would be back in the here and now.

"Then I heard about the models coming to Acapulco and had to try again for my modeling. You and I went to The Dive and you know that part.

"Late last night, Spencer called me in my suite and told me that a fashion designer was looking for me and wanted to do a contract with me as the new face of her fashion line. He insisted it was for real and that if I agreed to meet and pay him a finder's fee, all would be forgiven. We spoke for a long time. He finally convinced me, and I asked for the meeting for this afternoon.

"I spoke to Carlos and he agreed to have Juan escort me to the meeting. Oh, Petra, I told him the reason, but not who I really am. Then Juan went with me to the meeting. We met with Julie, the fashion designer, and her photographer, Manuel, who had taken pictures of me for my portfolio that she had seen somewhere.

"I went to change into one of her outfits. Then I heard loud voices, and shots were fired. I ran out to see Juan on the ground bleeding. Julie was on the ground. Manuel was tending to her. Spencer ran from the building. Manuel picked up Julie and left by the side door. I changed, helped Juan to the car, and Miguel from the front area helped me get him into my suite."

Petra's face went white. Julie was hurt somewhere with someone named Manuel. Simone was right, this was a mess. Far worse than she had even realized. She had to alert Quip. She wanted Jacob.

"Oh, Simone, how awful for you. I am glad you weren't hurt. That poor woman. Poor Juan." Then Petra quietly spoke, "Why couldn't you trust me to say who you really were? I thought we were friends."

Simone dabbed at her eyes knowing that she'd lost sight of how to trust, how to make decisions based on looking at the long term gains or losses. She'd done it with her father, her first true girlfriend, and even perhaps Carlos. The magnitude of her choices slammed into her heart.

Petra was concerned about JAC, her misplaced trust in someone who hadn't been thoroughly checked out, and the depth that she missed Jacob. She liked it better, she thought, within her programs and her logical knowledge flow.

"Petra, you are right. I haven't been a good friend. I can only say I was scared. Scared of being a failure. Afraid of not reaching for dreams at all. All I can say is, I'm sorry and I will try to do better. I want you as my friend. I will do better," Simone finished and then started crying again.

"Well, aren't you and I the odd pair?" Petra offered. "I guess neither of us had that much trust. I'm here with Jacob, trying to find out what a relationship with someone you care about deeply is, as well as trying to be more of a person and less of a technical geek.

"Of course I forgive you. I too would like to have a dear friend I can trust. Nice to meet you, Lara," grinned Petra.

"Thank you, Petra. Can you help me sort this mess out? I am not certain which of the problems I created should be worked on first."

"First, we need to eat. We cannot do anything on empty stomachs. I need to make a quick call on a customer issue. Why don't you start eating, pour us some more wine and then we'll take one issue at a time and make a plan."

Simone agreed and smiled. Petra stepped outside onto the Jacuzzi area and closed the sliding glass door. She phoned Quip and told him she was with Lara. She then alerted him that JAC was hurt and was last seen with a photographer named Manuel.

Quip worked in tracking mode trying to locate JAC's cell signal. He said he'd get back to her and Jacob once he'd located JAC. He was glad that part of the issue was resolved with locating Lara, but focused now on finding JAC.

Petra returned to Lara, and they both ate well. They then stepped through each of Lara's concerns. First on the list was Carlos, who needed to be told her true identity and some background on her family business. Then, if Julie was located, they needed to continue the contract negotiations for the fashion line. They discussed reconciliation with her father, but that was a bit tougher and no resolution was decided other than she would phone him soon.

CHAPTER 34

Knowing is better than imagining the worst

Quip had received the call from Petra and immediately tried locating JAC using her cell phone signal. ICABOD displayed her location by street names in the Acapulco area. That was a plus from Quip's perspective as Petra was nearby. Based on her quick discussion, she'd indicated that she was taking care of Lara and trying to sort out the rest of the events. Quip messaged both Otto and Jacob with the information regarding JAC and that Lara was in Petra's care. Otto was still in the Zürich lab and entered soon after.

"Quip, have you located JAC's position? Have you reached her?" asked Otto with grave concern.

"I have called her cell, sent a text to it and sent a secured email as well. No response as of yet," responded Quip as he was watching the location on the screen. "I had a brief conversation with Petra where she related that JAC was injured during her meeting with the model via that Spencer character.

"I warned JAC to take care, as that guy's background illustrated a mentally incompetent human with intent to hurt others, especially children. JAC knew the results of the background check. I don't know what else I could have done. I feel responsible, like I should have done live monitoring during that meeting or something. Her cell is on and right now she is roughly ten miles from Petra and reasonably close to where Jacob should be landing soon."

"Ok, we have her location. Her phone could be on silent, due to the meeting. She wouldn't have wanted an interruption," Otto suggested hopefully.

"I can go with that, but she was injured and carried out, Otto. I know the name and the address of the photographer, Manuel, but JAC had already told me the address was essentially empty and had an eviction notice. ICABOD shows her location to not be at that address, so he had another place to go, or he dropped her someplace."

ICABOD was painting the screen with location information and topology. The signal was not within a hospital or any industrial building. The screen showed what looked to be basic housing structures. No technology signals appeared from the buildings adjacent to her location. ICABOD grabbed more from the satellite imaging to make the picture of her signal's location as clear as possible and in real time. The few people on the streets looked to be going about their business oblivious to JAC. She was not showing in what Otto and Quip could make out on the screen.

"Can you get a position on Jacob and his estimated arrival time? I presume you already texted him the information that she was removed from the scene, right?"

"Yes. Otto, I sent him a message the same time I sent yours. He has not responded. I am trying to track into the plane and see if Carlos is doing his tunneling routine. Ok, it looks like ICABOD is grabbing that information and mapping it. Give it a minute."

"ICABOD, I want an ETA on that plane. Destination is Acapulco."

The screen balloon message appeared on the screen, and showed arrival estimated at 30 minutes, 22 seconds.

"ICABOD, continue tracking and report time updates every five minutes.

"Ok, Otto, we have him on track. When he lands, I would suggest he simply grab a car and go to the location. Do you have any other suggestions?"

"Quip, if Jacob was coming in alone, I would totally agree. However, he is arriving with a very distraught Carlos. I think Carlos will simply want to go to his brother or to Simone, aka Lara, as soon as he lands. He will expect Jacob to accompany him to see Petra."

"You make a valid point. Then I will send Petra a text, along with Jacob, suggesting they stay the course directed by Carlos, keep Lara in sight, and then one of them can go to locate JAC, once Carlos is set."

"Agreed. Jacob will likely go to JAC, and Petra will maintain Lara. JAC will be fine, Quip. Keep in mind how resourceful she is, especially in tough situations."

CHAPTER 35

Friends help friends ...

Carlos and Jacob landed and quickly cleared customs. Carlos rented a car and made his way to the resort. As they drove, Carlos discussed how he hoped things would play out.

"Jacob, I need to see Simone and reassure her that all is well. I would ask that you and Petra keep her safe. I need to see my brother and get him some special medical attention. It could take a day or so to complete that, maybe longer. Can I impose on you for that help?"

"Carlos, Petra or I will take care of Simone while we all get this mess sorted out. You just need to make certain you call and touch base with Simone, or she will worry. You know how females are."

Carlos grinned, "Oh yes, just like you. I would rather be holding her hand and stroking her hair than almost anything. But, my brother, is, well, my brother."

They arrived at the resort. As the men entered the suite, both ladies were in their arms almost before the door closed. Jacob and Petra went outside while Carlos and Simone remained in the sitting room. Petra had ordered some additional food sent up when Quip had told her how soon they would land. Carlos appeared relaxed as he spoke to Simone, but Jacob knew it was a facade.

"So how was your day, honey?" They both said at once and laughed.

"You first, Petra," offered Jacob.

"It was interesting to say the least. We will need time to discuss the details, but not now. Simone is a mess, and she is Lara, only Carlos has no idea. I don't think Simone will have time to enlighten him before Carlos will leave to tend to Juan. I never saw who picked Juan up."

"That would be JC, whom I have briefly met. I think he is an American. Tell you what – why don't I borrow a car from the hotel and get over to where ICABOD has tracked JAC's phone? If she is ok, I can bring her back here or to her hotel. Quip supplied me with the information to allow those options. I think every-one would feel better if we knew Julie's condition. If this Manuel has helped her then I will reward him. If not, then we'll look at other options later."

"I think that is best. Go ahead and grab at least a little to eat as you leave. I will take care of Simone until you return." Petra smiled as Jacob took her into his arms and whispered, "Sleeping arrangements might be odd for a couple of days, but I do have designs on you, my dear. It starts with not being separated for quite some time and goes on from there."

Jacob laughed, then groaned, "Ok, good distraction, babe. I didn't need that, but it worked."

He kissed her again and put as much into it as he could. If he was going to be distracted, so was she.

Jacob grabbed the car and called Quip. He wanted point-by-point instructions and knew Quip would want to hear all of it unfold. It took a scant twenty minutes to locate the signal from Julie's cell outside a rundown house in a very poor neighborhood.

"Ok, Quip, have arrived. It all looks quiet."

"Yep, ICABOD is tracking you. Now go find Julie, please."

Jacob knocked on the door which was answered by a man that looked like the picture Quip had sent. Jacob explained why he was there and then entered. On the couch he saw a very confused but very alive Julie.

"Well hello, Jacob. Have you met my dear friend, Manuel? He has been most kind and helpful to me. I didn't recall the details, but Manuel has filled me in and my memory is slowly returning. Apparently, I received a hit in the head from some debris. I have been trying to pay him for protecting me, but he is refusing."

"Nice to meet you, Manuel. Thank you for helping my boss, Julie. We have been working in tandem on locating this model she is so taken with. I hear you are the hero all the way around," Jacob grinned, then shook Manuel's hand. "I need to get Julie back to her hotel now, but she will be in touch with you soon."

"I am glad she has someone to look after her. She seems to be fine and doesn't appear to need additional medical care."

"Again, thanks to you, Manuel. I promise I will be in touch. Jacob, let's go and let me get some rest."

CHAPTER 36

Is the good ol' boy network worth the schmoozing?

Thiago was feeling much better following his latest treatment plan. He needed to focus on the company and the upcoming board of directors meeting. His legacy to Lara was based on either the company remaining successful or selling out. The company had achieved success so he could sell for a huge profit, but he wanted it to continue. For that he needed to remain in control of the board or simply walk away. As his health improved so did his determination to continue the company.

He'd reviewed the background on Wolfgang and found his financial and business background aligned with the core competencies required for the open board seat. However, Thiago had founded a successful Brazilian-based company and having that maintained was key in the current political climate. The world economic situation had proved weakened for many years, and the countries within Europe that failed to meet budgetary constraints had reached staggering proportions. Brazil performed well in the world markets and his company contributed to that success.

Most of the board had been in place for many years. Jorge Genio was his trusted friend, as well as a powerful businessman. Carlos Civita was CEO for another non-competing firm in Brazil, and Thiago sat on his board. The newest member was Arminio Fafra and during the last two years Thiago had mentored him. Paulo and Sergio were also strong in finance and government interactions, respectively.

As Thiago reviewed the board members, he felt his strongest support would be from Jorge, Carlos and Paulo. He wanted their feedback on his recommended board member if he pushed it. This really was a diversionary tactic to get the board to focus on something different. Obviously, Lara would be the best recommendation. She'd been groomed to take on a leadership role within the company through her education and the work she'd performed over her years with the company. It would be impossible to recommend her to the board until she was located. He'd finally decided if she wasn't located, he would sell his interest in the company.

Thiago had crafted a very personalized cover letter for the three gentlemen he planned to approach initially. The letter outlined the reasons that this candidate should be considered for the board seat. The reasons included Wolfgang's broader world view, his vast experience in financial investments, and the auditing Ronnie, Ltd routinely performed for their company. Once satisfied with the content of the letter, he sent each of the gentlemen individual emails with a request to phone at their specified time.

He worked through the morning on various business matters. He was finally current on all his required responsibilities. That was one of the things that helped him feel better, health wise. His medical team wanted his stress level reduced. For a man such as himself that meant clearing the To Do list. He was caught up on the list and had just finished a modest lunch at his desk when the phone rang. He glanced at the clock and knew the first call was on time and caller ID confirmed.

"And a good afternoon to you, Carlos," Thiago began.

"The same to you, Thiago," responded Carlos with good humor.

"Carlos, thank you for making this call. I simply wanted to discuss the reasons behind my email this morning. You, of course, are aware of the upcoming board meeting. My thoughts are for us to consider an interim board member who has a broader world viewpoint yet familiarity with our business overall. This candidate, I believe, is more than qualified from a background perspective."

"Thiago, I must admit at first glance the qualifications of this gentleman are broad and, frankly, impressive. I have not delved into the details as thoroughly as I will, as I wanted to better understand your thoughts. Of course, any recommendation by you would be viewed as a front runner. At this point I personally have not heard of any other recommended person for the slot, outside of Lara."

"Nor have I, Carlos. Of course, Lara is the long-term path. However, as an interim arrangement I wanted to bring this candidate forward. What I would appreciate is your careful review with that perspective in mind and ask that you let me know your thoughts in a week or so. You are more than welcome to perform a background check or speak directly to this gentleman."

"Thiago, I will certainly take my time to do that, then follow up with you. I am having lunch with Sergio later in the week. May I perhaps socialize it in discussion with him?"

"That would be great, Carlos, but not outside Sergio. I hope you understand my need to keep this close until the meeting. Thank you again for meeting my call time, as well as your careful consideration of my request. I expect an update early next week, either via phone or email."

After they disconnected Thiago worked on the approach to the next call with Paulo. Paulo had originally surfaced Arminio's name when a board seat had opened. Paulo always wanted the best for the company but had his own self-interests.

"Ah, good afternoon, Paulo. How is your day going? Mine has been very productive," offered Thiago.

"Mine as well, Thiago. I obviously received your letter of introduction and experience on Wolfgang. Interesting that he has no Latin American experience other than through the audits performed by his current firm, Ronnie, Ltd. What plans do you have around this candidate and the direction of the company?"

Thiago laughed, "It is always so hard to keep something from you, Paulo, and your insight is scary. As with your recommendation of adding a youthful perspective, when Arminio was put into place, I want a broader world view added, at least for an interim period."

"Interesting. I can see why that might be of benefit. So how may I help, my old friend?"

"I simply trust your opinion, Paulo. I would appreciate you taking a long look, perhaps call him and talk, do a background verification, or simply think about the possibilities. The business is expanding and we need to expand to service EMEA interests more broadly in the future. Now might be that time.

"I know that you will keep your own counsel on this and provide me your honest thoughts."

"Thiago, I will, of course, support your course for the direction of the company. I will do as you ask and get back to you in a few days. Thank you for your confidence in me as always."

After they disconnected Thiago mentally reviewed each of his board members. It was important to have them understand that he still ran the company. He wanted them off balance of his direction and thinking about something other than the succession plan. A short time later the last call arrived.

"Thiago, it is Jorge. What are you doing, young man?" admonished Jorge.

"Why, Jorge, so glad you still think I am young. I am having fun running my company of course. You obviously received my email then and perhaps read it?"

"Of course I read it and reviewed the background. Again, what are you up to?"

Thiago grinned, "I am trying to determine the character of the board these days. I need your ear to the ground, Jorge. I sent this to Carlos and Paulo and I want to see what they do with the information.

"Beyond that I am working, happy and healthy, my friend. How are you doing?"

"I am fine as well, thank you for asking. Perhaps we can have dinner next week some time. My wife is looking for another date for you and is quite focused on getting you with a lady of her choosing."

"Well, thank you for the heads up. I appreciate your wonderful wife's efforts, but you know I can find my own ladies if needed. I have never been to a function without a suitable companion by my side," he laughed.

"Glad you are doing well. I will let you know what I hear. You sound engaged. Need to go, my friend."

Thiago sat back and reviewed the day. As he considered his actions, he smiled, still longing for Lara to return soon.

CHAPTER 37

Men sometimes cannot put things back together again...

Carlos ordered, "Put him down gently on the best sofa over there. Use the one with the fewest snakes in it."

Juan sensed his brother's level of concern and croaked, "Bro, no need to go to all that trouble. I mean what's a few snakes among friends. Besides, what's all the fuss about? I've had worse hangovers than this silly little gunshot wound."

Carlos growled, "Yes, but you're not gonna feel better by tomorrow if we don't do something about the bleeding. I want you to be able to order cervezas while standing and hustling the babes at the bar, and not bleeding out on my favorite snake-free couch."

JC and Robert stood and watched events unfold.

JC offered, "Let me help on this one. I was an emergency vehicle driver for a while in the U.S. I know enough of first-line emergency treatment to bring this under control. Besides, I feel I owe you guys for pulling us out of that bad situation in Dallas and setting us up in your business. Hell, I even like him a little bit, except for that rude comment about me and Robert having a ménage à trois he made a while back."

Juan tried to laugh but it hurt too much. He took a breath and whispered, "So is the offer still good on meeting at the bar?"

The situation was so tense that they only smiled at Juan's brave effort to make light of the events. The On-Brothers began bringing in supplies ordered by JC and also showed concern at the gravity of the situation.

"JC, I didn't know you drove an emergency vehicle," Carlos said. "I'd like to hear that story while you work on Juan if you could."

Juan croaked, "So you drove an emergency vehicle in your youth? Did you have a neck back then that people could actually see? Maybe twenty kilograms ago, right?"

JC was quite focused on stopping the bleeding and let the taunts slide by, setting the stage for what has to come next, the cleaning and stitching of the wound.

"Well on one hand, it sure feels good to help people that are hurt or incapacitated. But after seeing one poor individual get patched up and sent to the hospital, you get another call to help someone else and so it goes on for ten to fourteen hours a day.

"Well, one day I was called out to a location to help someone, and it is a kid about nine years old. He was beaten pretty badly. Picking up kids without a guardian is always a poor idea so I tried to find a responsible adult at the location and sure enough I did. Turned out the kid's old man had been drinking all day. When the kid came home from school and didn't know how to make the right kind of sandwich for the drunk old bastard, he started beating the kid.

"I didn't handle it very well and hit the asshole really hard. The funny thing was that the kid grabbed ahold of my leg, crying his heart out. He begged me not to hit him anymore and that it was the only parent he had left since his mother had died the month before. The kid wouldn't leave his father because of their mutual loss so I tried to patch them both up right there before taking my next call.

"The next call was for another minor needing medical attention. I couldn't deal with it and just walked away right then. The emergency vehicle lights flashing, car door open, and the radio voice screaming at me to hurry up for the next call."

JC paused in the story telling to make certain his evaluation of Juan's wound was correct. He frowned and then returned pressure.

"Well good buddy, it looks like the bullet sailed on through you and didn't hit any bones or major organs. If we can get both entrance and exit wounds to seal up then there is a good chance you'll be regaling babes again with your cave-diving routine again soon. You'll have those girls showing off on the dance poles, just to get a chance with you."

At that moment Don of the On-Brothers approached, "Carlos, I think I can help here with the entrance and exit wounds and their healing process. My medicinal studies with the Yaqui Indians have given me insight into some powerful healing herbs and plants that should help enormously, if you will let me weigh in here. This herbal compound called 'ᶦᴸᵁᴾfǫ♥₂ẓṯЖŤ' by the Yaquis has been known to draw out poisons from wounds and help seal open wounds of warriors who have fallen in battle. With your permission?"

Juan and Carlos looked at each other uneasily while Robert and JC seemed confused.

Juan motioned Carlos close and whispered, "Bro, I am willing to try it but don't let him chant that stupid desert Indian crap while he dances naked around me. Got it?"

Carlos pulled back from listening to Juan and said, "Don, go ahead and use the 'ᶦᴸᵁᴾfǫ♥₂ẓṯЖŤ' on his wounds."

Don brightened up and explained, "You bet, just let me change into my loin cloth and we'll get started."

Juan had a panicked look on his face, so Carlos suggested, "Just apply the damn 'ꞙⵉⵍⵯPfɋ̣ɥ⚹ⵈ̣ⵓ𝕏Ŧ' so we can get him well!"

Don said, somewhat dejected, "Juan won't get the full effect of 'ꞙⵉⵍⵯPfɋ̣ɥ⚹ⵈ̣ⵓ𝕏Ŧ' without the customary tribal dance that goes with it! You want him to get well, don't you? He needs the full weight of the 'ꞙⵉⵍⵯPfɋ̣ɥ⚹ⵈ̣ⵓ𝕏Ŧ' and its healing power which means I need to perform the sacred ritual!"

"Oh alright, but keep the loin cloth on so we don't have to see your shlong flopping out. I don't want Juan barfing at us on top of everything else."

Don was delighted to be allowed to perform the full ritual and scampered away to suit up. As he dashed away he reminded Ron and Vaughn to get the instruments.

"Boys, show time, let's go!" Don announced.

Carlos grinned, "I hope you don't mind about Don and his Yaqui rituals, but if it does work then we are ahead of the game. In any event I thought I might video record this display to have a little memento of this solemn occasion. I hope you won't mind."

At this point Juan needed to be restrained by JC and Robert, who are also now grinning. What started out as a potential tragedy looked promising as a one-of-a-kind event. Carlos rotated the video camera to his shoulder and got into a good position to catch all the action.

"Don, I want to get this on the first take, ok? Oh, and do that stammering stomp twice per foot with your arms out to the side pointing forward and rotating. I find those undulating moves fascinating." Carlos confirmed, "I really think that adds to the regional colloquial realism of the ritual."

Juan desperately looked for a way to escape the total humiliation planned. JC and Robert enjoyed watching Juan's terrified look. JC wrapped the wound but held the gauze in place to stem the bleeding. He and Robert sat back to enjoy what promised to be Juan's mortal embarrassment.

Don came into the room chanting and stomped each foot twice with an authentic dance stutter only seen at true Yaqui rituals. Ron and Vaughn beat the drums and shook the rattles in high spirit, both focused on contributing to the healing process. Predictably, Don's loin cloth slipped away during the Yaqui medicine dance while Carlos filmed the comical scene to Juan's continued humiliation.

Carlos called out, "Good! Good! Don, turn so the lighting catches that terrific profile of yours. Yes, that's good! Juan, no worries. I have the one-eared elephant on video coming over to administer the 'ⵊⵝⵡPfáΨⵯⵥⵟӜϒ' to your wounds. Oh, terrific shots, guys! I wonder how many hits on YouTube we'll get. Wow! Good stuff, bro! Are you feeling better yet?"

Don knelt down, administered the 'ⵊⵝⵡPfáΨⵯⵥⵟӜϒ' to Juan's wounds and then replaced the dressings that JC provided.

Juan cried out bitterly, "Shit! That stuff burns like hell! And hey, throw that elephant trunk back over your shoulder. I don't want it draped over me!"

"Hey bro, what a great idea! I could provide a little voice over on the video talking about how the male African elephant uses its trunk to dust its back," Carlos suggested.

Carlos kept filming the event and added voice overs as if he were a wildlife naturalist filming the event in the African savannah in hushed tones.

Juan croaked, "I will get you for this, Carlos! I will fucking get you for this!"

Carlos lowered the video camera and grinned, "That's what I am counting on, bro. I want you to get well enough to whip my ass. Can you do that for me?"

CHAPTER 38

Remembering to say thank you is good manners

Julie felt so much better after a good night's sleep. She'd met with Jacob for breakfast in her hotel. They had discussed some options for getting Lara to reconcile with her father. At this point either Jacob or Petra would remain with Lara at all times, at least until Carlos returned. Petra had shared some of her insights to Lara's mindset as well as commented on Lara's strengths. As Julie headed toward Manuel's home, a plan formed. If executed correctly it solved several issues.

Jacob had also brought her up to speed on the requested changes for Carlos and Juan's identities. He had indicated where their funds were located as a part of what she needed to complete the changes. This would wait until Juan was healed. Neither of them could be reached easily at this point. Jacob wanted to remind Julie that her position as JAC was valued.

She arrived at the address and looked around. The area was very poor but the few people she saw smiled at her. Children played like all children, with laughter and bottomless energy. Julie hoped that Manuel was home. She'd had no way to contact him other than at his doorway. She had liked how he'd taken care of her and protected her, as she would expect of a brother. Mostly, she wanted to help him succeed. As Julie knocked on the door, she heard sounds from inside indicating at least someone was home. The door opened.

"Well, hello there, Miss Travelers Checks. I hadn't expected to see you again." Manuel's faced brightened and he smiled. "Would you like to come in for a few minutes? I have some coffee if you'd like it."

"Hi, Manuel. Yes, I'd like that. We need to talk about a few things, if you aren't too busy."

"I would always make time for you, pretty lady."

He directed her to a comfortable chair by the window and left to fetch the coffee. He returned with two mugs and some packets of cream and sugar. After he was ensconced in his chair, he looked at her, taking an assessment.

"Are you feeling better after the odd meeting from yesterday?"

"Yes, I am. I wanted to let you know that today and also to again tell you how much I appreciated your help when I was struck down. A lessor man would have ignored me and saved his own hide."

"I wasn't raised that way. I look out for children, elders, and of course, pretty ladies. And no, I require no payment for services rendered. Don't let this place fool you into thinking I don't have other resources because I have. I am just a frugal man that lives simply."

"I totally understand that. I live simply as well, but mostly because I tend to travel a great deal. I was raised to say thank you and to return the favor when possible.

"That brings me to my other reason to want to speak to you face to face. When we met with Simone yesterday, what did you think of her as a person?"

"Well, of course she is pretty, but I thought that before yesterday. When I had previously spoken to her, she had a certain refinement to her. Seeing her yesterday with the notorious Spencer made me suspect she was not as closely linked to him as he'd indicated to you. I doubt they have any sort of agreement in place."

"Ok, that makes sense. As far as the bastard goes, he had no place in our discussion. I have totally dismissed him." She smiled with a glint in her eyes that indicated revenge more than a dismissal. "And you, Manuel, what do you want from a career perspective? Could you work with her? I liked the designs you drew to highlight the fashions. I believe they helped accentuate the lines and the style marvelously, even though you'd spent limited time completing those designs. It seems you have talent, sir."

He laughed a bit. "Once I thought I had talent. I wanted to be the best photographer in Latin America. I studied hard, made some good friends in the fashion industry, and photographed many beautiful women.

"I let my ego get in the way though and ended up with a bit of a drinking problem. Being good is a slippery slope when there are others nipping at your heels, making the most of your faults to their benefit. To be taken seriously in this business you have to be good, work well with others and, as a mentor of mine once said, don't run with scissors. I have no one to blame but myself that the up-and-coming photographers simply walked over my drunken body.

"I overcame my problem but breaking back into the business is a difficult task. Winning the trust back from those that I let down is very slow. I have some recent opportunities that have worked well. I will get back some of my ground in a year or two, I think."

"That is a very straightforward response, actually." She looked serious as she continued, "You had a problem, but you believe it is resolved. I'm willing to trust that is the case.

"Your design layouts are effective and a bit different than most I have seen. You seem to want to bring light in at different angles to highlight a design aspect of the garment rather than simply make a great photograph. Why is that?"

"I find in fashion the whole purpose is to make the item desirable and help them sell. Anyone looking at the garment should see the setting, the model, but first and foremost the garment. They must be able to imagine themselves in the garments without discounting it due to the fact that the model may be a blonde or a redhead. That means the focal point of the photograph has to shift.

"I was getting some traction with this approach with a specific designer when fame, as it were, went to my head. Many of the shots I provided could be tracked back to the purchases. No doubt the designs were great as well, but the focal point made the consumer look at a shot and then start asking for a specific line at their favorite store. It is something I believe in."

Julie beamed. "That, sir, is a great explanation. I think we have common ground. I would like to propose something here."

Manuel nodded and smiled with hope in his heart. Taking photographs was his passion. He was pleased when he provided value using his talent. He couldn't say a word, as he feared breaking her train of thought. This crazy lady seemed to accomplish things others walked away from.

"I would like to see these designs launched. I think Simone may be the right vehicle. I would like to make a proposal to her and have you ready at that meeting to set up and start taking pictures to help prove the point to Simone. Would you be agreeable to that sort of arrangement? If so, then I would only allow you to participate if you were on retainer. I do not want to have to fit into your schedule. I think this could be lucrative enough that you would get your shot at fulfilling your passion."

"I think, pretty lady, what you are suggesting sounds marvelous. I will cancel all my appointments and commitments immediately to be at your disposal. I am ready to sign a contract right now."

Julie laughed, "Good. I am glad that suits you. Sorry, but I am not going to write a contract today with you. It is something that will occur, I feel certain, but it won't be directly with me. I will, however, provide the retainer, which should cover our commitments for the next thirty days. I also brought a phone for you so that you might be easily reached, in case I can't come by."

Julie handed him ten thousand U.S. dollars and a cell phone. He looked at the money in awe.

She explained before he could comment, "I know it is a bit less than what you might expect over time and with the contract, but I am hoping you will trust me for a month or less. I have a few things I need to get lined up and then we will have another meeting with Simone. By the way, I have located her. I just spoke with her to arrange a meeting. It may take a few days.

"I am also hoping we can be friends. I would very much like you as my friend and advisor," she finished with her trademark smile.

They agreed and shook hands at the door as she readied to leave. He waved as she got into her car and slowly drove off.

He whispered, "I'd still done it for just one kiss, my new friend."

CHAPTER 39

Being nice to others is often self-serving

Carlos cautioned JC, "Let me do the talking. If we don't do introductions the way they are trained, then you can expect them to checkout of the discussions. This opportunity would be lost."

JC acknowledged, "I understand, Carlos. I can see this as a good adjunct to our drug business, but I don't understand why you want to turn it over to me for just a percentage. I will send your percentage to the numbered account like you asked. But why go to all this trouble to make this business deal just to turn it over to me, Robert, and the On-Brothers?"

Carlos responded, "So about my percentage, that has to be our secret, based on what I promised. Understand?"

"I'll take care of your percentage on the nineteenth of every month like you asked, but I still want an answer as to why. Plus, once you have turned this over to us, your leverage is gone. I could easily renege on the agreement. So what gives?"

Carlos rested his gaze on JC as he formed the words. "First, I am doing this because I owe the On-Brothers, you, and Robert something after all that was done to take care of Juan. That effort helped him pull through.

"Second, Juan and I became collateral damage when Phillip Johnston got caught stealing the drug dealer monies we moved to the Caymans Bank. We had to make a deal with the Mexican and U.S. governments to exit the business after we helped them nail our clients.

"Third, which is the most important one, I promised Simone to exit my old line of work of moving goods and people. I don't know what I am going to do, but I don't want to starve. That's where that percentage you will pay me comes in. But the federales and Simone can't know of our arrangement for the reasons I just gave you.

"Finally, you should understand that the federales don't know anything about you, Robert, the On-Brothers, or the ongoing enterprise. I am good with that. However, if you try to screw me over after all that I have done for you, I will ensure that they will have all they need to know about the moving business. Now do you understand?"

JC nodded agreement, "Ok, got it! Let's go talk to the Egg Roll brothers and see how many Won-Ton's they want to move."

Carlos gave a serious look to JC out of the corner of his eye. The man's smartass mouth was the wild card in dealing with these Chinese. He needed to relate the issue at JC's level, dumbing it down.

"JC, I think all that time in the Caymans hanging out with Phillip Johnston must have infected you with that same idiotic sense of humor. Do we need to shave your head, make you give that hideous toothy grin, and have you clap your hands together in an effort to smear more oil on your hands every time you honestly believe you said something funny?"

JC's unadulterated, panicked look, reinforced by the fear that he might be mistaken for Phillip Johnston, drove his breathing to hyperventilation levels. After a few seconds JC composed himself.

He choked out, "Oh, Carlos, I'm sorry, man! I'll get a grip, man! I don't want people chewing on tin foil and having their head shaved with a cheese grater on my account."

JC shuddered at the comparison of him to the gnomish bank robber now being detained in Guantanamo.

"Ok, but if you do that again we will go back to only letting you use flash cards to communicate with the humans on this planet," insisted Carlos.

JC and Carlos arrived at the meeting destination a few minutes before it was scheduled to begin. They found Won and Ton waiting calmly for them as they entered. Their faces were inscrutable.

Carlos began, "Good day, gentlemen. As per my communication, I am pleased that your Operations Director was interested in our hard asset-moving expertise. We are agreeable to move our relationship forward. As a show of good faith, I have brought my moves coordinator, JC, with me so that I can make proper introductions. I trust this will meet with your approval?"

As usual Won remained quiet as Ton said, "We did not hear back on your earlier purchase and feared that the product did not meet your expectations. Were our efforts to accommodate your friend's needs well leveraged? Hopefully he is enjoying his new existence."

Carlos sighed, "He does have a new life but, alas, he is not enjoying his new circumstances. I did convey to him the more comprehensive services that your organization offered, but regrettably he was compelled to take the more expedient, lower-cost approach. Looking back in hindsight, his selection can only be categorized as a poor choice. However, on the bright side I have one less Christmas card to address this year."

Ton, displaying a modest show of regret, rebuked, "I don't believe we talked about you bringing another person along to our meeting. We are very discreet businessmen. We like consistency in our business dealings.

"However, we do see the value in introducing your moves coordinator at this stage. We will overlook this breach in protocol this one time. For all meetings with Won and myself, all attendees are to be approved prior to the meeting. Do we understand one another, kind sir?"

Carlos nodded his agreement. "I would like to apologize for my transgression in this matter. We will take steps to insure no protocol violations occur again. JC here is my witness for our concurrence in this matter."

JC also nodded his agreement.

Carlos continued, "Gentlemen, you should understand that our business offers are in demand. If I am unavailable for some reason, it seemed prudent for you to have another reliable contact that can be trusted to maintain consistency in our business dealings. He is dedicated to meeting your business service's needs. Permit me to give you his personal contact information as well as mine for your discreet communications when required. He is your primary account manager. Is that agreeable?"

Won nodded and Ton said, "Most agreeable. We find your business purpose to our liking and special needs. Your manner and attention to detail is thorough and alternatives are in place should the need arise. I believe we can do business with people like you and JC."

Carlos and JC both smiled at what appeared to be a small victory.

"Then, may I ask, do you have some moving business we can assist with at present, or should we be content on hearing from you?" asked Carlos.

Again Won said nothing, but Ton replied, "We have nothing at the moment. I do have a question for you. Are you restricted to operating only in the Caribbean theater, or can your expertise be leveraged in other areas of the world?"

Before Carlos could answer, JC responded, "If it's valuable and needs relocating, ways can be found to accommodate the customer anywhere in the world. Our motto is, If you can bag it, we can shag it."

Carlos half closed his eyes and shook his head from side to side. JC, however, needed to make his own relationships, so he didn't interject.

This time it was Won that spoke first with great enthusiasm as Ton exclaimed, "Excellent!" Then added, "We will be in touch."

Won and Ton rose, bowed to JC first, then to Carlos and departed.

CHAPTER 40

Why are humans the only animal who look for what is not lost?

Thiago was returning to his office from a meeting with the Operations Director when he was interrupted by his secretary.

"Mr. Bernardes, there is a call holding for you on your personal line. A Mr. Otto. He was most insistent on speaking with you now. What would you have me tell him?" asked Thiago's secretary.

Thiago smiled and said, "I already received an encrypted text saying to get to my personal land line in my office to take an important call. Apparently when Otto wants to talk it doesn't matter what I'm doing, so clear my calendar for the day, please."

The secretary frowned at the computer screen and said, "Mr. Bernardes, I will not be able to do that for you, since that apparently has already been done."

Picking up the handset, Thiago said, "Otto, good day to you, sir, and thanks for helping me navigate my business schedule, or should I say negate my afternoon business meetings. Usually we just schedule a time to talk. So what can I do for you on such short notice?"

Otto chuckled as he informed, "Thiago, this isn't about me or even talking to me. Please hold while I transfer a call and enjoy your afternoon, kind sir."

Thiago held a puzzled look until a voice come on the line.

"Hello, Papá. It's me, Lara, Papá. Do you have time to talk to me, Papá?"

Thiago was stunned at hearing Lara's voice on the other end of the line. He struggled to find words and barely contained his emotions.

"My filha Lara! My querido filha! You have no idea how good it is hear your voice. You have no idea."

Thiago paused a few seconds to recall what Otto had told him on how to conduct himself on this first call. He also needed to get hold of his emotions. It was not really about him, and that needed to stay firmly in the top of his mind.

"Lara, please let me hear your voice again. Are you well? I'm so happy to hear from you."

Lara was inundated with emotions, but she marshalled her feelings before speaking. Part of her had feared a hang up from her papá upon hearing her voice.

"Oh, Papá, so much has happened that I don't know where to begin! Thank you for taking my call. I wasn't sure you would want to talk to me after our last fight."

Thiago struggled to hold back the tears and not let his voice crack. He realized he had let her down.

"Let me clear the way between us. Let me begin with an apology. I would have you know that not a day goes by that I don't wish I could take back that petty nonsense that I spoke. Since the day I knew you would be born, I always envisioned a magnificent future for you. I knew I would do everything within my power to give you those possibilities. After we lost your mother, those future possibilities became all the more important. But somewhere along the line I started holding onto my fears for you rather than help you with your ambitions. How could I not have seen you had become everything I wanted my filha to be?

"You have so many qualities that I know so little of. Kindness, humility, warmth towards others. I became so wrapped up in smoothing the walkway for you, I forgot that 'trip ups' in life's journeys also teach valuable lessons. I would like to think that during your absence I may have learned something as well. I have no right to ask and you are under no obligation to provide, but I would ask for your forgiveness and permission to start over. Perhaps you can teach me some of what you know that has not been properly cultivated in me."

Lara cried and laughed softly with emotion at the words she heard. A great burden was lifted. This was what family was all about, unconditional love.

"Oh, Papá! We have lost so much time but look at what we have learned! Hopefully we have both grown! I love you, Papá. I always will. We will get through this, Papá. I promise."

Thiago smiled as he wiped his own tears. "Now, what happens next? Where can we go from here? I am extending the olive branch to you and will say that the next move is yours. If you need more time to think about what we have said, then I understand. If you are compelled to return, I have a large house here…wait, excuse me, WE have a large house here, and it will always be our home. But either way I promise not to be as I have been accused of by an old friend, a used car salesman, trying to hustle you to get my way.

"Anyway, that is my apology and since you have no reason to reciprocate, please tell me of your adventures and discoveries over these last eight months. I am elated to just hear your voice and your descriptions of your marvelous encounters. Or, perhaps

I could start with things I have recalled while you've been gone to not put you on the spot.

"Do you remember that summer when you were ten? That India Explorers Pith helmet you wore every day to go outside and play? Some mornings you put it on before you got dressed and I'd have a devil of a time helping get your clothes on when you complained they were stuck. That was the same summer you and your playmate wore out the walkie-talkies as you acted out your explorer fantasies."

Lara laughed genuinely. "Oh, Papá. I never did such a thing. But I do now remember the walkie-talkies. Oh, and the ladder over the fence you had built so we could sneak over into the pasture to play with the horses. That I remember!"

Thiago had a sobering thought. "I did? How reckless of me to build a ladder over the fence so you could play with the horses! Looking back on it you could have been trampled! Obviously, I will need to submit myself for disciplinary action for such a lapse in good judgment!"

"Papá, those are good memories I had of those times and places. So, no lamenting what should have been different," she responded with indignation. "Things don't always go according to plan and that is what's so remarkable about my time here.

"Yes, I will tell you many amazing stories and probably leave out the ugly stories and the associated pain, but not at this time, Papá. I want to do that in person so I can see your eyes and face while you hold my hand as we talk. Also, I have something I'm working on and I want you to look it over and offer me your council. Is that ok, Papá?"

Thiago was somewhat surprised and closed his eyes as hope filled him. He paused for a few seconds to gain his composure.

"Am I given to understand there is a chance that I might be forgiven for my words of anger and that you seek my counsel on an issue in your life? I sure hope I don't wake up from this dream any time soon!"

"If you weren't my Papá, I might call you a rascal for teasing me as you do. And yes, I did miss the gentle teasing by you, Papá. I will see you soon. I love you, Papá."

Thiago responded, "I love you, Lara. I will be here whenever you want me."

"I will call again soon, and thank you, Papá."

CHAPTER 41

The difference between winning, losing, and optimization

JAC picked up Haddy at the airport, along with two heavy bags. Like co-conspirators, they were both animated as they discussed the plan to get Lara on board with her real destiny. JAC was surprised and pleased that Haddy had agreed to travel and support this effort. Usually Haddy's responsibilities precluded her from travelling for something considered so far from normal R-Group business. Haddy had insisted with Otto that this was needed to fulfill his commitment to Thiago. She planned to enjoy each and every minute.

Haddy brought along some additional garments made using JAC's designs. All were to Lara's size specifications. Their first stop was to meet with Manuel and get him focused on the scenes to be used for each of the garments. JAC wanted everything in place for the shoot the next day. She'd rented some meeting room space at the resort which allowed for indoors and outdoors shoots, depending upon Manuel's staging requirements. He'd located some workers that promised to help as needed for any staging effects required. It would be tight, but Haddy and JAC agreed that would be the best part.

Petra had Lara sequestered in her suite for the day, though she'd been apprised of the plans. Lara was stunned at all the events. She'd spoken to her father and gained new hope, but there was still her direction and her dealing with Carlos to be resolved. JAC and Haddy were handling the direction and Petra was working with Lara on the Carlos portion. They arrived at Manuel's house and arrived at the door just as it opened.

Julie smiled, "Hi, Manuel, looks like you were expecting us. Let me introduce my makeup artist and dresser, Haddy."

Manuel was not surprised that the lady beside Julie was so pretty and elegant, even for one that he guessed was at least in her late fifties. She was dressed very nicely and far too elegant for the role Julie had just outlined. But who was he to doubt what Ms. Travelers Check could do?

He grinned as he reached for her hand. "So nice to make your acquaintance, Haddy. I understand you just arrived here and I must say you look beautiful and fresh. We might talk later about a few shots of you, if you would permit it, madam."

Haddy beamed, "Well, young man, how very gracious of you. Nice to meet you as well. I think the photos should be reserved for the younger set. Perhaps Julie here would make a better candidate."

"Haddy, that would be wonderful, but Julie has defined things between us very succinctly, though I would welcome a chance to take some photos. You work on her for me, alright? Now ladies, come in, let's get started. Julie has a very tight schedule. I don't want her disappointed."

Julie provided yet another of her megawatt smiles as they entered and started to work. Manuel had tables and chairs, along with drawing pads and assorted colors. They spent the next several hours as each garment was discussed, reviewed, and then positioned into one scene or another. They had a dozen setups that were agreed to and estimated the timing for each scene to be created from a background and lighting perspective. Manuel made a few calls and established a meeting time at the resort for midafternoon with the workers.

"Ok, Manuel, you have laid out some incredible ideas. If they look as good when they are completed, we'll have this aced," Julie indicated with a pleased look.

"The designs make it very easy. There are some very unique qualities in these designs that I feel can be highlighted with these scenes. I think you have a winner here.

"I want to propose that you two return to your hotel, rest up, and meet me at the resort this evening. I think we'll be completed by then. I also want to have the timing for the setup of each shot and the logical photo order to be most efficient.

"Haddy, I will have your area isolated. That way Simone can change, then you can revise make-up and hair as needed with some semblance of privacy. We will get the mirrors and lighting that you need, as well."

"Sounds perfect, Manuel!" Julie proclaimed.

Manuel met his team and they worked through the afternoon as they created the portable screens with the designs. The simplicity of the designs he had made them easy to create and assemble. The screens would make the change out between garments fast and efficient. He felt this was a chance for his career to get back on track so he pushed his crew.

When Julie and Haddy arrived, they walked through the setup for each of the garments. Haddy made notes on makeup and hair changes that aligned to the sequencing. The sun was setting so the light was not as vibrant as it would be, but Manuel had taken some timings during the day. They completed their efforts and Julie made the call.

"Hi, Simone, this is Julie. I hope you are recovered after our odd first meeting,"

"Hi, Julie. I am recovered. But you, are you feeling better after the bump on your head?" asked Simone with honest concern.

"All is well. I was hoping that you would be free tomorrow morning to resume our review of the fashion line and perhaps allow a few shots to be taken by Manuel."

"Oh my goodness! After all the problems, you still want to have me involved with your fashion line? Are you kidding me?" asked Simone with tears forming in her eyes.

"Well, of course, Simone, why would that change? I spent too much time locating you to walk away from seeing my fashions on the girl that I believe can speak to the line," asserted Julie.

"Umm, I don't know what to say. First though, I need to tell you that my name is not Simone, it is Lara. It is a long story that won't interest you as to why, but I wanted you to know my real name."

"That's fine with me. I suspect it would make a fascinating story over wine at some point, if we reach an agreement. It is you that will make this line come alive, regardless of your name. Just don't tell me that you are a rich heiress and have lost interest in this career."

Lara laughed, "I am most interested in your line and resuming our conversation on perhaps a contract. Where and when would be my two questions?"

"Ten tomorrow morning in the meeting rooms Cliff and Beach at the Divers Resort."

"That is the resort I am at. So, yes, I can be there," Lara excitedly responded. "May I bring a friend with me to watch?"

"Sure, the more the merrier. Thank you, Lara. I feel good about this. I hope you do as well."

After they disconnected Lara filled Petra in on the call details as she danced around the room. They ordered late snacks and wine to celebrate. Jacob toasted Lara, which helped make up for Carlos being gone. Lara tried to phone Carlos but ended up leaving him a detailed message that she hoped would make him smile. Petra urged Lara to go rest, as she needed to be at her best in the morning.

Lara and Petra arrived promptly at ten to the location. Once introductions were made, Petra was directed to a chair to watch the activity but stay out of the way. Lara was hustled off to begin. Julie was in her element as she directed activities. Haddy performed changes in makeup and hair that clearly complimented each of the garments. From lingerie to loungewear to beachwear, the ladies worked through their sequenced plan as Manuel smiled at shot after shot. Lara was a talented model and took direction well. It was a pleasure to work with someone less spoiled than the normal ladies, Manuel had commented multiple times.

They sat together for a quick lunch and commented about different shots. Manuel wanted to reshoot two garments as the sun shifted to gain some different light angles. He'd run through three hundred photos so far and knew he'd have to get the proofs out the next day. They set up and reshot with the changes for the light.

Julie thanked Manuel's team and paid each of them handsomely, even though Manuel objected. She shot him a brilliant smile and patted his arm as she continued to do her thing.

Petra applauded all the efforts and reassured Lara that she was awesome each time she looked concerned or lost a bit of her confidence. Petra admired JAC and her whirlwind approach. It was a side she'd missed along the way. She was equally impressed with Haddy's care as she adjusted Lara's hair and makeup between shots. It amazed her that this was actually more fun than her normal computer activity, though not something she wished to adopt as a steady diet.

They finished up and discussed the next steps, including the proofs for the next afternoon. Petra offered her suite as a meeting place for the reviews and selections. Manuel left while his crew promised to clean up and bring him the screens. The four ladies were getting ready to depart when Julie laid her bombshell.

"Lara, I am impressed with how versatile you were with each of the items. Your animated features worked for each of the personas you assumed. I think that Manuel also had the changes staged perfectly."

"Julie, thank you for everything. I think this could be the start of my destiny. I enjoyed the modeling so much. With each item, while Haddy finished my look, I thought of how I would sell them and discuss the item if asked. I think I could be your spokesperson; I really do."

"Lara, I think that you'd do quite well in that role, however I must admit I saw something different."

Lara frowned and looked concerned. Petra and Haddy both raised an eyebrow and silently questioned JAC for this conversation direction. But they knew better than to buck JAC when she was on a forced march with a target in view.

"To be honest, Lara, I think you are shortchanging your abilities. And honestly, I don't have all the funding to launch this line. I have some designs, good ones I believe, as well as ideas for more. I also have other work that I am passionate about. This is more of a lark for me," Julie offered with a smile.

Lara couldn't speak and looked crestfallen. So close and yet so far from her dreams being realized. She felt tears work their way behind her eyes. She refused to cry.

Petra suggested, "So, Julie, I am not sure I understand. Are you saying Lara is good with the fashion, good with her thoughts on discussion of the items, and you have designs in mind to move forward, but you don't have the time to spend working the entire line? Is that what I am hearing?"

"Exactly, Petra. I love to design. I hate the idea of doing books, securing models, getting shots organized, planning locations, marketing, and so forth. I lucked into finding a photographer with the depth of experience of Manuel and I think he is a keeper. It took forever to locate the face and body that I pictured would bring out the best in my designs. But I don't want to run a business, I simply want to do designs."

Lara's eyes got wide as she suggested, "I can run a business. I have the education and, frankly, the experience. I don't have the capital though. I like the idea of doing all the details, working with models, doing the marketing and overseeing the books. It is what I was trained for growing up."

Petra smiled, "Perhaps, Lara, you need to use this as a method to open up a dialogue with your father. Perhaps he can suggest funding sources. I am sure he would be proud of what you have accomplished, though we won't know for sure until we see the proofs tomorrow. What do you think of that as a way to find your destiny?"

"Petra, that's a great idea. I knew I liked you for a best friend. You just make me feel good about myself. I think it has possibilities. Now I'm excited again."

They all smiled and rose to leave with plenty of hugs and excitement. As they filed out of the room, Petra and JAC exchanged winks.

CHAPTER 42

Actions are far more effective than words

Petra was relieved as the door closed behind Simone and Carlos. Carlos had returned a couple of hours ago and the four of them had drinks while updated information on Juan was shared. The couple obviously were waiting to escape, which they finally had done. Jacob laughed softly as Petra harrumphed to herself and grumbled about time to vacation. Jacob pulled Petra close and she wrapped her arms around him.

"Finally, we are alone. Jacob, I feel like we haven't had hardly any time together on this vacation." She smiled as she looked into his eyes. "Are we done working for a while? I have some plans I would like to enact with you."

Jacob kissed her gently, then answered, "Yes, my darling. I think we are finished working for a while. Let's order dinner in, take a soak in our private pool and relax. You can regale me with all the fun you had with Simone…er, Lara."

"That sounds perfect. You order, I will change into my suit and meet you outside."

"Don't feel you need a suit on my account."

As she gracefully moved away she replied, "Oh, I don't. It is the waiter that I wish to avoid. Easy on, easy off, this wonderful suit. A JAC design that was promised to make you drool."

Jacob placed the order. When Petra emerged from the bedroom a short time later, he was stunned into silence. The suit certainly left little to the imagination, but the overall presentation she made was lovely and desirable. She moved toward the sliding door to the outside, picked up towels and turned toward him with that lovely smile.

"So, Jacob, do you like the suit? Get yours on, and let's go out to the Jacuzzi. We can talk and you can relax."

"Petra, you do understand that relaxing and looking at you in that suit just doesn't work. JAC obviously has some talent, but your body makes that suit, hmm, impressive," he practically leered as his eyes undressed her. "I'll change and do your bidding. Don't bother answering the door for room service, I'll take care of it. I certainly don't want to share any of you with the waitstaff."

He brought out wine and the snacks and turned on some soft background music. Petra had scooted the umbrella table so it provided some shade over the Jacuzzi. She was in up to her shoulders when he handed her a wine glass. As he settled into the Jacuzzi next to her and they toasted, it seemed as if peace had arrived.

"So, how was your time in the Caymans?" she asked sweetly with her hand brushing his arm.

"It was successful. Your Carlos and Juan are quite a pair. Busy boys," he grinned.

"They are not mine, per se, though I guess technically it was me that got us all involved. Simone, now Lara. Now there is an odd coincidence. What a time she has created for herself. JAC did a great job of getting the direction shifted. I think Lara will be on the right track now. At least I hope so."

As they drank and ate, hugged and kissed, intermingled with time in the Jacuzzi, Petra explained the JAC and Haddy show and all that occurred. Jacob laughed while she explained all the fun and banter that had occurred. He related well to the whirl-wind atmosphere that prevailed, having experienced JAC as his cyber assassin Julie. Jacob was sorry he'd missed seeing Haddy, but they planned to return to Zürich after their vacation ended.

Jacob told a few of the stories about his time in the Cayman Islands. She laughed at the descriptions of the people, especially Phillip Johnston. He explained some of his view of Carlos and Juan, as well as the deal that was created.

Then Petra decided she needed to explain about the events at The Dive. She also wanted to lead into some discussion with what Rita and Lara had said about men in general and what they liked. She'd been a bit concerned following that discussion that she needed to be more open. After all, if she wanted a long-term relationship, she needed to voice her concerns.

They moved indoors and settled onto the couch with fresh wine. They sipped their drinks, but before Petra could bring up the discussion, Jacob decided that he'd seen the suit enough and removed it.

"I think that drool is a total understatement for this suit," murmured Jacob into her ear as he nuzzled her neck and shoul-ders and moved his hands over her exposed skin. "I also think that I missed you far too much to spend any more time talking, unless you are totally not interested in my current activities."

"Oh, Jacob, just keep touching me. I missed you so much," she responded with more urgency. "I want to feel you now," she insisted as she helped push his suit off.

They kissed, touched, handling and licking one another, until Petra begged for him. He swiftly entered her. Together they lost time and space as they joined and he relentlessly drove into her until they both cried out with the force of their climax. Exquisitely spent, they remained intertwined until their breathing slowed and their skin cooled.

Petra scooted out from his grasp and retrieved some pillows for them to lean on as well as a lightweight throw. She smiled at the way they seemed to fit so nicely together. He made room for her as she rejoined him and handed him his wine.

"You have the best ideas, my darling, Yes, keep that suit. It is a marvelous distraction on your lovely form," he said as he smiled and ran his hand down her shapely hip.

"I think it was your idea, though I was certainly not opposed. Which brings me to the other subject I wanted to discuss with you," she grinned mischievously.

He raised an eyebrow as he asked, "Really, is this a good subject or a challenging subject? I only ask because I'll be worn out for a few more minutes, but either way I am all yours."

She giggled, "Well, you'll probably think I am so inexperienced you'll laugh."

"Honey, you can tell me anything. Between us there should be no fear of anything said in love. Go for it!"

"Remember, you said anything. Simone, I mean Lara, and I went off resort to a restaurant called The Dive. It was great. Good food, drinks, and the view of the cliff divers was incredible. It was so thrilling, and nope I don't want you to try it.

"After we ate, we decided to go to the dance area and listen to the music and have some more wine. It seemed like a really good idea until that wretched Spencer showed up to ruin everything. Stop, don't get all concerned. I was able to deliver a pointed kick that pushed him over the table while we left."

"What! Are you kidding? I had no idea you even saw that poor excuse for a man," Jacob replied with anger in his tone.

"Shh, don't worry about that. I want to talk with you about

our girl talk before that bastard arrived. He is so not relevant to this discussion," she implored.

He nodded, calmed, and pulled her just a bit closer as his arms protected her.

"So, Lara and I were talking in general about you guys when her friend, Rita, joined us. Rita discussed some of the things that she had been involved with in her work as a porn star. She explained that men like to go to gentlemen's clubs to see women dance, some naked, as well as fanaticize about other sexual activities. I asked a few questions, because my, er, experience is rather limited. None of my education has given me much insight in how a male thinks, aside from a technology perspective."

Jacob thought for a minute on how to best respond. He too was lacking in experience, but not unsettled by that. He thought things between them were great. He was focused on learning what she liked and how she responded. He knew that any couple needed to learn one another.

"First, I think your experience is just fine. I have absolutely no complaints. Just wanted that on the table. Men think differently. For example, you in that suit honestly made me jump from interested to out of control wanting, then to be in you in two seconds. Men think about sex a lot. I haven't been desperately active in that area, since my career development was foremost. But I can tell you it was and is certainly in my thoughts, often.

"So what did the girls say that has you concerned? Again, you are not lacking, my darling."

Petra sighed, "Ok, you will let me know when that is not the case, right? You are important to me and I want us to grow together.

"Rita was outlining one of the scripts that she was considering. She didn't seem all that committed to it though. The outline for the film was that she was in a club and doing dances on a stage and by request, as well as for extra tips, individual lap dances, which, by the way, I needed her to explain.

"This target couple that requested the lap dance was actually a male and a female. The man paid for the lap dance for his lady. Apparently, that is a very erotic experience for a man OR a woman. Anyway, the lap dance was so well-received that the ladies decided to take it several steps further with kisses and grabbing and pleasuring one another, followed quickly by the man joining in with the both of them for a wonderful three-way experience.

"Rita said all guys liked this, at least as a fantasy, and that was one of the reasons that porn films were sought after. My question then for you is, is that true? Is that something you'd want? I'm not sure I would ever be able to share you with someone, so I wanted to know if we have a problem to resolve. Perhaps we need to watch some porn films, though I am not certain that thought holds my interest."

Jacob chuckled, "I think that would be desperately exciting, but not something I'd likely do either. I can tell you that this wonderful story you've painted has restored all my energy, and I think we are going to bed. I will do my best to reassure you that you are all I need."

With that he rose and picked her up. As he carried her to the bedroom, he kissed her and pulled her close. They fell into bed together where they made love multiple times, explored different positions, then fell into blissful asleep.

Jacob slept, but his dreams were filled with vivid eroticism. The ladies in the suite were beautiful. One resembled Petra but with wild hair. He related to her presence and enjoyed the other woman. She had no face that he recognized, but she had a very pretty body, similar to Petra's, lean and very curvy.

The girls sat together naked and explored each other with their hands. They fondled each other's breasts and gently stroked each other's skin. For some reason, he was forced to remain where he was on an adjacent chair rather than with them. He watched them as they kissed and stroked. He realized he was totally excited with a tremendous hard-on.

The no face lady advanced on Petra and proceeded to run hands and fingers between her legs, reaching inside the panties he had missed at first, while they kissed. The level of excitement between them escalated until both ladies moved into position to lick and stroke each other. He noticed that each of the women suddenly held sex toys. He was amazed he hadn't noticed. They teased one another with the toys. They altered positions each time one of them climaxed and showed him every view possible.

They moaned and he found that he moaned and asked if he might join. They finally agreed he might join their fun and each in turn pleased him as they sank deeply onto him, or begged he drive into them. The lady that looked like Petra smiled at him and then groaned as she reached another climax, and he struggled awake.

He sweated, breathing labored, and as his eyes focused he saw the first blush of daylight as it appeared in their room. He reached over and found Petra on her side next to him. He sighed as he teased and stroked her without waking her. Her face looked lovely as she smiled in her sleep. Jacob hoped his overtures were writing something erotic in her dreams.

After his crazy dream he woke up focused on the real Petra. He trailed kisses down her body, paused at each breast for a time sucking her nipples into hard nubs. She sighed and whimpered in her sleep, which encouraged him further. His tongue and kisses worked down her body to the apex between her legs, which his fingers had already found warm and wet. He felt her growing more excited. He licked and lapped gently at her folds of sensitive skin as his tongue also darted inside of her. Her body responded and tightened, until she cried out his name as she climaxed. He attempted to lick some more when she pulled him up and whispered she wanted to feel him inside. He repositioned over her and slid into her wetness in one move. Joined together, he continued to slide in and out until he felt her tighten again. Her climax totally undid him and he followed her over the edge. When their heartbeats slowed, Petra looked at him with passion and love.

"Now, Jacob, this is a wonderful way to greet the day," she said with a sleepy bedroom voice. "Perhaps when I recover we can continue this oral exploration."

Jacob laughed lightly, "I agree. However, just so you know, your girl talk invaded my dreams. Two Petras was almost more than I could take and not wake up desperately hungry for you."

She raised an eyebrow, and asked, "Does that mean you want two ladies?"

"No, it means I want you. All of you."

CHAPTER 43

Let me tell you a story...

Simone closed the door behind Carlos and they both slumped onto the voluminous couch of the sitting area.

Simone asked with great concern, "So how is he? Tell me he is going to make it. I know how much you care for Juan and, well, I do too. I'm so sorry this happened. I feel like it must all be my fault. If I had just let that modeling nonsense go, none of this would have happened."

Carlos was rather stoic about the whole episode as he replied, "He will recover, though it may take a while. He is in the care of some friends.

"How could you have known how things were going to turn out? That is unfair blame you are heaping upon yourself and there is no point. Juan and I have done the same thing too. We've played the odds trying to earn a good win. Sometimes when you grab at the brass ring, you miss. So tell me, my sweet, what happened? I need all the details, please."

Simone tried to settle herself down to deliver an honest accounting of the events but stopped short. She knew what she needed to say. It was just so hard, so she took a deep breath and steeled herself.

"I should have been more honest with you, Carlos, about the meeting. I didn't tell you it was with Spencer, that man you tossed around like a rag doll that first night we met, because I was afraid you would say, 'No, you can't go because that man can't be trusted'. What Spencer described was what I had been dreaming about for so long. I just couldn't let it go by. Foolish, right? Just like the gambler who wants just one more throw of the dice. I should have let it go. That man is poisonous."

Carlos stated, "So that is why you asked for an escort like Juan rather than wait for me? Because this Spencer character would have ruined the deal if he had seen me. So Juan walked in as your escort, but he couldn't tolerate Spencer any more than I could that night we met. Only this time Spencer was carrying a pistole, and Juan had no backup. I can see how it must have gone down."

Simone had tears running down her cheeks as she explained further, "Julie, the designer, had given me some outfits to go try on, like an audition. When I came back Juan and Julie were on the floor. Spencer was screaming uncontrollably with a gun in his hand. I don't even really know what happened myself."

Carlos asked, "Then what?"

"Oh, Carlos, Juan is so brave! He was brave for both of us! He was giving me instructions that needed to be carried out like calling you, arranging transportation, and keeping all of this away from the authorities.

"The photographer, Manuel, called out that Julie was hit, and he would care for her. The next thing I knew they were gone.

"Juan suggested I grab the goods they had left behind so that at least Spencer wouldn't get them. He even mentioned that I looked pretty in the piece I had on and he was sure you would love it."

Simone stopped long enough for a couple of deep breaths. She wasn't finished and knew she had to tell him everything

"Carlos, you know the rest of that story, but what I haven't told you is why there is this story. It meant a lot to me when you told me to go and pursue that modeling dream. You have no idea how good it felt coming from a loved one. You see, that is what my Papá and I fought about before I left. He who had known me all my life, raised me by himself after mamá died, wouldn't listen to my dreams, much less encourage me to try modeling. I left home that night in Brazil to seek my fortune and become that which I was told couldn't possibly happen.

"I began using my mamá's name to ensure that what I made of myself was not based on my family's status in Brazil. My true name is Lara Bernardes and my Papá's name is Thiago Bernardes of Bernardes Ltd. I was taught that wealthy and affluent children are usually targeted for kidnapping. I used the name Simone, with no last name, to hide who I was.

"When we met, I was so used to being Simone that was what I told you without even thinking. I have been dreading this discussion with you because I didn't tell you who I really am upfront and that makes me feel deceitful."

Carlos smiled, "Simone…umm, Lara, both pretty names for a pretty lady. I figured there was more to the story and your background than you were letting me in on. Didn't you find it strange that I simply took you at your word and never asked about your family or even your last name? I figured that if you came to love me that you would tell me someday, and if you didn't…well, then it didn't matter anyway. You will always be Simone for me when we are alone and I can get used to calling you Lara Bernardes when we are in public. That is, if you still want me in your life."

A look of cold, dark fear crossed Lara's face, then she asked, "What do you mean? Why wouldn't I want you in my life? I'm the one afraid you won't want me because of not telling you the truth of who I was."

Carlos was now the one who had to come clean. He offered, "So where to begin with my secrets and deceit.

"First, the good news! My name really is Carlos Rodriguez, and I really am from Mexico. I really am in the financial world. The bad news is that all my financial advising has been to drug lords. I have been helping to smuggle drugs, precious metals, stones, hard currency, semi-priceless artwork and drug lords themselves to places of hiding. I find offshore banks to help launder their ill-gotten wealth.

"Juan and I recently got caught up with the Mexican and U.S. authorities, but they have agreed to not press charges if we help them track down the missing drug lords and their wealth. JC and Robert, plus some other anonymous associates, were part of our little moving business that I also must shut down as part of our deal to go free.

"To make the deal complete and for Juan and my safety we need to accept new identities that should help keep us out of prison should the federales change their minds. Ironic, isn't it? We are getting new identities and you are returning to your original one." Carlos studied Lara's face for a moment and then offered, "You're right, it does sound like a plot for a bad play."

Lara looked longingly at Carlos, "Oh honey, what are we going to do? Juan wounded for my foolishness, and your identity now being taken from you. Why didn't you tell me of your dark operations business?"

Carlos sighed, "Tell someone about my burdens when I know she herself is struggling with her own past? No, because I didn't want my sordid business dealings to ruin our chance together. I was looking for a way out so I could distance myself from it, but Juan made things more complicated.

"All he wants to do is fly and live on the edge. Of course, now he is recuperating from the wound. But before long we will have to reconcile, him and I, with his new career goals.

"With all that is going on in my life, you now need to reconcile with your father and I'm not sure how I will fit in with your life. It sounds like you are a rich heiress with a bright future. Unless I miss my guess, and I am just a moving man who has been on the fringe of the law way too long to be anything more than a liability in your life. Your upward social mobility will always be at risk having to explain me to others. How can there be any room in your charmed life for someone so tainted as me? When your father finds out who I am he will correctly point out my unworthiness and you know it."

She cried, "So does that mean you don't want me? Is there no chance for us at all to have happiness? Carlos, or whatever your new name is going to be, will you not give up on me? Yes, you're right. I do need to patch things up with my papá. That doesn't mean I am willing to leave you behind or push you out of my life. Please don't ask that of me because you are far too important. You have shown me love, affection, dedication to those close to you, and honor in your dealings with people. Carlos, I trust and love you and I never want you far from me. Will you give me another chance? Can we try beginning again?"

Carlos smiled softly as he took her hand, "Madam, it appears that your drink is empty. Would you permit a stranger to buy you a fresh drink for the chance to learn your name?"

Lara smiled with tears still in her eyes. "My name is Lara, young prince. May I know your name and something of your intentions?"

"Madam, you are obviously a lady of good breeding, and so I would tell you my name is Carlos. Now that you know that perhaps I would be permitted to join you in a libation so that we can talk?"

Lara was on an emotional high as she wiped the tears from her face. "Yes, Carlos, that would be wonderful, but I find myself lacking in suitable accommodations and wonder if I could impose on you to share your bed with me tonight?"

Carlos smiled knowingly, "That is a bit forward, but I do feel compelled to grant this request, as you seem to be a lady who is driven in her passion."

Lara smiled seductively, "Oh, my prince, it is because of my passion I wish to be driven!"

Lara turned into Carlos and started running her hands through his hair, brushed his neck with her nails, and kissed him with unbridled passion. He responded immediately, pulled her closer and stroked her back and sides. Their hands flowed over each other as they were each driven to touch more skin, muscles, and heat. Lara deftly unbuttoned his shirt and gained access to his chest while she continued to deepen the kiss. She persisted in her probing with her tongue to his. Her excitement mounted as he responded.

Carlos increased his touches and strokes through the folds of the silky fabric of her cover up. She ran his fingers over her legs and to her wet core where he stroked and circled in an ever-unrelenting manner. He felt her passion increase to where he knew her release was moments away. As her kiss deepened, he pressed his fingers into her and captured her release. As her climax flowed over her, she opened her eyes, which hardly focused as she murmured for more. Then she shifted to pillage his jeans and handle his manhood.

She pushed back slightly and rose with great effort, pulling him up. Quickly she released his fly and tugged his jeans down. He regretted for a moment that he had to release her in order to assist the removal of the barriers to his skin.

"Carlos, I want you. I want you now, naked, in our bed, and inside me," she implored as she pulled him to the bedroom.

She pushed him onto the bed and opened her cover up, naked before him. The passion smoldered in his eyes and equaled her determination. She climbed on top of him and impaled herself in one swift move. As their love dance continued, she begged him to touch her while she rode him with long steady strokes. As she reached her pinnacle, he held her and stroked a bit to prolong her enjoyment. She leaned over and kissed him as her hips began to rise and fall over him. As he was carried to the point of no return, her kiss deepened again with moans of pleasure in her throat. Together they rode their ecstasy with tightening pulses which exploded into fulfillment. As they lay together and waited for their breathing to slow, Lara looked at Carlos.

"I will never lose you, my prince. I love you to my soul."

CHAPTER 44

It's all in how you look at things

"Oh come on, Juan! Snap out of it, buddy," said Carlos. "Bro, the worst is over. We just have to look at our next steps and move forward. The deal was, hand over the drug dealers' locations, point to where their monies were stashed, and agree not to go back into our old line of business. They pinned everything on Phillip Johnston, we get to keep our brokerage commissions, and we get to disappear with no one hunting for us.

"I thought at least the pinning of everything on Phillip Johnston would cheer you up. I mean, think about how lively the conversation is going to be between Johnston and the drug dealers while they are bunking together at the Guantanamo Country Club waiting for their turn in the sauna. The bogus passport I planted on him went a long way to selling him as the mastermind of the operation. I know I'm ready to retire the cheese grater and pitch the aluminum foil as a liberating exercise. Don't you get it, we are clear."

Juan replied listlessly, "Yeah sure. Ok, I feel better. All I have to do now is pass my drug test and I can go to work behind the counter of a local stop and rob convenience store. Better start practicing my standard phrases, Ten dollars on pump number four, or, The feminine hygiene products are over next to the love gloves.

"Say, Carlos, you're right! I do feel better, but don't throw out the cheese grater or aluminum foil just yet. I sense that I'm not done with them yet."

Carlos offered a very sour face and all the sarcasm a person could squeeze in as he responded, "There, see? Isn't that better now?"

Juan responded, "Carlos, I'm not adaptable like you are. All I ever wanted was to be able to fly. When the airline that was going to let me fly that seven twenty-seven went into bankruptcy, my future as a legitimate pilot was doomed by the Pilot's Union for crossing a stupid picket line! If you hadn't set up our little moving business and asked me to be the chief pilot I don't know what I would have done. I liked having us work together. I liked the juice I got from flying our illegal cargo. And I liked being in business for ourselves. Now that's gone and along with it, our income. So yeah, I'm depressed. What about JC, Robert, and the On-Brothers? What are they going to do?"

Carlos cleared his throat and timidly offered, "Uh, yeah, about that. I only told the federales that we wouldn't take up our old line of business. I didn't promise to shut down the business, per se, Juan."

Juan rolled his head slightly to one side and looked at Carlos as he asked, "What do you mean, you didn't promise to shut down the business?"

Carlos sheepishly responded, "Well, you would agree that JC, Robert, and the On-Brothers were very helpful and supportive while you were holed up here. Since we needed to promise not to return to our old line of business, I gave the operations to them."

Juan studied Carlos for a few seconds and flatly asked, "You gave our business to them?"

Carlos fidgeted a little bit, "Well, they had helped to cover up the shooting from the nosey policía. We've all been like family for quite some time now."

Juan again asked, "You gave our business to them?"

"I had to promise the federales that we wouldn't go back to our old line of work of moving drugs, people, or money!"

Juan again asked flatly, "You gave our business to them? We didn't get anything?"

Carlos added a slow smile, "Bro, we do get a monthly percentage of the operation sent to our new accounts, per my agreement with JC. The federales didn't say that we couldn't take a discreet percentage of someone else's on-going business.

"I only promised that WE wouldn't return to our old line of work. So yes, we do have a modest income from JC each month, for a while."

"I guess that's something in our favor. But how can we trust him to make good on the arrangement? After all, he now has all of the operations. Here we are trying to go straight but holding out our hand for a percentage of an illegal business. How can we believe he will honor his commitment?"

"I told JC that if we don't get our cut by the nineteenth of each month that on the twentieth of that month, I will alert the federales of their activities and make sure they know where to look."

"Ok, Carlos, that cheered me up a little. I'm sorry that I am so down about this break with our past success, but it's just that I don't quite know what to do next. Anyway, before history rolls over it, thank you for taking care of us and me. I don't mean to be ungrateful, bro."

"I understand and we'll get through this together. I'm not quite sure how, but there are always possibilities, wouldn't you agree?

"So, one more question. You do want to fly again, right? I mean not as a freight dog, but as a people pilot, correct?"

Juan nodded his agreement with sadness written on his face.

"Then let me see what can be done. In the meantime, keep working out so you can pass your flight physical. Ok?"

Juan grinned, "Ok, bro."

CHAPTER 45

Dreams without actions are just dreams

"Lara! I'm so happy to see you. Please come in, I'm so glad this day has finally arrived," greeted Thiago as he reached to hug her. "Let me savor the moment lest it slips through my fingers again. I hope to always have a chance to see you and feel like your Papá, my filha!"

Lara beamed at the greeting, returned the hug and exclaimed, "Oh, Papá. It's good to see you too!" She handed him a package and explained, "I've brought you something. Please don't open it until we talk. I have many things to tell you about my adventures, my friends, and what I've learned. Oh, where to begin?"

Thiago mused, "Odd, I can't think of anything important to tell you that happened to me over the last eight months. It's as though I was in suspended animation and awoke at your arrival. Come in, sit, be comfortable, and regale me with stories and learned adventures."

They settled in the beautiful living room with its plush furniture of cream and colorful accents of flowers and modern art. Windows on two sides of the room overlooked beautiful flower gardens and ponds. Thiago placed the package on the coffee table and, though he itched to open it, he would wait.

"Papá, I was so angry after our fight and our harsh words that night. I was mostly angry because I was afraid you were right. I wanted to be a model and I wanted people to point at me and say, There she is, the famous model. But just wanting is not enough. I knew I had to act on that wanting and that I couldn't have anyone hand it to me. It's like you've always said, it's sweeter when you earn it on your own.

"I made up my mind that night to leave and either earn my destiny or fail at it. I wasn't really angry with you, Papá. I was terribly frustrated with myself, as well as very childish. This was more about proving something to myself rather than to you. I had to know if I was right or not. Do you understand, Papá? My leaving was not to lash out at you, but to see if I could realize my dream and reach my destiny."

Thiago reflected on her comments and responded, "Yes, Lara, I think I am beginning to understand. Strange though, I had not considered that maybe you had given yourself the challenge rather than delivering a hostile emotional blow to me. My vanity, I suppose."

Lara apologized, "I am sorry if I hurt you, but if I had stayed, we would have had the same argument again. As I said, part of me was afraid you might be right, so I had to go find out for myself.

"I went to Buenos Aires, Santiago, and a few other cities looking for jobs, determined to make a go in this line of work. Most of the people I petitioned were polite, even kind, when they said 'no thanks.' But I had one jerk tell me I was too fat to be a model and to leave. Me! He told me I was too fat! When I couldn't argue anymore, and was ready to cry, he must have had a change of heart and pulled out a huge stack of photos. Almost without exception the models were thinner, younger, and mostly flat chested. He spoke softly when he told me he was sorry to tell me the truth. He said three to five girls a week roll through with the same ambition and it bothered him to ruin their dreams. He told me to go home, that there is nothing but grief waiting on the path I was taking.

"I gave him a hug for his honesty, and he gave me his handkerchief to dry my eyes. He gave me one last lead and told me if I could get to Mexico there might be some modeling work there, and because it was closer to the U.S. I might have better luck. He also gave me the name of an old friend of his, Manuel, who was pretty good at photography and creating a portfolio for someone trying to break into the business. So I made my way to several key cities in Mexico, then finally Acapulco. I paid Manuel the last few dollars I had for some photos that I could use for my portfolio. I was able to do a few extras shots for some pay, but it was limited.

"Well, Papá, things didn't go much better in Acapulco than anywhere else I had tried. But I could see there was much more going on throughout the season, so I kept trying. I tried so hard, but all the premier modeling was done by thinner girls who were several years younger. Most had started as small girls and had built reputations over time.

"I was so disappointed. As the despair started to take over and my self-worth spiraled in, I became vulnerable. I had said I had done some extras shots, which I am sad to admit were nearly nude. As the despair increased, I almost accepted a really offensive job offer of adult filmmaking for a sleazy man that promised it would launch me to stardom. Then, a prince stepped into my life. He intercepted my downward spiral and recued me from a really poor decision I almost made.

"Oh, Papá, I have never met a man such as him. All he wanted to do was refresh my drink and take me to dinner. His name is Carlos Rodriguez. He was so wonderful that night and still is. In all the time we have been together, he never asked me my last name or where I came from or anything about my history. He simply took me at face value and never tried to pry into my past. When I told him of my dreams to be a model and that I had a chance at a contract, he was supportive and encouraged me to pursue the opportunity. After he told me that, I felt that I could do anything. All this time all he ever has called me is Simone. Funny, isn't it?"

Thiago asked with a gasp, "He calls you Simone? You were using your mother's name? I never considered that. How foolish of me."

"I didn't want people trying to look into my past or discover who I really was. The urban training that Oscar gave me stressed that when important or wealthy people are out of their element, they are vulnerable. So, my alias was Simone.

"Anyway, I went to meet with this fashion designer, Julie, to talk about being a model and spokesperson for her loungewear line. Julie had Manuel with her and claimed she had been looking for me based on a portfolio picture I had done earlier with Manuel. It all sounded too good to be true and of course, it was. It finally came out that Julie was actually engaged to look for Lara, and she was good enough to track me down. There is more to this portion of the story, but I'll save that for another time."

Thiago started to speak but Lara stopped him, "Papá, it is ok. I understand why you did what you did and it's fine. It actually helped lead me to an incredible revelation. At our second meeting, Julie pulled out more designs, some photo mock-ups and asked my opinion. Julie indicated she really didn't have the funding to launch a designer line of clothes, but it occurred to her that Lara Bernardes might. I was dumbfounded by her statement. I was astonished at what I was seeing, and a new thought occurred at that same moment. Modeling wasn't the end game. Selling products based on the model is the end game. My business degree finally got me to thinking more long range and told me that this was my destiny.

"Julie painted a scenario where she and her contacts will help with design consulting for a small percentage, but that I needed to build and run this company myself. She pointed out that many high-end fashion brands were coming to Brazil to have high quality, generic clothes made. Julie suggested that I should be thinking about building a brand name in my own country. Before I could digest everything I was hearing, seeing, and thinking she shoved a phone into my hand and told me to talk to you. The next thing I knew you and I are talking and a great burden was lifted from my shoulders.

"After we hung up, Julie again did all the talking. She said we had a lot of work to do to get me ready for my discussion and presentation. She had Manuel set up for the photo shoot and told me I was to model everything she brought. Both Julie and Manuel said I would look awesome. Honestly, I couldn't get a word in edgewise. She opened the door and had a makeup artist ready to fix my hair and makeup. Once that was done she instructed me to go change into the first item. I tried to speak several times, but nothing came out of my mouth."

Thiago smiled, "You? Speechless? Oh, my filha, you had me believing this yarn until you said that!"

Lara laughed, "Yes, speechless. I was so caught up in the production events that I went with the flow. And now for that package I brought you to review. Will you open it, please? This is months of work put into a portfolio mockup."

Thiago carefully opened the package, removed the contents, started flipping through the pages, and walked slowly towards the window for better light. Finally he looked up and smiled at his grown up filha.

"Lara, this is impressive! Most impressive. But I sense this is not just a souvenir photo album. What are your intentions?"

"I would like to produce this line of clothes and make Brazil a fashion destination like Milan or Paris or New York. I need to find an angel investor to help me drive this forward. Will you help me, Papá?"

Thiago brought the portfolio back to Lara and handed it to her. His face was gentle with a pasted, rueful smile, but obviously he was deep in thought for several minutes.

"You mean I don't get a chance to help you make this work? I don't get to be the angel investor?"

"You would be interested, Papá? I mean, this is a crazy scheme of mine and, well, if it fails you would be part of that failure."

Thiago laughed, "My querido filha, every one of the major lines of business of our company has either been close to bankruptcy or bought out of bankruptcy. I have no fear of failure, but I can tell you that simply putting together a photo scrapbook is not enough to get any investor interested, angel or otherwise. Where is the business plan? What is required? How long a time frame are we talking about for profitability? Where do we want to establish this new brand line? By the way, what do you want to call this new brand line? These are important considerations in order for you to take this to the next level."

"Oh, Papá, I would be proud to have you in this project. The name I would like is Destiny Fashions. You are right. I will start on the business plan right away. Thank you, Papá. Thank you for everything."

They continued to chat for some time over modest refreshments. Thiago updated her on the progress of his health and that the doctors were pleased with his progress. As Lara readied to leave, she hugged Thiago with a fieriness he recalled when she was much younger. She promised to return soon to visit, but that she would write her business plan in Acapulco.

CHAPTER 46

A diplomat thinks twice before saying nothing

Eric Pettingrübber hadn't forgotten how Otto and Quip had strong-armed him into allowing Carlos and Juan to skate on the Mexican drug dealer operation. He hesitated to re-engage the R-Group for another project. However, there simply was no other organization that delivered as effectively, especially for this issue. He reluctantly called Otto.

"Mr. Monty, how nice of you to call again! How can I help you today, kind sir?"

"Otto, thank you for taking my call. I have been asked to lend some of my resources to a new project and would like to have another Statement of Work with you added to our contract, now that the mystery of the missing Mexican drug lords and their monies has been resolved," Monty said, hoping it would remind Otto of his obligation.

Otto positively responded, "As it happens, we are finishing up on another successful project which should free up some resources. I have a few team members that I expect to complete their current activities fairly soon so they could possibly be made available, depending upon your scope requirements. What is needed for this new Statement of Work? What date would you like to set as a goal? Can you provide some details, please?"

Mr. Monty responded, "Well, actually, I am being moved up in my responsibilities. I have been given a new direct report. I would like to have her attend the meeting and deliver the briefing to you and your team. As per our agreement, I believe I am entitled to have a designee work with you and the team just as if it were me. I believe you will find her competent and efficient. She has my full confidence in this new assignment. However, I must insist that you do not discuss previous assignments or other work efforts that you have done for me in the past.

"I would appreciate her not knowing how poorly you behaved on the missing Mexican drug lords and their funds. I have had to endure several snide comments from peers of mine and had to completely resist discussing the reasons for allowing one drug dealer and two transporters to go free. Let's just say I am owed a favor sometime soon for my complicity in that matter."

Otto feigned a crestfallen attitude as he replied, "Mr. Monty, I'm sorry to hear that our discussion on overlooking the missing drug dealer and two transporters has left you with bruised feelings. Perhaps a good turn from our organization to you would help the wounds you have had to endure. Would you like us to help you find the money-laundering thief, Phillip Johnston, who has vanished from your custody?"

Stunned, Mr. Monty slowly responded, "Otto, how do you know that? I was only informed this morning, and you make it sound like old news. How did you come by this awkward piece of news?"

Otto chuckled slightly, then said, "Mr. Monty, our association with your government is based on delivery of timely information. For that to be true, we need to be scanning all communication channels for relevant information. Sometimes we don't know what to do with that reconnaissance we capture until a request is made. Sometimes we know exactly what to do with it based on its relevance.

"It seems your transportation arrangements had Johnston routed through Guantanamo on his way to your Justice Department. Due to a few missed connections, he was being held there at the same time the missing drug lords showed up for their extended visit. The next series of events are a little vague, but it appears that someone alerted the drug lords as to the identity of Johnston and his role in their incarceration.

"Quip, in an effort to help you, got a lock on Johnston's tracking watch, but it seems to be fading rather quickly, which suggests salt water got into the device, ruining the battery. His last known position would put him on a slow drift, at the same speed of the ocean currents, around the south east corner of the island.

"I can imagine the drug lords being quite upset with Johnston, perhaps uttering harsh language at him. After doing some physical harm to Johnston's person, they likely invited him to swim to his forwarding address. We suspect the reason you can't find him in the camp is because he is not in the camp but floating on the currents around Cuba. I hope this clears our debt and that your bruised ego will not trouble you going forward, sir."

Mr. Monty slowly shook his head, clearly relieved, "Otto, I am so glad we are friends again. Yes, you perceive correctly. My bruised feelings are doing much better now. Please give me a date and time for my new direct report to meet with your team at the usual facilities. Oh, and I want to recommend her suitable avatar name as Prudence, unless you object. Thank you, Otto."

Otto smiled, then said, "I will forward several dates and times within the hour to meet with Prudence. You let me know which one is suitable. Good day, Mr. Monty. And good luck with your new responsibilities."

CHAPTER 47

When you aim at nothing, what should you expect?

Lara had been on a high since she'd departed São Paulo. She believed her papá liked her ideas for a fashion line, but she needed to prove to him that she was capable of a solid business plan. Papá loved her, of that she was convinced, but she wanted the respect of her papá as much as she wanted his love.

With the five thousand-mile trip, as the crow flies, between Acapulco and São Paulo, she'd been delighted that Carlos had suggested Juan fly her. The commercial flights would have taken twice as long, as it required stops at a minimum of three different airports. The aircraft was not as luxurious as Papá's private plane, but it was efficiently comfortable. She had more personalized amenities than she'd have received on a commercial flight, which included the flowers Carlos had provided at departure. She'd visited some with Juan and enjoyed the front window view as she ate, drank, slept, and outlined her plan, as well as stretched periodically when they'd refueled.

Lara had wanted to have the plan outline completed and notated where different information components could be potentially found. Carlos had said, if all went well, that he would help if needed for her to realize her dream. She wanted him involved. He'd reassured her that it could happen. She missed him and feared that this venture would take a toll on their relationship. Lara had asked that Carlos join her, meet her Papá, and see her family home, but he'd suggested she take the first step toward reconciliation alone. He'd been right.

Juan had indicated they'd land in an hour or so. She'd put aside her outline for the time being and rested. Juan had looked very fit and seemed pleased to fly her both ways. She woke with a start as the wheels touched ground. Carlos had promised to meet the flight. Juan deplaned first and greeted Carlos.

"Hey bro, glad you could meet us. I brought her back safe and sound like I promised."

Carlos grinned, "I had no doubt that you would. How are you feeling though? Any lasting issues from your recent wounds?"

"Nope, feel great. This was exactly what I needed to return to the living. Don't know how long the juiced sensations will last, but until things get finalized, I'll take what I can get. I'd like to stick around and see the lovebird reunion, but I need to get the ground crew to perform some special maintenance." With that Juan headed toward the hanger with a smile on his face and lightness in his step.

Lara scrambled down the steps and flew into his arms. He grabbed hold and swung her around as they both laughed. He was pleased to note that she was beaming, which was exactly how he felt.

"Carlos, it went better than I expected. Papá isn't mad at me. Best of all, he wants me to hurry up with a solid business plan. I think he might back me, if the investment looks like it will provide a positive return. Will you please help me find some details, please help me review. I am so excited," she said in a rush of words and animation that suited her.

"Of course, my love. I am glad it went well. Madam, let's head toward the resort. I would like to review your plan and hear all the details. I also missed you so I cannot necessarily be held responsible for my actions when I get you alone. You look ravishing when you are happy and animated."

Lara laughed, "Oh, Carlos, I missed you too. Great idea."

They gathered her belongings and headed toward the resort. Once in their room, it was obvious that their passion gave thoughts of the business plan a back seat. Later, they ordered room service and relaxed some before they re-engaged in her recant of her trip.

"This is so nice, Carlos, to be here with you," she said as she moved a bit closer to his side.

"It is nice. However, my beautiful lover, we have work to do. That is what you wanted, right?" Carlos grinned.

"Well yes, and now no. Ok, yes for now."

For the next few hours they worked from her outline. He was impressed with the level of detail included. They researched the market areas for valid supporting numbers for the investment, which they'd agreed were paramount. Then they reviewed the manufacturing options she'd considered based in and out of Brazil, the name of the new company, operation plans, shipping, marketing and, of course, defined roles. Carlos had seen her portfolio of shots with the garments and was impressed. He was surprised at her determined focus on the business end of this business and impressed with her abilities. Lara said she intended to do some cameo shots for each season and in each line of garments, so they planned the costs for other models and locational shoots.

"Honestly, Carlos, I think that Manuel would be best if he was on the payroll as my permanent photographer. If the scheduling was done as it should be, he could choose to remain in Mexico or relocate to São Paulo. What do you think?"

"So, you are committed to a São Paulo base for operations, right? Your photo shoots would make sense in the most cost-effective location. That might be São Paulo or here or even someplace else. I agree he would have the flexibility. His cost of living is likely cheaper here, so the cost for his annual, exclusive-to-your-company salary would be likely lower."

"I think so as well. In my brief discussion with him, he had no problem with being exclusive in order to take his career to the next level."

"Agreed. I actually did some follow up conversations with him. His main requirement is that he wants a voice in the artistic presentation of the lines. If you have him located here then the technology tools needed would require video conferencing and large file transport. Because of the industry's penchant for stealing designs, the security of the systems used is also critical. Perhaps Jacob can assist with that on a contractual basis; we need to check."

"Great idea. Communications between us are also important during normal operations, as well as when new lines or seasonal shoots are occurring. Can you work on those costs for this plan? I want to keep this as a dedicated infrastructure, not necessarily hooked into Papá's infrastructure. The costs then are worse case, right?"

"You're right, Lara, and I can help get those details for you. I think you also need to consider the other people you want as dedicated staff."

"Julie wants to provide designs but is open if I find other designers I want to also use. Haddy, her assistant, was really good at fabrics, accessories, and the finished look. I know her fees at this point, and I doubt I will find anyone cheaper until I start prowling the schools to get new interns. That is also attractive as a growth area for new talent, which should make the plan more readily accepted by the board of directors."

"Good idea to highlight that detail.

"Lara, I have an idea that I'd like you to consider," he paused to insure her attention. "I think there might be a valid need in this plan to consider a full-time pilot, namely Juan. I am hearing of location shoots, transport of models perhaps, garments that need secure transport until market realization, and perhaps additional transport you might require. Could you consider this, even as a personal favor to me?"

Lara flung her arms around him and giggled, then laughed.

"Yes, what a great idea. Carlos, I have looked for ways to thank Juan, but this is truly perfect. I need him to help this succeed. I hadn't considered the transport needs of the shoots yet, so this is a solution to an as yet identified problem. Do you think he'd consider it?"

"After looking at his face when you arrived back, yeah, I think he'd jump at the chance. He is a flyboy to his very core. Thank you for the favor. I wanted him secure in his next great adventure. He seemed a bit worried about how to reinvent his life."

"Ok, then it is in the plan," she agreed with a smile. "I will make him an offer and build that cost into the plan as well. I suppose he will wish to be based wherever the pretty girls are located," she laughed.

They continued for the next few days to complete the detailed plan by day and make passionate love at night. Carlos made certain meals were delivered so they could be focused. Then she decided to pull together a professional-looking presentation to go along with it. Her papá was used to hearing and seeing an overview, then digging into the details. Lara practiced on Carlos, and he provided constructive criticism which she used or they discussed. It was a blissful few days.

"Lara, that last run through was great. The business plan itself looks amazing and the numbers are viable, if a little to the pessimistic side. When are you returning to São Paulo?"

"I knew you were going to ask me that. I am so pulled. I think I want to do it soon while it is so fresh.

"You are going with me, right? You will meet Papá and see my family home?"

Carlos slightly frowned, "I don't think you need me for this, but I will go if you still want me to."

Lara smiled, "Carlos, I want you to come with me. I will always want you."

With that, they took a break from business. She proceeded to show him how much she wanted and adored him.

CHAPTER 48

Consider me the go-to guy

"So what's up, Carlos?" Juan asked as he and all the guys converged in the room.

Carlos said, "I'm bored. Let's go find Spencer and change his status in the universe."

Juan responded, "You mean like put him on a self-help talk show? That kind of change?"

Carlos added, "Yeah, you know, no arms or legs. Mumbles a lot because all of his teeth went missing after he ate his own genitals."

JC jumped into the conversation, "I kind of favor a Nascar race scenario. We chain him to the bumper, then we see how fast and how many times we can lap the track. Of course, someone has to follow behind me to make sure we know exactly how long he lasts."

Robert then suggested, "Don't we need to be somewhere else with alibis when he changes universal status? Let me take him at five hundred meters with my long-range rifle. I should be able to discreetly slip away in the police confusion. By the time they are finished waving their arms in the air and cordoning off the area we can be halfway to Panama."

Juan argued, "If anyone is going to do him at five hundred meters, it's going to be me. Besides, I can use my antelope hunting rifle O' Death to Many. It's perfect for this kind of work. You're just a shotgun-wielding bank robber. What long range shooting expertise could you possibly do here?"

Robert mused for a moment. "I know you have some expertise at shooting a few pistoles, shotguns, rifles, and have perhaps a little over four thousand rounds of ammunition in reserve. In my world we would call you an informed novice. People who know how to re-load their own shells for everything in their inventory from an AR-15 to a long-range, single-shot fifty caliber, who owns enough handguns and semi-automatic and automatic assault guns to outfit his own platoon of thirty guys, and forty thousand rounds of ammunition in reserves, are what we call the go-to guys. Gentlemen, you should consider me your go-to guy in these matters."

Juan was little miffed at being outclassed. "Well, just because you have a larger inventory doesn't mean you're going to be the best choice. You know what they say, it's not the gun but the gunner. I'll be the lone shooter."

Robert placated, "I understand how you feel, Juan, since you are the one who was shot. Tell me what happens if you miss or he doesn't die? You won't get a second shot, and he will blab to anyone who will listen that it was you who tried to kill him. This is a one-n-done, all you get is one try shot, or they are after you for the rest of your life. Let me cover this for you. I owe you for getting me out when you did."

"I appreciate the offer, but what makes you think you can do it, one-shot-bubba?" asked Juan.

Robert reflected, "I was on the SWAT team for the police after leaving the military. We got a call one night, and I was the leader of the SWAT team that had to go in. It was a bad one.

The old man was drunk out of his mind and holding a pistol to his kid's head, screaming that he would kill him just like he had done to his wife a few minutes earlier. It was dark and I got into position on the next house.

"The duty officer keeps an open channel with the SWAT member. You don't shoot until he says to. The son of bitch was so drunk that he kept staggering around and changing the target pattern, putting the kid in the line of fire several times. The light to dark environment also made it a problem to set the shot so as to not hit the kid. I can see that kid's face today still, crying and calling for his dead mother with a pistol held to his head by something that used to be his father.

"It took everything in me to suppress my fear and then finally the question came through. 'Robert we can't get him to put the gun down. Are you in position? Can you take the shot?'

"Juan, sometimes all you can have is only one shot.

"I don't remember how long I took to respond. 'Yes, I have the target. Permission to take the shot?' Then the answer came back. 'Take the shot and save the child.'

"All was calm and quiet when I squeezed off that round. His head snapped back like I planned, ending his grip on the kid. It took me hours to stop shaking because I knew that a slight miscalculation would have taken both of them out.

"That was the last time I worked SWAT, but I know how to do it. Juan, I am the best for this role."

Everyone was quiet for a several moments. Quip, on the conference bridge, interrupted. He and Carlos had been discussing some of the satellite communications methods Carlos had employed when the other gentlemen had come into the room. Quip had stayed silent for as long as possible. Now he was engaged in the discussion and had to add his commentary.

"Gentlemen, I don't want to intrude on your thoughts and discussion here, but I will maintain that simply shooting Spencer isn't good enough. If all you do is take him out but leave the pornography business and distribution infrastructure intact, there is always someone willing to step in and take over the reins of the operation, in my experience. I would maintain that you are thinking too limited and that we need to take out everything associated with Spencer's exploitation service. Therefore, a single gunshot will not suffice, as pleasing as that effort might be. What is our plan B?"

Robert expressed, "Hmm…trying to shoot five to eight people and still get away is impractical, plus it would take too long for one shooter. We could use more shooters but then we have too many people to extract and dodge the police. We still need a single event to take them all out at once, but only one individual needs to launch the event. I've been saving some C-4 explosive for a special occasion. You know, like birthdays and christenings. I could rig the building to go once we have everyone inside and then we still only have one person to extract.

"From what you described to me, Juan, it sounded like the building was one of those concrete tilt-wall constructions. If that is the case, a few well-placed timers on the C-4 on the inside, and I think I can contain the blast within the building but disturb the infrastructure in such a way as to have the twelve-foot walls fall to the inside, one after the other. If the blast doesn't take care of them on the first round, the concrete tilt-walls should complete their transformation into blasted concrete sandwiches.

"I think I want to add some high-octane accelerant in the middle of the building just to make things interesting. If by some miracle the blast doesn't take them out and the walls don't fall exactly as expected, but instead pins them under the walls, the fire should complete the job. Yes, I think that's doable. I'll need a little time to build the devices and program the sequences. So how are we going to get everyone there and when do you want to do this?"

Carlos smiled and asked, "Sounds like an original end to our drama, but won't you need transport, spotters, and helpers to stage this so it gets pulled off in a well-choreographed manner? It will take more than simply one person to make this go smoothly, and I would like to help.

"Quip, if I can take a very nice satellite shot of the building, can you maybe help double check our charge placements for maximum containment of the blast, along with time sequencing? I am sure that Robert knows what he's doing, but if we have two great minds working the numbers, we should be able to minimize errors in cooking our blasted concrete sandwiches."

Quip agreed, "Robert, let's you and I collaborate on placement, charge size, and timing of the devices. Then I can run them through my computer for a simulation of Armageddon for this low-life bunch."

The On-Brothers chimed in as well, offering to be transport and spotters for the people inside setting the charges and the high-octane accelerant. JC offered to help deliver the semi-finished devices before the final detonators were installed.

Juan felt a little left out of all the planning and finally interjected, "Hey, I want to be in the party as well. What am I supposed to do here?"

Carlos smiled, then said, "Bro, you are providing the bait. Simone…er, Lara told me that she wanted to call a friend of hers, Rita, and offer her a job in this new clothing line enterprise that she's putting together. Lara feels she owes Rita for warning her not to get involved with Spencer, because Rita knew he preyed upon the dejected and naïve. Quip dug around and has confirmed this about Spencer in spades. We know that Rita has worked for Spencer in the past, but that he has never paid her in total what he owes.

"Lara let me listen in on her conference call where they talked about this new business plan. Rita sounded excited until she learned she would need to relocate to São Paulo or Rio de Janeiro. Lara heard Rita's tone change and asked if she needed money to make the move. When Rita didn't answer right away, Lara offered a loan to get her there if that would help. Rita bristled a little at the offer, but said she knew she could get the needed funds from Spencer.

"I thought since we hadn't been able to find Spencer, perhaps we could get him to come to us. I did a little surveillance tracking on her call. I mirrored the conversation to a computer so I could play it back to see what was going on. Spencer agreed to pay the money owed, if Rita would do that distasteful scene he wanted done for his next upcoming film. After the call from Rita, Spencer set the wheels in motion to round up all his production help two nights from now.

"So, Robert, the answer to your question is the night after tomorrow. Juan, Spencer has promised Rita he'd pay everything he owes if she completes the scenes, he wants for his porn film. For that production he will have everyone there that we want for the final event. Juan, you have to intercept Rita, then stall her long enough for the operation to conclude and not let her get hurt. Can you do that?"

Juan grinned, "I like this part of the plan! I get to schmooze with a porn star babe! Uh…can I borrow the car, dad, and a few bucks?"

"Only after you clean up your room, Juan, and take out the trash like your mother asked!"

Everyone chuckled at the banter between Juan and Carlos.

Quip asked, "I hate to ruin what seems to be a very nifty plan, but I thought that the goal was to get away clean? What do you think the authorities are going to do after you blow up part of their neighborhood? In my experience, they typically send in a bunch of folks to look for not only the cause of the blown item or blowee, but also the blower."

Carlos looked hard at the conference phone, then asked, "Why does your question sound so dirty? Every TV show I've ever seen says 'victim' and 'perpetrator.'"

Quip snickered, "Oh, ok dad, then 'victim' and 'perpetrator' need to point to someone other than us. I usually like to point to the same person."

Carlos said, "I don't follow you."

Quip explained, "If we point everything back to the bastard as, say, trying to do a little insurance fraud, then when they investigate, they find that his own stupidity got him killed and the investigation gets closed.

"Here's what we do. I have my ICA…um, computer, make some voice-synthesized calls using Spencer's voice and ask the insurance company to purchase insurance on the building and contents that will go in effect immediately. My computer makes the call look like it came from Spencer's phone. We pay immediately with a bank-to-bank transfer from Spencer's account.

"The slimy bastard has seven figures in his bank account, but he still tries to cheat everyone out of their wages. Anyway, we do everything in a hurry which should make the insurance company suspicious, so they will tag his file. As soon as Armageddon has run to completion, the police and the insurance investigators will converge on the scene and put two and two together. They will deduce that Spencer was going to do a phony insurance fire claim to collect against the loss of the building and his contents, but inadvertently blew himself to hell where he belongs.

"QED, they close the case, no insurance monies are disbursed, and the authorities don't look for anyone else. Oh, and once the case is closed, the bank will get his last will and testament, requesting all of Spencer's funds to be disbursed to the widows and orphans' homes in and around Mexico. It will, of course, have the stipulation that no plaques be displayed with his name, since his last wish was to remain anonymous."

JC and Juan at the same time questioned, "All of his money donated?"

Carlos negotiated, "Well, Quip, there will be no small expenditures here, and costs out of pocket are costs out of pocket. I would suggest that a small amount could be diverted to compensate for our expenses. That would be fair, sir."

Quip's voice through the phone was unwavering. "Which part of pedophile porno producer's stolen money do you think we could earmark as fair for your trouble in this matter?"

The faces of all the men in the room turned sour, and they looked like they wanted to wash their hands.

"Well crap!" resigned Carlos. "I just hate it when you put it like that! Fine! We are all ok with funding all of this out of our own pockets. Shall we get started with our pro bono work, gentlemen?"

Carlos and Robert were on with Quip via a conference call, as they discussed what had now become Project Armageddon.

"Carlos, thanks for that satellite location and picture of Spencer's building. One of these days soon I need you to show me how you do that. Anyway, I had my computer hunt down the building blueprints, so we can work with actual dimensions for our modeling sequence.

"So, you and Robert know, I asked ICA…er, my computer to leverage the building's construction dynamics to give us a best use case of imploding the building. The goal being that nothing could live inside based on ceiling and wall collapse just seconds before a fire races through the interior. I also included a caveat to have no collateral damage to the surrounding areas. Much like what they do when they bring down a high-rise building in a downtown city.

"Now, Robert, the program that was generated requires a lot of C-4 and appropriate detonators to be able to get the ceiling to fall first, and then collapse the walls on top of the ceiling. I have run the sequencing a couple of times and this sequence will give us the most favorable result. However, that will take the most C-4 and require a little more timing and finesse with the explosives.

"On the other hand, if we just go for bringing everything down on top of them and have a raging firestorm inside the building, we can use less."

Robert frowned, "Quip, I was given to understand that your machine would be able to give us the perfect sequencing with little or no chance for escape. What happened?"

"Well, Robert, the program also takes into consideration the unknown X-factors. The most troubling one is if the explosion is too well choreographed, using too much C-4, then Project Armageddon looks too professional to be done by Spencer the sleazeball.

"So, one of the important criteria had to be done so that it looks to the investigators that, while semi-clever in his use of C-4 and accelerant, Spencer must also have the tragic look and feel of a classic Darwin Award recipient. In other words, it can't look too good to the investigators. That said, I suggest we rule out the ceiling collapse scenario in favor of a clumsier one with a lower probability of success, but up the quantity of accelerant, which would be more consistent with an investigator's experience. How do you feel about that?"

Robert, feeling humbled, said, "Looks like from now on, you will be MY go-to guy."

CHAPTER 49

Is there something you're not telling me?

Juan easily located Rita in the bar of her hotel. Obviously, she was getting fortified for her upcoming scene. Juan grinned at the accuracy of Carlos's information. She was a beautiful woman, which made his task of delaying her hardly an arduous duty. As he slid into the bar seat next to her, he offered to buy her next drink as he ordered his own. She accepted with a smile and they introduced themselves.

Juan soon had her laughing and exchanging banter that was light and non-threatening. She seemed so young and full of life to him that he knew that getting her transplanted would bring out her best. Sometimes he appreciated his ability to make females laugh. They were so cute when they became animated.

She glanced at his watch, "Oh my goodness, I am so late. I have to go. I need to find a ride and get over to my appointment." Her angst was growing by the second.

"Go where, madam? I thought we were having a fun discussion," Juan asked as he paid the barkeep.

"Yes, we are, er...were. I had an appointment and was due there an hour ago." Rita smiled, "It has been great fun talking with you. Now I need to find a ride."

"If I might be of service, madam, my car is right outside," offered Juan.

"Great. If you can drop me off I would appreciate it."

Juan was sorry he'd missed the actual event, which should have occurred thirty minutes ago. Boom! Collapse! Barbeque! Spencer and his team of low-life associates completely eliminated. The fire trucks were returning to their stations while an investigator prowled around.

The area was cordoned off as Juan and Rita drove up.

Juan exclaimed, "Wow! What happened here? Rita, honey, was this where you were supposed to be? Do I have the wrong address?"

Rita looked on, stunned at the collapsed building and a few smoldering fires here and there.

Rita mumbled, "I'm late. I'm just too late."

Trying to help refocus Rita's dismay, Juan suggested, "That is one phrase every un-married male dreads hearing from his lady, but in this case I'm very glad you're late."

Rita sighed with a barely perceptible grin at the comment. She looked so crestfallen.

Finally Rita reflected, "I had one more distasteful gig with that prick to get what was owed to me. Now that avenue is gone, dammit! Where am I going to get the money now to go do that modeling job?"

Juan consoled, "What job are you talking about and where, honey?"

Rita yelled, "You know, it's your fault that I'm not going to be able to fly to Brazil. That bastard owed me money. I needed it to pay my own way. Now I'll miss my opportunity!"

Juan asked in a puzzled but reflective manner, "Rita honey, did you say you needed to fly to Brazil? Such an odd set of circumstances.

"Well, I should tell you that as private pilot I am asked to fly people many places. As luck would have it, my next charter flight is to, of all places, Brazil. I am sure that the people I am taking on this flight wouldn't mind if my lady were to discreetly fly with us on the charter. Since, as you have said, it's my fault that you didn't get paid, it's the least I can do to make things right."

Rita, surprised by the generous offer, asked, "In exchange for what? I just told you that I don't have any money and very little to show for my time here in Acapulco. I don't think I'm your lady either. So what are you looking to get for this favor? To take it out in trade?"

Juan displayed a staged look of hurt. "Madam, you wound me with your coarse accusation of my intentions! I would offer to be your escort until you have other arrangements. I expect you to allow me to buy you dinner and a drink. I will not ask for anything other than that. However, if you do not want the kindness of a stranger, I will understand. My intentions are as I have stated."

Rita was a little ashamed of her accusations. "Juan, I'm sorry. If the offer is legitimate, then yes, I would very much like to take you up on it, with thanks. It's just that it sounds too good to be true. Honestly, I'm tired of being hustled by handsome men."

"Handsome men! I like the sound of that! Can you get packed and be at the airport on the charter plane side at nine in the morning tomorrow? That's when we are leaving and that's when I need you on board."

Rita smiled, gave Juan a small hug, and then replied, "I can be there, Juan. I don't have much to bring, and I can get it into one small bag. Drop me off at the place where we met earlier, and I'll see you tomorrow."

Lara spotted Rita and they both fell into each other's arms in a warm embrace.

"What are you doing here?" Rita asked.

"What are you doing here, Rita? I have a charter plane going to São Paulo, and Juan said he had a surprise for me! I now know who the surprise is! Will you come with me now? The offer is still good. I still need friends and associates if this new fashion business is going to work."

"Juan said he was a pilot and would take me to Brazil even though I had no money. I was going to try and squeeze it out of Spencer, but I got to his place just after all the fire had been put out."

"Ladies, I am sure you have much to talk about. We have a long flight ahead of us so may I suggest that we all load up and be on our way? This way, please," interjected Juan.

CHAPTER 50

Speaking your peace is often contrary to going along

"Lara, please come in. I have everything set up for your presentation as you requested," said Thiago.

"And you, sir, please come in so we can be properly introduced," Thiago said to Carlos as they shook hands. "Will it just be you two for the presentation?"

Lara responded, "Yes, Papá, it will just be us two on this round."

Carlos added, "Actually, it will just be Lara doing the dog-and-pony show, but if there are any follow-on questions that I can answer, I will contribute. This is Lara's business plan. I will help her wherever I can, sir."

Lara smiled somewhat possessively. "Papá, let me introduce Carlos Rodriguez, friend, confidant, and partner. Without him in my life I would still be adrift and still looking for that which was in my own backyard all the time. Carlos, may I present Thiago Bernardes, my Papá, and other most important man in my life. Gentlemen, I hope it pleases you both to know that while there are many who are loved in my life, you two men are the most treasured people in my heart."

Thiago beamed with pride.

Carlos spoke in a reserved tone, "Mr. Bernardes, I would hope that someday I would have such a delightful, charming daughter such as yours, to introduce me the same way to her significant other. She honors me by having me here to be by her side at her company's launch. I have other items on my personal agenda to discuss with you later. I would maintain we should focus first on crafting the ideal business plan, so this dream can become a reality. I hope I have stated my position fairly?"

Thiago smiled at the support Carlos offered to Lara. "I will point out one troubling detail that we must dispense with in our interactions. It would please me if you call me Thiago, rather than Mr. Bernardes, as it makes me feel too distant. Other than that, I would agree that we should now focus on the business plan since introductions have been made."

Carlos smiled, "Thiago, thank you for helping to remove the distance between us. Lara, what can I do to help with your efforts at this point?"

Lara said, "Let me get into character here and get set up for a walk through. I want to apologize up front for this lapse into formality, but I will speak to each of you using Mr. Bernardes, or sir, for the duration of the presentation. I know this is corporate combat, and I want to treat it that way. Gentlemen, let me introduce myself, my company's product line, and our business vision for Brazilian designer fashions."

Over the next two hours, Thiago and Lara dug into the financials of the business plan after a brief marketing overview and an in-depth product review. Short-term and long-term goals were reviewed and weighed, which yielded some modifications to the overall plan. Carlos contributed now and again, but mostly he watched as Lara and Thiago communicated back and forth like two high-speed computers. Carlos was both proud of his Lara and somewhat lonely in the isolation he felt during the overall discussion. There was a growing, gnawing doubt that there wouldn't be any room in her life for him.

Thiago noticed that Carlos was increasingly withdrawn from the discussion but tactfully waited for the appropriate time to pull him in. Once the presentation, marketing overview, and financials had been covered, the opening was presented.

Thiago asked, "Well, Carlos, what do you think?"

Carlos was a little taken aback at being asked for his opinion. "Well, if everything goes to plan, then it should be fine."

Thiago studied Carlos a minute, then said, "You know, that observation ranks right up there with, no matter where you go, there you are. What I meant was, what do YOU think? Are you in the business plan? Would you be interested in investing in this as a venture capitalist? What has been overlooked? What I am asking is to help us see what we have not seen or accounted for."

Carlos hadn't expected to be put on the spot. "I am not sure what additional value I can contribute here. I have not seen a role in this business venture for me, nor has it been discussed. Thiago, my ambition here is to help get Lara teed-up for a business launch of her dream company, not to insert myself where there is no room.

"But you asked me what I think. I will tell you that the ambition and boldness of the plan make it compelling. When you add in the regional and nationalistic pride factors of establishing a fashion industry in this part of the world to compete with Milan, Paris, and New York, I will tell you, I am all for it. I see opportunity for wealth and power in an industry that can be cruel to people not prepared to face it down. I see that Lara and you are the kind of people who can survive and thrive in this type of industry. But I have to be honest here, Thiago. What I cannot see is any room for someone like me in this kind of company. It requires none of the skills which I possess."

Lara went pale, but Thiago smiled, "Now Lara, you told me he would fight for your honor, but you didn't tell me that he was an honorable warrior as well. So let me get this straight. You fight for her, support her dreams, and care for her as a human being. Here you discovered she was a rich, driven heiress, determined to build a company that you helped her work towards, but you won't put yourself into a management chair, for fear that you would appear to be a fortune hunter? Is that about it?"

Carlos fidgeted in his chair but responded evenly, "When you put it like that, yes. When I found this woman, your daughter, I was only thinking about having her at my dinner table to help me celebrate a business venture that I had created for my brother and myself.

"I have never thought about elbowing my way into her business plans for a seat at the management table, or to be offered a reward for finding a lost heiress. I have never wanted or accepted charity, as there is no honor in that approach to life. I cannot and will not ask to be included in this business plan. If there is somewhere that I can add value and earn my keep, then we have something to talk about.

"The final issue I must surface here is that my past has, shall we say, some baggage in it. Lara is aware, but this baggage can only be classified as damaging collateral for your good names should it be discovered. Perhaps I am more of a liability to your business plan that you suspect."

Thiago chuckled a little. "Lara, the man has pride as well! I knew you would choose well.

"Carlos, if you think I got to be the top of my industries with Bernardes Ltd based on a completely squeaky-clean background, then you need to cut back on your naïve medication. I have and continue to play to win, usually on my terms. So if you don't think you have that in you, then why does my daughter think you do? But I'll tell you, I can see what she sees in you. So if you can demonstrate what we can see in you, then at some point you will no longer address me as Thiago, but you will call me Papá as my son-in-law is destined to do."

Carlos nodded thoughtfully, then said, "I would rather be asked than assume I'm wanted. I love your daughter and would have her in my life, but not if it is to feel like an obligation. I put everything on the table for your daughter and am willing to stay. But I want mutual consent between us with no suspicions or hint of alternative motives. Now you know how I feel, Lara and Thiago."

Lara finally smiled again and responded, "Oh Carlos, you frighten me sometimes! Of course I want you in this business launch. Please help us make this business work. I do so need you, my prince."

Thiago smiled too, "Carlos, I feel you have honor. It is apparent you have earned my daughter's heart. Yes, please stay and help us with launching this business. Who knows, maybe after a while, I might even like you myself. Now you know how I feel."

"Thank you, sir. I believe you have this well in hand now for the upcoming meeting. It is time, Lara, that I took my leave so I can take care of some business before the meeting. Plus, I know the two of you have a need to make up for lost time. We will speak often. I know you will do your best."

Lara rushed into his arms as he opened the door. With tears in her eyes, she held onto him, trying to will him to stay with her. She knew he was still leaving. So, she held her tears in check, then stood on her toes and kissed his cheek.

"Thank you, my prince, for all your help. I love you."

CHAPTER 51

Today is the tomorrow you worried about yesterday

Carlos and Juan were very sullen as they reflected upon their upcoming identity change that had been arranged by Jacob. Even Juan didn't have much to say about the pending erasure of their born identities. The pending loss of their life-long identities had made them very somber and somewhat intimidated by the future. All that they were was to be altered from this point forward. They both felt like they were losing a part of themselves. They had agreed that this identity change was for the best. Now that it was about to happen, they were both anxious about the effect. It was Juan who broke the silence.

"You know, this whole identity change thing, I think we are making too much of it. I mean, it's not much different than getting a vasectomy. The doctor is gonna come in, snip, snip, maybe a little bit of discomfort, but in the long run I'll still be who am, bro. I will still always be Juan. Of course, I will be shooting blanks from that time going forward, but what the hell? I won't have to keep buying condoms by the gross container each week. Now I can just go with the flow and not have to stop to do the sausage stuffer routine. I betcha this identity change thing is going to be very liberating, bro."

Carlos tilted his head as he rolled it to one side to give Juan an incredulous look.

"Juan, I have known you all my life, but you never cease to amaze me with your deep philosophical approach to life-altering events. That distinct rationalizing you are capable of has a wonderfully calming effect. In short, you're like a laxative, so stop it! I don't need any more visits to the porcelain convenience."

Juan adjusted himself in his seat and with a little indignation said, "Well, you try to look on the bright side of things, and the grumpy people of the cosmos get irritable. You remember what our mother told our married cousins?

"She always said, 'Honey, you have to please your husband and there is absolutely nothing you can do about it, so you should relax, lay back and simply enjoy the event.' Yeah, Mom sure knew how to navigate through life. Since there is nothing we can do about this event, I want to try and enjoy it!"

Carlos couldn't even find words to respond. He shook his head as if he might be able to un-hear Juan's pithy musings. About this time, they alerted as someone knocked at the door and called out their names.

"Hello, it's JAC. I'm pretty sure you are both inside. May I come in?"

Carlos didn't move so Juan went to the door and opened it. His demeanor was relaxed with the exception of the wariness expressed in his eyes.

"Hi there. Are you looking for your next two victims? Come on in! We are ready for our vasectomies! Which one of us do you want to see naked?"

JAC held back a little bit as she suppressed a smile. She hesitated, uncertain of Juan's intentions, but immediately took charge.

"Ah, Juan, I see you have mended well and that your sense of humor has not been impaired at all. But let's get down to business. This may take some time for you to absorb," she stated as she turned up her smile.

Juan was a little taken with JAC and quickly recognized a verbal sparring partner who was also quite pretty. Juan liked her brilliant smile and wanted to flirt with her. Carlos, on the other hand, was sullen, unmoving, and said nothing.

JAC ventured, "Gentlemen, I know this seems difficult, but we have tried to put together some clever documents, credit cards, and background histories for both of you that should allow you to be reinvented and fly under the radar of most authorities."

As she handed each of them their specific information, she continued, "I took the liberty of cannibalizing all of your liquid assets and converted them to these debit and credit cards. Your monies are completely safe and accessible from around the world. If new monies happen to find a way into the old accounts, the transfer will automatically occur to the debit card account. Carlos, you should understand that this identity change is more sophisticated than the one that Won and Ton were going to sell you for a quarter million U.S. dollars.

"I would recommend that you destroy your old docs and begin practicing the new identities I have given you so they are natural and easily stated with conviction."

Carlos had a sour look on his face after studying the new identity.

"Why couldn't you get me an ID with a cooler sounding Mexican name? This gringo sounding name is going to stick in my throat every time I have to say who I am. What's wrong with a name like Eduardo Pizzaro, Jorge de Columbia, or Remondo al Riveraro?" complained Carlos.

Juan picked up on the absurdity of the request and chimed in, "Yeah, or even BEEF JERKY for a name!"

Juan had always tweaked and teased Carlos. On most occasions, it lightened his anger. This time it hadn't worked.

"Oh, screw you, Juan, and your fucking wit!"

Juan quickly fired back, "You wouldn't like it, and I'd just lay there while you screwed me."

Carlos couldn't bear being bested in a verbal match and responded equally fast, "Oh yeah, well at least I'd get off!"

Juan sensed one more taunt might salvage the situation so while he nodded his head up, he said, "Say, Carlos, can you show us how the guards do it?"

Carlos laughed at the absurd exchange they were having and blurted out, "Don't make me laugh when I'm pissed off, Juan!"

JAC, who had watched and listened up to this point, was resolved that now was the time to be assertive.

"Perhaps I can come back some other time when you two children can be a little more adaptive to the circumstances you find yourselves in."

She moved to take out the documents, background history, and credit cards, but Carlos grabbed her wrist to stop her. Before she could react, Juan grabbed Carlos's hand but said nothing while he and Carlos stared into each other's eyes.

"Ok, boys. As a cyber assassin I am perfectly capable of delivering a spin kick to the side of your chin with enough force for you to check into la-la land, so turn me loose."

Juan asked, his interest piqued, "Really? That I would like to see."

Juan quickly stood and assumed a defensive stance for the demonstration. Carlos had relented, and JAC was now forced into a karate demonstration with Juan. She was somewhat confused by the turn of events but refused to back down from the challenge. JAC stood and faced Juan.

Juan smiled, "Well, come on, honey. You said you could do it, so show me whatcha got. I mean if you show me yours and I like it, I might even show you mine."

Carlos shook his head at Juan and his flirtatious nature. He settled back, ready to watch the show.

JAC was uncertain of Juan's capabilities or his intentions but quickly decided not to hold anything back and sprang at Juan. JAC delivered a well-placed, chin-high frontal kick where Juan was standing. Juan moved quickly and positioned himself right beside her, as she flew through the air while he watched her technique. She landed rather ungracefully, having missed her target completely, but quickly snapped back up into a fighting stance again. Juan wrinkled his brow indicating he was giving her efforts good consideration.

"JAC, your balance is off. You should have more weight on your back foot, and you should not kick quite so slowly. It should be a fast out, then back, in case you miss. Your frontal assault was not bad, but you spent all of your time and effort looking good rather than judging if I would hold still for you to land the kick.

"It is evident that you have had some training, and I am sure that Pedro Average would have stood there waiting for impact. Now I want you to try it again but be a little more focused on the target. And remember, don't hit at me, hit through me."

JAC was dumbfounded by Juan's critique of her fighting style. She was now embarrassed and annoyed to be dressed down like she was a mere student again. This time she moved at combat speed. Juan didn't try to move but instead took her frontal kick to his chest with almost no effect. JAC again landed improperly and scrambled back to her feet. Juan stroked his neatly trimmed goatee and contemplated her efforts. The mock combat had become a teacher-student exercise, and JAC found that she accepted the role of the learner.

"Honey, I think you have been taught fairly well, but the body differences between us will tend to favor my weight over your determination. Most probably when fighting with someone closer to your weight, these moves are going to be more effective. Honestly though, forty-seven kilos against my seventy-seven kilos is not going to let you win.

"We need to practice on your landing better and have you target more nerve areas for a better delivery effect even if you are outweighed. However, I think your speed is quite good and with a little practice, we should be able to channel it and make you a formidable opponent. I know of a good gym where we can spar and workout. May I call for you tomorrow? Is there a time you would prefer, my gorgeous featherweight?"

JAC lowered her hands but was unable to articulate any useful speech. After a couple of attempts Juan grinned at her plight.

"Honey, I'm sure if you would add in some vowels to the consonants that you have obviously mastered, we should be able to communicate. Although I must admit that I am used to my females being unable to articulate when they are in the throes of passion. However, until I can get you into those throes of passion, please try adding in the missing vowels. Ok, honey?"

JAC looked at both of them and added with anger in her voice, "Ok, fine then! Pick me up at ten thirty, and I'll whip your ass!"

Juan smiled, "Whip my ass? I like the sound of that! Yes please, honey!"

CHAPTER 52

Wealth, leisure, and the velvet Elvis

"What are you doing here, Carlos? And more importantly, how did you find me? And now that I think about it, why were you even looking for me? Furthermore, I would guess that based on you being here, there is something wrong. Right?"

Carlos gave Jesus a puzzled look but said nothing.

Jesus asked, "Well?"

Carlos retorted, "Ah, well, that's a pretty deep subject for such a shallow mind. Anyway, you were having such a nice conversation with yourself, there was really nothing for me to say. I figured I'd let you continue conversing with yourself until you finished telling me my side of the discussion. Maybe I should just get some cue cards so you could continue talking and answering yourself."

Jesus smirked and chuckled while he added, "Same ol' smartass Carlos. I'd recognize that wit anywhere, or at least half of it anyway. Let's try it again, shall we? What's up, Carlos?"

"This is actually a social call, Tío, with a little bit of business to discuss. May I sit and have one of those fruity chick drinks with you? I want a parasol on my glass too. They're so cute."

Jesus looked mildly indignant and explained, "It's too early in the morning to be drinking mojitos here on the beach, so I settled for one of these fruity chick drinks or FCDs. Besides, the babe that brings these to me has to bend way over to deliver it so it doesn't spill. She gets just close enough for me to smell her terrific cleavage which sets the stage for me to hit on her. In another ten drinks we are going for it right here on the beach in my cabana."

Carlos gave Jesus a puzzled look, then asked, "How the heck do you smell cleavage?"

Jesus grinned, "With my nose right in between her tits! That's how I deliver her tip so if she won't let me get my beak in between her boobs, then there is no tip for her on that run."

Carlos shook his head as he tried to shrug off the nonsense from Jesus. He hoped it was not something that he would do in his old age.

"I forgot why I came here to see you."

"Ok kid, come on, sit down, and tell me all about it."

Carlos laughed, "Well, Jesus, I had to move your money from Cayman Bank. Here is your new account number and here are the instructions for accessing your funds from anywhere in the world. This bank is in Switzerland and has the necessary strict banking laws for your cover."

Jesus looked at the information and the total amount. He was surprised.

"This is the same amount I had in the Caymans, plus a bit of interest. You didn't take a commission as you did the first time. How come? And again, what's wrong?"

"Well, the bank was being fleeced by an employee there and because of him our whole operation got discovered by the U.S. feds. Juan and I were caught. They pressured us into working with them to hand over the five drug dealers and their cash wealth to the Mexican government who was working with the U.S. federales."

Jesus moved the parasol to one side of his glass so he could take a drink. He thoughtfully reviewed the exact words Carlos had just used.

"If memory serves you moved six drug dealers and their personal wealth. How is it that I am not part of this round-up?"

Carlos sighed, "That was the deal. They knew there were six dealers, and I told them that I wanted Juan and me out and that number six had to remain off the radar forever. They didn't like it, but I had some friends persuade them to accept my position. I couldn't leave your money there in case they changed their minds, so I moved it. Part of the deal is that Juan and I no longer work that operation we built up. They let us keep our inheritance commissions, but we can't be operators anymore. So, to honor the deal, I didn't take any commission when I moved your money."

Jesus contemplated the story from Carlos while he sipped his FCD. He wondered what Carlos had up his sleeve. Family or no family, Carlos was just like his dad and himself.

"I thought you had a nice little transport business going on for moving people who needed to run. What happened to that?"

"Juan and I turned our business interests over to our buddies, JC and Robert, for a clean break with our old lifestyle, per our agreement. Juan got shot in all of this mess. That was a wakeup call to go find something else to do with our lives."

Jesus' eyes widened as he probed, "Juan, shot? Is he ok?"

"It's a long story that I don't want to go into now, but he is recovering and doing a lot better."

"And you? How is my favorite nephew doing with all this?"

Carlos's face assumed a faraway look as he quietly said, "My future seems uncertain at this point. We can't go back to what we were doing, and I'm not sure where my new friends will take me as a contractor to them. Juan is having trouble with the loss of our business. I also have a lady who may move far away to gain her future. But other than that, everything is wondrous."

Jesus stared at the bottom of his glass and noticed it was empty. He looked around for his waitress.

Jesus mumbled, "Well, I'm now ready for my next FCD, so where is the waitress with her nice girls?

"Carlos, you are a smart guy with what sounds like new opportunities. I might suggest that you run with it and see where it goes. You might like your new lifestyle. You might enjoy this lady and find your new life together. It could happen."

"Oh, that reminds me, Tío. We need to get you a new identity before anything else happens. Just before I was forced to give up our moving business, I made a connection with an identity-laundering group that we can use to outfit you with a new identity. JC and Robert will be laundering IDs for people, and I want you to have a new identity in case either the U.S. or the Mexican governments come looking for you."

"Which reminds me, nephew, where did you stash the hard assets that we couldn't move to the Cayman Bank? You know, the gold, silver, diamonds, and artwork of mine. Specifically, my velvet Elvis painting"

Carlos gave Jesus a disdainful look. "I have all your precious mementos hidden in an underground vault, along with a few other holdings that no one seems to be able to find. But maybe you can tell me what's so special about a velvet Elvis painting? You're not counting that as artwork, are you?"

"It is artwork but, more importantly, it has sentimental value. Besides, I always liked Elvis."

Carlos rolled his eyes. "Oh alright, have it your way. It's artwork of inestimable value and in high demand. Should I contact one of the online auction houses to start the bidding at ten pesos?"

Jesus was distracted. "Oh good, here come the girls with my FCD. I signaled to bring you one too.

"You need to relax and accept this new business that you are going to do. It also sounds like you need to if work things through with your new lady. You know, it occurs to me that I need to stay mobile for a while. With a new identity, it might be awhile before I can get back to pick up my hard assets. If you don't see me in, say, six months, why don't you start charging me a storage fee? Now, if I am unreachable, then start selling off some of the gold or jewels to cover those storage fees. Will that be agreeable?"

Carlos studied his uncle and the offer for a few seconds, then firmly stated, "Only if I can send the velvet Elvis to you right away. I am afraid that all the affluence that it would provide from a frenzied bidding match would ruin my moral fiber and have me expire from advanced vertigo from some roulette wheel."

Jesus chuckled, "Same ol' Carlos. Always the smartass. Yes, send me the velvet Elvis, and I'll take it with me when I get my new identity. Deal?"

Carlos accepted the FCD from the waitress and watched as Jesus accepted his drink and politely tipped her fifty U.S. dollars. Carlos tilted his head to one side as he puzzled over the gentlemanly way Jesus dealt with the attractive waitress.

"You don't think I'm as crude as I let you think, do you?"

They toasted each other's health.

CHAPTER 53

Pulling a rabbit
out of the old hat trick

"Mr. Bernardes, there is a call holding for you from board director Jorge Genio, and he stressed that it was urgent," said the secretary.

Thiago picked up the phone. "Jorge, what a surprise. Do we have a pressing issue or is it something that can wait until our regular board of directors meeting?"

Jorge responded, "Thiago, you know that I don't call with trivial issues and ask to be put right through to you without good cause. I have it on good authority that our banker, economist Arminio Safra, is putting together a consortium of malleable directors and private investors with the intention of staging a proxy fight. The reason I know this is that I was among those approached to see what my position would be on your successor."

Thiago sighed, "Arminio, the loose cannon, who acts like this is his company. It is hard to believe that his humble beginnings and our collective mentoring over this past year have only made him an adversary rather than a trusted advisor. Well, Jorge, how do you feel about this coming proxy fight? May I count on your support or has his agitating given you cause for concern?"

Jorge choose his words carefully and cautiously. "Thiago, I have never forgotten the opportunities that you gave me and I have always supported you. I must confess these last eight months have been awkward for everyone. We have noticed a lack of focus for the business. Without knowing what is on your mind or your intentions for the future of the company, you have inadvertently provided ammunition to that unsavory individual to wage a proxy battle. I don't want to side with him, but if he engineers a coup d'état, those of us loyal to you will be cast out. The succession issue is actually a cover up to bring in more of his loyal followers so he can wrestle control of the company."

Thiago mused over what he heard, then asked, "Jorge, what are board members saying about that idea we floated of having Wolfgang join our board?"

"Permission to speak candidly, sir?"

"Yes, of course, Jorge."

"Thiago, no one liked the idea of Wolfgang joining the board. That's what sent Arminio into overdrive for his own agenda. I must admit that I found the recommended individual a poor idea myself. Wolfgang is European, so even though he has the expertise, he is not from our country or familiar with our culture. I must report that you will find no support for your nomination should you try to pursue it."

"I see and I appreciate your candor. Then may I have your recommendation as to a proper course of action?"

"Thiago, I personally want someone from Brazil in the open director role. Frankly, I don't understand why it isn't Lara. With her in the director role, the succession discussion simply goes away, and we can all return to business issues rather than back room politics. However, I must tell you that while I and many of the other board members would find favor with such a proposal, Arminio will not.

"There are so many things that he takes personally but just the mention of her name makes him noticeably bristle. He has even tried to have us believe that she has left the country with no intention of returning. He paints a very bleak picture of the company's future with no blood line successor and you…uh, uninterested in the company's health. So, with all that, I would recommend that you set the agenda discussion topics and pull a rabbit out of the hat to make the boardroom meeting flow in your favor and discount Arminio's scheming."

"Jorge, as usual you give excellent counsel in these matters. I will set up the agenda accordingly and go look for my old trick hat per your recommendation. Now, sir, if you will excuse me, I have much to do."

After the call with Jorge had ended, Thiago called Otto.

Otto answered on the first ring. "Thiago, you must have anticipated our need to talk. I have the background material we talked about on the board members and, candidly, we have some surprises in our findings. I will send it all encrypted as usual for our communications, and while there are some blemishes here and there one name does seem to rise to the top for your consideration. It will probably come as no surprise that it is he who is leading the proxy battle as well. We have taken no action, only reconnaissance per your request."

Thiago responded grimly, "Well, this board meeting is going to be festive! I'm actually looking forward to the combat about to take place. You will convey my thanks to Wolfgang for the diversion you two helped to orchestrate. The diversion has helped to set the stage for Lara's return.

"Otto, knowing your capacity for curiosity, I would like you to be a fly on the wall. I am confident that I would not be able to stop your remarkable resources from listening in and since I will need recorded evidence from the planned event, may I count on your clandestine audio surveillance of the boardroom meeting? Once you have captured the audio, can you put it in an accessible location for me in an encrypted mode? I would be most grateful for your efforts, kind sir."

Otto grinned, "Why Thiago, I am shocked and wounded that an esteemed colleague and friend would ask for something such as this from me and my organization. You know perfectly well that all of your boardroom meetings are already being recorded and stored in a secure area under the control of the comptroller. We could not possibly be expected to do a second recording to compare to the first highly secured recording to see if it had been tampered with. Certainly your financial economist has high ethical standards that would preclude him from altering a taped recording. So my organization and I must decline such a request for this type of covert operation. I trust you will understand my reasoning, kind sir."

Thiago looked down at his personal cell phone to read the text from Otto that said "Consider it done."

"You're right as usual, Otto. Let me withdraw the request and pretend this conversation never happened. Good day, sir."

CHAPTER 54

It must be that male bonding thing

Carlos was out sitting by the pool after he'd returned to the resort in Acapulco. He was proud of all that his Lara had accomplished with her business plan and the steps toward rebuilding the relationship with her father. He was pleased that her business would require services from Juan. Juan had been so delighted when Lara had asked for his help in that regard and told him he could be located wherever he wished as long as he met the scheduling requirements. Juan would essentially be on a retainer.

He sipped his wine and thought about the many problems he had solved and smiled. That the annuity from JC would at least keep him in a good wine now and again. The new identity would keep him out of jail if he stayed on the straight and narrow.

As he looked out toward the ocean, Carlos thought about how important Lara was to him. She was like no other woman he'd ever met. He wanted to continue their relationship, but he felt he couldn't work in her business, based on its requirements versus his skills. True, he could learn almost anything, but honestly, it didn't hold any appeal. He was so absorbed in his thoughts that he failed to see Jacob approach the table.

"Hey man, mind if I join you. Petra is busy trying to get everything organized to pack and suggested I find someplace out of her way."

"Jacob, how interesting that you would be here now. Please join me and fill me in on your plans," Carlos said with a smile while he signaled for the waitress to bring another wine.

The drink arrived moments later, and they sat quietly for several minutes. Jacob recalled their many conversations in the Caymans and knew that Carlos had a need to take care of everyone. When they'd discussed the possible terms required to square things with the U.S. array of alphabet-soup agencies, Carlos had negotiated with honor. Jacob respected that Carlos felt inclined to take care of family. Though he'd shared that piece of data with his team, Carlos's personal statements would remain confidential to their team. He also knew that Carlos was a bit like a fish out of water at this point.

"So, we are still on for this afternoon for the meeting with the Bernardes Board of Directors, right? I really need your expertise on the satellite element, Carlos."

"Yes. Since Petra would like her own time, we can do it from my suite if that is agreeable."

Jacob chuckled. "Man, I was hoping you'd say that. I have my laptop with me.

"How was the meeting with Lara's father?"

Carlos looked a bit grim. "It was a good meeting overall. I like the man and I love his daughter. However, they are much wealthier than I'd imagined. She seems to fit in there perfectly. It is a very different lifestyle than I've ever lived. She doesn't seem to notice it though. Almost like it doesn't affect her. Hard to explain, that part of it, but the business venture is everything to her right now."

"Well, I think that is good. The girl struggled to find herself and almost made some major bad choices. You have kept her centered. No small feat with a strong-willed female. She obviously wants you in her life. She's phoned Petra half a dozen times asking if you are really ok, saying how much she misses you and so forth. Petra has reminded her that you are a man that makes his own decisions."

Carlos smiled. "I think Lara and I will be in it for the long haul, at least I hope so. I just cannot be a part of that business. I bring nothing to it, and I would get bored. Bored for me is a bad thing."

"You know, Carlos, we talked about some of this in the Caymans. You are a very intelligent man. You pick up things very quickly. You have a great eye for finance, and that portion of the negotiations for moving your uncle's funds into their present vehicle was agreed to by folks that have worked that field far longer than you've been around.

"I think though you have more fun with the satellite hook ups. From what you said you took some random training opportunity then maximized it further than anyone else. Andrew, who has been in that field for years, was totally amazed at what you accomplished. When I think about your doing that without the background he has, I have to agree that in this area you are brilliant," Jacob offered with all candor.

"Coming from you, the penetration-tester par excellence, that is indeed high praise. I do honestly enjoy the whole realm of telecommunications. I think the meshing of the older technology of telecommunications with what can happen in the future is fascinating. It is like putting together a five thousand-piece puzzle of a picture of hundreds of carrier pigeons with only subtle differences to make the overall picture come together. Putting that into the context of global communications is mind boggling as well."

"I couldn't agree with you more. I have studied, as you know, technology and programming and the learning curve is still straight up to stay on top and ahead of the technology changes. Added to that is the human factor with its random needs and desires. It is a never-ending challenge."

Carlos thought about that a moment and then started his slow smile that was reminiscent of the confident Carlos that Jacob had first met.

"Challenge. Exactly! That is what I must have to feel right. Whatever I take on I must be able to freely explore it, figure it out, test it, and evolve it. I just don't quite fit into the normal corporate mentality. That is the underlying problem of working with Thiago and Lara."

"Then go find what you want to work in. Explore the possibilities and then negotiate how you want to have it to meet your personal goals. I think it is perhaps closer than you suspect right now."

"Perhaps you are right, my friend. I don't say that lightly, Jacob. I don't have many I call friends."

"Neither do I. I am honored, my friend. We need to get a move on though if we are to get connected for this meeting in time," added Jacob as he rose.

"Agreed. And I appreciate your thoughts. I surely do."

CHAPTER 55

If at first you don't succeed, you're about average

Otto and Quip were in the control center in Zürich. Quip placed a secured conference call connection to join Andrew, Carlos, and Jacob and secure the recording.

Andy said, "Are you sure this is ok to do? Is this what you people do when you are not playing with computers?"

Quip rolled his eyes and said, "Just for the record, we don't play with computers, we leverage them in determining or predicting future outcomes. Now are you going to help or not?"

"Well, young feller, I just got saddled with a new assistant that I am supposed to train and mentor so I can have some time off. I don't want this green bean being led astray by the likes of you and cost me my vacation."

"Now, Andy, how can you say that after all the luncheons we have brought you to? I might admit that this is a little unorthodox, but this is perfectly ok for you and your helper. You can trust me, Andy."

Before Andy could respond, the most seductive, southern belle drawl said, "Why, Dr. Quip, I must protest my categorization as only a lowly helper in the telecom world! I am an accomplished unified communications specialist, well versed in multiple modes of communications from instant messaging all the way to high definition audio and video.

"Dr. Quip, my name is Eilla-Zan. I would prefer that you consider me Andy's protégé. I promise you, Dr. Quip, that I will be able to deliver a positive contribution to your team's efforts and that I am the epitome of discretion in all sensitive operations. Will you accept my petition to be called Eilla-Zan, the protégé?"

Quip was mentally derailed at hearing that Georgia peach accent dress him down for a belittling comment, and at the same time being called Dr. Quip. For a male that usually only ran the gambit of emotions from A to B, being high tech and surly to just surly, he had gone way past his normal comfort zone with this engaging voice. He struggled to shake off the effect Eilla-Zan had unexpectedly had on him. He decided introductions were definitely in order.

Quip asked, "…uh so, gentlemen, and madam, is everyone online now?"

Looking at each other with big grins on their faces, Jacob and Carlos agreed in unison, "Yes sir, Dr. Quip."

Carlos smiled and added, "Are you ready to share bits and bytes, Dr. Quip?"

Quip rolled his eyes at the subtle teasing being received from Carlos and Jacob. While he was resentful of being called Dr. Quip by them, it was strangely engaging when it came from Andy's protégé. The funny part of the whole conversation was that he had the degree to prove the title. He hated coincidences.

"Quip, I don't rightly recall you being a doctor," Andy expressed. "I apologize for not using your full title in our conversations. So let me make amends by asking, are you ready to launch this operation, Dr. Quip?"

Quip gave an incredulous stare at Otto.

Otto chimed in, "Yes, Dr. Quip, are you ready? The meeting is about to start."

As usual, Andy, and now his protégé, had spun up Quip but this time in a larger audience that made his feelings of mortification even more acute. He took a second to get into character.

"Dr. Quip here! Ok, let's get started and no flub ups, madam and gentlemen. We will run this recording activity at our facility using your links.

"Andy, you and your PROTÉGÉ will thread your way through their onsite phone system to connect to the conference phone in the boardroom and open up a one-way recording path from that room that has been established by Jacob.

"Carlos, you will be leveraging the satellite link to move the conversation signals between the ground and satellites that will get it to us here in the operations area.

"Does everyone understand their roles in this exercise?"

Eilla-Zan suggested, "Just one thing, Dr. Quip. In Georgia we don't say flub up, we always say screwed the pooch."

Andy jumped in with a disapproving tone, "Now Eilla-Zan, we've talked about this. These folks are gentlemen of good breeding. I, for one, do not want to have to explain your vulgarities to them, so please curb your use of overly colorful analogies. Are we clear, young lady?"

Otto struggled to keep from laughing. He couldn't make up his mind if it was because Andy was trying to defend Quip's honor or if it was because Eilla-Zan got Quip to blush beet red. Carlos and Jacob were noticeably quiet, which suggested they had muted their line.

Eilla-Zan acknowledged, "Gentlemen, please accept my humble apologies. I will declare my intentions to conduct my speech in accordance with the high social norms you gentlemen have set."

Otto prompted, "Dr. Quip, I believe we are at zero hour. Shall we begin?"

Quip again forced himself back into character and stated, "Yes of course. Let's begin."

Everyone was finally seated in the corporate boardroom except Lara. Thiago wanted a dramatic entrance and a crisp presentation for maximum effect. The skimpy agenda he published the night before had left everyone wondering if he was going to try and postpone the board meeting again.

Thiago took the lead as usual in opening the meeting. He distributed his agenda to try to preempt Arminio's pending proxy fight. He carefully left topics open and vague so that he could bring up his topics with proper dramatic effect. Arminio didn't allow him that chance and promptly commandeered the meeting as he tore up the agenda in front of all the members.

"Thiago, I do not intend this to be another wasted board meeting," began Arminio. "This company cannot afford to spend time with vague discussions and lost opportunities for filling the open director's seat on this board. I speak for many on this board and while we respect what you have done for this company up until now, we need to put someone on the board that will bring some energy that will help move the company forward. You floated a candidate that no one liked.

"We still have no successor, so we believe our best course of action is to take matters upon ourselves and do what you seem incapable of doing. I want to nominate Pedro Cervanez to the open seat for the board's consideration. He is Brazilian by birth and is an eager leader who will bring direction and purpose going forward. I don't even want to entertain the European you suggested we look at that is associated with the Ronnie, Ltd. financial firm. That recommendation is a little too self-serving for everyone's taste, for this is a Brazilian corporation."

Thiago smiled knowingly. "I am pleased to hear you prefer a native-born Brazilian for the open director's position. I have such a candidate in mind and since you are anxious to get to this portion of the meeting, let me introduce Lara Bernardes as my board member candidate. I would highly recommend that the board select my candidate not only because she is Brazilian born, but also because of her extensive working knowledge of the corporation. She has served in many roles in this company and has a vision that is aligned with progressing the business forward.

"Allow me to add that she is to be brought in to also become my successor, which should alleviate the anxiety of succession should anything happen to me."

Lara entered the room in very businesslike attire, carrying her PC and her presentation. She smiled at each of the board members as she quickly connected her PC to the presentation screen in the room. While the majority of the board members smiled and nodded in approval, Arminio was stunned.

Trying to derail what was apparently going to be an easy selection for the board to make, Arminio sneered, "So Lara has finally surfaced after all these months. Well, a lot has happened in all the months you have been gone. I personally doubt the conviction of anyone who would run off and simply leave things hanging, while the rest of us try to keep the corporation running. So tell us, Ms. Lara, what was so important that you couldn't be bothered with coming into work?"

Thiago strained to hold his temper at the attack stance from Arminio, then placated, "An excellent question, Arminio!

"Gentlemen, Lara has been on assignment for this corporation to find its next product line and to research it thoroughly before delivering her results. But rather than me put it to you, let our new board member make that delivery. Lara, will you go ahead with your presentation of findings, please?"

Lara had rehearsed this presentation with Thiago several times, getting it down to crisp bullet points along with hard facts and figures. Lara knew that boards of directors for large corporations had so many sales pitches tossed at them that they wouldn't focus any longer than twelve minutes. Her presentation was just exactly that long. Lara knew that the board would simply rubber stamp the business plan for a Brazilian line of clothes because her Papá said to. She wanted the board to agree that this was not only a good business proposition, but also potentially a source of national pride.

Lara opened, "Gentlemen, for the last several months we have looked at building not just a clothing product line centered here in Brazil but driving our country to be a fashion destination alongside the likes of Milan, Paris, and New York. Many named labels pay a lot for our outstanding workmanship in garment manufacturing here in Brazil.

"What if that was our label? What if fashion design starts here and flows outward? Let me show you some Brazilian examples of what our first introduction of loungewear can be, to be followed by other Brazilian designer clothes that leverage our clothing manufacturing capabilities. This is Destiny Fashions of Brazil. This corporation is going to help create a fashion destination for men and women. I propose, with all my research in this area, I will be your first choice to head up this new venture. Our use of high-fashion design will cut time to market design issues and our labor cost advantage will bring a high profit margin to help offset some of our cyclic product lines of business. It will also highlight the distinctive Brazilian style and beauty that is present in our people and respected by the world. Fashion manufacturing is a ruthless business, but what business isn't?"

The perfectly choreographed slide presentation was slick and the numbers were believable. All of which was completed in exactly twelve minutes. The only person that had not nodded with approval was Arminio. He clapped his hands slowly, with a sneer present on his face.

He spoke contemptuously, "So you want us to fund daddy's little girl's pet project so you will sit on the board of directors? Is this what I'm hearing? This is a joke, right? We are a mining, shipping, and energy company! Where does that fit in with your fashion design company?"

Lara smiled, "I was hoping you would ask that question. Our energy company is already creating some new synthetics, of which I am sure you are aware. They have taken patents out on specialized recycling technologies to make this possible. I am sure you are aware these synthetics are already being incorporated into some fabrics and clothing lines in our competitor countries.

"Our shipping business is at sixty-five percent capacity for the ore we mine, so we have unused capacity that can be leveraged for moving goods to other markets. You ask how our existing business works with fashion manufacturing. I would ask, how does it not?"

Arminio dismissed, "This is too ridiculous to even consider. Young lady, why don't you try selling this to someone who is interested in what you are selling?"

Lara again smiled like a cat that had swallowed a canary. "You mean like the time you tried to corner me at my house under the pretense of waiting for my father? You remember what I told you then when you tried to grab me? I told you to try and sell yourself to someone who might be interested in what you had to sell. Do you remember that exchange when you lunged at me with your intention of forcing yourself on me? Or did the defense training that my head of security taught me cloud your memory? I had to ask Oscar to load you into your car and made him promise to keep the incident classified.

"However, since you have made this an adversarial event, I would have the board of directors know that I will be a formidable opponent to any and all that threaten my family or my corporation."

The strong exchange between Arminio and Lara left no doubt as to how the board would vote. Lara sensed that her hand was successfully played. By the looks of the rest of the board, Arminio would not be around to muddy any more meetings.

"Gentlemen, I thank you for your valuable time today, and I am prepared to withdraw unless you have further questions for me on this business venture," Lara finished.

Thiago beamed with pride, then said, "I believe we have heard all we need at this time. Thank you, Lara. If you will excuse us for a few minutes we have some items to finalize."

After Lara left, Thiago addressed the board, "I trust you gentlemen are interested in the proposed business venture and are agreeable to having Lara join the board of directors, particularly since Arminio is tendering his resignation to go in search of new business opportunities."

The board members all turned their gaze to Arminio and watched his jaw drop open. He closed his mouth to reel in his surprised look and steeled himself for what promised to be a fight for his survival.

Arminio then offered, "I am unsure of your information sources, but I can assure this board that…"

Thiago deliberately cut Arminio off before he could go any further.

Thiago explained, "You do recall that this meeting marks the one-year anniversary of your being allowed to join our Board of Directors. All junior members are evaluated at their one-year mark. The senior members grade the usefulness and contributions of a junior member to see if they should be retained.

"It is with some regret that this board will not be asking you to stay in this role. We felt it fair to give you the opportunity to resign so that when this becomes public knowledge you can indicate with a clear conscience that you left our organization to pursue other interests. We will maintain the same story so as not to injure your business reputation."

Arminio barely contained his anger as he emphasized, "I already have half the board members on my side. This ridiculous attempt to force me out will only help me galvanize the remaining votes I need to throw your ass out! Don't think I'm going to give you my resignation when it is you who is on the way out!"

Thiago's face indicated a slight frown and he sighed as he renounced, "I had hoped we could have kept this on a more professional level. Since you seem reluctant to participate that way, I guess we will have to do it the hard way."

Thiago reached into his briefcase and brought out enough thin dossiers to give one to each board member. As each one opened and read the dossier, they, without exception, cast offended looks at Arminio. Arminio, who was also given a copy to read, could not raise his eyes from the document's content to face the board members.

Thiago offered some sympathy to Arminio, "The ethics and moral standards agreement we all signed to be on this board states that you will set high standards for others to follow. The insider trading you have done by betting against the stock price is clearly a breach of your fiduciary responsibility as a board member. You have been selling corporate shares short for some time. Your accomplice is poised to buy up those shares at depressed prices because you think you will win the proxy battle and the stock will soar, profiting you greatly.

"It appears that your accomplice is the same person that you are trying to have nominated to this Board of Directors, which is also a conflict of interest. We have also found some accounting … irregularities that prompted us to search your corporate computer to get to the bottom of these allegations. The monitoring of your corporate computer has unhappily uncovered the fact that you also spend a great deal of time on websites that are not business related, such as online gambling and pornography sites.

"And for the final show of how you dishonor this corporation, we now have several sexual harassment charges being leveled against you based on your unwanted advancements to several young employees, both male and female. I should have thought you would have learned your lesson when Lara demonstrated what she considered her response to unacceptable behavior from a bully.

"Now, let me ask you again. Did you want to resign, or do you want to refute these charges?"

Arminio realized there was no recovering from the overwhelming case presented by Thiago. He looked at each member of the board with animosity in his eyes and a fatalistic smile.

"Gentlemen of the board, I wish to give my resignation so that I may pursue other business interests. I have no intention of refuting these charges."

Thiago smiled at his inside joke as he went to the door, opened it, and allowed the police to enter.

He pointed at Arminio and stated, "Gentlemen, this is the individual you need to charge for the crimes he has committed. Insider trading, theft of corporate property, and sexual harassment of company employees. We wish to pursue these matters to the fullest extent of the law."

Arminio was dumbfounded. Finally, as the handcuffs were secured, reality sunk in as he reasoned, "What are you doing? I said I resign and that I wouldn't fight the charges! You lied to me!"

Thiago smiled again and advised, "Actually, you misspoke when you said you wouldn't fight the charges, which basically means that you admit your guilt to the allegations and resigning was just a formality."

Thiago leaned over to one of the conference phone speakers and said, "Thanks all for capturing all of the audio for this meeting. Please see that it is forwarded to our corporate attorneys for use in having this degenerate put away for a long time."

The lights on the speakers all flashed twice in acknowledgement.

After the police bundled Arminio out of the room, Thiago addressed the board, "I am sorry to have had that episode ruin what is normally a very sedate meeting. I feel it is important to know who you can trust and who is untrustworthy in our corporate environment. Wouldn't you gentlemen agree?"

Some of the board members were perspiring after the confrontation and some even showed a little fear, but they all appeared to be in agreement with Thiago, lest he pull out more dossiers for discussion.

Thiago returned to a smiling, friendly mode and cheerfully asked. "Now how about our vote on the business proposal and Lara as our board member candidate? Unless someone feels a need for more discussion, I will begin the voting with a 'yes' for both options."

After the ritualistic execution of Arminio, all the board members were very receptive, even enthusiastic in their support of the new business line and Lara joining the board.

Thiago was gratified by the positive vote. "Thank you, gentlemen. As a show of good faith, I expect that you all will want to purchase stock in our company, particularly since we had a rogue director try to drive the price down. With our new business coming online soon, it seems fitting that you all own more shares in this company than you currently do. Wouldn't you all agree?

"Besides, a show of good faith from the board will help increase the price and at the same time add to the losses of those who would short-sell our stock. Oh, and don't forget to do the proper registration prior to your purchase so everything is on the up and up. Good day, gentlemen."

CHAPTER 56

To assemble a complex puzzle you must have all the pieces

It was a good thing that the whole team was back to meet Mr. Monty's replacement, thought Otto. She was not quite what he was expecting, he silently mused. He had to admit the avatar name that Monty had picked fit perfectly.

Prudence said, "Otto, thank you for having your people transport me to your facilities. I am looking forward to briefing your people on the work we need done.

"I was told that you and your team require an avatar name for all communication and in real time meetings for security purposes. My supervisor did not say how my avatar name would be generated, so it occurred to me that if I offered one up, then our opening conversations could begin quickly and efficiently. Therefore, I request that my avatar name be Lady Stardust from this point on."

By this time the other team members had gathered to greet Prudence and had carefully assessed her physical characteristics and some of her speech patterns. Prudence, real name Arletta Krumhunter, was carefully dressed in a conservative grey blazer and skirt. She was wearing heavy brown-rimmed glasses that rode too low on her nose, which made everyone suspect that she would peer over the top while speaking. Her hair, a mousey brown, was worn in a severe bun, almost too tight across her eyes. At 1.65 meters, she was an easy height to talk with and probably had a nice figure eighteen kilos ago.

The R-Group team members, including Otto, all conducted discreet, searching looks to each other to reassure themselves that Prudence would never be mistaken for an exotic topless dancer named Lady Stardust.

In fact, Prudence's social skills were such that Quip speculated that she likely managed to alienate her prom night escort to the point that he left her at the one and only dance she had ever attended, and went home by himself. Her dad had likely been prudent not to pay him the promised fee until after he dropped her off at her house.

As usual, it was Quip who spoke first. "Madam, apologies, but we have already assigned your avatar name as Prudence. It is custom around here not to change it for fear of bad luck."

The group members all mumbled Prudence loud enough to hear, almost as an incantation to ward off an evil presence. Prudence was disappointed that her first choice for an avatar name was not accepted, but she quickly adapted and introduced herself as Prudence to the team. The team members, all visibly relieved that they had thwarted whoever had played this cruel hoax on Prudence, in turn introduced themselves. Otto escorted Prudence to the meeting room with Quip, Raja, played by Jacob, and Sasha, played by Petra, following close behind.

Once everyone was seated, Prudence began, "I hope our business relationship will move forward comfortably and that my being Mr. Monty's replacement will not be an awkward transition for you.

"I was given very little background on previous assignments with your organization, but I was told that was for my benefit. The phrases, don't know, can't tell, and don't remember, shrouds all of your past activities with my government. So in many ways, this is a fresh start for all of us. With no history to draw upon, shall we proceed to create some?"

Again, Quip quickly responded, "That does sound prudent to me."

Otto glared at Quip so he would settle down to business, but the glib comment was lost on Prudence.

Prudence launched into her briefing. "Actually, Otto, Sasha, Raja, and Quip, I have two assignments. The second one was only handed to me literally as I was getting on the private jet. So let me cover off on the main objective first and then we will discuss the secondary one last."

Otto interjected, "Excuse me, Prudence, but if the second assignment is smaller in effort it might be easier to cover it before lunch. That would then leave us the afternoon to cover the more complex project you have in mind. Your thoughts, madam?"

Prudence said, "Yes, and quite right, Otto.

"So this secondary task is a more modest assignment in that it involves an incident that happened a few weeks ago. It cost us in our relationship with Mexico. A Mexican operative was lost. She was to be protected as a part of our joint government effort to prosecute a long-running pornography ring. Our details are very sketchy. What we do know is that the Mexican government believes that their operative on the inside was lost when a building was blown up and incinerated a group of questionable and distasteful individuals involved in child and adult pornography. The Mexican government is furious at the thought of having the CIA operating in their country unbeknownst to them.

"We want to get to the bottom of this issue and prove that the CIA was not involved. The internal reviews do indicate that the CIA wasn't involved, but an outside review might find the actual culprits. It seems a trivial matter, but the events surrounding the explosion and subsequent fire that killed a pornography producer and his crew are such that our curiosity has been piqued."

Quip's breathing started to accelerate, and he felt lightheaded at hearing the information. Quip innocently asked, "So you seem to be saying that this was not an accident? May we know why you believe it not to be an accident?"

Prudence offered, "Well, the C-4 residue found in key places in the building rubble suggests a professional effort. Local fire team authorities initially thought it was an insurance scam gone wrong by the owner, Spencer something or other. However, when the Mexicans found the C-4 residue, they naturally suspected that it was a CIA operation and we clearly know that it was not. I can tell you, coming from that organization, they are funny about being blamed for things they didn't do. The CIA is usually blamed, rightly so for many things, so that when it's not their fault they become tenacious at preserving at least a little bit of a good name.

"For this assignment, we need to know where the C-4 came from and who orchestrated the staged accident before emptying Spencer's bank account. We want to know who killed their operative, lady and gentlemen, so we can feed them to the Mexican authorities."

Quip had visibly paled and was clearly short of breath. Otto picked up on the fact that something was not quite right. Perhaps Quip was ill but afraid to miss the meeting.

Otto interjected, "Thank you, Prudence. That takes us up to our planned break. Would you like to adjourn for lunch, or do you prefer to do the American lunch-style and eat while we talk about the larger assignment?"

Prudence said, "Otto, I am your guest so I would like to take your lead in this matter."

Otto, now interested in keeping the conversation light and away from Quip, said, "Then, Prudence, allow me to suggest that we change gears from the business environment and go enjoy a carefully constructed meal, designed to appeal to American tastes. However, I must warn you there will be no packaged vending machine fare on the table so I am hoping you can adapt."

Prudence showed open concern on her face as she asked, "Otto, am I given to understand there will be no bagged, god knows how old, cellophane-wrapped food to choose from? Will I be able to get my daily supplement of artificial coloring and toxin-based preservatives on the side then?"

Otto was clearly brought up short with the absurd request. When Prudence didn't smile, it added to his confusion.

Otto then asked, "We do have some wine with sulfites in it. Will that help with your dietary requirements of preservatives?"

Prudence responded with only a partial smile, "Oh no, Otto! No wine at lunch. That would be imprudent!"

Otto tried to pull Quip aside on the way toward lunch, but Quip brushed him off.

After lunch the team and Prudence reconvened in the meeting room. Quip was still distracted and clearly uncomfortable. Quip had avoided Otto during the break. Petra and Jacob sensed something was wrong with Quip when he hardly said anything throughout lunch. Prudence seemed indifferent to Quip's mood as she started the primary assignment briefing

Prudence said, "We are working on a rather important initiative for national interests. I am not at liberty to provide much in the way of details, but its significance cannot be overstated. The project is based on a thesis written by a young doctoral candidate about fifteen years ago and has been of great interest ever since. The concept is based on Competing Architectures Leveraging Mutually Exclusive Deterministic Probabilities and Outcomes Developed in Parallel for High Gain Results. Internally, we refer to it as 'CALL-ME-DINGY.'"

Again, no smile from Prudence was detected, so no one was compelled to laugh at the absurdity. Quip was now so distracted that he was hardly focused on the briefing, much less able to comment on the appropriate title.

Sasha said, "I'm familiar with the theory of that doctoral thesis. Basically, you're suspicious that a competing power with similar resources is building a similar solution and might in fact be ahead of your team. Is that where you are going with this?"

Prudence finally smiled, then said, "Well, I must say I'm not disappointed in your knowledge base, Sasha. Yes, that is exactly what we are concerned about. We have been working on this project for some time. We have a lot invested in it. We keep finding, however, little snippets of code here and there as well as seeing chatter on the Internet suggesting we have competitors working on the same topics. We typically monitor Internet searches on topics of interest, but we also watch the kind of questions being asked.

"I am sure you are aware that we have assembled a reverse algorithm that takes questions or topics being fed into a search engine to figure out what someone is working on. From the questions being asked, we can deduce what a person or a government is researching by applying this reverse algorithm. So that's how we know we are in a race. However, what we don't know is who or how far they've gotten with the prototype. That is what we want your team to look into."

Raja added, "That explains the reason why you are concerned, but for us to be useful in this delivery order we need to know what the project is you are working on and who you suspect is in a race with you. Without understanding the project you are worried about, I am at a loss to understand what to hunt for."

Prudence nodded in agreement, "Yes, Raja, I thought that might be a problem. Telling you to go look for something in a haystack but refusing to tell you what to look for is ludicrous. My instructions were to not tell you about the project. That is true, but I wasn't told not to give you contextual clues from the project. So toward that end, I have a list of key search words that should allow you to search effectively for this topic."

Quip was now reengaged and listening to the exchanges, so he suggested, "So if we use these search words in our hunt and we find something, how do we know if it is the right something? More importantly, if we find the right something that is in parallel development, then we would know what you are working on. How will that be treated since your government is obviously worried about someone discovering what you are working on or beating you to the punch?

"And by the way, I am also intimately familiar with that doctoral thesis, and I don't think the 'CALL-ME-DINGY' tag line would be appreciated by the author."

Prudence again gave a slight smile, then responded, "Yes, we know it's your paper."

Quip was again feeling uncomfortable but masked his discomfort.

Prudence added, "In answer to the last question, this team is under non-disclosure and we expect that to be honored. It would be unfortunate if we lost our confidence in such a valued special contractor, don't you agree?"

Quip was stressed and had trouble swallowing after he'd heard the thinly veiled threat.

Prudence continued, "So the key words that I think you will be most successful with include: nano-technology, grasshopper, biometric implants, peer-to-peer mobile communications, satellite uplink tethering, near-field communications in combat situations, po, and pilotless drones.

"With your computing ingenuity and obvious collective intellects, I believe those key phrases should lead you to that which we are concerned with. It is believed that if these key words were searched for heuristically for points of intersection you should find something of great interest to us. Namely, our competitors. Oh, and one more thing, we believe that these terms may correlate in various manners, so cross-referencing is critical to validate high probability corroborating results."

Now it was Otto's turn to blanch a little bit when he heard the terms in play from Prudence.

Otto swallowed hard but maintained his composure when he said, "I thank you for your innovative thinking at keeping your organization's confidence, but yet providing us a clear opportunity to be successful. So team, do we have any other questions for Prudence?"

CHAPTER 57

Nimble and quick … is that you, JAC?

Julie was headed to the gym for her the third workout with Juan. She mentally reviewed all of the different moves she'd practiced since their last meeting. She was pleased with the way she'd improved some aspects of her style but was disappointed that she'd missed taking advantage of openings. At this point her pride was on the line. Granted, Juan was larger than she was, but they were both ranked as brown belts. She wished she'd continued her studies, but up until now no one had bested her.

As she entered, she noticed that Juan was already there and stretching. He looked up and nodded in her direction while doing a quick appraisal of her from head to toe. She flashed him a smile and headed into the back, removed her outer clothing and stored it in a locker. She quickly returned to the main room. Last night when they had worked out, a small group had gathered to watch. Tonight that group had doubled in size.

"Hey, Juan," she greeted.

"Julie, you look wonderful as always. Are you ready to show me some improvement?"

She moved in a bit closer while she maintained eye contact, then responded, "Oh, I do hope so. I am tired of your cleaning, um…"

She moved at the last word and did a total sweep on him unexpectedly, which connected perfectly and landed him on the mat.

Then she finished, "the floor with me." She grinned as she jumped back out of his reach and allowed him to stand.

"Very nice, madam. I knew you could do it if you focused. Good eye contact was maintained," he encouraged. "Let's see if you can keep it up. I do though think your eyes are quite lovely when you are mad. Perhaps I can make you angry and see that fire."

She successfully blocked his next three moves and even landed two well-positioned kicks. He smiled at her efforts and provided an opening that appeared too good to pass up. After she landed hard on the mat, she realized she should have passed it up. Her eyes flashed; he had succeeded, she was angry. She also knew, from two previous lessons, that getting angry caused her to forget basic defense postures. She stepped back and took a breath, then focused again.

"Good, Julie, better on the control. I love the fire in your eyes, but it does impact your focus. Glad you remembered," he said with sincerity.

Julie had worked on picturing him as a workout bag suspended from the ceiling. No chiseled face, no well-formed muscles, no eyes that reminded her of melted chocolate, and no kissable lips. If she kept the right image in her mind, she knew she would not be as distracted. She'd also worn a multi-colored top that caused his eyes to move with the color as she moved. The objective was Juan being distracted and off base, rather than her.

Julie kept her feet under her as they continued some good exchanges, with the offensive and defensive moves evenly distributed. The crowd had clearly picked sides, and each side shouted approval for successful moves from their champion. Juan's smile of approval when she did a move correctly or effectively evaded his assault helped emphasize her mastery of each move. If they'd been in a match, she felt her score would be close to even with him, yet she knew his strength in the long run would win. They were both breathing hard and sweating like crazy when Juan called a break. She gratefully accepted the respite. Juan waved away the gathered crowd, then moved closer to Julie.

"That was much improved," Juan offered.

"Well, I should hope so after all the practice I have put in. You, sir, are a tough but fair task master," Julie said as she flashed her megawatt smile.

"That is, of course, part of the secret. Practice. Not just individual practice, but practice with a worthy opponent." He smiled, then added, "I certainly volunteer to be a worthy partner in any activity you might wish to practice. I find that you are well-formed, funny, tenacious, and quite beautiful."

"And you, sir, are a rogue. Your flattery is appreciated, but I suspect that you flatter all the females."

"Flattery. Madam, you wound me. I would never flatter such a magnificent rose. I speak nothing but the truth. You are a good student and you learn quickly. I, umm, do not think of you as a female per se, but rather an equal," he suggested with a grin that was hardly meant for an equal.

Julie laughed. "You are such a liar, Juan. Cute, no doubt, but a liar."

"Now, Julie. We have worked out on three separate occasions. Have I been anything less than a gentleman? Have I once tried to take advantage of you?"

She shrugged, then said, "True, you have been awesome as an instructor, and as you said, I have worked hard.

"Let's try a few more moves, then call it a night, alright?"

"From your beautiful lips to my ears. Of course, sweetheart. But, tonight you will allow me to take you to dinner to celebrate your accomplishments."

"Oh Juan, there you go trying to get me off base again."

She tossed her towel over to the side, flashed him another smile with a gleam in her eye, and then swept him again. As he was unprepared, he landed soundly on the mat. He looked up and smiled, then moved so fast to his feet and behind her, that she was pinned against him. It was a move he hadn't shown her previously, and she had no built-in counter move.

As he held her tight from behind, he whispered in her ear, "I love having you off base, or anywhere else I can get you. Your best defense here is to go limp, make your opponent believe they have won, then with your feet planted and knees bent, flip them."

His whispered directions had allowed his warm breath against her ear and neck. The gym disappeared from her mind for a second. His arms were warm and secure as they encircled her, and she felt anything but threatened. In fact, she suddenly felt very warm and pliable. He released her and stepped back.

"Alright, Julie, let's try again." He grinned, knowing he had distracted her and that she had liked it.

The crowd loosely re-formed, and they continued to work on various moves. He called out some tips and she adjusted. He had no doubt that she moved well. She would be superior to most opponents.

After a particularly difficult sequence, she stepped back and held onto her knees with labored breathing. She didn't move from the spot for what seemed to Juan like too long. He moved close to see if she was in trouble. As he leaned in to ask if she was finished for the night, she moved like lightning, and flipped him onto his back. Then she pinned him for a moment.

She looked in his eyes, flashed her smile, and then whispered into his ear, "Play fair. This is a workout, not a bedroom. If I wanted you to whisper into my ear and make me feel all feminine, I promise I'll let you know, Juan."

He laughed and asked to be released. She laughed too. The crowd joined in and clapped at what they saw as a well-matched workout.

She stepped back as he got up and held her hands up, indicating she was finished. He nodded agreement.

"So, I think you owe me dinner, Juan."

"It would be my pleasure, madam. You are a worthy opponent, my equal now, perhaps."

As she headed into the ladies' side of the locker room, she looked over her shoulder. "Juan, that is a nice comment from you, thank you. See you in ten, and I'll let you buy me a cerveza as well. We'll swap lies and see what else we have in common."

"I think we have lots in common, and what isn't in common will still fit well together."

"Juan, I think women have been too easy for you. Please remember, I am anything but easy."

The ten minutes Juan waited for Julie quickly became forty, but when she arrived at the car, Juan quickly decided it was well worth the wait.

Juan smiled with appreciation as he lightly quipped, "I see that the concept of the time/space continuum is consistent among females everywhere. I must say, however, your time/space gear is highly effective, and your landing approach is heartily approved. Please put your classy craft in the #1 stall of the hanger, madam."

Julie stood patiently by the passenger side of the car until Juan grasped the concept of chivalry. He jumped from the driver's side and opened the passenger side door for Julie while taking another head-to-toe appraisal.

Julie smiled as she got into the car and said, "I thought you could be taught."

Juan grinned and under his breath added, "This evening is going to be a hoot."

"Madam, you should understand that we have a vast array of dining choices that range from an excellent five-star restaurant, specializing in Northern Italian cuisine, to vending machine food, specializing in botulisms and everything in between. We can even go hang out at the local mom and pop shop, wait until shift change, and look to purchase whatever rotisserie item is unsold after being there for eight hours. Those are usually discounted quite heavily and come with a dining experience that is without equal. The ensuing intestinal cramps will be an additional bonus.

"After that the sky is the limit with your choice of my favorite bowling alley Biker Bowling, Babes, and Beer, where they have the most exquisite nachos, always a date pleaser, but time con-suming as we'll need to fly into Texas. Or, you're in luck as my favorite Roller Derby team Wenches on Wheels is supposed to be in town to face off against Beelzebub's Boil Suckers. The roller rink specialty is chili cheese dogs covered with jalapenos, served with a Maalox ice cream shake. What do you feel like, madam?"

Julie struggled to suppress laughter and answered, "Juan, I am so disappointed! Nothing at the bus station among our dining choices? Hmm, if we do the roller rink, may I add raw onions to accentuate my buffalo breath for the remainder of the evening? Are you always this outrageous when entertaining your ladies?"

Juan, with a contrite grin, said, "Well, I do that sometimes to see what kind of response I get. If the lady cannot see that I'm only jesting, as in she has no sense of humor, we really do go to a bowling alley so there won't be a second date. But seriously, I already have reservations."

Julie retorted back, "No, I'm the one with reservations about this date, Mr. Juan!"

"Like I said, this evening is going to be a hoot. Let me state it a different way, madam, I would like very much to take you to a nice Italian restaurant where they have a table waiting for us. I believe you will find the food there most agreeable. Will you consent to join me?"

Julie touched his arm and grinned. "I would enjoy having dinner with you, Juan, as you have offered."

Once they were seated and working on their first glass of wine, they started to settle in comfortably.

"So, Julie, will I get to know more about you? I mean, you have spirit, intelligence, wit, a good command of martial arts, and all heavily layered with a thick skin of beauty. But you show up with answers to questions we haven't thought of yet. You engineer new identities for strangers. And, unless I miss my guess, you're a loner who moves fast through life. Can you tell me who Julie is, if indeed your name really is Julie? I would really like to know."

With a quizzical expression, Julie looked from her glass of wine to Juan. "You know, you're not who you pretend to be. You act and talk like you're a devil-may-care pilot who is always womanizing when he is not in the air. But then you pull out the sensitive male routine to talk to a sparring partner in a caring, insightful, and thoughtful manner. Why do you cover up those very fine qualities, so that they only come out on rare occasions?"

Juan looked rather reflective. "Makes me too vulnerable, I suppose. Let me answer the question you have on your mind. Yes, she hurt me when she picked up and left. I was struggling with my career, no near-term financial opportunities, and she wouldn't let me into her life. She very sweetly kissed me, told me that she had the pregnancy terminated and that it was no longer my concern, then she got into her car and left. I never saw her after that. So, yes, there is a part of me very scarred, and I don't let it out often."

Julie was a little taken aback and saddened. "Juan, I'm sorry. I didn't mean to pry into old wounds.

"So you want to know about Julie? Well, she was abandoned at a very young age, as in days old. When they found me I was nearly dead. Those people wouldn't give up on me, thankfully, and I pulled through. I never understood why I was unwanted, or why I was left to die in a dumpster behind a restaurant. The family who took me in never treated me any differently than their own child, and I never felt like a castoff child growing up.

"But I suppose, to a degree, I'm like you because those scars are so ugly that I don't want anyone to see them because I...I...I..." Julie's voice trailed off and tears filled her eyes.

Juan reached out and gently touched her hand, then extended his monogramed handkerchief for her use without saying a word. He waited for her to compose herself before he spoke.

"Wounded souls need to have good friends, don't you think? Julie, would you let me be that friend? I would esteem it an honor, madam."

Julie struggled to get control of her emotions, although she did a good job of soaking Juan's handkerchief.

"But if you're going to blow your nose in my handkerchief and wipe your beak on it, I don't want it back. Ok?"

Julie laughed and wiped her tears as she realized Juan was the only man who had gotten her to laugh and cry at the same time. The rest of the evening passed far too quickly with jokes, funny stories and a genuine interest in each other. He took her to the front of her hotel and jumped out to open the door. He bowed as he extended his hand to help her out of the car.

"Madam, thank you for joining me for dinner. I enjoyed it and would petition you to do it again at your earliest convenience."

Julie flashed her brightest smile, then dropped his hand as she stepped back so he could close the door.

"Juan, I enjoyed it as well. Sorry for ruining your handkerchief. I will replace it. Dinner was surprisingly delicious, but the company was better."

She leaned into him and gave him a tentative kiss, then turned toward the door of the hotel. She took a few steps and looked back.

"Goodnight, Juan."

"Goodnight, Julie."

CHAPTER 58

Why can't I have it my way?

"Quip, what were you thinking?" asked Wolfgang. "Can we hear the logic process you used to keep this to yourself, please?"

Quip had all eyes from Jacob, Petra, Otto, and Wolfgang focused on him for his explanation. "When I got on the phone, I was angry. I was angry about what I found on Spencer's kiddie porno business, along with everything else he photographed naked. I was angry about JAC being at risk from that maniac, and I was angry that he'd shot Juan. So when Carlos asked me to listen into their discussion, I did."

Wolfgang said, "But you did more than just listen, didn't you? Tell us how you went from listener to participant, please."

Quip was beginning to tire of the cross examination but knew that it was futile, so he explained, "Carlos stated flat out that he wanted to extract revenge. Then Juan and Robert argued about who would pull the trigger. Robert won the argument based on being an ex-SWAT sharp shooter. That was as far as they intended to take it."

"So then I'm confused. It sounds like you were just a listener and not a plotter. Or is there more to the story?" asked Wolfgang.

Quip was feeling a little ashamed. "Well, at that point I interjected that if they only took out Spencer and left the organization intact, someone would move into the role of Spencer and the exploitation would continue.

"I'm afraid I recommended that Spencer's whole team and the facilities they operated out of be erased from this planet for the greater good."

Wolfgang nodded with understanding, then suggested, "Yes, of course, that was the most logical course of action to stop the exploitation."

Quip was more pragmatic in his thoughts as his story continued.

"Robert offered to plant C-4 explosives in key places so as to have the building crumble on top of the crew once they were all inside, with the extra touch of high-octane accelerant to ensure that no one survived.

"It was at that point I moved from listener to participant. I offered to model the explosions, building collapse, and subsequent fire to minimize exterior collateral damage, maximize the terminating effect on the attendees, and have the blame fall on Spencer so the authorities would not investigate any further. I used ICABOD to assist in the C-4 placement to minimize the usage, thus better containing the blast. I also modeled how to make it look sloppy enough to suggest that Spencer was his own victim."

Wolfgang again nodded and agreed, "A very well-thought out plan indeed. You accounted for the follow-on investigation efforts after the fact. Good.

"Tell me, Quip, how many people did you model for Project Armageddon? Five? Six? Ten, more? And most importantly, did you analyze all the background of the targeted suspects?"

Quip hesitated for a moment, furrowed his brow, then he clarified, "I can tell you that Carlos baited the trap that should have lured all of them into the building. They were supposed to film some big porno scene with someone named Rita. Rita was not present when the building went up because she was distracted by Juan just long enough for her to miss the blast.

"But, as for the actual number of his crew and a background check on each one, no. I did not dig that far."

Wolfgang questioned, "You dug deep on Spence but not on the others. So, is this pure hearsay guilt-by-association and no research prior to making them all casualties? How is that justifiable, Quip?"

Quip swallowed hard, then he added, "They were all Spencer's cronies and cogs in his machinery to crank out films of exploitation of children! The people who showed up there to watch knew this wasn't a harmless game show! Everyone who was there was there to satisfy their lurid, prurient interests based on the degradation of another human being!"

Wolfgang asked in a subdued tone, "Did you know that a Mexican operative had been assigned to infiltrate the Spencer machinery, as you call it, to uncover evidence of wrongdoing to the authorities? This operative was building an exploitation of children and pornography distribution case with the U.S. Department of Justice, and the U.S. State Department was working on extradition of Spencer and his organization."

Quip straightened and his eyes widened. "I knew some of this after our briefing with Prudence, but not all the U.S. representation that was working on it.

"Now let me ask a question. Did Prudence ever say who their operative was? Because I never heard a name."

Otto interjected, "We were not given a name so we really don't know who or if any Mexican operative was truly there. The additional information I gleaned from other resources that I could reach out to discreetly."

Quip defended, "Actually, after our meeting with Prudence, I started sifting through the information that I could find. I was able to find and verify that their operative was Rita, whom we know wasn't in the building. So she is safe."

Wolfgang showed some surprise at the information and asked, "So Rita is allowing the Mexican government to believe she was in the building and not checking in with them? The Mexicans will learn of the deception soon enough and what will happen then?"

Quip suggested, "Rita must have wanted out of her contract since she took that job with Lara to work that new apparel line in Brazil. I guess she didn't feel inclined to tell the Mexican government goodbye. That would be under the heading of not my problem, wouldn't it?"

"Perhaps," Wolfgang considered. "How are you going to account for the C-4 that Spencer is reported to have? The CIA are themselves being blamed for the incident and want to be exonerated from this suspicion."

Quip admitted, "I arranged a very hurried, sloppy insurance request using a synthesized Spencer voice from his cell phone and used his bank account to pay for it. From an insurance investigator perspective, it looks like an insurance fraud issue. There is no reason I can think of why we can't simply point to Spencer as having sourced the C-4 himself. The insurance company's report can be leveraged to place the blame for the blast on Spencer."

Wolfgang sternly responded, "Well, there obviously are some loose ends to deal with. What other details do you have on this unilateral project of yours?"

Quip felt increasingly embarrassed but offered, "Well, the topic of Spencer's bank accounts came up, and the guys wanted to share in the spoils of the exercise. I was able to persuade them to allow all of Spencer's funds to be disbursed to charities around Mexico. They would have all been tagged, if they had split those funds."

Wolfgang reviewed, "So, to summarize, to make certain we have it all.

"You took on a project of assassination without discussing it first with anyone in our organization.

"You didn't research all your intended victims thoroughly, leaving one infiltrator at risk.

"You may have a good enough alibi for the C-4 issue, but not confirmed.

"And you may have kept the Spencer monies from showing up in close proximity to the R-Group. Is that almost everything, Quip?"

Quip now sensed that the end of the trial was close. Somehow though, listening to the list from Wolfgang, he felt worse than when they had started.

"Pretty much. All except for Rita. She is still unaccounted for by the Mexican government, and we really can't approach her without compromising our operation. So while I don't know what to do about that one, I am glad she was spared and now doing what she really wants to do in her career."

Wolfgang asked, "Quip, do you see why we want to work through all the issues together before an operation is launched? Doing damage control after the fact puts us in a reactive mode and reduces our operating efficiencies.

"One thing, above all else, you made a conscious decision to eliminate other human beings just because of their supposed association with Spencer. I will tell you that is exactly the attitude the Nazis had in World War II and why I find it so abhorrent in the actions of others. Quip, when you make those kinds of decisions without consulting this group, you are no better than a Nazi. This group has always been comprised of members that were angry with those that took advantage of others. Angry at those in power that acted as judge, jury and executioner, based on their whims. We do not deliberately execute humans, though we will set them up for justice within their countries, based on the laws of the lands they were born to. It is a fine line at times. Do you understand our concern in this matter, or does our charter no longer interest you?"

Quip felt his self-esteem lying on the floor. He weighed each word that Wolfgang had said against his moral fiber. He realized that he'd acted incorrectly and used tools for his ego, not for the betterment of humanity. The silence in the room extended for several minutes.

Finally, Quip lifted his head up and responded, "Yes, sir, I do understand. I apologize to this group for my actions in this matter. Not in what I helped engineer for Spencer's demise but for disregarding our group dynamics and not seeking our collective wisdom. I am truly sorry for being so angry and selfish in this matter, and I should have sought your guidance. I ask that you forgive me in my indiscretion and that I be allowed to stay. I won't make that mistake again, ever."

Wolfgang smiled slightly, and queried the team, "Well, all, we have everything on the table, I believe. Based on what was heard, how can we proceed?"

Petra questioned, "I, for one, want to know what we are going to do about Rita."

Jacob suggested, "How about asking her the truth? It seems to have worked here today at this table, so perhaps we can get it to work again. We just need to decide who is best to contact her to get her to come clean with her former bosses."

"Perhaps," Petra offered, "I can get that seed planted when we girls talk over the next couple of days. To be honest here, I would like to keep Lara as a friend, unless someone objects."

Wolfgang smiled broadly at the junior team members. "Otto, I do believe they can be taught!"

Otto nodded in agreement, but his features remained more closed than normal.

Wolfgang then leveled the final problem on the table and asked, "So how are you going to deliver this escapade to Ferdek? What will you tell him?"

Quip's emotional low was now in May Day! May Day! We're going down! mode. Wolfgang had already drained him of all his emotional strength with piercing psychological comments, so there was almost nothing left in him to fight this mental broadside hit.

Quip was barely able to keep himself from hyperventilating but meekly forced out, "Do we really need to tell him? I mean he is so ill right now. Besides, what possible value can there be for him to know?"

Wolfgang was quite icy at this point, and adamant. "We will not tell him. You will tell him. This is a point of honor for you and for the group. He must know because he saw firsthand fighting the Nazis what happens when an organization takes inappropriate actions and then simply rationalizes after the fact to suit their purposes. Ferdek must know of Project Armageddon so he knows that you are not hiding issues from him. You already hid, or at least tried to hide this issue, from the operations team so you must come clean with him. Do you understand, Quip?"

Ever since Quip had been a little boy, just the thought of having to face his grandfather to admit even the smallest misdeed would make him physically ill. In Quip's mind, there was no greater punishment than having to confess a transgression to Ferdek and then having to endure the emotional skewering that came out of the follow-on discussion. Quip had nothing but honor and respect for his grandfather. He simply couldn't bear disappointing the man with his mistakes.

"I will deliver this story of my transgression to my grandfather, but I will tell you all here and now, I would rather eat a nail than have him disappointed again by me."

Wolfgang said, "Yes, Quip, we know. Ferdek has honor, and we need you to have it again as well. He needs to know that you can and will carry on in his place when needed."

Quip knocked quietly on the door and said in a whisper, "Gramps? Do you have time to visit with me, Granpa? I can come back later if you're busy." Quip was hoping that he wouldn't be heard, but while Ferdek's health was quickly deteriorating his hearing was still quite good.

Ferdek said in a low but audible voice, "Come in, boy."

Quip entered and took the chair by the bed. Ferdek seemed very frail but alert.

"It's been awhile, my Quip. I would hear of your exploits as a digital mechanic and ladies' man!"

Quip thought to himself, Oh great. Not only am I hear to be dressed down for being a Nazi, I am going to have to hear about my lack of sexual prowess!

"Grandfather forgive me for I erred. I was foolish and vain. I let my immediate team members down. In a fit of anger, I became a part of the assassination of a low-life porn producer and his team of parasites. Worst of all, I tried to keep it from our family. Wolfgang said that based on my actions I was no better than a Nazi. Perhaps he is right."

Ferdek struggled slightly to speak, licked his lips, and then asked, "So who told you he was a bad actor? Did you seek consensus in your theory, and did they too confirm the facts with you?"

Being emotionally filleted twice in one day was not something Quip wanted to endure ever again and said, "There was no one telling me this had to be done. And no, I trusted my own judgment based on all the details I unearthed on this individual. I camped onto a group of others who were plotting to kill him anyway, but I over-contributed to his demise, as well as the rest of his team. I failed to perform a team member review."

Quip offered Ferdek a sip of water as he struggled to get his voice out. He coughed for a minute but held onto Quip's hand.

"You joined a lynching party? Quip, do you remember what I asked you when you and your brother were boys and were caught doing something foolish? I'd always asked you, if your buddy Jacques Bruno jumped off the balcony, would you follow him in that dumb stunt too? Just because someone else is vectored on a fool's mission is no excuse for following!

"Did you stop to think that they might have been using you to be the scapegoat? Or perhaps that the lynching party was a ruse to get you and your resources to do their bidding?"

Quip was astonished at the question and mumbled, "I…I…I hadn't considered that possibility…I thought that this was a porn producer and that…"

Ferdek interrupted, "You fell into the classic trap the Nazis used on many of our comrades-in-arms! Pull a stunt that makes you believe what your eyes think you've seen and then get you to pull the trigger! Once that is done, they have something on you to coerce you to do their bidding. This is why we don't work individually, because once your emotions have been launched you can be herded like cattle!

"A team can explore the X-factor and examine a situation from multiple angles! My dear boy, I love you so much, but I can't stress this enough. I believe you have the right honor. I must know that you are safe from the Nazi thinking that nearly destroyed…"

Ferdek was overcome with a coughing fit and struggled to catch a deep breath but held onto Quip's hand. Then he stopped coughing, the hand relaxed, and Ferdek was gone. It took Quip a second to comprehend that his grandfather had died in their last ever conversation. Quip shook with guilt, anger, fear, and tears at this last instance of communication with his grandfather. He knew their conversation would haunt him until his last breath.

Even though Ferdek could no longer hear Quip, he said quite deliberately "Grandfather, I will never let you or my teammates down again. I swear it!"

CHAPTER 59

Age is a high price to pay for maturity

"**D**amnit!" Carlos muttered to himself after the stewardess had serviced his wine. "If Juan was piloting the plane, I could have the entire bottle."

After he'd returned a few days previously from São Paulo, he'd mentally reviewed the conversations with Thiago and Lara a dozen times. Lara had stayed behind to work out some of the details following the successful board meeting. They'd spoken daily, missed one another, but he was dissatisfied thinking of simply being a prop to her business. He was unable to define a true role in her work world. He had his pride.

Andrew Greenwood had contacted him following his return and asked for a meeting. He was quite adamant that Carlos should come to Atlanta and meet with him to discuss telecommunications technology. After the third phone call from Andrew, the follow-up conversation with Jacob, the receipt of the travel voucher, and the promise of southern hospitality, Carlos agreed to the meeting. Rarely in his life had he felt this unsettled, and he categorically disliked the feeling. At least he could use this opportunity to try out his new identity, which so far seemed to be flawless.

During the long flight, he thought about the possibilities of this meeting with Andrew Greenwood and his protégé, Eilla-Zan. Jacob had encouraged him to attend the meeting when Carlos asked his opinion. Jacob provided a bit of his perspective on Andy, as he preferred to be called, from his modest interactions with him. Jacob had asked Carlos to make certain and listen to the guy's stories as they promised to be funny.

Jacob had also advised Carlos that participating in the discussion didn't mean he was committed to it, but rather he should look at the possibilities.

A short time later, Carlos deplaned and headed toward the exit marked for passenger pick up. His cell phone rang.

"Hi, young feller, this is Andrew. I am outside on the far lane in an electric blue Chevy truck. You can't miss me," drawled Andrew.

"Thank you, Mr. Greenwood, sir. I am headed that way."

"Take your time, young feller. We are on southern time, relax a bit."

"Yes, sir."

Carlos had been raised to respect people overall, especially their time. He located the vehicle and was surprised when he saw Andrew. Jacob had described him well with the shock of white hair, braided, worn Levi jeans, faded blue plaid shirt, twinkling bright blue eyes, and a grin that seemed to welcome Carlos without a word spoken. They shook hands firmly, each taking the measure of the other.

"Welcome to Georgia. I am glad your trip was uneventful. It is so nice to get to meet you face to face, thank you."

"Sir, it is my pleasure. I look forward to our discussions," Carlos said, and he was surprised that at that moment he meant it. "I like your truck. It is considered old school, right?"

Andrew beamed. "She's a good ol' thing. She runs like a top. Her name is Sapphire. I have had her for over forty years.

I travel some and am always sad I can't take her along. Wait 'til y'all hear the sound system. I even had a DVD player put in that I use sometimes when I take her camping. I finally had to give up my eight-track player."

They both got in and as they headed out, Andrew talked about the truck, showed him all the bells and whistles it had. It ran as he had said and provided a cushioned ride with its air suspension system. Carlos appreciated good vehicles, but he'd never considered a vehicle as a member of the family like Andrew did. Andrew pointed out a few landmarks along the way out of town. As they changed roads, they ended up on a two-lane road with rolling hills of green on either side. Carlos noted the healthy livestock that field after field supported. Far different than the desert area where he'd grown up and spent much of his time in, when not in a city.

"Beautiful country, Mr. Greenwood. Are these all shared lands?"

"Now, young feller, you need to call me Andy. That Mr. Greenwood stuff is just not needed. We are going to be friends, Carlos, so let's not stand on that sort of formality.

"These lands are not shared, but large parcels are owned by individuals. They mostly employ part-time help for their crops and livestock. I myself have several hands that keep my parcel up when I travel. It's been in the family for three generations. I just can't part with it, though I don't spend nearly enough time here any longer."

A couple of miles later they turned onto a gravel road and passed under an archway that announced entry to Words of Wisdom. It was a well-kept, long entry way bordered with evenly spaced trees and white fencing that curved slightly up hill. The drive ended at a two-story white house that appeared to built circa 1880 or 1900, but was pristine in condition. Well-manicured lawns, bushes and flowers surrounded the house. A traditional red barn was visible behind the house. A large dog of brown and yellow loped next to the truck until they stopped.

"Don't y'all worry about Wrinkles there, Carlos. He's just a big and slobbery mutt who wouldn't hurt a flea. He might jump up on you and lick ya to death if he takes a shine to ya."

Andrew laughed, "Come on, let's go greet the mutt and I'll take ya in and show you your room. Then we'll start talkin' shop."

The mutt was huge. He sniffed Carlos all over and was apparently satisfied when he stood on his hind legs and rested his forefeet on Carlos's shoulders. Carlos patted him, spoke softly and laughed as Wrinkles planted a lick on his cheek. He told the dog to get down, gave him a pat, and walked toward the house. As the dog wasn't allowed inside, he lay down at the door with a forlorn look as Carlos stepped inside.

"Quite a dog, Andy."

"Yep, and it looks like he's taken a shine to you. He won't move until you come back out, 'less a course he hears the grass growin' or sees a squirrel. That dog purely hates squirrels," chuckled Andy. "Here, this room is for you for tonight, son. Feel free to settle in a bit, and then when y'all are ready, head straight across the hallway. You'll find a door on your right. I'll be in there getting some stuff set up for us to poke around in."

Carlos settled into the large room dominated with a king-sized bed. There was a flat screen TV on the wall, a laptop computer, and a sound system with a remote control on the table by the bed. Comfortable and tasteful in somber browns and dark blues. He grinned at the thought of a channel flip later. He hung up his alternate slacks and shirt, washed his face, and then went to seek out Andy. As he walked past a couple of rooms, he noticed the same care in simple decorating prevailed.

As he entered the room, he took in the electronics, laptops, and screens that were scattered about. Andy was looking at a screen with his back to the door. Next to him was a mane of red wavy hair that almost covered the back of the chair. They both seemed absorbed in the screen and didn't hear him enter.

"Andy, your home is lovely," he said.

"Ah, Carlos, so glad you like it. My wife, Flo, rest her soul, did all the decorating when we modernized it some years ago. Nowadays I have a housekeeper that helps maintain it for me.

"Carlos, I'd like to introduce you to my protégé, Eilla-Zan. We were working on mapping several dial plans for customers that are planning changes.

"Eilla-Zan, honey, please stand up and shake hands with Carlos."

The redhead stood up and turned around and smiled. Carlos noted her heart shaped face and startling green eyes that reminded him of the sea. She appeared about 1.65 meters or so and not an ounce of fat anywhere, just luscious female curves. He grinned as he pictured Quip if he ever met this lady. His mouth would surely get stuck in open mode with no words escaping. Quip had been so funny during that call just listening to her voice. Seeing her would likely undo the lad.

"Nice to meet you, Carlos. I believe we met when Andy let me listen in on that remote recording, we did of that board meeting. I think you were working with Dr. Quip, right?"

"Madam, your memory is perfect. The pleasure of your company is all mine," he said as he shook her delicate hand. "Though we all worked from different locations it seemed to work very well.

"You did a great job on that, Andy. How did you complete that remote tap on a closed system?"

"Here now. Take a seat there, young feller. Let me show you a few of my toys. Then I want a walk through on your satellite connection."

For the next few hours, Andy showed both of them some of his different connections to various switches all over the globe. He explained the history of telecommunications for the last forty plus years. They laughed when Andy described his first cell phone as a ten-pound brick that couldn't be used in the wind.

Eilla-Zan said very little, but Carlos found he was getting quite interested in what Andy shared. Carlos mentally summarized him as a straight up man who was hard not to like.

Carlos then showed both of them, to a degree, how he connected to the satellite to create the tunnel using a SYN-FLOOD attack on the admin port that caused the operating system to restart in default mode where he took over as root. From there he was able to launch all the normal services and build a backdoor for himself so he could come and go when needed.

It was an impressive demonstration of how to create a satellite blackout tunnel and how to chamber it, so it only held a small segment for tracking at any given time. He then pointed out to them how the segment could be narrowed or expanded, depending upon what you wanted someone to think they were tracking. Complete satellite outages were rare, but communication irregularities were commonplace and easy to use for 'cloaking' a moving object like a plane.

Eilla-Zan asked good questions, as did Andy. Their questions were based on how he programmed the algorithm. Carlos explained that what he'd done with his operation's planes, which Andy brought up, what to use to mask the signal, then distort how it was transmitted, and then remove the digital fingerprints so the activity looked like a simple anomaly. Many of the inflight satellites had been launched into orbit two decades ago with technology that was now quite vulnerable to hackers who had been trained post-satellite launch. Once a satellite was launched it typically didn't get an on-site visit in space to upgrade its systems for hardware or software and so quickly became museum pieces for state-of-the-art technology frozen in time. A well-informed, determined hacker could use that to their advantage.

"So, son, tell me how you came across your expertise. That there is a right fine piece of cloaking technology. I haven't seen the likes of it, and I've seen a lot," requested Andy.

"For a while I was under service to my government. I happened to qualify for a special six-month course as part of the NAFTA agreement with the U.S. boys out of Houston. They showed me a few things with regards to tapping into the satellites that impressed me. I messed around with it while I was there and then revised it when my duty was up." Carlos grinned, then he added, "I suspect, sir, that you would understand that once some puzzle gets a hold of you, you simply must figure it out in total."

"That I do, son. That I do. Why, that makes me remember that time when I was asked to participate in a special project to start fiber cable deployment and transfer the communications for a large, not-to-be named government entity that uses only three letters.

"We had to move all the telecom equipment and the mainframe stacks to a nice new shiny data center with raised floors. The data center was so old school that the data and power cables were laid down across the floor to the power distribution unit, also known as a PDU, and the telecom drops. Each one of them mainframe stacks had two 220-watt, custom-made power cables coming out the back and were secured to the floor so people wouldn't trip over them. 'Course, you couldn't hardly walk on them since each was the diameter of a silver dollar.

"There were probably fifty guys on that project and one totally ignorant captain. Not a lick of telecommunications ability in his background, yet he was calling the shots. Well, we had done some really cool testing in advance in the labs. We tried to mimic the deployment sequences and cutover sequences several times to ensure that we would be efficient with the live project.

"Now to give you some idea of the kind of person this captain feller was, when he was a freshly minted second lieutenant working in the motor pool, the story goes that he walked into their offices one day to find the non-coms emptying all the filing cabinets of their files. When he demanded to know what on earth they were doing with all their paperwork that had been filed in triplicate, he was told that orders from the base commander had been received and due to the newly mandated Paperwork Reduction Act passed by Congress they had to throw out all their files from the previous three years. Now this then-second lieutenant, being the dimmest of the light bulbs on the string of Christmas tree lights, said, 'Ok, orders are orders but copy everything before you throw it out'.

"We had roughly ten mainframe stacks that had two of these 220-volt, custom-made power cables for a total of twenty expensive power cables bolted to the floor. Each one was just the right length to get to the power distribution unit. Each of these stacks could hold two central processing units, or CPUs, two controller units, and two disk drive units. A man shoulda been able to lift one controller or one CPU by himself, but it always took two of us to lift just one of the disk drive units and load it into the bay before sliding it into place. You pack all the units into a single mainframe stack, and you had some serious gravity to overcome. Which is why they had these ten mainframes resting on the cement floor, 'cause they were afraid they would have crushed a regular raised floor.

"We talked through how we were going to pull out the disk drives, the CPU, and the controllers after carefully powering down the units in sequence so they would come back up and work again. Boy, were those things temperamental, as well as being heavy beasts. Once we got the bays emptied, we could pull up the cables after removing the floor ties and wind up the power cables for re-use in the new data center.

"That ignoramus captain decided it would be better to save all of us from making that trip, so he used his towering intellect to go out to bid for some local moving company to move the equipment. We found out later that the low bid was won by this big burly guy named Seth and his wife.

"I'm there to make sure the telecom equipment is disconnected correctly and act as a sort of overseer so this mom and pop moving company can get paid if he does the job right. Don't think I'm making this up 'cause I saw it firsthand and to this day I am still not believing what happened next.

"Well, I'm in the computer room getting things straightened away for the contract company to arrive when I hear this knock at the back door to the data center. I stuck my head out, and there was this big burly feller and his hand truck, you know the kind used for moving refrigerators, his wife, and she wasn't much smaller than him, and their pickup truck. I didn't grasp the concept at the time of our brief introduction, but he was here to move the computer gear and he produced his work order.

"Something you should know about me is that I am almost never at a loss for words, but at that moment in time I couldn't have yelled 'fire' even if I was the one that was burning. I finally managed to say, 'Wait here while I go get my officer,' and did a double time to the front of the building.

"Do either of you know why data centers are locked up and access is tightly regulated? Well, let me tell you why they should be even if they aren't! I hot foot it through the mainframe area and just get through the other unsecure interior door to the area when I witnessed what they call a data center apocalypse. And me, I have a ring side seat through this big plate glass window that had been installed so visiting dignitaries and high level muckity-mucks could come see the data center and watch all the flashy-lighty things without having to listen to the drone of the drives and fans.

"I hadn't counted on Mr. and Mrs. Hand Truck coming through the door right behind me to begin the moving process. They didn't exchange many words, and he mostly bobbed his head up and down like she was doing all the thinking for both of them. Scary, now that I think on it.

"You know you just can't move sometimes when your mind doesn't believe what your eyeballs are serving up to you. That's what happened to me. She hands a big pair of bolt/wire cutters, you know the kind for cutting padlocks off, to him and points to those desperately expensive, handmade power cables. So he cut 'em not once but twice so he can throw 'em out of his way to maneuver his refrigerator hand truck back behind the units. I watched in disbelief as he cut those 220-volt cables BEFORE powering down the mainframe units or unplugging them.

"I don't know how he kept from being electrocuted because there was sparks flyin' everywhere, and circuit breakers going out as fast as you could count. You would think that with circuit breakers blowing and being bathed in a shower of sparks that, well, you might wanna ask yourself, 'Am I being stupid here?' But it didn't even register with either of them. For some folks you just know in your bones that their elevator don't reach the top floor.

"By this time all we have is minimum light in the data center. I didn't think I could see anything more incredible, but I was wrong! Ol' Seth kicked the chopped power cables out the way and moved his little refrigeration hand trunk back behind the first mainframe stack, and she pushed it over on top of him and the hand truck. He staggered a little under the weight of that mainframe tower but shook it off like he was some old hound dog that just came out of a fast-moving river. He wheeled that heavy unit over to the loading dock and muscles it onto their pickup trunk, then went back for another. I've never seen people so businesslike and matter-o-fact in their activity as I did with those two. He had half of them units loaded up before the bed was full, and they simply drove them to the moving destination.

"I would probably still be standing there except my faculties came back online when I started smelling smoke. Ol' Seth had caused a couple of electrical fires, and I got to see if the fire extinguishers were still charged.

"When the team showed up the next morning to see the mass destruction of the data center and some of the charred bits, we told the captain the project might have to be delayed. He fumed and yelled at us. All I did was hold up a charred connector and reminded him that each of those babies cost the government about a grand a piece. Amateurs, you gotta love them for their comic relief.

"Right after I told everyone what happened, the captain got a call to go talk to the base commanding general. We never saw him again. We did hear rumors that he had asked to be transferred back to the motor pool, but word was that an honest-to-god mutiny was waiting to happen. We were never quite sure of what happened to him. However, one day a piece of mail showed up for that captain and the base postmaster re-routed it to the Kurile Islands off the coast of Japan."

They all laughed and decided it was time to call it a day and go eat. True to his word, Andy provided a great dinner of smoked brisket that had been on the pit all day, baked potatoes and rolls that melted in the mouth. It was delicious. Carlos was pleased that they seemed to get along well. Eilla-Zan had proven to be very sharp on unified communications and remote connections, whereas Andy was more old school. Carlos felt like he complemented their expertise.

They sat outside enjoying the evening and drank the last of their wine. Wrinkles had stayed close to Carlos from the moment he came outside. Apparently, he'd made more than one friend.

"Well, son, I must say you have a sharp mind, and you know those satellites far better than either of us. I think my little operation could use someone with your skills."

"Andy, that is very nice of you to say. I must admit that I have enjoyed our exchange today."

Eilla-Zan offered, "I think you could help me hone my skills a lot, sir. Especially as methods for telecommunications change."

"I think, Carlos, you should sleep on the idea. When I take you back to the airport in the morning, you can decide if you would like me to flush out the details for you of responsibilities, salary, etc. Is that fair, son?"

"Sir, I think that is a good approach. Honestly, I think at this point, I'd like you to start outlining the details and specifics. You and I can discuss it over the next week or two. I would like to stay close to my home, if possible, but I am willing to travel."

"Yep, we can make it work."

CHAPTER 60

Don't treat the symptom, instead find the cause

"Friends and family, we are gathered here to honor the passing of a man…" Father Waltham began.

Quip felt a little ashamed that he couldn't do the eulogy, but he struggled to hold back his grief and feelings of loss. He had really tried to stand and deliver but at the eleventh hour he caved in and had the family priest perform the last speech for Ferdek. The service was going as planned but now he was dreading the funeral reception where he would be expected to meet and greet all the well-wishers and not crumble in front of everyone. Petra seemed to know or understand the inner turmoil he was experiencing as she sat next to him and gave him comforting pats and even a hug or two just at the right moments. Jacob sat next to her and gave Quip nods of reassurance now and again.

It was a little embarrassing to have his emotional armor so transparent to so many, but they were a close-knit group and as he thought about it the thought occurred to him that it was as it should be with family. Otto, Haddy, and Wolfgang were nearby, also providing glances of support now and again. There was something sad but elating to see and know that in this time of loss there was family and so many friends who had set aside everything to pay their respects and honor the surviving children.

The number of people at the funeral reception was crushing. Haddy and the staff at Wolfgang's estate had done a phenomenal job of taking care of everyone's needs. Haddy greeted each attendee, had them sign the guest book, and requested that they might make a note in the main room of their relationship with Ferdek, or perhaps send to her later as she wanted to compile some of the events for the boys.

Quip and Erich were the focus of many of the attendees, who approached them to shake hands and pay their respects to the brothers and the rest of the extended family. When Quip's childhood friend, Jacques Bruno, extended his hand, Quip felt compelled to hug his friend. Quip related with tears in his eyes that Ferdek had mentioned Bruno in their last conversation. Bruno spent several minutes with both Erich and Quip, telling some stories of their childhood and Ferdek's view on guidance for young men, which made them smile. It truly helped lighten the burden a bit, which surprised Quip.

Some people related stories not commonly known about Ferdek and how he'd touched their lives. Quip and Erich felt mixed emotions of awe and hurt as they heard these unfamiliar stories. They were astonished that Ferdek had interacted, befriended and supported so many people in so many different ways. The folks that came may have interacted with him on the financial aspects of business, but they truly came because of the man.

After what seemed to be an eternity, the last guest had gone and everyone took a well-deserved break in the first comfortable chair or sofa they could find. Erich found that he too needed to return to the city. He had spoken to his brother and was briefly reassured by the rest of the family. Wolfgang escorted him to his car. Quip had been uncharacteristically quiet and withdrawn throughout the day's events and practically laid down in his chosen chair with his arms and legs extended and his field of vision aimed forward at nothing in particular but the flames that danced in the fireplace. Everyone was prepared to give him his psychological space, so they remained quiet and circumspect.

After a while Quip blurted out, "I sure hope I get one-tenth of the turnout of people when it's my time to exit. I've heard more stories about Ferdek from more people disheartened about his passing than I thought one human being was capable of receiving. I didn't know how many people he had personally helped with favors and simple kindnesses. All of them wanted to pay their respects and give me and my brother their prayers. It was nothing less than astonishing, and I will tell you all it was extremely humbling.

"How could one man have done so much and helped so many and me not know of it? Every story I heard made me more ashamed of how selfish I have been with my life, and the only person who could have eased some of that guilt is now gone. And I'm sorry to all of you for the way I behaved in Project Armageddon, but if you will forgive me there will never be another lapse in my commitment to this group."

Otto and Wolfgang each gave nods of acceptance and glanced around to Petra and Jacob for their concurrence.

Wolfgang offered, "Quip, I believe I speak for all when I say we hear your sincerity and a deeply honorable commitment to this organization. I think we can put that episode behind us, as it appears that you will keep that lesson as sub-text to all your thinking going forward. Additionally, I want to also give you my personal note of loss to Ferdek's passing. He taught me as well the many things I needed to be who I am today. I too will miss his warm friendship and thorough logic to solving enigmatic puzzles of ethics, finance, and political power."

Just as Otto was about to speak, the head butler of Wolfgang's estate, Bowen, entered the room with a package.

Bowen moved quickly to Wolfgang and said, "Pardon me, sir, but this package just came, and the courier was most insistent that the delivery instructions be followed to the letter. Apparently, the courier had been outside the gate waiting for all guests to leave before delivering it to the house. Under the circumstances, sir, I am quite suspicious of the package and of the sender's intentions, even though it is very lightweight. You will note there is no identification on the package, and the delivery person is not someone we have ever seen before. A regular delivery service is usually in a hurry to get a signature to prove timely delivery and move on to the next destination. When I gave my signature on the non-standard receipt, he merely checked it against another list he had with him to satisfy himself that it had been delivered. Sir, I can take it outside and have one of our hounds sniff it for safety's sake."

Jacob calmly took out his pocket dress knife and opened the package to look for clues to the sender's identity. Jacob found a letter addressed to the group and opened it as well. Jacob smiled knowingly and read the letter aloud.

To my European benefactors,
I hope this letter finds you well even though the reason for all
of you being gathered together does represent an emotional
low point for the family members. I know that our association
on recent events has only been for a very brief period, but I
must confess that I sense a kind of honor in your organization
that I can trust. Your collective efforts have helped me and my
brother, as well as my lady, with no thought of recompense. Your
clandestine activities have helped to chart new careers for all
when we all thought there was no hope of a happy ending. For

that tremendous gift I am compelled to give you my heartfelt
thanks.

In my culture and how I was brought up, I need to clear the
way between us to reinforce our bond of friendship. In this box
there are several gifts for those who are there that have contributed to my family's wellbeing. I know that conventional gifts
denominated in some government currency would be an insult to
our relationship and so what I am sending are gifts as directed
by Yaqui mysticism that will demonstrate my feelings.

I realize that this group is firmly grounded in a
twenty-first century Western culture heritage and as
you hear this you may be tempted to disregard a 14th century
Meso-American religious way of life out of hand. I would submit
that you should not seek to cloak yourselves in your Western
European cultural cushion but instead learn to accept that
we human beings have had many evolutionary paths from the
dawn of man. Some paths are built upon cultural evolution, some
are built upon technological advancements, some are purely
economically based, and some are built upon mysticisms in con-
junction with spiritualization. All of these humanistic, evolutionary
paths contribute to progress of the human condition, and most
of the time they operate in parallel modes to each other and
each have something to offer the others. Some paths flare up
and then go dormant while others may simply vanish or fall into
disuse. The enigmatic looping of these parallel evolutionary paths
can be very subtle and very rewarding to a person or a country's
development. I would maintain that enlightenment can only be
achieved when multiple development paths can be considered
simultaneously and worked in concert with each other. It is only
when we have one development path to the exclusion to all
other possibilities that we have slavery and war.

I have tried to journey with an open mind to see what can be known and who can be a part of my life. So it is with this introduction that I tell you of being visited by the 'Dreamer White Wolf'. In these rare encounters information and directions are given during what can only be described as a Yaqui mystical experience. There are two parts to the Dreamer White Wolf sequence. One is designed to solidify you with your warrior clan, and the other is to point you to your next quest. Let me deal with the bonding to my new warrior clan.

The first gift I offer is to my lady's best friend. Petra. You have given warmth and friendship to Lara at a low point in her life with no thought of anything in return. In Yaqui mysticism you would be called "ﻝﺑﻗﻡ‌ﺃ" which means "the heart". The earrings made from fire agates mined in Northern Mexico are meant for you.

Jacob, you were honest and protective of me and my brother just as we were ready to fall into the abyss. You negotiated safe passage for us and then offered a place with your organization doing interesting work. In Yaqui mysticism you would be called "ﻍﺩﻙﺷﻡﺯﻡ" which means "the crow". The Crow is high flying, all seeing, and very intelligent. The Abyssinian amulet with the crow etched in it is for you.

Quip, you helped to extract revenge for my brother and remove a pestilence from this planet. I would understand that you probably have some second thoughts on providing help for such a permanent solution for one so cruel as Spencer, but your thoroughness of thought processes and attention to detail helped to bring all family and extended family members through that difficult time. In Yaqui mysticism your wiliness and cunning would earn you the right to be called "ﺉﻉﻅﺏﺷﻡΩ" which means "the coyote". For you, sir, you will find a translucent stone with the likeness of a coyote etched in it.

Otto, we have not met but the services you rendered to Thiago and the determined search you launched to find Lara clearly show you are the patriarch for the organization. I am grateful that you helped so unselfishly to put people's lives back together who are very important to me. In Yaqui mysticism you would be called "ꚇrɔφßжд", which means "the eagle". The Eagle is regal and has great strength that others depend upon. The eagle feather in the box is small but the power it has is strong. It is best worn in your hair but may not create the best aesthetics in your European settings. Therefore I recommend you carry it in your pocket.

Then a large estate loomed in my vision and Dreamer White Wolf said you would all be in this place and my destiny would soon be included at this structure. The Dreamer White Wolf then made a reference to three warriors, now two, which I interpreted as meaning another member of your group who I have not met. I would expect that person would be a peer to Otto and because of how you were described by the Dreamer White Wolf, I must believe your name is Wolfgang. There is no magic talisman in the box for you because Dreamer White Wolf said you were "жзйжɔΩшφ" which means "the wind". In Yaqui mysticism the Wind is unbounded thus everywhere.

The second part of the Dreamer White Wolf sequence is more difficult to interpret since it is either cloaked extremely well or is in the future yet to be. The images begin with a female huntress leading something, but she is only hunting for little things so I call her 'small hunter' just for reference sake. The images after she moves through clear up and I see hundreds of human beings all dressed the same and apparently readying for battle, but they are all looking up and touching their left ear as though hearing a voice from above.

Dreamer White Wolf closed the sequence at that point and left me with much gladness in my heart. Because of how this vision was given to me and in two parts I understand that I will be part of your extended family and that you have an important quest to embark upon.

The final gift that I have for the whole group is that I would accept a role with your organization and do all I can to help make you successful. Yours is a closed group so my role would be more on an as needed basis. Apologies that my message was not in digital format but Dreamer White Wolf can only protect analog communications.

Your loyal friend and mystical partner in the journey,

Carlos

While the letter was no cause for alarm, the impact of the letter was unsettling to everyone.

After a few minutes Jacob asked, "So does anyone have any serious heartburn in our having Carlos as an extended member of our team, functioning as a contractor?"

Otto replied, "I have to admit that I am uncomfortable at being analyzed by a White Wolf and don't even ask me about wearing an eagle feather."

Wolfgang nodded thoughtfully as he commented, "Jacob, you must understand this group should not and cannot just show up on someone's radar screen. It is dangerous for anyone to map us that closely, particularly since we did not choose to allow that to happen. What information did you give this Carlos about the family and our location? How would he know about me or even the funeral? I cannot think of a reason, Can you explain?"

Petra stiffened a little and questioned, "Wolfgang, what makes you think we told him anything about our family business? We simply wouldn't do that. We are too seasoned."

Jacob nodded in agreement, then offered, "Yes, you're right. The most logical answer is that we provided in-depth information to Carlos. That we discussed our operational parameters, and disclosed our center of operations because of our dealings together.

"It does make sense that we would have either knowingly or unwittingly served up classified information to someone we like, because how else could he know so much about us and, more importantly, our newest assignment. However, the simple truth is, I didn't, Grandfather."

Petra added, "Nor did I, Wolfgang!"

Quip rather solemnly said, "In mathematics there is a theorem that states, 'With all things equal the simplest answer tends to be the right answer'. I have no reason to doubt Jacob and Petra's statement. I doubt seriously that Otto and Wolfgang would have given any information away, and I am sure I did not either, even with my culpability in the one issue. So the simplest answer is that his mystical vision of the Dreamer White Wolf is probably the answer.

"Furthermore, we didn't get the Prudence assignment until after we were all back here, and we certainly didn't get any hints from her that might suggest that this is a military secret. We haven't gotten that far into this project yet so my tendency is to accept his offer at face value, realizing he has jumpstarted our investigation.

"Additionally, I noticed that he didn't ask for anything, but instead gave thanks to us. I would categorize him as something of a remarkable individual, and I don't mind having him on our side."

Wolfgang smiled knowingly, then suggested, "And that is exactly how a seduction works. Give gifts and plausible information to gain trust and once inside, the friend becomes foe. This is a classic attack strategy that was first made popular by the Greek siege of Troy.

"Jacob, you should be familiar with Trojan horses by now, based on all your penetration-testing for financial institutions."

Jacob nodded his head and then asked, "Then you believe we should disregard the information and the offer to help our organization?"

Otto said, "I don't believe he said that, Jacob. What he said was, have you considered the fact that this might be a very well-staged attack? We may all like him, and he has made us feel good about ourselves in our dealings with him. But let's not forget that he orchestrated the permanent solution to Spencer and his crew. I admit that there is good cause to want to leverage what he knows and can do. But understand, he is not and cannot be privy to our actions or our thinking. We all each have been groomed to participate in this organization, and that process has taken years to build this group. Someone we have interacted with for just a few months can hardly be counted on as one of us or be privy to so much detail.

"I can honestly say that I know and trust each and every one of you. I know that you will look out for our collective interests. I cannot say that about Carlos."

Petra questioned, "So how do we proceed? Keep him and his help at arm's length from us or look to neutralize his association with our group?"

Quip said, "I will point out that he does have skills in leveraging satellite communications, and we did have Andrew give him the once over. Andrew has made him an offer to support his efforts as well as delivered a good recommendation. Now, I can ask Andrew if Carlos was fishing for information if you want, but he would have said something if Carlos was asking too many questions."

Wolfgang grinned and said, "No, I don't think Carlos could pull the wool over Andy's eyes without a comment to us. But in answer to your question, Petra, my recommendation is that we should always be on the lookout for new talented resources and wisely tap into them. We need to keep our emotions carefully guarded so they don't compromise this group or our future. Nothing hurts more than being betrayed by someone you thought you could trust, and I am trying to limit our exposure."

Jacob looked thoughtful, then recommended, "Well, we could explore our leads and Carlos's and see where they take us. There is nothing that says we have to loop him into our project until we need his specific expertise. We proceed as we always do under our own counsel and only request assistance when and where we need it, thus limiting our exposure."

Otto smiled and suggested, "I think they are going to be ok, Wolfgang."

Wolfgang also smiled and responded, "Of that, I had no doubt. Let's move forward with the Prudence project and see where it takes us. We do have a complex contract to fulfill."

Specialized Terms
and Informational References

http://en.wikipedia.org/wiki/Wikipedia

Wikipedia (wɪki' pi: diə / *WIK-i-PEE-dee-ə*)is a collaboratively edited, multilingual, free Internet encyclopedia supported by the non-profit Wikimedia Foundation. Wikipedia's 30 million articles in 287 languages, including over 4.3 million in the English Wikipedia, are written collaboratively by volunteers around the world. This is a great quick reference source to better understand terms.

EMEA – Europe, the Middle East and Africa, usually abbreviated to EMEA, is a regional designation used for government, marketing and business purposes. It is particularly common amongst North American companies. The region is generally accepted to include all European nations, all African Nations, and extends east to Iran, but including Russia. Typically this does not include independent overseas territories whose mainland is in this region such as French Guyana (part of France)

Enigma Machine – An Enigma machine was any of a family of related electro-mechanical rotor cipher machines used in the twentieth century for enciphering and deciphering secret messages. Enigma was invented by the German engineer Arthur Scherbius at the end of World War I. Early models were used commercially from the early 1920s, and adopted by military and government services of several countries — most notably by Nazi Germany before and during World War II. Several different Enigma models were produced, but the German military models are the most commonly discussed.

German military texts enciphered on the Enigma machine were first broken by the Polish Cipher Bureau, beginning in December 1932. This success was a result of efforts by three Polish cryptologists, working for Polish military intelligence. Rejewski "reverse-engineered" the device, using theoretical mathematics and material supplied by French military intelligence. Subsequently the three mathematicians designed mechanical devices for breaking Enigma ciphers, including the cryptologic bomb. This work was an essential foundation to further work on decrypting ciphers from repeatedly modernized Enigma machines, first in Poland and after the outbreak of war in France and the UK.

Though Enigma had some cryptographic weaknesses, in practice it was German procedural flaws, operator mistakes, laziness, failure to systematically introduce changes in encipherment procedures, and Allied capture of key tables and hardware that, during the war, enabled Allied cryptologists to succeed.

Encryption – In cryptography, encryption is the process of encoding messages (or information) in such a way that eavesdroppers or hackers cannot read it, but that authorized parties can. In an encryption scheme, the message or information (referred to as plaintext) is encrypted using an encryption algorithm, turning it into an unreadable ciphertext (ibid.). This is usually done with the use of an encryption key, which specifies how the message is to be encoded. Any adversary that can see the ciphertext should not be able to determine anything about the original message. An authorized party, however, is able to decode the ciphertext using a decryption algorithm that usually requires a secret decryption key that adversaries do not have access to. For technical reasons, an encryption scheme usually needs a key-generation algorithm to randomly produce keys

Hackers and Crackers – Hacker is a term that has been used to mean a variety of different things in computing. Depending on the context although, the term could refer to a person in any one of several distinct (but not completely disjointed) communities and subcultures Cracker, or Hacker (computer security), a person who exploits weaknesses in a computer or network. People committed to circumvention of computer security. This primarily concerns unauthorized remote computer break-ins via a communication networks such as the Internet (Black hats), but also includes those who debug or fix security problems (White hats), and the morally ambiguous Grey hats.

Immersive Audio System and Telephony – Open Wonderland, (originally *Project Wonderland*) is a 100% Java open source toolkit for creating collaborative 3D virtual worlds. Within those worlds, users can communicate with high-fidelity, immersive audio, share live desktop applications and documents, and conduct real business. Using the open source VoiceBridge, not only do you hear recorded audio in stereo at CD-quality, but you also can hear other live people at this quality. VoiceBridge adapts to allow remote users with lower bandwidth connections to use lower audio fidelities, including telephone-quality.

near field communications – *Near field communication (NFC)* is a set of standards for smartphones and similar devices to establish radio communication with each other by touching them together or bringing them into close proximity, usually no more than a few inches. Present and anticipated applications include contactless transactions, data exchange, and simplified setup of more complex communications such as Wi-Fi.

Open Source – In production and development, open source as a development model promotes a) universal access via free license to a product's design or blueprint, and b) universal redistribution of that design or blueprint, including subsequent improvements to it by anyone. Before the phrase open source became widely adopted, developers and producers used a variety of terms for the concept; open source gained hold with the rise of the Internet, and the attendant need for massive retooling of the computing source code. Opening the source code enabled a self-enhancing diversity of production models, communication paths, and interactive communities. The open-source software movement arose to clarify the environment that the new copyright, licensing domain, and consumer issues created.

Pen-testing – Penetration testing is one of the oldest methods for assessing the security of a computer system. In the early 1970s, the Department of Defense used this method to demonstrate the security weaknesses in computer systems and to initiate the development of programs to create more secure systems. Penetration testing is increasingly used by organizations to assure the security of Information systems and services, so that security weaknesses can be fixed before they get exposed

Satellite blackout tunnel and Satellite cloaking event – Communications satellites are satellites stationed in space for the purpose of telecommunications. Modern communications satellites typically use geosynchronous orbits, Molniya orbits, or Low Earth orbits. The use of a blackout tunnel and cloaking event were used in this story to track communications signals as well as to hide or cloak those activities. The terms as used in this story are conjecture on the part of the authors.

SYN flood – A *SYN flood* is a form of denial-of-service attack in which an attacker sends a succession of SYN requests to a target's system in an attempt to consume enough server resources to make the system unresponsive to legitimate traffic.

Yaqui and Yaqui mysticism – The *Yaqui* or *Yoeme* are indigenous people whose ancestors originated in the valley of the Rio Yaqui in the northern Mexican state of Sonora. Many Yaqui still live in their ancestral homeland. The Yaqui conception of the world is considerably different from that of their European-Mexican and European-American neighbors. For example, the world (in Yaqui, *anía*) is composed of five separate worlds: the desert wilderness world, the mystical world, the flower world, the dream world, and the night world. Much Yaqui ritual is centered upon perfecting these worlds and eliminating the harm that has been done to them, especially by people. Words within this story attributed to the Yaqui language are pure conjecture by the authors.

Read a snippet from the third book in the series…

the Enigma Ignite

Breakfield and Burkey

There's no time like the present

"Ling, we gotta go. We have to get out of here! Can you stand?" asked JAC.

Ling was having trouble staying focused or comprehending much of anything. As the mental fog began to lift, words started to make sense again. Responding however was another matter. It was only after several minutes and with a great deal of struggle that words could be formed.

Ling finally questioned, "Where and when am I?"

JAC realized that Ling was still weak and in no condition to move under her own power.

"I can see you need a moment to gather yourself. You must understand the diversion will only last a few minutes and then the guards will return. You probably should have answers to get your thinking de-fogged, but time is of the essence, Ling. I can explain later when we have more of it. Right now, we gotta go."

Ling was lying on the table and rolled her head to the right in order to orient herself to the surroundings. It was an oppressive room with a stink of neglect and disuse.

"You are already too late," asserted Ling. "There is a video camera just over the door. They must know already of the escape attempt. You should make your way alone. I can just barely move my head and you look like you're ready for a marathon. Thanks for trying, whoever you are."

JAC was frustrated with Ling's attitude, but advised her, "We knew there would be a camera inside this area and right now we are feeding a video loop through it that still shows you lying on the table with the narcotic drip stuck in your arm. We expected that your muscles might have atrophied after this length of time, so I gave you a shot of B-complex with an adrenaline boost as a chaser to help get you amped up. With what I shot into you; it wouldn't surprise me if you wanted to run down to the beach for a ten-kilometer swim. By the way, we are one hundred kilometers from the beach.

"How are you feeling now, Ling? Can you stand? We gotta go."

Ling smiled, then responded more coherently, "Now I know who you are. You're JAC, aren't you? Why would you come to rescue me and Grasshopper?"

JAC's smile quickly turned to a solemn, dark look as she apologized, "Ling, I'm sorry about your assistant. They must not have valued him the way they did you. They saw to it that Grasshopper did not make it this far."

Ling was awash with remorse at the loss of Grasshopper and with guilt at having survived by the whim of her abductors. Her resolve to get up melted.

Ling's voice cracked, "Then my fate is here, and I shall follow behind my dear Grasshopper. All I see ahead now is emptiness, and I don't want to face it without his strength."

JAC's eyes flared from her temper, escalating to fury as she commanded, "Soldier! Colonel! I gave you an order! You will stand up and you will follow me out of here so we BOTH don't suffer the same fate as Grasshopper! Maybe you should understand that they tortured him before they killed him. I am giving you a chance to escape and extract revenge from your abductors!

Don't you want to get even? Don't you want to live for Grass-hopper, so they can pay for their crimes? Don't you owe that to Grasshopper?"

Ling began to feel the adrenaline boost kick in and the goading from JAC about revenge ignited a storm inside her. Ling swung one leg down and then the other, which gave her the momentum to sit up on the side of the table. Her eyes burned with hatred for those responsible.

Ling stared into JAC's eyes and responded in crisp military fashion, "Colonel Ling Po reporting for duty as commanded, sir! Get me out of here!"

JAC smiled knowingly and placed Ling's arm around her neck to assist as she stood to walk. They moved slowly and carefully towards an opening in the floor that allowed them to drop into the underground drain/sewer systems that snaked below the structure. The underground system lead to a shallow river. Going with the current, they finally located an area that was flat enough to make it up onto dry land. Ling's strength was almost all gone, but she grinned from ear to ear at their good fortune. JAC flashed a light signal into the dark, and a signal was returned. Shortly after, they were taken on board a craft and placed under cover as it moved downstream.

Ling used the last of her strength to ask, "What happened to my original escape plans? How did I end up here? Who was it that had me?"

JAC marshaled her features as she solemnly conveyed, "As far as we can tell, it looks like someone among the exit personnel compromised the operation and sold you out to Chairman Lo Chang. You have been here for months. We got a snippet about your location from the Internet chatter and staged this exit strategy. Now all we have to do is find a new place for you to operate from and a new identity."

Ling Po smiled as she said, "Thanks for getting me to go. Making me move was not easy. I will trust you for now."

Having spent all her physical and emotional energy, Ling dropped off to sleep while the boat made its way down river to freedom.

Web spinning usually expands with concenttic circles...
The Enigma Chronicles

Otto sat in his Zürich office. He casually ran a hand through his thick stock of well-cut white hair and reviewed the plan he'd put together to fulfill the requirements requested by Prudence under one of the United States government contracts. The R-Group's contract was primarily focused on gaining information on where each of the global players was militarily with nanotechnology. He struggled with understanding the goals that each of these major players envisioned for the use of nanotechnology, how it might be applied, and what the potential downsides or risks were to each of the global powers. This was always the backdrop to their assignments.

The R-Group was a closed-family operation that had been founded during World War II by two brothers and a best friend. It had all started with the capture of an Enigma Machine that the Germans used to encrypt communications. As the founders of the R-Group, which included Otto's father, fled from Poland to Switzerland, this acquisition did as well. They formed their operation to encrypt information and used the expanded capabilities they created to help preserve and transport the wealth of those under Nazi scrutiny.

Over the years the family operations had grown to include real estate and financial investments, along with the banking aspects, financial security, and, these days, a huge focus on information technology. They had many businesses established around the world that were subsidiaries of the primary family business. Trails from any of those subsidiaries back to the R-Group were obscured from the most in-depth reviews available to anyone outside the family. The overarching mandate of their organization was for human rights and options for good succeeding over evil.

R-Group resources for information technology were impressive by any standard. As their operations had grown, they had shaped bleeding edge technology and leveraged it far ahead of the intelligence agencies of any country in the world. As a result, they provided information services to those entities or countries with a goal of continual assessment of the capabilities of world powerbrokers. Decisions on which projects they would accept or reject was a review process with a voting right tied to the original founders. Each member of the inner circle of the family was highly educated in a general sense of the family interests, yet typically had a primary talent at which they exceled. The three primary members at present were Otto, Wolfgang, and to replace the recently departed Ferdek, Quinton Ferdek Watcowski, who was better known as Quip.

Otto himself had a real head for finance and was the primary contact for direct dealings with their clients from the world's intelligence communities. He also sculpted the vision for the organization expansion yet maintained focus on their core mission.

Wolfgang was primarily focused on all financial matters with his ability to find even the most deliberately buried money trails. Additionally, he was brilliant in real estate and ensured the moral ethics of the family and its associated business endeavors were held in high regard.

Quip, the youngest of this voting arm of the team, was the architect of their information infrastructure as well as an advanced technology integrator. His ability to access systems without detection, join programs and information together for analysis, and maintain the highest security levels was without equal.

Otto's daughter, Petra, was an encryption guru with the ability to create programs and algorithms to secure information. Her abilities were equally valued by the clients she assisted, based on their requirements. She was valued as a consultant to many individual customers worldwide.

Jacob, Wolfgang's grandson, had recently joined the family business after growing up in the United States with his mother. His mother had been killed, essentially in the line of family duty. Jacob was educated in both structured and unstructured programming, and gained significant experience as he worked with financial institutions on security of their systems. He was renowned for his ability to perform near exhaustive penetration-testing.

Additionally, all the family members were educated to be multilingual for reading and speaking, which allowed them to easily work with customers all over the globe. Their manners and attire spoke of wealth without being gaudy or trendy. They were masters at hiding most of their feelings from all but each other. For the few skills they did not have within the family, such as advanced telecommunications, they developed strong contractor relationships. They supported those that helped mankind and helped detour those who carried the same mind-set as the Nazis.

Prudence, an avatar identification for interactions with the R-Group by those in the Western intelligence community, had contracted for two services. One service was verification that the CIA was or was not involved in a terrible explosion in Mexico that could possibly derail the joint efforts by the United States and Mexico. This effort had been completed and would be provided in due time to fulfill that assignment. The other service, which was the one Otto was focused on, was the information requested around the terms "nanotechnology", "grasshopper", "biometric implants", "peer to peer mobile communications", "satellite uplink tethering", "near field communications in combat situations", "po", and "pilotless drones". The information from simple searches of these terms was certainly within the capability of the agencies at Prudence's disposal. So without further guidance, Otto had presumed that she required a broad deliverable for the service across world powers and their respective use of communications for identity and location of people and things.

Otto had outlined many of the possibilities that he thought might be applied with use of these technologies in part or total combination, but he wanted the insight from the key staff assigned to focus on the project. As he walked toward the conference room, located in the primary technology center in Zürich, he was absorbed with the direction he planned to take with that discussion as he took his seat.

"Good morning, all. I trust that you are refreshed and ready to tackle this new assignment. Of course, as other pressing matters arise from customers we will decide if any of you need to break away for those issues. Otherwise, I would like you all to focus on this assignment," began Otto.

Quip offered, in non-typical seriousness, "Otto, I have shown both Jacob and Petra my current modifications to our Immersive Collaborative Associative Binary Override Deterministic, or ICABOD, system. The enhancement made with facial recognition, as well as some enhancements Jacob made for handling rapid review of the Big Data collected, dovetailed well with the updated next generation encryption from Petra. It seems to be performing well with these additions, and Jacob will continue to modify as things are processed to continually improve. I believe this will be key to not only gathering and classifying the information by the sources and owners, but also for the modeling of where each of the leaders is in using these technologies and what their plans are."

"Good," Otto replied as he smiled and continued, "So, we all seem to be on the same page, which is important."

Jacob suggested, "In looking at each of the aspects of potential application of nanotechnology, the use of locating people rather than objects seems to be the focus. Problems to overcome that seem most obvious include: how to easily maintain power, how to be used with a person, and how to avoid falling into the wrong hands or effectively hiding. At least, I believe these would be initial critical category questions."

Petra chimed in, "All of this development would be ripe for stealing by different entities if they think one group is ahead of another. The encryption would be extensive by any group to help avoid information theft. At this point, given enough time, we can open any file and create the needed encryption keys.

"Toward that end, I have been doing surveillance on several of the most easily identified targets for military and non-military development. So far the feedback is meager, but the content is fairly rich from sources in the U.S., England, Middle East factions, and China."

"If those are the targets at present, then I will start tracking all the money sources for each of these primary players," Wolfgang offered. "As other players are added, we can expand the financial aspects."

Otto grinned and declared, "It is so nice not to have to pro-vide assignments since you each know where you can provide the most help. I suspect we will begin receiving other requests from these entities as they are hitting walls in developing or deploying the newer technology. We also need to determine if England is working independently, or augmenting efforts for the United States."

Each of the professionals at the table nodded in agreement. They didn't know what the full value would be for this project but felt that frequent reviews would help direct their efforts. For the time being, they would work out of this operations center, which would also hone the team further to make them a more cohesive force.

"I, for one, would like a meeting for updates at least every couple of days until we see where these trails take us," requested Wolfgang.

"Agreed. I also need to think of the best ways to get a bit of an update on our friend Su Lin at Texas A&M. I would not like her to become a target for any of these players," advocated Otto.

"We've kept a fairly close eye on her activities, but she is very adept and clever when she gets focused. So you might be right. Though nothing is present on the radar screen with her," confirmed Quip.

Wolfgang asked, "Don't we also owe Prudence an update on the CIA involvement in Mexico? I know Quip and Jacob were working on the report completion and the presentation framework, but I didn't hear if that was finalized and ready for delivery."

Both Jacob and Quip grinned at the same time, then looked to each other to see who was going to speak first. Quip nodded toward Jacob to do the honors.

"As you know, the CIA was not directly involved in the operation that brought down the building in Mexico and killed several pornography-linked criminals. However, we have been able to create the impression, if we all agree, that the CIA potentially was behind the incident. We don't want to report a lie by any means. However, we were able to secure some facts which might make this the best option for the slant of our final report.

"One, there was trace evidence, found by the authorities that investigated the damaged site, that indicated the C-4 was part of a shipment that the CIA had stockpiled in a southwestern U.S. location. Additionally, there were several CIA operatives that were identified as being in close proximity, though assigned other tasks, during the time of the incident. That information came from CIA correspondence. It would be a short step to weave these elements together to suggest this was an inadvertent communications glitch that resulted in a tragedy. There is no other evidence tying to any other source, and we dug really hard."

Quip offered, "The other option is to simply point out these facts in our report and that no other culprits could be identified, which is totally true. Jacob and I agree that outright lying on this would be wrong, but assembling the facts, along with the evidence of the activity, would arm the U.S. agencies during any subsequent discussions with the Mexican authorities. The evidence of the pornographic criminal activity has only partially been identified by those governments, so the report would include new information for Prudence on the actual victims of the activity."

Silence reigned as each participant thought about the options. It was a fine line. However, it made sense for conveying the information. Each of them wanted this chapter closed. Finally, Otto broke the silence.

"I think this might be the best choice to go forward. Complete the report then as you would like it to be submitted and send it to Wolfgang and me. We will read it very carefully and let you know the decision in the morning.

"Let's get started, folks, on the new assignment, update as needed, but we will regroup together day after tomorrow. Thank you."

CHAPTER 2

Start over as in a fresh sheet of paper

Dawn, with the light reflecting off the Yangzi River, promised to be a beautiful start to a productive day. The light from the east scattered through the low clouds on the horizon producing magnificent colors. The warming land generated a light mist over the river that spilled over onto the banks, much like the Scottish moorlands. What a great day to be alive! It seemed as if ying and yang were totally aligned for the troops that were assembled for practice maneuvers. What a shame!

The captain followed closely behind by the lieutenant, ran into the command center and both screamed, "Get me ambulances now! Do you hear? Now!"

The major was ashen white and could barely get any words out, but finally said, "We saw it on the cameras. They don't need ambulances, but we clearly do need autopsies. We need to understand what happened and why."

The captain and lieutenant stopped in their tracks as their eyes burned with fury.

The captain reprimanded, "We saw it firsthand! They are all dead! And the ones that didn't die instantly from the goddam chip in their neck died trying to claw it or cut it out before it could kill them! Shit! A hundred men killed not by the enemy but by their own people!

"This was just supposed to be standard maneuvers to try out a new communications system. Some great new weapon this is! Now all we should have to do is get the enemy to use it! What in the hell happened?"

The major struggled to keep his emotions in check at this outburst, then solemnly ordered, "I want all of them taken back to base, and the chip set removed for analysis by the engineers. We have to know why this new communications system malfunctioned. Additionally, this project and its results are to remain classified. Understood?"

The captain brought himself under control with some difficulty and finally responded, "Yes, sir. I understand, sir. Will there be any more executions today, sir?"

The lieutenant, however, was still seething with anger as he barked, "You ordered it, didn't you? The communications chip with its own battery implanted in their neck for battlefield communications wasn't working as expected, was it? It worked fine in simulations and at first while we were still in pre-deployment formation. So what happened when we progressed with our standard tactical deployment and spread out?

"We started losing communications with the edge points and …and then you boosted the signal, didn't you? You amped up the power to receive and transmit in the chips so that all points could be reached, didn't you? The chips didn't have thermal regulators to dissipate the heat that the damn things generated so they started burning through the flesh in their hosts' necks! These son-of-a-bitching chips were imbedded right alongside their auditory canal in close proximity to their carotid arteries! You murdering bastard! I should kill you myself!" he shouted as he pulled his weapon, only to be shot by one of the guards in the room.

The captain swallowed hard, looked the major in the eye, and said, "I really wasn't looking for an answer to my earlier question. I have my orders, Major. Will there be anything else, sir? If we are finished, I really do need to go outside and throw up."

The major, now recovered from the debacle on the simulated battlefield area as well as the execution of the lieutenant, waved on the captain to complete the assigned tasks without saying a word. The major wondered if there was a quiet place for him to go and throw up as well. The lieutenant had been right. He had pushed the power up on the chips to get the full range of communications. All those trusting volunteers had been killed by expedient field testing of a new communications methodology and it had been done on his watch.

This wasn't like the software world where you just recompiled poor code and tried again. You needed willing volunteers, or at least volunteers. True, the military, regardless of the country, always had volunteers willing or otherwise to *try* stuff on to see if it worked as designed. The trick was always to not discuss how the previous group fared in the testing. As the old phrase goes, with progress, someone always gets hurt.

In the primary examination room, the doctor affirmed, "Major, your field observation of the chip overheating and burning through the surrounding tissue is fairly accurate. The chip needed a certain amount of size, circuit density, and a modest power source to even function correctly. We encased the chip with a non-toxic polymer coating to keep the electronics from the hosts' immune system, as well as to keep the chip clean. We didn't expect to have a great range with them, nor did we expect them to overheat when pushed to maximize the radio range.

"We understand the problem of battlefield communications and personnel location if they are wounded or captured, so miniaturizing communications with position awareness devices that can be worn on or in the human body is very desirable. But this technical approach is just too limiting and, as you saw, not without its drawbacks. I am afraid I must tell you this is a dead-end approach, quite literally."

The major nodded his head and reviewed, "Our first generation of wearable communication devices weren't bad so long as you didn't lose it or forget to put it on. We needed to be confident that the device would be on or, in this case, *in the individual as a* set-and-forget technology. Implanting the chips seemed the best way to track the individual. Placing the chips near the auditory canal should have made it convenient to the host for speaking and hearing battlefield commands."

"So, doctor, what about the soldiers who tore at their ears, or those we found bleeding from their ears? How would you explain that finding?"

The doctor explained, "Well, it looks like there was no thought given to volume control when the power was boosted. Some were getting good reception at the same time some weren't. When the power was boosted, those with the best reception essentially had their units turned up so loud that the communication reached hyper-pain levels that had them clawing at the devices trying to remove them. Those soldiers simply experienced a sonic boom inside their auditory canal that ruptured everything."

"So it's back to the drawing board, huh? This was not what I wanted to report back to division headquarters. Device placement and a volume control would be critical from a centralized location."

It seems so unjust that criminals get so much more help than regular citizens...
The Enigma Chronicles

As a part of his standard process, Jacques Bruno reviewed the most recent notice on criminals from the Interpol Watch List. Each of the one-pagers identified the culprit, the crime, last known location, possible destinations, and background summary. He had captured many a criminal by consistent review of the watch list. As the Interpol Chief in Zürich, Bruno made it a point to stay briefed and make certain his team kept abreast of current events everywhere in Europe. The Top Ten List changed based on several factors and that included movement between countries.

Two of the criminals added to the most recent list had known affiliations with a splinter militant Islamic group that claimed responsibility for several deaths from bombs in London, Paris, Munich, and Hamburg. One of Bruno's closest associates in Interpol had been killed in the Paris bombing incident, which made the search for these criminals personal. The two men were identified as traveling together, a last known address in a poor neighborhood in Paris. They had simply vanished the morning of their pending arrest.

Oxnard Kassab, at first glance, seemed unlikely. He was from a reasonably good family in Iran, with some formal education at Oxford, and great interactions with his fellow students from all over the world until illness in his family sent him home. Several years later this devoted Muslim, identified as a leader in an al-Qaeda factional group, became a force against Western cultures. Oxnard was very vocal, very dangerous, and, to date, elusive for capture. He had been captured once in London where his prints were taken, along with the photograph provided in the summary. His known associates were primarily al-Qaeda affiliated members and known arms dealers throughout Europe and Asia. Several aliases were listed, so he was apparently connected with someone skilled in providing suitable identity papers. It was noted that he was vehemently against the United States, which was standard for most al-Qaeda members.

The other man was identified as Salim Bashir. His education was unknown, but he was also a Muslim zealot with a history of petty crimes, having been arrested in several cities in Europe, but with the ability to pay his fines to avoid incarceration. He had only been jailed for a total of one month for six incidents. His affiliations were not listed, nor was there any direct connection with Oxnard outside of the neighborhood in Paris from which he had vanished. With no real evidence, it was presumed they had teamed together on the Paris incident that had killed his friend. At the very least they should both be apprehended and questioned, perhaps providing other leads.

For all the years Bruno had been connected to Interpol, this was the first time a close associate had been caught in the crossfire. This caused him to be more focused on the list from the viewpoint of trying to find leads that others might have missed. He had put out feelers to all his informants to see if additional information could be garnered. After two weeks, no additional information had surfaced, but he kept searching under all the rocks. He'd even detained a few others that fit specific profiles to see if their sources might prove helpful. Like most agencies, Interpol rallied everyone when one of their own was taken out.

Zürich was in a quiet period for international visitors, so Jacques had accepted a lunch invitation from his childhood friend, Quip. They had tried for several weeks to have lunch and catch up on friends and family. Bruno hadn't seen Quip since Ferdek's funeral, so he wanted to make the effort. Ferdek had been like a father to Bruno, as well as Quip and Quip's brother, and had been a good mentor. Bruno knew he could count on Quip for some ideas with regards to how to look for and ideally apprehend these fugitives.

Quip arrived at the restaurant to see Jacques already seated in a corner with not only a good view of the room, but also of the entrance. He smiled and realized how predictable his friend Bruno was as he strolled to the table.

Quip extended his hand, "Bruno, my friend, how are you?"

Bruno shook hands as he partially rose. "Fine, my friend. So glad we could finally align our schedules. Please sit. Let's order and spend some time catching up."

As if on cue, the waiter appeared and took their beverage orders while listing the specials of the day. They each selected one of the specials. To these two men, food was necessary and enjoyed, but not worth wasting time over selecting.

"Quip, how is your brother and the rest of the family? I almost feel guilty not touching base to see how you, since um… well, you know."

"Things have been busy and actually fairly good, Bruno. Yes, there are changes, but isn't that part of life? I am working hard on some technology inroads and even expanding efforts to secure new clients. You know me – I enjoy tweaking technology and solving problems. And you, Bruno, what has your brow wrinkled and caused the extra stress lines? Has some bad guy stolen your favorite parking spot at the office?"

Bruno chuckled, "You always lighten things up! I am never at the office, so how would I know who parks where. As long as I don't get a ticket, I am doing ok."

They chatted back and forth like the old friends they were, updating each other on current events. Their lunch arrived and they continued the friendly banter. After the plates were removed and coffee was served, Bruno became serious, which immediately alerted Quip.

"One of the reasons I wanted to see you was, of course, to catch up, which we do far too infrequently, my friend. The other reason is that I was hoping you might help me a bit. It is somewhat personal."

"Of course I can be your best man, but I had no idea you were even dating," offered Quip without missing a beat, knowing it "would lighten his friend's serious expression. "Oh, thank heavens, it's not that," he added as he saw Bruno shake his head. "Tell me all then so I can cease my wild guesses."

"An old friend I worked with for years on and off headed up the Paris office. He was involved in an event and killed in the recent bombing there. Two suspects recently showed up on the Interpol Watch List with high probability of being involved in the incident. The problem is they have vanished, but even without confirming their presence there, I feel compelled to help at least bring them in for thorough questioning. With the ongoing problem with Taliban related groups and violence in Europe and the United States, I and my team always keep an eye out. However, with Pierre Renaud now a casualty, I want to do more."

Quip recognized the conviction in his friend's voice and the determination in his eyes. He mentally reviewed the recent Watch List that ICABOD had absorbed a week or so ago. As a matter of standard process, he had added uploading of the list to leverage the facial recognition element of ICABOD. With all the data sources ICABOD was tasked to use, it was always possible that he could offer locational information on any of the wanted suspects. From Interpol lists to the FBI Most Wanted, ICABOD had them all.

"I am sorry to hear about your colleague, Bruno. It is always a blow when one of the good guys get taken down. I will keep an ear to the ground and even put out a few feelers if you think that might be useful. Can you perhaps provide me a bit of detail on Pierre Renaud and the suspects you feel are culpable?"

"Quip, I can and will as soon as I return to my office. Is the secure drop-box you provided me long ago still available and secure? If not, I can bring it by Wolfgang's house tonight on my way home."

"It is still available to you, my friend, though Wolfgang would enjoy seeing you, I'm sure."

"Ok. If it looks like I will get home at a reasonable hour, I will take it by and say hello. Otherwise, I will call you and let you know if I am going to use the drop-box. Thank you, Quip."

"No problem, my friend, I am happy to try to help. I do need to get back to work; however, we need to do this again soon," Quip responded as he signaled the waiter for the check.

CHAPTER 4

Settling in for the mad rush of fun or work

Petra combed her long blonde hair and pampered her skin with all the lotions afforded the guests of this home. Wolfgang's home was large and lavish, but it felt comfortable, like a well-worn pair of shoes. The room she shared with Jacob was tastefully decorated in earth tones and older, European-styled furniture. It was so nice to be back in friendly territory, she thought as she added a couple of small logs to the hypnotic fire. The vacation in Mexico had been so much fun on the one hand and so crazy on the other. Spending time with Jacob, though not as much as she'd hoped for, had allowed her to see him in a different, more provocative light. Totally hooked on him, Petra was pleased that it seemed like the feelings were mutual.

After the meeting with the team, she had wanted to talk with Jacob about some of their approaches to the project. However, Jacob had suggested she relax for a bit while he played a game of chess with his grandfather. Wolfgang hardly appeared like a grandfather in the traditional sense as he was so close in age to Otto. He started young, she guessed. She knew full well that

Jacob enjoyed spending time with Wolfgang and hearing his stories. Since Jacob had only met him recently, he took advantage of any time available. The life he had adopted with the family business seemed to agree with him in more ways than one.

Petra decided to tie up her hair and find something slinky to put on. Perhaps something Jacob could easily remove when he came upstairs. She smiled when she located an emerald-colored teddy and admired how it looked in the mirror. Even though she enjoyed working side by side, she found their lovemaking wonderful and, frankly, could hardly wait for him to join her. She slipped under the covers and started to read a somewhat steamy novel her friend, Lara, had recommended.

An hour or so later Jacob came into the room and stopped to gaze at the pretty lady all tucked into bed with a paperback resting on her chin. She looked so peaceful as she snoozed with the firelight dancing across her face. He added a few more pieces of wood as he pictured them naked on the rug in front of the fire. Now the question became should he wake her up or take care not to disturb her. He continued the debate with himself as he undressed and went for a shower.

If he woke her, she'd probably be annoyed, if she didn't like to be wakened. This was a first for him with Petra, his first adult relationship. He was desperate to cover her from head to toe with kisses and touches, but then, he always responded to her in that way. He was still arguing in his head as he toweled off and headed toward bed. Looking down at his erection, his answer was abundantly clear.

As Jacob slid under the covers, careful not to let in too much cold air, she shifted into him. He wrapped his arm around her and plied her with caresses using his other hand. He let his fingers lightly glaze over her skin, and she soon emitted little mewing sounds of enjoyment. He shifted slightly to free his other hand with the desire to touch her in an effort to extract more sounds from her. During the process she rolled onto her stomach, which allowed him full exploration of her back and her pretty, round bottom. As he added light kisses to his gentle touches her skin responded with small goose bumps and her mewing moans increased, yet her eyes remained closed. Her legs opened with the slightest provocation allowing him access to her warm, wet center.

The sounds and writhing increased as he continued his kisses and touches, focused on her pleasure. As he explored and played more his own excitement increased. Soon he could feel her tension as it increased, and her hips moved as if looking for the right connection. Her breathing increased to panting and his name fell from her lips as he felt her climax. He stroked and petted her until her breath slowed.

"Oh, Jacob, that was magnificent, part dream and part reality," she whispered and rolled to face him. "Please, I want you inside me."

"Yes, love," he whispered back as he slid deeply into her.

They kissed and touched as he continued to thrust into her over and over. She was so wet and wild under him, meeting each of his thrusts with a shift of her pelvis to get him as deep as possible.

"Oh, darling. Don't stop, please don't stop," she murmured just as she peaked again.

Petra grabbed his bottom and pulled him in tight as she continued her pulsing climax, taking him totally over the edge as well. Jacob shifted his weight and they hugged each other close as their breathing returned to normal. He hoped they would always find so much pleasure in one another.

As she kissed him again, she quietly spoke, "I'm so glad you woke me up, especially in such a delightful way. It's so nice to be home with you."

"Love, it is always home wherever we are together. Do you wish to rest again or do you want to talk? I am sorry about earlier, but I did want some time to visit with Wolfgang, I hope you aren't annoyed."

"Not annoyed. I know that your time with Wolfgang is important," she sighed as she snuggled closer. "I think I am good for a while after my cat nap."

Jacob straightened up the pillows so he could sit against the headboard. Petra snuggled up to him, pulling the covers over her shoulders. Neither of them spoke for a few minutes as they enjoyed the quiet, one another, and the glow of the fire while a flame danced now and again around the logs.

"Jacob, what do you think of this assignment from Prudence? I believe we are going to have to work together, much like we did before in New York, to find all of the information and code streams around this technology, depending upon who all the players are."

"I agree. Can't think of anyone I'd rather work with on this project, though I suspect we will need to be flexible and open in our thought processes. No premature conclusions on this one.

"I can see the interests of the U.S. Military, the Brits, perhaps China, Israel, and even the Arabs to one degree or another. Optimized, timely communications are key. It is how the groups approach it, where their investments are, deployment models, and uses that will vary. I think that is what we need to keep an open mind to.

"I recognize that I'm, like, the newest member of this team, but I think the information trail will be a long curving path."

"You may be new, Jacob, as you say, to this team, but you have continued to demonstrate clear insight into many situations. I happen to agree with you. I think that we are going to be creating some very interesting scenarios as we review more and more of the information. I am just pleased that we can work together on it.

"Now, however, I am getting sleepy again, so make love to me, and we'll talk more in the morning."

"My pleasure, madam."

About the Authors

Breakfield – Works for a high-tech manufacturer as a solution architect, functioning in hybrid data/telecom environments. He considers himself a long-time technology geek, who also enjoys writing, studying World War II history, travel, and cultural exchanges. Charles' love of wine tastings, cooking, and Harley riding has found ways into the stories. As a child, he moved often because of his father's military career, which even helps him with the various character perspectives he helps bring to life in the series. He continues to try to teach Burkey humor.

Burkey – Works as a business architect who builds solutions for customers on a good technology foundation. She has written many technology papers, white papers, but finds the freedom of writing fiction a lot more fun. As a child, she helped to lead the kids with exciting new adventures built on make believe characters, was a Girl Scout until high school, and contributed to the community as a young member of a Head Start program. Rox enjoys family, learning, listening to people, travel, outdoor activities, sewing, cooking, and thinking about how to diversify the series.

Breakfield and Burkey – started writing non-fictional papers and books, but it wasn't nearly as fun as writing fictional stories. They found it interesting to use the aspects of technology that people are incorporating into their daily lives more and more as a perfect way to create a good guy/bad guy story with elements of travel to the various places they have visited either professionally and personally, humor, romance, intrigue, suspense, and a spirited way to remember people who have crossed paths with them. They love to talk about their stories with private and public book readings. Burkey also conducts regular interviews for Texas authors, which she finds very interesting. Her first interview was, wait for it, Breakfield. You can often find them at local book fairs or other family-oriented events.

The primary series is based on a family organization called R-Group. Recently they have spawned a subgroup that contains some of the original characters as the Cyber Assassins Technology Services (CATS) team. The authors have ideas for continuing the series in both of these tracks. They track the more than 150 characters on a spreadsheet, with a hidden avenue for the future coined The Enigma Chronicles tagged in some portions of the stories. Fan reviews seem to frequently suggest that these would make good television or movie stories, so the possibilities appear endless, just like their ideas for new stories.

They have book video trailers for each of the stories, which can be viewed on YouTube, Amazon's Authors page, or on their website, *www.EnigmaBookSeries.com*. Their website is routinely updated with new interviews, answers to readers' questions, book trailers, and contests. You may also find it fascinating to check out the fun acronyms they create for the stories summarized on their website. Reach out to them at *Authors@EnigmaSeries.com, Twitter@EnigmaSeries,* or *Facebook@TheEnigmaSeries.*

Please provide a fair and honest review on amazon and any other places you post reviews. We appreciate the feedback.

Other stories by Breakfield and Burkey in
The Enigma Series are at **www.EnigmaBookSeries.com**

We would greatly appreciate
if you would take a few minutes
and provide a review of this work
on Amazon, Goodreads
and any of your other favorite places.

Other stories by Breakfield and Burkey in
the Heirs Series are at **www.EnigmaBookSeries.com**

MAGNOLIA BLUFF CRIME CHRONICLES

MAGNOLIA BLUFF CRIME CHRONICLES

9 781946 858283